# THE PHYSICS OF WHY

## SALEH R SHAHID

Beezer
Books
Press

The Physics of Why

Copyright © 2024 by Saleh R Shahid

ISBN: 979-8-9905204-0-0

All rights reserved



This is a work of fiction. Names, characters, places and incidents are either the product of the author's imagination or used fictitiously. Any resemblance to actual events organizations, business establishments, events, locales, or persons, living or dead, is entirely coincidental.

Published by Beezer Books Press

Knoxville, Tennessee

# List of Named Characters

Aisha: a wealthy teenaged girl living in the capital city of 16th century India

> Omar Azim Sahani: Aisha's father and a general in the emperor's army
>
> Karnavati (Karna): Aisha's stepmother
>
> Malik the Great: Aisha's langur monkey
>
> Tarik: a security guard at Aisha's residence
>
> Sultana: a servant in Aisha's household
>
> Rubina (Ruby): a servant in Aisha's household

Sunil (Sunny): a poor boy living in the kingdom of Mewar

> Bansal (Bunny): Sunny's best friend
>
> Pankaj (Punk): Sunny's other best friend
>
> Bola: a friend of Sunny's and one of the Bhil people
>
> > Maru: Bola's wife

Jalal Ud-din Akbar: emperor of India during the Mughal (Mongol) dynasty

> TodarMal: Akbar's finance minister and diplomat
>
> Bagwant Das: one of Akbar's vassals in the Amber region
>
> Man Singh: son of Bagwant Das and supreme commander of Akbar's army

Pratap Singh: the rana (king) of the Kingdom of Mewar

> Chaudry: a top adviser to Rana Pratap

# One

At the center of your brain, there lies a small structure, no bigger than a grain of rice – the pineal gland. Ancient civilizations thought it to be a special, mystical organ – a third eye. Indeed, it does contain photoreceptors just like your eyes. That makes sense since it regulates the hormone melatonin. Melatonin has important, light-dependent functions in some lower vertebrates, regulating their sleep cycles and skin complexions. But there isn't that much melatonin activity in humans, and so our pineal glands have largely been dismissed by most scientists as an evolutionary remnant – another vestige left to us by amphibian ancestors.

But it's not just its location that argues its central importance. The pineal gland receives more blood flow than any other brain structure. It contains tiny calcite crystals, crystals that can generate an electric charge and can detect electromagnetic waves beyond the range of visible light. And when you lie dying in bed, your pineal gland will release a hallucinogen called N,N-dimethyltryptamine (NND) that will provide your near-death experience.

Dr. Dustin Nye is lying in bed, but he isn't dying. He's deep in sleep, and the NND is giving him dreams. His heart races and his body squirms as he dreams of a woman he's never met… at least not in this life. He *had* loved her intensely, hundreds of years ago, but he has no memory of her. Long ago, his brain and all its memories were extinguished, then buried, then eaten by worms, then excreted into fertilizer which later became part of a lovely banyan tree. No, all he has left is this dream, a dream which features vague images, but a vivid sense of belonging.

She had been a girl named Aisha and, in the Spring of 1575, she found herself packing for a trip. Finally, at the age of fourteen, her father was bringing her on one of his excursions. She had been too excited to sleep but felt great anyways. Her servant Sultana helped her follow his instructions. There was to be no flowing fancy fabrics adorning her tiny, fragile form, no silk shawls or scarves of delicate gossamer. She could pack a few of those things, very few. Sultana returned from the market with some boots and a plain tunic, inconspicuous in color and durable enough for a four-day ride. She helped Aisha wrestle her thick, black, overwhelming hair into a braid. She slipped off her bangles and packed them away. Aisha loved bangles and people liked giving them to her, but she never could get them to stay on her little wrists.

Through all the excitement, Aisha kept, as always, soft-spoken and well-mannered, as slight as her build. Only her eyes, serpentine and green, hinted at what lied within – a titanic soul and a backbone of titanium. She took after her father, and he was a seasoned soldier.

In fact, he had risen high to military prominence. She figured he was a general by now. Unlike her, he looked his part. His eyes, big and brown and intimidating, were set deep in a commanding brow. His jaw stood proud, manly but subtle, like the cleft that it displayed. But, to her, his most powerful feature was the moustache he wore. It flowed from his lip like a mighty waterfall. She sometimes wished she could borrow it… just for a while.

She was right, he was a general – General Omar Azim Sahani. He served in the great army of the Mongol emperor Jalal Ud-din Akbar. Sahani began his career around age twenty in 1556, the same year that Akbar took power. In the nineteen years since, Akbar had grown the empire beyond what anyone had imagined – anyone except Akbar. He had accomplished much of it through diplomacy, and now he was sending Sahani as security on a diplomatic mission. And Aisha was coming along.


They rode through Rajput country, in the northwest of what is now India. The Rajputs lived as a warrior people and, according to their Hindu religion, a class of some nobility.

It was the noble, not the warrior, that usually showed in the Rajput kings when the emperor came around with his usual offer – join the empire, keep your land and your religion, but surrender your title. You're not a king anymore. You're a governor and you have to pay the Akbar tax. But if you refuse to join, well…

Because most of them had accepted, Sahani felt secure as they traveled. But the sweetness of safety, like life itself, was soured by the knowledge of its imminent end, for he was headed to Mewar. The kingdom of Mewar, ruled by the Sisodian clan, stood as the biggest and most important of the Rajput kingdoms to resist the empire.

And the most defiant. In fact, this was the fifth diplomatic mission sent by Akbar in three years. Sahani looked over at his protectee, TodarMal, the emperor's finance minister and a good diplomat. His hair was greying, something Sahani considered a needed advantage, especially since this would be TodarMal's second attempt at peace. The first one almost reached a breakthrough but for one sticking point – Akbar had required the rana (king) of Mewar to journey to the capital city of Agra and genuflect in person. The proud rana, Rana Pratap, had refused.

General Sahani did not opine too much about politics, and he took care not to let his views affect his performance or his loyalty. But to him, this saga came largely from two men beating their chests like monkeys. "Pride," he would tell his young daughter, "is the kid sister of Arrogance. Both are Satan's children. Always remember that all credit and praise is for Allah. Then you will be secure." In this regard, Sahani definitely believed he worked for the better side. After all, the emperor had been the one to make the overtures and did so repeatedly.


But Pratap's resistance did not come from simple pride or fear or religious concerns, or even independence. There was also anger. The emperor had already conquered a large part of Mewar six years prior in not-so-diplomatic fashion. That conquest included Mewar's capital, Fort Chittor, a battle in which thousands of Rajputs perished.

Sahani had been there, and he well-remembered the siege of Fort Chittor. Years of war had tempered his gut and crusted his heart, but still left one weak spot in his emotional fortress – his teeth. Only thoughts of Chittor made them grind.

The siege had lasted months. It took that long for the engineers to dig through the steep hill on which the fort stood. The resulting trenches and mines allowed him to safely move canons and troops within striking distance of its massive walls. The defenders fought to the death, down to the last man, as was their tradition. But his most vivid memory was the smell of burning fat and hair, the hair of Chittor women who had cast themselves onto a suicide pyre, and the hair of their children who were pushed into it. It is a smell that stays in your nose long after it leaves your clothes.

The sight was no better – a powerful contrast he beheld when he finally entered the fortress. Ancient temples and grand palaces stood as testaments to timeless civilization, but in the courtyards between, those structures were mocked by piles of smoldering monuments to barbarity.

This time, they would not pass near Fort Chittor on their journey. The land they crossed this March of 1575 simmered hot and dry, desert in some regions, greener in others. The hilly terrain would get steeper as they rode towards the Aravalli mountains. Along the way, they would pass several lakes and a few wetlands, places that had retained some of the rain from last year's monsoons. They rode horseback only – no elephants – in keeping with their low profile. This low-key conduct was more than just a diplomatic strategy. It was a semi-furtive attempt to minimize embarrassment for the emperor, should Pratap reject him a fifth time. In addition to Sahani and TodarMal, they were five soldiers, four servants and a guide. And there was Aisha.

The general did have sons, two of them, from a different wife, and they were already working their way up the military ranks. They would have been fitting company for him any other time. But this was a sensitive mission and a mission of sensitivity. To him, it seemed like a good idea to bring Aisha instead. It was a softer approach, but also a jolt to Hindu preconceptions. It also seemed in keeping with the emperor's style. Akbar, who had many wives, was no feminist. He did, however, lean towards religious progressivism and he liked to use the soft jolt.

Sahani used these arguments to persuade the emissary as well as himself. But really, he just wanted to please his daughter. She never got to go anywhere, and she always wanted to come. TodarMal, himself a Hindu, also saw a blessing in her being the thirteenth member of the company. As they traveled, she tried to maintain a reserved composure to please her father, or at least not embarrass him. But at times, she couldn't help but tug on his sleeve and point at all the animals they passed, many of which she only knew from books. She saw gazelle, antelope, foxes, hundreds of different birds and several wildcats. Of course, there were also the inevitable traffic jams of goats and camels.

They stayed the first night with Bagwant Das, one of Akbar's vassals, who lived in the lavish, amber-colored Amber Palace. A massive complex built high atop a hill, it overlooked the serene Lake Maota in Amber City, the capital of the Amber territory. As they began the steep ascent up the hillside road, they raised the emperor's standard – a golden lion and a golden sun on a green field. They entered through a side gate and were received and sorted. Aisha and her aides were escorted to the women's section, the soldiers to their quarters, and Sahani and TodarMal were welcomed into the main residence. All guests were given supper, then retired afterwards for chai and chit-chat.

TodarMal joined Das in a lounge. Like every new guest who enters any room at Amber Palace, he paused a moment to soak in the intricate design and exquisite workmanship. Every inch of every surface was carved or colored or tiled into floral patterns, vineal patterns, hypnotic mosaics and bas-relief images. The ceilings arched. The doorways, shaped as pointed domes, reflected the Byzantine architecture outside. The two nobles sat on giant pillows and talked politics.

Sahani instead went with Man Singh, Das's son and a top general of the empire. The two of them withdrew to the study for a meeting. It was, in fact, a business meeting since the emperor, while making this peace effort, was also preparing for war.

Meanwhile, Aisha sat outside in the night, in a courtyard, in a pavilion draped with netting. The marble gave cool relief to the hot air. She was surrounded mostly by older women and a few children who were up late. The women ignored her, talking in a language she didn't understand, about people she didn't know. Rubina, another servant and companion for the trip, talked with her, marveling at the clothing and home of their hosts. Aisha listened a bit, but her attention soon drifted over Ruby's shoulder to a far wall on which some gray langurs lounged. The monkeys sat about two feet tall, their gray hair glinting in the moonlight. She sighed with worry as she wondered about her baby, Malik the Great, whom she had left back home in Agra. At four years old, the gray langur wasn't much of a baby anymore, except to her.

When he *was* a baby, he was nearly killed by another male langur who was taking over the group, a langur practice which often includes infanticide. In a park near his home, Aisha's father had been sitting under a tree, eating dates and watching from a few meters away. For some reason, he didn't like it. So he grabbed a big stick and intervened, striking and shooing away the would-be usurper. The mother also fled, and Sahani brought home the abandoned baby monkey and presented him to Aisha, who adored him instantly. His shriveled black face and deep brown eyes conveyed an illusion of venerable wisdom. He had been mauled and would drag a lame leg for the rest of his life. He had also sustained some brain damage and would remain a little dim. This allowed him, as he got older, to be an easy pet as monkeys go. She loved to talk to him, telling him everything on her mind, and to take him for walks around the grounds.

She eventually became the only family he could remember. He slept in a tree outside her window and spent some of his day monkeying around the compound. But he spent more time with her, for she was the most beautiful thing he ever saw, and very interesting. He watched her cook, waiting for her to slip him a radish or potato when nobody was looking. He watched her practice her archery and sew her clothes. He sat in bed with her and held her hand as she read. He patiently watched her play chess, waiting for her to make one of her thinking faces so he could have a good laugh. And he watched her do calisthenics, or so he thought. They were actually her prayers, but he didn't recognize them. He knew about God and regularly prayed himself. But he prayed monkey-style.

He subsisted mostly on leaves from the various plants on the compound, and from the millet seeds that she kept on hand. But his favorite treat rested in a bowl on a stand, at the end of his daily mango trek. He once learned that, at a certain time of day, The Man would be out of the house and the mango would be in The Man's room. But Malik's little black hands were too small to open the door. So, at the same time every day, he ventured to the dining room and climbed four meters up a pillar in the corner. From the top, it was a short jump onto a transom, which he crossed to the other corner. There, the wall didn't quite meet the ceiling. He climbed through the space onto a small ledge in the bedroom. From there, a giant leap onto the bed canopy, then slide or climb down the net, depending on his mood. A quick dash, grab the prize, then out the window and onto a tree a meter below.

Now, as Aisha sat and gazed and worried, her worries were warranted. In the years they spent together, Malik could not remember her ever being away this long, and he had stopped eating. He felt ill and spent more time in his tree. When in the house, he got underfoot, and The Woman swatted or chased him away.

The Woman, named Karnavati, wasn't Aisha's mother, but one of Sahani's two other wives. At age fifteen, she married him in a wedding that had been arranged for political reasons. The emperor liked intermarriage as a tactic for improving diplomatic relations, and she came from the Sisodian clan, the same family as Rana Pratap. She didn't take very quickly to her new husband, who was twice her age. Besides, she loved another boy. But that was not meant to be, so she eventually made an effort. She dutifully converted to Islam and became a pretty good Muslim. In time, she came to love her husband enough to be happy.

She more quickly took to Aisha, who was five years old and motherless when they met. After a couple of years, it became evident that Karna could not conceive. The more she failed, the more she resented the little girl. For a year or so, they both had difficult lives. But Karna eventually accepted her fate and, with this acceptance, their relationship grew stronger than before. She would become the closest thing to a mother that Aisha had. She taught Aisha religion, skills and games. She cared for her when ill or sad. And she didn't mind the monkey… until now.

TodarMal and company departed from Amber the next day at dawn and made camp that night. The following night, they stayed in a village much like any of the dozens of others through which they had passed – small, thatched homes of wood and clay, fields of wheat and rice. By this point, the hills had grown quite tall and difficult, and the roads narrow and winding. The next day, the fourth and final of their journey, went worse. Travel was slow and hot, and the horses needed frequent rest, the sweat stinging their eyes. Furthermore, the party now rode in hostile territory, and they lumbered under the weight of that knowledge. And though they proceeded with permission and under protection of the rana, they were being received, not welcomed.

Aisha became aware of that distinction as they passed local peasants, peasants who always stared, frequently glared, and defiantly crossed their arms. More than once, her father reassured her that these gawkers did not know them. "They're just miserable," he told her. Indeed, they did look wretched and poor, as did their desolate homes.

The prior year had been worse when, in preparation for war, Rana Pratap had ordered the crops burned, the villages emptied, and the villagers dislocated into the surrounding hills. The idea was to make Mewar inhospitable to invaders. But war had not come – just a few skirmishes – and eventually the threat of starvation outweighed the threats of Pratap. Little by little, his people resettled their homes and replanted their crops. And the looks they gave now, when fancy people rode by, were not born of hatred for the empire. They simply feared Pratap's wrath.


In the late afternoon, TodarMal and company arrived at their destination, a small military encampment on a large hill. On an adjacent hill loomed Fort Kumbal. Aisha saw it as just another giant castle on another giant hill. To her father, it was a formidable foe and a smart move. Pratap had recently moved his seat of government there and, as a wartime capital, it was nearly impenetrable. It rested comfortably within a double ring of protection. A great wall, as much as five meters thick, stretched thirty-five kilometers around the fortress. Beyond the wall, a dozen hills surrounded it - colossal, rocky guards standing eternal posts.

They were received by three serious men with stern faces. As Aisha dismounted, the first thing she noticed were their heights – tall. They dressed in the same, familiar attire as most upper-class men of northern India. They each wore a jama – a type of frock, sleeved and fitted around the trunk that spread below the waist into a long skirt, under which they wore pajama trousers. The jamas, like their genie slippers, were thoroughly embroidered. One man, wearing light armor, carried an armigerous shield and sword.

She thought the next man quite striking, even more so than her own father. The man had a noble face which exuded competence and confidence. His moustache was spectacular. A crimson turban crowned his head, the front of which displayed a round, golden ornament. She noticed that it matched the golden sun painted on the red shield of the first guy. This second man was Rana Pratap Singh. He embraced TodarMal, who introduced him to Sahani and Aisha. On being introduced to the girl, Pratap leaned over to the third man and muttered a question in a foreign language.

"Is this is supposed to be some kind of back-handed insult?"

To Aisha, this third fellow, named Chaudry, was just there – boring. But Chaudry had wisdom, wisdom enough to advise a king. He paused and thought. He then rephrased the question and posed it in the common tongue of Hindavi. "Did she come for marriage?" he asked.

TodarMal replied before anyone else could. "Possibly. She is very dear to her father, and he has been telling her all about Mewar, the beauty of the land and the majesty of its people. After all that, he felt compelled to show her. How could he not?"

Pratap seemed unimpressed but satisfied. "Tomorrow, you shall rest," he said. "You shall ride to my father's city and enjoy the day. We have a nice guest house there. The next day, men shall return here for business and women stay there."

So decreed, so settled. The three women settled into one tent, where they dined and drank tea. The men did the same in another, taking care to avoid serious discussion. The next morning, the guests left for Udai City.

# Two

In a small city in the Mewar kingdom, a young man sat cross-legged on a barrel, flanked by two friends who also dutifully held down their own barrels. He was seventeen, though he didn't know it. His black hair with auburn highlights fell to shoulder length. The barrel, full of apples, stood against a building on the perimeter of the city's bazaar. He was a part-time farm hand, part-time thief and part-time loiterer. Right now, he was working hard at the latter. He sucked on a slice of sugar cane and picked at his bare feet. Most of the bazaar's streets and alleys only spanned wide enough for foot traffic and donkeys. But here, the road was amenable to the occasional horse or other large animal, sometimes with a carriage in tow. Here was a good place to sit if a young man hoped for something to happen. Today, something did.

A beautiful, white horse pulled up with a covered tanga (carriage) in tow. This was not royal extravagance, but obviously someone of note. Maybe someone interesting, maybe someone boring but wealthy, maybe even someone to sell to or steal from or both.

The boys put down their sugar and their feet and stretched their eyes and necks. Between the curtains, Sunil and his friends managed to get glimpses inside – a girl and a man. The girl looked about their age, perhaps a bit younger. She wore elegant, new clothes but not much jewelry. The shawl draping her head could not restrain the intelligent loveliness of her face. The man looked old enough to be her father, maybe her husband, probably her uncle. He wore a big ole scimitar.

One of Sunil's buddies nudged him. "You put a baby in that one, you'll be set for life."

Of course, they all knew the truth, but Sunil felt the need to say it anyways. "If I put a baby in her, I'd be dead and so would she. Besides, where would I put it? She has no meat."

But their truth was not actually true, for they didn't know her father. He had already lived a lifetime's worth of honor and glory. If jeopardized, he would gladly sacrifice it all and find a way to spare his daughter. He loved her more than anything, largely because, to him, she embodied the spirit of her beloved mother who had died in childbirth.

Sunil's friends promptly jumped down and went to work, enthusiastically offering their services to guide the new guests, or to fetch, carry, or squeegee something. Sunil himself suddenly had a new instinct – to slink away down a path where he knew there sat another barrel. That one collected rainwater and he used it to wash his head and take a drink. He returned to find his friends still at it. They had already been smacked in the backs of their heads … twice … each, but still had some alacrity left. Sunil stayed back, a stone's throw away. He watched and waited until his friends had tired and she had escaped. He diverted around a building to avoid the inevitable questions from his friends, then proceeded to follow her and the man. He watched as she did the usual things – browsing and buying, tasting and eating. Each vendor gave a familiar, suspicious look as Sunil passed.

She was just becoming acclimated to the unpleasant concentration and combination of smells – spice and stool, food and feces – when he sidled up. She was watching a man put color to an idol he had just carved – an image of a man with six faces and six pairs of arms. The artist rubbed colored sticks to make colored powder, then mixed chemicals to make colored paste. He worked the paste into the wood.

Sunil began shyly. "Excuse me, is that your uncle?"

A bit startled, she nonetheless maintained her nerve and etiquette and ignored him…for a moment. She then thought better and replied without looking. "No, my dad."

"Oh, your daaad," he said, and flashed a meek smile. "That's a huge sword he has. I wish I had one."

She thought better again and resumed ignoring him.

He pointed at the idol and spoke to its maker. "Dude, you're a bummer!" He turned to her. "A bummer, yes?" No reply. He continued to dance alone. "Festival is coming and he's making war gods."

For the first time, she turned her head to face him. "I'm sorry, but you're standing too close," she said politely.

She was again startled, this time by her father. He had been standing about three meters away, looking at something else. He announced his return with a single slap to the side of Sunil's head, which knocked him to the ground. With one foot on the boy's chest, the general pulled out his huge sword and held it to his neck. "Get lost!"

Sunil scrambled away like a squirrel, his retreat laced with many apologies to both father and daughter.

Aisha also apologized. "I'm sorry, Daddy. I don't know where that boy came from."

He replied with contempt. "This is not a boy. This is trash."


The next day, the general was gone, left for the rana's camp along with the emissary and most of the party. Aisha remained in Udai City with two servants and a guard in a house on a lake. Her father, meanwhile, sat in a tent on a cushion, in a circle with TodarMal, Pratap, Chaudry and another. At the meeting, Pratap spoke with calm tone but harsh words.

"We have frankly had enough of your Mongol masters," he lectured. "They plague us like they plagued our ancestors. They know nothing but violence and conquest."

TodarMal raised an eyebrow in disbelief. "Come on," he said. "We Hindavis have been killing and robbing each other long before the foreigners came. I humbly ask that you look through the other side of the lens. The emperor has unified most of our land, and with that unity comes peace. Let him bring peace and prosperity to Mewar."

"If the emperor wants to bring peace, then let him stop his attacks."

"And he will. You only need go to him and pledge fealty."

Pratap snorted at the idea and stroked his long stache.

TodarMal paused to review his mental list of talking points. At moments like this, he usually looked off to the left, but now he kept his gaze locked with the eyes of an intimidating opponent. Pratap was an accomplished and respected warrior and a charismatic leader. On the death of his father, he had been thrust into power by his family and other leaders, over the head and objection of his older brother.

TodarMal continued. "Do you deny that His Highness has brought peace to his subjects?"

"I do."

"I humbly disagree, and I ask that you beware of selective outrage. You should ask yourself 'Do I care about who is being killed, or only about who is doing the killing?'"

"I care about both," said Pratap. "I don't want to be ruled by Muslims."

On hearing this, TodarMal had a sudden, secret desire to laugh, shake his head, put a friendly hand on Pratap's shoulder, and tell him "Girlfriend, Akbar ain't no Muslim." Now his gaze did drift leftwards, and a little smirk slipped as he fell into a brief daydream.

"His Highness is far from dogmatic," was his actual reply. "In matters of religion, he seeks not victory but truth. This is a widely known fact and you know it; so please at least give him credit for it. He's a renaissance man. Most of his administration is composed of Hindus. The emperor himself has taken part in Hindu rituals. He regularly convenes interfaith forums. Just last month, he hosted a discussion with some Christians called… um… J-sweets." He relaxed, sat back, and continued confidently. "This is a subject in which I think you will easily find compromise."

Pratap wagged his finger. "You are mistaken, my friend," he said. "You are trying to make a point but you don't have the ingredients. Compromise is achievable between things that are different, not opposite. When two things are opposite, you can only gain ground or cede ground. Our two religions *are* opposites. The Muslims' central tenant is that their god is the only god. Our way, our gods and idols is not just a sin for them. It is *the* supreme sin. It is number one of their ten commandments. I think the reason that you think and he thinks that compromise is possible is because neither of you have yet realized the truth. The truth is that Akbar's true god is Akbar."

TodarMal's face soured. "I'm afraid we may be getting carried away," he said. "These are words of war, not diplomacy. May I suggest that we break for tea? Give ourselves a chance to reset the tone and direction."

The others agreed.


Aisha's day was more pleasant. She started her morning sitting by the window of her second-floor bedroom gazing over a lake, Lake Pichola, only fifty meters away. Its expanse reached to the horizon in several directions. Its ripples shimmered, entrancing her as shimmering ripples tend to do. A warm breeze further lulled her into sedation and nearly squashed her motivation before the day even started. But she was young and excited to explore the young city, and she broke the stealthy spell of beauty. She washed up, threw on her dupatta (head scarf), wrapped a sari, chugged some goat milk and a half a chapati, and grabbed Rubina by the hand. She would have dashed out the door, but Ruby convinced her to wait for Sultana and for their brawny guard whose name nobody knew.

Once outside, they saw a site of enormous construction along the shore to their north. It teemed with busy workers. Aisha figured (correctly) that it was going to be another palace and she wanted to investigate, but her guard advised against it, and she was wise enough to heed counsel. They followed a road into town instead. The city felt more familiar to her than the countryside she had just crossed, with most of the buildings and many of the roads built of stone. Much of it choked with congestion, with homes built so closely that traffic and news flowed almost as easily by rooftop as by street.

She marveled at the pomp and color of everything. Bright, magnificent decorations tugged her attention in every direction. Banners and tapestries and statues of every size and quality stood or hung or danced in the breeze. Doorways were freshly painted. "What fancy people!" she thought. Or perhaps it wasn't always this way. She remembered hearing something about a festival. She then realized how plainly everyone dressed in contrast, and it made sense – whatever was coming had not yet arrived. She hoped it would before she had to leave.

The bazaar had the usual carnival atmosphere. Vendors barked from stalls, pitching their wares and deals. The merchants who had no store simply planted their merchandise in the middle of the road, in spots they had staked out long ago. The ones from out of town sold their goods off the backs of carts.

On one road, a young man struggled with a donkey who would not budge, despite all the pulling, pushing, whipping and begging the man could muster. The obdurate creature was already pooped from the sacks of flour and rice she carried. But something else had stopped her – a memory. The day before, at the same spot, she had seen an elephant cross her path. She had not gone any further then and would not now. She simply worried less about whipping and whining than about elephants.

Aisha pitied both man and beast and approached to help. She stroked and tousled the animal's frowsy hair and fed her an apple. She leaned into her ear and whispered for about a minute in soft, lilting tones, words of encouragement and reassurance.

During that minute, the young man watched Aisha. During that minute, he succumbed to a stealthy spell of beauty, one that would never break.

At the end of it, she gave the donkey a gentle pat on her bum and the donkey walked away. She then noticed the man and recognized him as the same boy her father had whacked the day before. She hadn't really looked at him then but saw him now and felt something strange and pleasant in her stomach. But he was staring, so she squirmed until they both realized that his flour, rice and ass had walked away. He thanked her quickly before running off. He didn't have far to go, as his stand was right around the corner and the donkey knew where to go. He tied and unloaded her hastily, and ran back to where he hoped the girl would still be.

Aisha had not gotten far, and he called out as he approached, so as not to startle.

"Excuse me! You'll come to my shop for tea, yes?" he asked as his pace slowed. "Please. Let me thank you for today and to be sorry for yesterday, yes? You must come and I'll serve you."

Aisha hesitated.

Again, "You must come, please. Have tea in my shop. Please."

She glanced at the adults, then made a decision. "Yes."

They followed him to his stand, aptly named since there was no place to sit among the large sacs of lentils and grains and such that filled the place. It turns out that such sacs make very comfy chairs when tied shut, so he did just that. He only had enough chai supply for himself.

"Please stay," he said, running off to a neighboring merchant to borrow more cups, ingredients, and a bigger pot. He was back in a jiff. While the ladies sat, he stayed outside with the guard and donkey, where there was room to cook. Everyone remained quiet in this strange situation. Squatting at a makeshift stove, he bounced up intermittently to converse with Aisha over the counter.

"How did you make the donkey go?" he asked.

"I don't know. I'm just good with animals. They like me."

"Oh, I see."

Back to the tea. Up again.

"I'm Sunil. My friends call me Sunny. I have two friends and seven brothers and sisters. We live outside the city with my parents and grandma. We grow most of what you see. Some of it's from the neighbors."

As he went down again, Rubina leaned over and whispered "Miss Aisha, this is very inappropriate." Sultana nodded in agreement.

"What are your names?" he asked.

Aisha introduced everyone except the guard, whose name she still didn't know. Sunil repeated her name with slow enthusiasm, savoring the sound. "Aishhaa!" He then savored some tea and continued. "Have you come for Gangaur?"

She looked confused. "What?"

"The festival! No? But you *must* come, yes? It's tomorrow, after all. Maybe Gauri will bless you, I think."

Rubina spoke up. "We are leaving tomorrow."

Aisha corrected her. "We *might* be leaving tomorrow."

"Then you might stay," said Sunil. "That's a good start. If not for the festival, then why have you come?"

Aisha gave the adults more than a glance this time before answering. "We're here on business." Sensing another question, she quickly added "I really can't say much more than that."

Sunil flashed a sunny smile that melted Aisha and Ruby too. "I see. Your father's business?"

"Yes."

He suddenly realized something about his guests. There had been something odd but familiar – their air, their mannerisms – that he couldn't quite pinpoint until now. They were Muslims. There were a few Muslims living in Udai City. They mostly kept to themselves; they certainly didn't come to festivals. They also dealt very seriously in their businesses, he felt. No nonsense.

But he most remembered that "they" killed thousands of his fellow countrymen at Fort Chittor when he was just a boy. They were murdering bastards who could be trusted with money but not power. This is what he had been taught and what he knew until now. Now he served them tea and they seemed harmless, and *she* was magnificent.

He wanted to show off, but he didn't own much or know much. Then he remembered his knife, an antique Persian dagger, once owned by a prince or something. It had a curved blade, single edge, pointed tip. The ornate handle contained some writing that he couldn't read and a few craters where jewels once lay. He kept it shiny and sharp and tied to his calf. His show-and-tell was short-lived, however, when the guard took notice.

"I think you should put that away, Son," he said with calm authority.

Sunil complied without hesitation. "Where are you headed?" he asked.

"We're just looking around."

"Then you must let me show you around please. It would be my honor. I'm a very good guide," Sunil said, his hand placed sincerely and proudly on his bosom. "I usually do it for money, but not today, of course."

"NO," said Rubina and Sultana in chorus.

Aisha looked annoyed. "Yes," she sternly countered.

The scene made Sunil a little uncomfortable, but only for a second. "Come on!" he said with excitement, waving them to follow. "There's a lot of beauty here, some great food and some terrific freaks. There's this one guy. You give him a couple of coins, and he'll eat broken glass. There's another guy who has this box, no bigger than this. It's totally airtight. For a mite, he'll squeeze himself into it. He slows his breath and his heart and stays in there for like ten minutes."

He closed up his shop and took them around. He showed them things garish and others noble. They saw artists and artisans. He brought them to temples, elaborate structures of Hindu and Jain devotion. At lunch, they stopped at his cousin's stall to fill up on greasy junk. After, he brought them down to the water to spy on a nesting colony of black-headed ibis, a striking bird with a white, puffy body, ugly black head and a long, curved sword for a bill.

Overall, the group had a very nice day and became somewhat fond of him. He remained a gentleman throughout, except perhaps that he only spoke to Aisha. He watched her at every opportunity. He couldn't help it. She never sensed his stares but felt nervous all the same – a sweet anxiety, something new.

Dusk arrived. Time to part. He spent the remaining minutes steering a circuitous conversation – talking first about her family, then his family, then his older brothers, then his older brothers' wives, then their marriages, then marriage – steering it gently to his target question.

"Are you arranged to be married?" he asked.

"Yes," she replied with deadpan seriousness. "A short, shriveled, gray-haired man. He's disgusting."

Sunil looked more lost than defeated. "Gray-haired… um…"

She couldn't hold it any longer and burst into laughter.

"Sunny, come on. No. That's my monkey." She gave him a shot in the arm.

He didn't surface very quickly. For a few seconds, he kept an expression that could pass for either confusion or the smelling of a fart. "Monkey?" The face soon morphed into a shy smile, and she melted again.


Aisha's father didn't return that night, or the next. The rest of that first day of diplomacy devolved into exhaustive discussions about manifold squabbles and petty grievances involving relatives, friends, and other prominent people on both sides. A large list of concerns and proposals had been compiled to bring to the emperor. The next morning started with an equally light, but not so petty subject – Aisha.

"What about the girl?" inquired the rana.

"Girl?"

"His daughter." Pratap pointed to Sahani. "I have a cousin. His wife died a while ago. Consumption."

At the start of this day, like the day before, the rana and the emissary agreed that they could speak with their respective associates in unfamiliar languages without permission. Now, TodarMal turned to Sahani and spoke in Persian. "What about the girl?"

Sahani hesitated a minute, weighted by the same internal conflict felt by most doting fathers of teenaged girls. "Yes, we can have a look."

TodarMal turned back to Pratap. "The general would be honored to meet your cousin," he reported.

At this point, Chaudry chimed in, speaking to Pratap in Bhil. The Bhil were the indigenous people who lived in the surrounding hills and forests of the region. They were poorer than the Rajputs, with different gods and customs. Their shorter stature, darker skin and broad noses made them somewhat recognizable. The word "Bhil" means "bow" in some ancient Dravidian language. It is a name given to them for the archery skills of their men. But they didn't call themselves Bow; they called themselves Dudes.

"If I may," said Chaudry to his king. "Intermarriage is fine, and useful in many ways, but we should always avoid taking their women when possible. Always send them our women."

"Why is that?" asked Pratap.

"Because Your Highness is noble and wise. Sure, in the present, it makes no difference. But in your devotion to the Rajput people, and to Lord Shiva, over years and generations, it can strike a great impact. Faith is not spread by the pointed swords of men, but by the loving arms of mothers."

Pratap digested his words, then turned back to TodarMal and back to the common tongue. "We'll get back to you on that." He then turned to a bigger topic. "I think it's time we stop dancing around the main issue, the real reason that you want my land and my loyalty. Let us face it. I am literally, physically in your way; the last stop between you and the ocean."

"I think you misspoke," replied TodarMal. "When you say 'real' reason, that would mean it's the only reason, and that would suggest that all the other reasons we've discussed were disingenuous. I don't think that's what you meant. But you're right, a trade route to the ocean is a big goal and perhaps the biggest. His Highness wants prosperity for his people as well as peace. That means international commerce."

"Which explains why his finance minister is also his chief diplomat. But why push us around? Why not use a little imagination and a little honey? You Mongols like to collect taxes but you don't like to pay them. How about you let us keep our independence, and you just pay us a toll? We can all make money. We can hammer out a treaty right now."

TodarMal thought for a moment. "I will present your proposal to the emperor," he said. "But I must tell you that I will advise him against it."

"Why is that?" Pratap sounded annoyed.

"Because when we open this traffic, commerce will blossom and millions of our people will become dependent on it. That would put the stability of the empire at your mercy."

"Well, perhaps we can figure out some safeguards."

"Perhaps we can."

They discussed the subject for another hour before moving on to others. Sahani daydreamed through the discussion, running through his worries and his task lists. He wondered about how his wives and sons fared. And he wondered about Aisha.

Aisha didn't sleep well the night before. She didn't dream about boys; she dreamt about flying, and about her teeth falling out. But before that, the thoughts of a boy had kept her awake. Even before her night of insomnia, she was already tired from a day of walking in the sun. Now exhausted, she planned to do absolutely nothing. Suddenly, a voice restored her vigor, raised her spirit and also made her somewhat nervous. It was his voice, and it called her name.

The voice didn't come from her western window where she watched the lake, but from the east, facing the courtyard. He was calling with one of those absurd, hushed voices that people use that don't make any sense. You only want one person to hear you and you think that, if you yell a whisper, the sound will only go where you want. She dashed across the room and looked out. He faced the south wing of the house, not knowing where she was. He had brought a friend.

"Hi! Um. What do you want?" she said.

He turned towards her and smiled. "Today's festival! Will you miss it?"

"Get the hell out of here!" yelled Rubina in the same hushed yell from a downstairs window. "Or I'll have you beaten!"

Aisha threw on her shoes and a dupatta and ran downstairs to Ruby in the kitchen. "Please, Ruby, let's go?" she asked humbly.

"No, Miss Aisha! I have to cook, and your father may be coming home, and it is improper," she said. "This behavior does not suit you. This boy does not suit you."

Aisha scampered down the hall towards the open door. "Sure, we'll come!" she said cheerily.

Ruby chased after her. "You must not go alone with a boy. It is forbidden!"

"That is why you have to come with me," said Aisha, and she grabbed Ruby's forearm with both hands. Aisha proved strong for her small frame, and she managed to pull Ruby several steps before Ruby could stop her. Aisha let go and stood straight, arms folded.

"If I go without you, who is going to get in more trouble, you or me?" she challenged. "Come on. You were with him all day. You know he's nice. Do you really want to cook while the whole city is partying?"

Ruby made a face like she had swallowed a bug, then she relented. "Ok, just let me get dressed."

Sunil had also slept poorly; in fact, hardly at all. He had spent all night thinking about her, whether to pursue her, how to go about it, and whether or not he was just crazy. Eventually he decided he *must* be with her, and that the only possible way was to simply find her house, jump the gate and call her name. He also decided that he was indeed wacko. That notion was extinguished as she emerged from the door.

"Who's your friend?" she asked.

"This is Pankaj. We call him Punk. He's my best friend."

Pankaj was about the same age. Shirtless, he wore a long, white loin cloth that hung to his knees and a plain white cloth tied round his head. On his feet were two worn, black army boots that he had scavenged off a fallen soldier years earlier. He had spent most of his teen years clunking around in those oversized boots, looking quite odd. Now he had grown into them and almost never took them off. He gave a quiet hello and a nod. Aisha recognized him as one of the boys who had begged from her father.

Sunil cautiously attempted a compliment. "You look… well, anyways … you look pretty really nice."

Aisha looked down with embarrassment and thanked him. She and Ruby kept a respectable one-to-two meters distance from the boys, and they maintained that social distance as they followed them off the grounds. They all took one look back at the house. Nobody else had heard or stirred.

They followed the same route as before, crossing the meadow behind the house, through the tall grass, being wary of snakes. Then along the creek to the makeshift bridge, then across to the dirt road, which joined the stone road, which led east into town. The townsfolk now dressed in their newest and best, especially the women. Their clothes were adorned with gold, wrapped in bright designs of color and glitter, and faces to match. Even the oxen were dressed up, and the elephants were painted in gay patterns. Food and drink flowed all around, and small clusters of people sang and danced together.

Ahead, something was afoot, but Aisha and friends couldn't see what. The backs of spectators blocked their view. The sound of drums shook the air. As they weaved through the crowd, they came to a circle of eight men dancing in the square. The dancers wore spectacular, matching silver dresses, red turbans, red sashes and red slippers. Their skirts flowed and their blades flashed as they twirled, bowed, stepped and waved their swords in synchronicity. In the surrounding buildings, people watched from windows and roofs. From their view, the dancers looked like a kaleidoscope.

In another part of town, they found a contest where women competed in balancing stacks of clay pots on their heads. The winner wore seven pots for fifteen minutes while nursing a baby.

They eventually met up with Sunil's other best friend. Like Sunil, he was barefoot, donned in pajamas and wrapped in a shawl. His face looked smart. His nickname was not.

"This is my best friend Bansal," Sunil reported. "We call him Bunny."

Aisha stopped, put hand on hip, tipped her head, and peered at Sunil under eyebrows cocked in disbelief. "Wait a minute," she said. "Sunny, Bunny and Punk? Is that a joke?" The three friends just looked at each other and shrugged.

They went all over town, taking in a variety of street shows, and the day passed quickly. Even Ruby couldn't help but have fun. As the day grew long, the local revelers began heading for the center of town. By late afternoon, everyone had gathered there and separated by gender. Each woman held a female idol on her head.

"That's Gauri," said Sunny, pointing to the idols. She's the goddess of fertility and love. The virgins ask her for a good husband and the married women ask to bless the ones they have." He paused. "Perhaps she will bless you, I think," he said sheepishly.

Aisha shivered. She had spent the day being entertained by paganism, spent it with a boy, and a pagan boy to boot. She felt a little dirty and a little fearful of God. But she was also well-mannered and in love, so she measured her reply. "I don't think so."

The women of Udai began to sing in unison and dance down the street, a merry chorus parading through the city, praising the sculpted scouts atop their heads. Aisha and company followed, tugged along by curiosity and the lure of joy. For a while, they shed their mores in an effort to stay together in the crowd and not get squished by it. For one brief, chaotic moment, Aisha and Sunny even held hands. That was interesting.

Eventually, the crowd reached its destination, the Gangaur Ghat. The celebrants took turns, a dozen or two at a time, descending the broad steps to the lake, dunking their idols in the water, then saying a prayer. Most returned to their homes after that. A few hung around for a while.

Aisha sat on the ghat steps, leaned back on her hands and contemplated. Away in the distance, across the water, a flock of flamingos crossed the sky; black silhouettes against a broad, pink sun setting behind the mountains. Down the ghat, a stone's throw away, Bunny and Punk laughed about something. All was still and quiet, and their voices carried. In the other direction, Ruby picked flowers in the twilight. Aisha felt relaxed, so much so that she hardly noticed or cared that Sunny had taken it upon himself to sit closer to her than acceptable. He sat for a moment and enjoyed this subtle accomplishment. He whispered her name across the lake. "Aishhhhhhaa."

"Yes?"

"Nothing. I just love the sound of your name. I made a poem about it, you know. About you."

"You what?" She turned to him.

"Yah, I stayed up late thinking about… it. Will you hear it?"

She hesitated a second. "Ok."

*Aishhhsaa sounds like the blowing breeze.*
*The leaves hear its song and applaud with glee*
*Announcing the stormy dance of the trees*
*And the march of the waves across the sea.*

*By the day which reveals it*
*And by the night which conceals it,*
*My love for her is a natural force*
*Eternal and sure as a planet's course.*
*Like the moon which follows with calm devotion*
*And stirs the tides of a roiling ocean,*
*Or the radiant sun which shines bright and hot,*
*A more heavenly thing was never wrought.*

Aisha was well-read and recognized a couple of the verses. She would have been amused by his plagiarism had she not been so taken aback by his forwardness. In her young life, she had never been so flattered or moved. She sat there, agape and aghast, and could only squeeze out one letter. "I…"

He broke the awkward silence. "I didn't really have anything to give you, so I made that. And I also made this for you. I know how you like bracelets. I think this one will fit you better than the ones you have."

He presented a red, wooden bangle, thicker and smaller than her others. He had carved a fairly intricate design into it and had obviously spent a lot of time at it. He had also carved her name in it. "I can't write, so I asked someone to show me. I hope it's right." It was. The bangle was also oddly shaped – round with a twist, a Mobius loop.

"Its shape is like a mystery," he explained. "It has only one side. You'll just run your finger along it and see."

She did so, then marveled, then thanked him sincerely. She was growing bashful and he was growing confident. He tried to touch her head.

"Why don't you remove your scarf, yes?"

"My master forbids it," she said, and pulled away.

"What master? There's no master here."

She scoffed. "He is always here. His eyes are always on me. And on you."

"What kind of...?" he asked, scratching his chin. "Oh, you mean God? Are you a God girl?"

"Yes, of course."

He puffed his chest. "I have no master."

"We are all slaves," she chided. "You're either a slave to someone else, or a slave to your own desires, and *that* is the cruelest of masters."

He looked skeptical. "And you don't have desires?" he challenged, lifting an eyebrow and trying so carefully to inch closer.

"That is none of your business."

He recognized the mildest hint of annoyance in her tone, and quickly agreed, apologized, and changed the subject. As they chatted about smaller things, their comfort levels met an equilibrium. They were talking about their families when she let it slip that her father was a general.

"A general? Really?"

"I'm pretty sure. Anyways, he's a really important man in the emperor's army."

"Wow, the emperor!" He was too impressed to remember his hatred for Akbar. "I heard he's got like a hundred wives."

"I don't think it's that much."

"Well, it's a lot. What I wouldn't give for that life."

Upset, she gave him a shove. "You just got done saying how much you love me! And the beautiful poem and the beautiful bracelet and la dee da."

Sunny turned palms to the sky and pleaded his defense. "But I *do* love you! Can't I love more than one woman?"

"No, you can't. Duh."

"Why not?"

"Because true love is for only one person."

"How do you figure?" he asked. "I can love my mother, yes?"

She started to think him absurd, and it showed. "That's different."

"Why?"

"Because motherly love is different from romantic love." Her eyes rolled.

"I disagree."

"That's sick." She stood up.

"No, it's not. I don't believe there are different kinds of love. Love is love, and you can love anyone. These other things – romance and motherly instinct and the bond of brothers, and the bond of veterans – these are ornaments for love. They are not love itself."

Aisha contemplated his words for a second. At any other time, from anyone else, she might have found them interesting. But now she folded her arms and quickly decided that he was just full of it. "You're just rationalizing. You're not ready for love and you're not serious about me."

Sunny believed what he said, and he didn't think that she was being fair or logical. But he also realized that this ship was sinking fast, and that she meant more to him than being right. So he dropped to his knees and planted his face and forearms in the ground at her feet. "I swear that I will never love any woman, in this life or the next, except you."

This gesture quickly eased her young mind, and she realized that she did indeed love him, and she realized why. At that same moment, a large figure came running through the dark towards them, arms waving in the air.

"Miss Aisha!" yelled her guard, "I have been seeking everywhere for you! I was so scared!" He turned towards Ruby, who had returned from her floral pursuits. "How could you let this happen?" Back to Aisha. "This is very dangerous! Your father—"

"Is he back?" Aisha interrupted, alarmed.

"Not yet. Not that I know. I've been gone much of the day seeking you."

"And now you've found me, and now you're keeping me safe, so you need not fear," she said. A hint of arrogance sullied her voice.

"Miss Aisha, you must go back now!"

Aisha, now certifiably in love, did not want to look like a child in front of Sunny. "I'm not ready yet," she countered.

The guard's face grew red, his eyes bugged, and his finger raised to point at her. "Young lady," he said, "there is nothing that I can do to you, *but…*" He turned his pointer to Sunny "I can take this one and throw him in the lake right now and watch him drown, right now."

Aisha became frightened, not just by the nature of the threat, but because it was delivered by a man who she had always known as quiet and pleasant. She knew he meant it and she straightened up quickly. "No, please! I'm sorry. I'm coming."

Aisha and Ruby turned to go with him. He quickly calmed and returned to his affable self. He liked Sunny and felt kind of bad. He turned back towards the boy. "It's nothing personal, you know. It's just a simple choice. If I have to choose between losing my head or taking yours, I choose yours." He shrugged.

Sunny pushed out a half-hearted smile. "I get it, Dude. Say, what *is* your name, anyways?"

"Caligula."

"Caligula?"

"Yah, it's Roman. My mother heard it once and thought it sounded noble and important."

"Well, goodbye Caligula, Rubina, and goodbye Aishhhhaa."

Aisha turned, waved a sad good-bye, and left.

Bunny and Punk had already scattered. Sunny stood alone.

Sahani returned the next day. He didn't see his daughter much and when he did, her mood seemed dim. However, he was too tired from the trip to give her much notice, and too occupied with business to give her much thought. No one uttered Sunny's name.

# THREE

The journey home was quicker than the egress. On arrival, Aisha was pleased to find Tarik on gate duty. Young Tarik was the only member of her dad's security team whose name she knew. He had always been friendly and kind to her, and he remained so now.

"Welcome home, Miss Monkey," he said with a toothy grin. He had begun working there around the time that she adopted Malik the Great, and he was tickled by the sight of a ten-year-old girl with a pet monkey, so she quickly became Miss Monkey. She had grown a little old for the moniker, but she still didn't mind, especially now being exhausted and glad to be home.

Keeping to his tradition, he reached in his pocket and presented her a glass bangle, sparkly and green. "Here you go, Sunshine. I'm sure you broke a couple on your trip."

She cried when she saw the state of her monkey, who had become gaunt and ill in a very short time. She devoted her attention to caring for him and about him. But in the back of her mind lived Sunny, and her own appetite deteriorated, as did her sleep. Malik, however, rejuvenated nicely, at least for a while. A month or two later, as the summer rains began, he began to decline again, slowly and for no apparent reason. This time, he didn't recover. He died in the fall.

Aisha wept for days. Feeling alone, she latched on to her stepmom, even sleeping in her bed. Karna consoled her as best she could with food and hugs and words. The best of these was her reassurance that if Aisha led a good life, she would likely see her little friend again one day. This consoled her, for she had not thought there were animals in Paradise.

"But Mom," she asked, "how can that be if they have no souls?"

"Oh, my love, of course animals have souls. All of God's creatures do."

Her father's words, though not as warm, also helped. "You must remember that Allah did not give you this creature; He only loaned him to you. You should be thankful for that."

Aisha grew quickly that year and into the next. She outgrew most of her clothes and spent much of her time making new ones. Her menarche came. That was fun. She eventually stopped dreading the inevitable, imminent, arranged wedding engagement. She came to accept it and also accept the loss of her baby, Malik. And she got over her first crush, What's-His-Face. That winter was bitter cold.

But spring soon debuted in full regalia, erupting with color and life. The house livened with sunlight and visitors, the grounds bustled with workers and the nights hummed with insects. Aisha learned how to load and shoot a musket. Tarik taught her and her friend, after much nagging and securing her father's permission. She didn't like it as much as she thought she would. It was too loud and a bit scary. Her ears rang for days and she was teased for weeks by the servants and some of her friends. People didn't normally tease her much; they had simply come to expect her to do weird stuff. But not this weird.

She also took up gardening. She didn't take interest in flowers or other pretty, useless things. She grew food. She liked it for the same reason she liked to cook – she looked forward to internalizing and sharing the tasty results of her effort. Her fruits would not break like a glass bangle or fade like the remembrance of a gift once given. They would become a lifelong part of her physical existence long after memory of them had left, like the mother of whom she had no memory.

Like all her endeavors, she dove into this one thoroughly and cluttered her room with a plethora of seedlings. She was tending to them one night when she was suddenly struck in the head with a realization. It was the realization that she had been struck in the head with an object. She looked down and saw that it was only a pebble, but it stung. She spent a moment in confusion, trying to discern what had just happened. Another rock whizzed past, coming from the window. She looked down, through the tree outside, into the dark. Standing there in the yard were Sunny, Bunny and Punk.

She stood there, mouth agape with astonishment as Sunny smiled and waved. Eventually, she spoke. "You hit me in the head with a rock!"

"Ooh, I am very sorry! I was trying to signal you without noise."

"What are you doing here?" she whispered. "How did you get past the guards?"

Once again, Sunny fell to his knees, his hands clasped in supplication. "I have come for you," he declared. "Please come with me and never leave my side."

Aisha felt a sob building. A long pause ensued, sad for her and tense for him. Her cracked voice broke the silence. "I can't go anywhere with a man who I'm not married to."

Sunny pointed to his friends. "But, as you can see, I brought two witnesses. Let us have this done right here and now."

Now the tears came. She shook her head. "I can't. I can't marry a pagan."

Those words brought another grin to his face, for he was ready for them.

"Like I said, two witnesses." His countenance turned serious as he pointed to heaven. "I hereby declare that there is no god except *The* God, and I declare that Mohammed is the prophet of God."

Her weeping turned blissful, her face turned bright, and she nodded in affirmation. "Ok. Yes. But I don't know how we can do this. If I come down through the house, we'll definitely get caught."

He thought about it for a moment, then proceeded to climb the mahogany tree outside her window. With strength and agility, he climbed into her room almost as easily as Malik had done so many times before. He bowed, then turned his back to her. "Hop on," he said.

She hesitated. She had climbed that tree several times herself when she was younger, until the day she fell and broke her arm.

"Don't worry," he said. "I'm skinny but strong as a bull."

She climbed on his back and rode him down to the ground. Then, there, under the great mahogany, they swore in whispers their allegiance to each other.

Afterwards, he grabbed her hand, and the four of them ran quietly across the yard, through the brush, then skirted along the outer wall and passed through the gate. The guard was gone, which concerned her, and she wondered how many previous nights she had slept unguarded. They continued to run another kilometer or so through the dark, quiet streets, passing only an occasional vagrant, until they reached a thicket where two camels stood tied to a tree.

"You guys came all this way for me?" Aisha asked.

Bunny grinned a grin as warm as Sunny's. He had undergone a huge growth spurt in the past year, and Aisha didn't recognize him until now. "We are your friends," he said. "We are friends for life now."

Punk didn't smile. "Yes, friends," he said. "Do you got any money?"

"Um, no I, uh. No."

Punk looked at Sunny. "You should've made sure she brought money," he said.

"There was no time. You know this."

"Well, we'd have a better chance of getting back with our heads attached if we didn't have to steal everything along the way. Anyways…"


They rode back to Mewar by day. They got about halfway home before Bunny and Punk got drunk. It was on day three of their journey and the newlyweds had gone off honeymooning and foraging for food, leaving Bunny and Punk behind to get bored, get drunk and abuse the camels. But one camel was poorly tied and the other not at all, and both were scared off. Thus, the rest of the trip was made on foot. The whole expedition took eleven days. It would have been nine, but Aisha had never walked so much before, and she didn't have the shoes or the feet for it. Her husband carried her piggy-back for long stretches, but not enough. She needed time to rest and heal her blisters. They traveled mostly at night to avoid predators and heat. In the cities, they stole bread and pies. In the country, they stole vegetables and eggs, or ate wild fruit. One day, on the plain of Ajmer, they found the remains of an abandoned hut. On another, they found a cave hidden deep in the lush foothills of Mewar. The other days, they slept under the sky, shielded by their shawls from view and sun.

When they were a few leagues away from Udai City, Punk pointed to a hill. "I'm kin to some folks who live just past there. They can feed us and hopefully lend a horse or mule. Then I can ride ahead."

"Why ride ahead?" Sunny asked.

"Because she is a general's daughter and we kidnapped her as far as anyone's concerned. She might be a big deal. I don't know how long we have been gone, but it sure seems like plenty of time for some important people to be looking for her and raising a big fuss. You ain't gonna just walk in your front door and introduce her to mama."

Sunny rubbed his chin, which had five hairs growing from it. "I see your point. What's your plan?"

"Nobody knows me," explained Punk. "I only spent a few hours at festival with her and some lady, and I didn't talk. But they know you, they know your store and who knows what else. I'll ride ahead and look around. I'll talk to my mom, and you can stay at my place till we know the situation better."

It made sense.

Punk's cousins lived in a hamlet with about a dozen kids, one blind and crippled from leprosy. She lived in a shed out back. They all lived in squalor but still had class, and they shared some turnip soup with their guests. They also did indeed have a mule to lend, and lend it they did without hesitation.

"Stay here," said Punk. "I'll be back in a few hours." And off he went in cantering stride. Meanwhile, Sunny, Bunny and Aisha found a quiet place to sleep in the woods, away from the busy locals. Punk had not returned by the time they awakened, and they spent the rest of the night worrying and wondering whether to wait or to go. The noisy woodland creatures taunted them.

He finally came back as dawn expelled the dark. "Festival is on!" he proclaimed as he dismounted. "It's a blast!" Nobody else seemed interested, only exhausted.

"Festival again?" said Aisha. "You guys are always celebrating."

"What about your mom?" asked Sunny. "How did it go?"

"Oh, yeah. It's cool. She hasn't heard anything. Everything seems quiet… except festival!"


And so they left, and Aisha began her final march to her new life. It was on this last leg of her journey that she began to feel the gravity of her actions, and the guilt. Until now, her father had not crossed her mind much since she left. She didn't normally consider him much when he was away, and he had been away when she left home. In fact, he had been away much of her life. Nonetheless, she loved him, and Punk's words had stirred an awareness in her. For many days, her husband's embrace had been her opiate, shielding her not only from fear and cold, but from all unpleasantness. Now, more and more, she worried about her father's worry, and she grieved for his sorrow. She didn't worry as much about her mother. She somehow knew that Karna would be ok, though she would miss her. But her father... Aisha began to wonder if she was, in fact, the good person she had always thought she was, and she felt Satan's pointy finger run down the back of her neck. She also became increasingly concerned whether she was equipped to handle poverty. She hoped that sore feet would be the worst of it. She walked over to Sunny and pulled his arms around her.

As they trudged into Udai City, even Punk was no longer in the mood for the merriment which assaulted them from all directions. Following him, they wound their way through the singing and dancing and clapping and drumming and cooking and eating and smiling and waving. Aisha was relieved when they turned down an empty lane. The narrow alley felt less cramped than the broad thoroughfare from which they emerged. It continued for thirty meters, then made a sharp turn to the right. It was at that bend that Punk suddenly stopped, turned around, and looked into Aisha's eyes.

"Aishhhhha. You got any money?" he asked in a slithery tone.

Bansal, who had brought up the rear, struck Sunny in the back of his head with a rock the size of a fist. Sunny fell forward onto his face, stunned. Big Bansal straddled his back. With his right arm, he leaned on Sunny's head, which was turned to the left. With his left, he grabbed Sunny's left wrist and secured it behind his back.

Aisha bit her cheek, confused and frightened. "No, Punk. You know I don't."

Punk sauntered into Aisha's personal space, his eyes grabbing hers, his foul breath on her face. "The thing is," he said, "I don't believe you."

Sunny struggled to breathe under Bansal's weight. He mustered enough air to cry out once. "Pankaj, by the gods, what are you doing?"

Punk ignored him. "I'm betting that you do have something of value under all that fancy fabric. Of course, I wouldn't know if you did, but Sunny would. But Sunny's not a sharing kinda guy, are you Sunny? Even with your best friends, who sacrificed and risked so much for you."

Aisha froze and Punk sensed fear. He proceeded to frisk her with caution. Even now, there was a line he dared not cross, and his hands grudgingly complied.

Sunny couldn't see what was happening, which made him terrified, which made him wild, which made him dangerous. And Bansal, despite his size, had positioned himself too high, leaving Sunny's waist free. Sunny managed to twist and flex his hips until he lay nearly on his right side. He held that position for a second, long enough to flex his left knee and, with his free hand, reach his left shin, to which his knife was strapped. With a firm grip, he drew the blade across the only piece of Bansal he could reach – the left quadricep, just above the knee. He cut deeply through muscle and tendon.

Bansal gave a yell, from fear more than pain, and grabbed the wound with both hands. The pain soon arrived, and with it anger, as Sunny turned on his back to face him. Still clutching with the left, Bansal released his right hand to grab Sunny's throat. Under the pressure of the broad, bloody claw, Sunny felt his consciousness slip away. He made one limp attempt to save his own life and stab Bansal's chest. Fortunately, his dagger was wickedly sharp, viciously designed, and happy to do most of the work. Bansal suffered a laceration to his left lung and a pulmonary artery. His skin became pale and clammy as his nervous system struggled to maintain his blood pressure. He crawled a few steps to a pile of wood and sat himself up against it. As he sat, bleeding out his life, he watched the celebration stream past the alley, paying him no notice. He watched until his vision faded. His breath became desperate and erratic as blood and air filled the space around his lung, compressing and collapsing it. Then he breathed no more.

Meanwhile, Sunny grabbed Aisha and fled back the way they came. Punk stood there like a punk, shocked and dumbstruck. Aisha looked back as she plunged into the crowd. In the alley, she saw two uniformed men who must have come from the other direction. One examined Bansal while the other talked to Punk. She thought she recognized one of them, but it couldn't be.

Sunny ran fast, sometimes too fast, hurting Aisha's shoulder as he pulled her along. They wound through the crowded city streets, barraged from within by adrenaline and from without by sounds and sights and smells. The mixture created a toxic intoxication. The world swirled and they kept running.

Until they finally stopped. Aisha recognized the shop. Its proprietor was Sunny's friend or cousin or something, a man in his 30s, wearing nothing but a loin cloth. The man, named Bola, stayed there all day with his pariah dog, selling baskets, winnowing fans and other woven bamboo stuff. Sunny jabbered furiously at him in a foreign language. The two conversed for a while until Sunny finally said something she understood. Placing his hand on the dog, he said "Dude, I swear on your dog."

"Ok then," said Bola, and the conversation finished. He strapped on his bow and quiver and closed his store.

Sunny turned to Aisha. "We're going to stay with him for a while," he explained. He took off after Bola, who was already halfway down the road.

"Oh" was all she could say as she joined the chase. There was no more handholding as she struggled to keep up. They marched at a brisk pace, led by the lean, tan dingo, its ears erect with constant vigilance. When they reached the city limits, she realized, disappointed, that this would not be a short trip. As the day and the miles grew longer, disappointment grew into dismay. She finally became exasperated when they turned off the trail and plunged into the small, rocky mountains to the west. She demanded a rest, and they stopped.

Sunny held his bride as she cried in his chest. His face, no longer sunny but grim with worry, was a new and scary sight for her. Several days would pass before they spoke about what had happened. Even then, he would only say "I cannot explain it. I grew up with those guys. I knew those guys for my whole life."

For now, they rested quietly while Bola wandered off with his dog. He soon returned with a rabbit, which he shared with Aisha. Sunny, who had never eaten meat, was not about to start. After the break, they resumed their trek upwards, through patches of brush and scrub, past thickets of cactus and small trees. Bola's dog scampered ahead, quick and agile as any other mountain critters. They reached the crest by dusk and slept securely through the night, under the ears of a well-trained canine.

The next morning, from this vantage, Bola could more easily convey the remaining course of their trip. He spoke to Aisha for the first time, in broken Hindavi. "One more mountain we cross. This mountain." He pointed across the valley to the next peak. "After this mountain, my village is. This my home."

The descent was quicker but trickier. Aisha endured a few slips, scrapes and bruises but no spraining or limping. They didn't actually cross the next peak but mostly circumvented it, only climbing it at a low point near its southern end. Along the way, Bola acquired a peacock, a squirrel, and three more hares, one of which they ate. By this point, Sunny was ready to try some. The texture made him shiver but he kept it down.

As Bola skinned the hare, Aisha noticed that he seemed to be speaking to it. She recalled that he had also done so before.

"He's thanking the animal's spirit," Sunny explained.

She later noticed similar language when they stopped for water and Bola thanked the spirit of the stream. And when they finally arrived at his one-room, mud hut, he placed his hand on a large stone and greeted the spirit of his home.

The Bhil village consisted of a dozen similar homes, each with a small farm or large garden. Broods of meandering community chickens were scattered throughout. Bola himself had two goats, and a cow who protested loudly for having not been milked in days.

Inside, the hut looked a mess. Tools and utensil littered the dirt floor. In one corner lay his only furniture – a pile of twigs carefully woven into a nest. In another corner squatted his wife, Maru. She was attempting to weave something, but spent more time holding her head in pain. She was emaciated and her skin appeared unusually dark. A smell of sickness permeated the air. She looked up and smiled, and spoke in Bhil.

"You're back early!" she said cheerfully. "I'm feeling good. No fever in days."

Bola turned to his guests. "She has Black Fever."

She stood up, revealing a distended abdomen. She was not pregnant, as Aisha mistakenly thought, but full of swollen liver and spleen. Months earlier, unbeknownst to anyone, a tiny sandfly had given her the kiss of death, injecting a parasite into her blood.

While she and Aisha tried to get acquainted without a common language, Bola and Sunny set out to meet the village chief – an elderly, scrawny, happy man with two teeth. The chief sat under a tree with several others, all dressed the same – one cloth wrapping the groin and another round the head. Bola explained the situation and the chief granted Sunny leave to stay.

So they all lived together in that one room. Bola taught his new roomies to build their own nest. In the months that followed, Aisha's soles and soul got tough. She learned a lot about farming and weaving and speaking Bhil. She learned how to care for a husband and to care for, or at least comfort, a dying woman.

The husband was trickier. Familiarity revealed a whiff of arrogance in him, which became more apparent when he and Bola would return from a hunt. He would tease his new wife, for example, about the superiority of men, a notion which he knew irritated her.

"Of course men are superior," he would say. "God is a man, yes?"

To which she would reply "The Master of the Worlds is a man?"

"Well, *He* surely isn't a woman."

"Look," she would explain "Allah speaks to us in ways that we can understand. But *He* has no gender."

This would make Sunny incredulous. "What scrolls have you been reading?"

She always remained calm and patient, but persistent. "Look, He created gender for the purpose of reproduction. He created reproduction to perpetuate things that die. But He does not reproduce, because He does not die. Get it? He always was, and He always will be."

This would make Sunny think, and for a moment he would understand. But then he would forget and bring it up again later.

And he was a fussy eater, though he did eventually learn to eat meat and even like it. But for every new dish she made, he had the same response. "I will not like that."

To which she would reply "How do you know if you haven't tried it?"

"Because it does not look like something that tastes good."

"Do you suppose your mouth serves you better when it tries things, or when it opines about things you have not tasted?"

She had learned that retort from her stepmother, Karna. Aisha occasionally channeled her when speaking. She missed her and thought of her often. She had always assumed that their relationship was like that of any other mother-daughter. After all, Karna had raised Aisha as her own and Aisha loved her. But Aisha didn't know any better. Since birth, she had never basked in the warmth of her own mother's love and could not imagine the experience. She could only guess at it, much as a blind man guesses what it means to see. Had she known that bond, even for a small while, she might have been able to sense that something was off, though she could never have guessed the truth – that Karnavati disliked and disdained her.

# FOUR

There was actually nothing wrong with Aisha except that she was the doting daughter of her father. Karna loathed Omar. Her hatred had not grown gradually, but developed in bursts over the ten years of their marriage. It originated in the tense circumstances surrounding their matrimony, wounds that eventually healed. Or so she thought. Having a child would have helped, but that was not to be God's will. Omar showed neither kindness nor cruelty about her barren womb. They never discussed it; they never had any serious talks. The nature of their relationship was that of the man himself – pleasant, quiet and distant.

The first blow to their marriage came from the seizure of Fort Chittor. Several of her own relatives perished there, and she could only wonder what hand he had, directly or otherwise, in their deaths. As the news trickled in over those terrible months, any love or respect she had held for him gave way to contempt and distrust. She would maintain a holding pattern in that state for the next five years. She held her tongue to preserve peace and security, and he remained unaware that any problem existed at all.

It was a gorgeous day in late July, 1573 when a man knocked her from her orbit, sending her careening to destruction. It was unusually cool, a respite from the vicious, imprisoning heat that had reigned all summer. Karna grabbed the chance to escape, setting out across town to visit a friend. She had not gotten very far when her tanga pulled over and stopped. She hardly noticed; tangas often did that, especially on a nice day when traffic tended to be thick. Sometimes, a dead or stubborn animal blocked the way. Sometimes the driver would stop to talk to someone. But then she caught a glimpse outside and saw that she was not en route, not even in town. Instead, she was in the lonely countryside on the outskirts of Agra. The driver turned around, stuck his head through the drapes and smiled a toothy smile. "Hello, Karna."

Karna took a wide-eyed gasp. She tried to speak but couldn't. She tried again and whispered "Tarak!"

Tarak leaned in, revealing two broad shoulders. "Karna, I always love you." A brief silence ensued after which Karna regained her composure and looked appalled.

"Tarak, I am *not* a fifteen-year-old girl, and this is *very* inappropriate!" she protested.

Tarak thought for a moment. Then his faced turned serious and determined. He lunged forward and kissed her thoroughly, running his fingers through her scalp. Like an old song or a forgotten scent, the kiss released a flood of memories for her. Karna's servant, an older woman, was quite alarmed at all this and hurried out of the tanga. She marched a few meters away before realizing that she didn't quite know where she was and didn't quite know what to do. She sat down under a tree.

Karna sank into her seat under the weight of the moment. A moment later, she began to sob. "I've been married for years and you're the only man who's ever kissed me," she confessed, stroking his cheek.

"That is another one of your husband's crimes, but it's my blessing and it's the will of Gauri."

"Oh my, Tarak. My mind forgot what my heart could not. I have yearned for you without even knowing it."

"I go by Tarik now. It sounds more Muslim."

"Oh. Are you Muslim now?"

"No, baby, I'm a spy, and I've been watching you for a year. It's been sweet torture." He sat down beside her.

"You what?"

"Hang on," he said. He shifted his attention to peek outside the curtain. "I'll be right back." He hopped off the carriage and walked towards the servant. Seeing him come, she stood up, because she didn't quite know what else to do. He drew his short sword, cut her down in two strokes, and dragged the corpse into some tall brush. Karna watched the deed from her perch. The servant was nothing, a lower caste, but still Karna had never seen a murder. She was not nearly as horrified as she thought she would be, and that troubled her. She also fretted about this new side of Tarak, and it tempered her feelings a little. Any scruple she had soon dissipated, however, as he told her his story and much more.

After she left to get married seven years prior, he joined the army, first serving under Rana Udai Singh, and then under Udai's son Pratap. Tarak never married. He eventually became a scout and proved very proficient, so he trained in more advanced forms of intelligence. He moved up the ranks and never forgot her. It was inevitable that he would eventually combine his skills with his loves, for Karna and country, into a single idea. He would infiltrate the general's staff, serve as a mole and flip Karna if possible. He presented it to his superiors who then ran it up the chain.

"I told them 'I know she still loves me' and I was right."

Eventually, a spot opened on Sahani's security detail thanks to the mysterious disappearance of one of the guards. A sympathizer in the emperor's cabinet made a recommendation, and Tarak secured the job. He spent a year gaining trust, gauging Karna's situation from afar, and then waiting for an opportunity to approach her.

He spent another three years rekindling their relationship. During that time, he filled her in on a variety of gruesome details about Chittor and other Mongol atrocities. He also filled her head with propaganda, and she learned to seethe with hatred. She also learned deception and became quite good at it. Lies rolled off her tongue as easily as a drunk off a curb.

It was a change of tune when she approached her husband one day in the spring of '76 with a bolus of cruel honesty. He had returned home the day before to learn that Aisha had been four days missing. Ironically, it was Karna's belief that all had gone as planned that led her to deviate from the plan and start blabbing. She found him lying in bed, unkempt and unslept. She sat down beside him – this time without permission – and stroked his hair.

"Aww, worrying about your little girl? Well don't. She's safe for now."

He rolled over to face her, confused and hopeful. "How do you know?" he asked.

"Because we have her."

He sat up. "We?"

She remained unafraid, partly because she knew he had no temper – emotional violence had been trained out of him years ago – and partly because she believed that she had his heart in her grip.

"*We* are the patriots of Mewar, the mighty Rajput people. Aisha will remain safe and pure as long as you do what you're told."

He was incredulous. "What have you done? How can you do this to her? To me?"

"Because I am a patriot, Omar, and you are a demon. I know you're a demon because you won't die. Lord knows I've poisoned you enough."

"Poisoned me?"

"The mangos, Omar. Anyways, we learned about your daughter's little romance. (She's been a bad girl, Omar. You'll need to have a word.) How foolish of you to bring a girl into a war zone. And you thought no trouble would come of it? In a sea of mighty Rajput men? Alas, your arrogance has always been your weakness." She paused a moment to gloat. "We saw an opportunity to control you, which in retrospect is far more useful than killing you, I suppose."

Mangos? Romance? He found this all to be very confusing, but also knew a quick way to un-confuse. He had her arrested and tortured. Karnavati knew a lot about her husband. She knew that he valued Aisha more than his reputation, his job or his emperor. What she didn't know, to her doom, was what he valued even more – his oaths, especially oaths he had made to Allah. During his career, he had been required to make several, and he would not betray them or Him.

From her interrogations, he learned about Tarak, learned that he was in Mewar and would not return, and that he probably had custody of Aisha. Karnavati had not received word from him but expected to any day. He also learned about Sunny and how rumors of their forbidden romance had predictably spread all over Udai City. In fact, they spread all the way to the rana's inner circle where an idea was born.


The idea became a plan. It was a long shot, but low-risk and cheap. Sunny's friends were recruited and promised riches. Their assignment was to sow the idea of elopement into Sunny's mind and help it grow.

Bunny and Punk were young, so they were carefully and constantly coached through the process. That task was assigned to the mayor's manipulative wife.

"Don't just come out with the idea," she would tell them. "Start with reminders. Ask about Aisha. Make comments about her. Don't be too anxious. Pace yourself. You should even make a schedule. Know what you're going to say and when."

She helped them make such a schedule and met with them every couple of weeks to discuss, revise and to keep them on track.

Even the conception itself was cautiously crafted. First, they invented a story, a rumor about the elopement of a fictional Persian princess named Layla. Then they told it to three of Sunny's cousins, but not to Sunny himself. For step 3, they were to wait two weeks and see if the rumor came full circle out of Sunny's mouth. It didn't, so they went on to step 4. Step 4 sounded something like this:

"Hey, Sunny, did you hear about that Persian princess Laila who..."

He hadn't heard.

"We heard it from your cousin So-and-So. Imagine if you and Aisha did something like that? That'd be crazy."

With the soil prepared and the seed planted, they proceeded to cultivation – a slow crescendo of supportive words and increasingly serious discussions about What-Ifs. This continued for two months before Sunny finally came to them and said "Let's do it."

Had the elopement been as thoroughly planned as the conception, Bansal might have lived and Aisha been arrested. But the mayor's wife excelled in manipulation, not in elopement, and certainly not in the foolish actions of young men. To my knowledge, no such experts existed in the kingdom.


After Karnavati had confessed all she knew, Sahani let her live another two weeks, locked her in an unused stable, and awaited enemy attempts to contact her. The contact was to be a woman she'd never met who would come calling as her Aunty Ganga. No such person ever came, and Karnavati was beheaded unceremoniously, alone. Sahani assigned the task of executioner to the "safai karamchari," the one who cleans out the latrines, a final humiliation for the proud, young Rajput. The poor guy didn't want the job and half-expected to find his own head next on the wood stump. He wondered if he was being tested or somehow scapegoated. But the job went smoothly and no consequence ever came, and he couldn't wait to get home and tell his wife about his crazy day.

Sahani was crippled in his quest to find his daughter. He had very little information and she was leagues away in hostile land. The emperor did have some spies of his own in Mewar, but Sahani doubted about how much help he could get with such an embarrassing situation. Worst of all, he had to get back to work. The preparation for war was ramping up, and he had to return to Amber right away. He had no choice.

# FIVE

It was almost summer when war came to Mewar. On a steamy day in mid-June, the kind that makes you stick to your clothes and sick to your stomach, Bola returned to his village. He had been on a routine vending trip to the city and, once again, came back earlier than expected. Maru, delirious with fever, took no notice of him, or of Aisha sponging her. Sunny was lying around, panting and thinking about all the work he had to do. Embarrassed by his sloth, he jumped up to greet Bola.

"We have to go," said Bola.

"Go? Where?"

Bola whispered in his ear, after which Sunny turned to his wife and said "I must go."

"What? Go where?"

"This is the promise I made," Sunny explained, "when he agreed to take us in. I'll be back."

He offered no further explanation, but grabbed her hand and gave her a quick kiss while Bola washed up. Each man grabbed an apple and then, without another word, they left. Aisha, dumbstruck, stared out the door until she could see them no more. Then she stared some more. Behind her, Maru groaned in pain.

Bola traveled quickly and quietly. He didn't normally talk much anyway, nor did his dog. They were hunting partners, and hunters don't make noise. But they didn't hunt this time; they hardly even stopped to sleep. All of this frustrated Sunny, who was full of anxiety and questions. He didn't know where they were going, how to fight, or what would be expected of him. He had no armor or weapon except his knife.

The next day, they met up with more Bhils marching to war. The pace of the larger group was not much slower, but Sunny did get some information. He learned that the empire had invaded Mewar with an army of tens of thousands, including Rajput traitors, hordes of elephants and possibly a wizard. The army camped on the north shore of the Banas River, north of Udai City. The Mewar army camped nearby.

The Bhils reached camp by nightfall. On arrival, even Sunny's untrained eye could see that Rana Pratap had picked a brilliant location. Although they were only about five kilometers from the enemy, "nearby" was only as close as two people on opposite sides of a castle wall. Pratap had camped at the southwest end of Haldighati Pass. The surrounding terrain was a treacherous, rocky labyrinth, nearly impassable by horse and providing numerous, natural ramparts. They could not have built a better fort.

The only other approach was through the pass, a gorge through the hills about a kilometer long with walls rising seven meters high. At its narrowest points, it only allowed horses two abreast or elephants single file. It extinguished any size advantage of a larger army.

Sunny felt the sickly mixture of fatigue, hunger and adrenaline. The excitement came not just from the anticipation of battle, but also the sundry wonders around him. He had never seen so many elephants in one place – at least a dozen. He had never seen an army; they numbered five thousand. The Rajputs were drilling, another sight to behold – rows of glorious warriors on horseback, shiny armor vests, pointy helmets and long spears. Sunny hoped in vain they would issue him something fancy. He was corralled into his division, comprised of Bhils and grunts, and led by the Bhil chief Rana Punja. He was given a short sword, a bowl of rice and a place to sleep.


Trumpets woke him the next morning. He hadn't slept well, and it took him a moment to get oriented. He sighed with relief on seeing Bola still at his side, and he hoped they could stick together. Bola's dog had wandered off to look for scraps. It was still dark, and Sunny couldn't understand why they had been wakened. Then he heard it. The enemy had crossed the river but had not advanced further. The rana planned to attack.

Suddenly, Rana Pratap didn't seem that brilliant anymore.

"We have the upper hand here, yes?" Sunny complained to Bola. "We must not discard it."

He repeated this concern to a couple of other people, neither of whom had any authority or any interest in what he had to say.

"The Mongols will not turn around and go home," he said. "They'll come to us through the pass. We should wait for them." Throughout the morning, he continued to repeat these truths to the only person who would listen – himself.

The entire army assembled battle formation. It would resume the same formation upon exiting the pass. The cavalry rode in front. The horses were now donned with prosthetic headgear designed to resemble an elephant's trunk – a trick to fool enemy pachyderms. Behind the cavalry marched the pike men, then drummers and trumpeters, then the elephants. In the center of it all, for the first time, Rana Pratap himself could be seen, mounted on a spectacular white horse, shaded from the dark by a servant bearing his royal umbrella. In the back, Bola and Sunny were separated as the rear guard formed, with Bola and the other archers moving to the flanks. Swordsmen stayed in the middle.

Row by row, the troops filed into the pass. As they proceeded, another problem occurred to Sunny, one nearly as frightening and nearly as certain as death itself. It's the problem that comes from walking in the dark, in a narrow file behind a dozen elephants. This one he kept to himself. Fortune almost smiled on the rear guard that morning, as eleven of the beasts marched through without a hitch. But the twelfth one, ironically named Lucky, had discovered a cache of ripe bananas two days before, and this was his moment to learn what a cache of ripe bananas does to elephant bowels. Through it all, the Bhils remained stoic, if not entirely fresh.

Sunny emerged from the pass to see that dawn had arrived. The army reformed, then turned and marched northwards. Here, the ground was better but still uneven and woven with brambles. For a brief moment, a downhill turn allowed him to see over and past his own troops. In that moment, in the distance, he saw the enemy assembled in a dale, twice their number. Twenty minutes later, everything happened.

The Mewar cavalry charged. The Bhil archers ran up the hills to either side and began sniping. The rear guard ran to keep up, but didn't join the fray. Rather, it hung back and waited and watched. For the first time, Sunny heard the crack of muskets and smelled the odor of burnt gunpowder. It must have been a rout because they charged forward again, as if the empire was retreating. Again, Sunny had to run.

Eventually, the running stopped, and the battle stalled on a new field. It continued for hours and the fighting intensified, a rout less evident. The elephants joined the fight, and the spectacle of those battling beasts terrified him. Occasionally, the churning mass of war that raged before them would spit out an arrow or a musket ball, which would either whiz by or fell one of his comrades. By mid-day, a haze of gun smoke hovered in the field, torturing the sinuses and stifling the senses. It kept him, and more importantly his commander, from seeing that the enemy was breaking through Mewar's left flank and starting to surround its main force. A minute later, they attacked the rear.

All around Sunny, a sea of chaos suddenly swirled as riders charged with spears. He saw a pike lying on the ground and he dropped his sword. He lifted the pike, planted one end and aimed the other, impaling a horse that nearly trampled him. The rider flew off and broke his leg. The horse landed on Sunny and quickly died. Nobody noticed him trapped under its massive torso, which made him feel safe in a way. He thought about just staying there. On the other hand, if anyone did see him, he was defenseless. This dilemma soon resolved as his breathing became labored, not just from the animal's weight, but because he had broken a rib and it stabbed him with every breath. He would have surely died there had he not found the strength to wriggle himself out, a process that took four minutes. He staggered around a bit before regaining his senses.

In the center of battle, General Sahani rode an elephant from which he shot a bow and arrow. He was there to lead a division and to take control if the supreme commander, Man Singh, perished. The situation had looked a little hairy at first, but Man Singh was a brilliant tactician and they had superior numbers, as well as muskets. Now it appeared that Allah would favor them after all. The muskets were spent and the smoke was fading. Most of Pratap's elephants had been shot, and Sahani could move about safely. He was now more free to turn his attention to a more important matter. He had waited weeks for war to bring him to Mewar so he could find his little girl. His eyes darted around, scanning the mayhem. He ordered his mahout (driver) to take him this way and that.

He searched for a familiar face; he searched for Tarak, his only lead to Aisha. He didn't know what Tarak looked like, but he didn't know anyone else in Mewar, and he figured he would recognize a man who had worked for years at his home. An hour passed, which felt like a year, and he began to get discouraged. Then he saw someone.

It wasn't Tarak. It couldn't have been. The boy was too young. But he certainly looked familiar, though Sahani couldn't remember when or where. He strained to keep sight on him across the field, over the bodies, through the haze, the swarms of steeds, and the bedlam of hand-to-hand combatants. The boy just stood there, even stumbled a bit. He never looked up, never saw Sahani.

"Go that way!" the general barked at his mahout. "No, that way!" But it was too late. He could only watch helplessly as another boy of similar age walked up behind Sunny. With his left palm, Punk grabbed Sunny's forehead and pulled it back, securing it to his chest. With his right, he drew a knife from Sunny's left ear to right, severing both carotids. Sunny died instantly, and Sahani slumped over.

He quickly perked back up, though, determined to accost this new boy. But he never got a chance. Word spread across the field that Rana Pratap was wounded and retreating. New orders came down to regroup and pursue, and Sahani's chance was lost.

# Six

The monsoons came abruptly in early July. They made a pond in the center of Aisha's hut that would stay all summer, replenishing itself with each daily rain. She didn't mind it too much, for it meant that she didn't have to go far for water, and she didn't want to go anywhere. About one third of the village men had returned from the battle. Others had been killed or were still off fighting. Bola had died. No news arrived about Sunny.

With no men around, there was more work to do and less to eat, and she was malnourished and weak. Maru had a son who did return from battle but was nearly as useless as before. He occasionally came over to help with the cattle but would not come inside, would not see his mother. He feared that the spirit that was eating her would eat him too.

Aisha was also pregnant. She had already miscarried once, but this baby was sticking and growing. Between the vomiting and the malnutrition, her teeth were decaying, and the pain gave her headaches. She developed some unwanted habits, including licking her bowl, picking her skin and crying herself to sleep.

Maru died in August.

It wasn't a great summer.

In September, the nausea and the rains began to subside. Aisha started thinking seriously about leaving. Before then, she had certainly not been in traveling condition. Even if she had found the strength to climb one side of a hill, she figured she would probably mudslide down the other and end up drowning in a stream. Now, the ground was drying and she was eating more. But she still wasn't ready.

By October, she knew the time had come. Her belly had already grown to a significant size. She feared that, if she waited any longer, her tiny, emaciated bones would not be able to lug that baby over mountains. She had no food to pack. Her garden had withered and rotted over the summer, and she had survived the past month by "borrowing" from her neighbors at night. She never took enough to raise notice – an onion here, an eggplant there. But the night before leaving, she took plenty, which she packed in a small sack. She didn't sleep at all. At dawn, she strapped it on, along with a bow and quiver, and lit out.

Driven by privation, not planning, she didn't know where to go. She had not been out of the Bhil village since spring, but she remembered that the city lay towards the rising sun, approximately. Towards the setting sun lurked the unknown, perhaps paradise, perhaps starvation. She chose east. She circumvented the mountains as much as possible, following the Sabarmati River northwards until she could cross east. She couldn't completely avoid climbing or falling, but mostly she managed to find the safest, easiest route, albeit long and circuitous. By noon, she reached a vista from where she could see a city, or maybe a town, to the east. She couldn't tell how far, but she could see it. At the age of fifteen, without knowing where she was or what she would do, she experienced a sensation somewhere between relief and salvation. Then she saw the leopard.

Unfortunately, the cat also saw her and was quite interested. He didn't care for the taste of villagers, and this one looked kinda puny. But it had been a slow day and you take what you can get. He watched from his vantage atop a rocky cliff, no more than ten meters up and a hundred away. She froze and gasped, and he sensed that this would be easy. He bounded effortlessly to the ground and slowly began his sinister, feline advance. She lost sight of him through the trees, then caught it, then lost it again. She dropped her sack and drew an arrow. He reappeared only fifteen meters away. She said what she always said before releasing an arrow. "In the name of Allah, The Most Loving, The Most Merciful." Her well-practiced hand trembled.

She fired. She missed.

The cat was startled by the flash and sound of something whizzing by. Not sure what just happened, he decided that playtime was over and started to sprint at her. She drew again. He leaped a full five meters through the air. He lived for three of them.

The ordeal gave her a pounding headache and she had to sit down. For an hour, she rested as much as she could while still keeping guard.

Her thoughts turned to her baby as they often did, mixing worry with excitement and a little sadness. It was then that she first felt it kick.

It actually felt more like a wave, a ripple, and she couldn't even be sure if it had actually happened ... until it happened again. She didn't know what it meant, and it frightened her. She thought she might deliver right there. After all, she didn't quite know how long she had been pregnant, nor did she know anything about pregnancy, for the topic had always been taboo. With new urgency, she got right up and resumed her hike at quickened speed, occasionally prodded on by her suddenly bossy passenger.

She reached the outskirts of the town before dark, fighting hunger and exhaustion. Each lonely farm that she passed beckoned her to beg or steal. But both options were too risky for a solitary woman in a strange and solitary place. Instead, she found herself a secluded stack of hay, buried herself in it and slept.

The next day, as she made her way into town, she found that it was, in fact, a town and not Udai City. That fact gave her some comfort, given the circumstances of her departure. On the other hand, towns are small, and town folk know each other; and she wanted the security of anonymity, or at least the option of it. She avoided the south side, which was full of soldiers and a grand palace. She opted instead for the north where life appeared more normal. But on closer look, it wasn't. It was full of people doing nothing – just sitting around in front of their homes, watching each other sit around. Most of the shops had closed. The first one she found open didn't even have anything in it, just a man. She begged him for food.

"Ain't no food, fool," he jeered. "The Mongols ate it all."

She tried three more shops and a few passersby, but everyone ignored her or chased her off like a dog. But she was still hungry, so she tried again.

One shopkeeper eyed her abdomen. "Where's your husband?" she asked curtly, never looking up.

Aisha replied with what she thought to be true, though she wasn't sure. "Killed in the war."

The woman reached behind the counter and brought out two mangos. Forgetting her manners, Aisha grabbed and devoured them. Now the woman watched her. Shoeless and filthy, Aisha was the picture of pathetic.

"Why aren't you at Beggar's Lane?" the woman asked.

"What's that?"

"That's where the war widows are. It's on the south side. There's nothing over here."

Beggar's Lane had evolved spontaneously, as people from the surrounding war-ravaged areas had come to town seeking relief. The soldiers who quartered in town didn't have much, but they often had something. The beggars tended to gather where there were other beggars, who tended to gather where traffic and money flowed. Eventually, someone would evict them, or the soldiers would simply reroute their routines. Then, Beggar's Lane would dissipate and organically form somewhere else.

Aisha found it and learned what to do by imitation. She took a couple of slaps to the face when she eventually, inevitably bothered the wrong man. But she soon figured out who were the more veteran beggars, and watched who they avoided. The other beggars mostly ignored her and each other, though they sometimes pushed in competitive moments. They tended to sleep together, but she didn't join in. Instead, she walked out of town every evening to the same secluded haystack where, thus far, she hadn't been bothered.

Not quite sure what else to do, she continued to beg for a week. During that time, she learned the town's name, Gogunda. She learned that all those soldiers worked for Rana Pratap, the man with the crimson turban and the spectacular moustache. She usually collected more than the other vagabonds. Besides being young and pregnant, she was also fairer and taller than most of the others, most of whom were Bhil. Even in her destitute state, she was easy to recognize. After a week, someone did.

"Aisha?"

It took her a second to place his face. "Tarik!" She squeezed him so hard she could hardly breathe.

"Okay, okay, Miss Monkey." He gently pushed off her embrace. "Mind your manners now. You're not a child anymore."

She had no reply except to cry, which she promptly did. And kept crying. It was quite a scene, and everyone stared.

Tarak laid a kind hand on her shoulder. "You come with me now. Calm down. That's it. Come to my home." And he led her away.

"Have you seen my mom and dad?" she asked as they walked.

"They have been chewing off their fingers with anguish, child. Your father was here."

"Here? When?"

"He was looking for you. He was here all summer. He's gone now. Home. Since last month."

Aisha felt sick with guilt, and with worry of her own. "Can you help me get home?"

"Don't fret, Sunshine. Everything will be alright."

By the time they reached his house, a two-room stone dwelling, her mind had calmed enough to notice his clothes. He wore a different uniform than she had seen on him before. "Are you a soldier?" she asked.

"I'm more like a kind of policeman. Now I have to go back to work. You can stay here. Clean up the house very nice, and make me something nice for supper, okay?"

Then he left and she relaxed… sort of. Having exchanged one set of problems for another, she felt both grateful and distressed as she lay back on a hay pile. The distress won. She got up and got busy. The house was fairly clean but sparse, containing only the hay, a stool, some clothes and weapons, some lentils, a few spices, and a few supplies for cooking and cleaning. When he came home, they slept in separate rooms and he behaved as a gentleman, except that he took the hay. The next day, however, he thought to bring her a sheaf of her own. Otherwise, the routine stayed the same, and it stayed that way for another three days without a word about any plan. He didn't quite know what to do with her, and she relished the tranquility. Unfortunately, it was not to last.

She was already having headaches and a new backache on the day that he came home early. He came home furious.

"Your father is coming!" he said in a nasty tone, slamming the door. His news was wonderful, his demeanor frightening, and the incongruity sharpened her headache. She got dizzy.

She squeaked "But that's great, isn't it?"

"No, it's not great, you stupid kid. Do you know where you are? Do you know who I am? I am Sisodian. I was born in this house! That castle you saw; Maharana Pratap, my king, was crowned in that castle. Gogunda was once the capitol of a great kingdom. Your father took

Gogunda, but he couldn't keep it. We kicked his butt out, and now he's coming back for seconds. Him and his precious emperor."

"But…"

"But what!"

She kept her face down, afraid to see his. "But I don't care about politics."

"Oh, but politics cares about you, my friend. You may be a Mewar citizen, but you are the spawn of the enemy, and the man who—" He choked a bit. "The man who murdered the woman I love. You are also an accessory to murder."

With those last words, she remembered and realized. It was Tarak who she saw in an alley, in Udai City after Sunny's crazy friends attacked her. She suddenly got warm and tingly as her heart pounded blood to her skin. Her stomach protested and threw her breakfast at the floor, just before she fainted.

She was only out for a couple of minutes before Tarak roused her with slapping.

"Wake up! That's better. Aisha, you are under arrest," he declared. "That means that you are my slave, my property." He proved his point with beatings and rape.

When he finally, finally calmed a bit, he started looking around. "I must have a couple of nails around here. You cleaned the place. Where are my nails?"

She didn't know.

"That's okay." He grabbed a hammer, broke apart the stool and retrieved two of its nails. He picked up a pot and handed it to her. "Here. This is your toilet. I'll bring you another for food." With that, he stepped outside, nailed the door shut and left.

Aisha was terrified and despondent, but not broken. He had left his weapons behind – a sword, a couple of daggers, a spear and even an old mace. She tried to chip and pry at the door using what she had. She even tried to hammer it with a grinding stone. When her efforts proved futile, she determined to fight. She knew that if he kept beating her, he would kill her baby, if he hadn't already.

She practiced the use of his weapons. She had her bow but no arrows. The mace and the rock felt too heavy. She settled on the spear – nice and long. He wore a leather vest, so she would have to plan for a smaller target, the head or the groin. She chose groin. She picked a position and posted herself. She kept guard all day, imagining him coming through that door, imagining his height, his frame, his reaction. Night came, though she didn't know it. She had no way to tell time, or to know how long she crouched there, watching that door, bruised and swollen and sore all over. But she maintained her vigil…until she fell asleep.

She awakened to the sound of him prying those nails, and quickly resumed readiness. He walked in and she attacked, breaking the clay pot that he was holding at exactly the wrong level. Unfortunately, the spear went no further, and he grabbed it from her. He wasn't angry though, and didn't react any further. He looked somber and serious.

"I notified my commander," he said. "They have no use for you. I have been ordered to carry out your execution…now."

This time, she felt no rush of blood. Instead, she felt it drain from her body, along with any remaining hope.

He pulled out a small bottle and held it out. "This is Datura," he said. "It's the same poison I gave your mother to kill your father. I'm going to give you the choice that I'm sure she was never given."

"My mother?"

"Never mind. Listen. You have a choice. You can choose to die by my hand. It will be violent but quick. Or you can drink this."

She thought for a moment, then took a deep breath and stood tall. "I will not have my last deed in this life be a sin. You'll have to do it yourself, Mr. Tough-guy."

He brought her out into the night and picked a spot – a large stone behind the house. By his order, she placed her head on it as he drew his sword. Shadows of flickering torchlight danced frenetically with infernal glee. She squeezed her eyes tightly.

"Oh Master," she begged. "Please forgive me. Grant me your generous mercy."

A flicker of pity crossed Tarak's heart. "I'm sorry, Miss Monkey" he said. "I cannot. I have orders."

She turned to him with that contemptuous look and sneering tone that is the specialty of teenage girls. "I wasn't talking to you."

# II

# List of Named Characters

Dr. Dustin Nye: a nuclear physicist in Oak Ridge, Tennessee

    Ilka: one of Dustin's classmates

    Dr. Frank Archer: a scientist on Dustin's team

    Dr. Beeks: a scientist on Dustin's team

    Autumn Sumner: an assistant on Dustin's team

    Brady: Dustin's dog

    Ahmed: Dustin's travel guide

Anna: a maid in the hotel where Dustin is staying

    Eduardo: Anna's son

Dr. Pia Pacelli: Senior Director of Medical Services for Liberated Loins

Cookie McGuffin: television journalist for the show Good Morning Today

Krystal: owner of a crystal shop

    Maggie: Krystal's daughter

    Dr. Joseph: Krystal's friend and mentor

    Dr. Francis Metheuen: esteemed anthropologist and Krystal's father (deceased)

Officer Dibble: a Baltimore policeman

Honcho-ipitch: chief of the village of Janepsto

Yopokay: namero-o (shaman) for the village of Janepsto

    Ohmati: Yopokay's sister

Dr. Jorgensen: neurophysicist in Copenhagen and pioneer in the field of Connectomics

Dr. Shah: a physicist in Bangalore, studying Y-waves

# SEVEN

It's 11:00 and Dr. Dustin Nye finally wakes up. He's usually a morning person, but has been sleeping late since he came to Boston, maybe because he can. After all, he doesn't have to get up early until he goes back to work in Oak Ridge, Tennessee. He's in Boston (Cambridge actually) to take a two-week class at his old alma mater, the Massachusetts Institute of Technology. It's a night class, so he might as well mess up his sleep schedule. But he doesn't like messing it up, and this is unusual for him. He's never been a late riser, regardless of his work schedule. He thought about setting an alarm, but he's been having nice dreams, and they seem to happen in the morning near the time he awakens. This time, she had blue eyes and blonde hair. She's had different looks, but it's always her. Mostly she's been amorphous, like an angel might be – too perfect for human detail. Only once was there sexual steam. More often, the dreams have been innocent and cozy. She's been a refuge, giving him haven from loneliness with her arms, from insecurity with her words, and from vampires with her home that's also a church. This is his sixth day in Boston, and he's dreamt of her for five of them. The thing is, he never did before he came. In fact, before this, he rarely dreamt at all, or at least couldn't remember if he did. For that reason, he's sure he must be dreaming about someone in his class, but he can't figure out whom. He's looked around, taking inventory of each classmate, even the men. None of them have looked particularly familiar or attractive. Not that he's anything to look at himself. At age thirty-five, he's almost six feet, kinda fat, kinda bald, pasty-white and single.

He's also a scientist, analytical and curious by nature. But this isn't just a curiosity for him. These dreams have touched him deeply and he's eager to find their source. Today is Friday and he has one more chance before the weekend to study his classmates – oh, and the lecture. He bought himself a small handheld mirror yesterday. He plans to sit in front and use it to watch them without being noticed.

He gets up, throws on some pants and opens the door. Good, the housekeeper left some towels, toiletries and caffeine. He has a "Do Not Disturb" sign on the door of his room at all times, and he was running low on supplies. He's staying at the Kensington – just a nine-minute walk to MIT – and getting all his food delivered. He scratches his head, washes up, and spends the day doing what he's done most of his life – reading. He reviews the online class materials, then inhales two research journals. He's always preferred paper, and frequently spends money printing things out. He never had a laptop as a child.

In fact, there weren't a lot of decent books in the poor public schools he attended in the Appalachian hills of East Tennessee. He managed to satiate his voracious appetite for knowledge early on with the help of a supportive mother, who would pick up books at yard sales and take him to the library on her days off, when she had enough gas money for the trip into town. As he got older, he learned the value of writing letters, asking for material from corporations and a few pen pals he'd acquired – professors at the University of Tennessee and researchers at Oak Ridge National Laboratory (ORNL). Every tome and every periodical he obtained felt like an accomplishment, whether crisp and shiny and smelling like chemicals, or wrinkled and faded and smelling like dust. He relished each one and carried that love into adulthood.

He grew up in a two-room cottage, one of many such homes that dot the rolling pastures of Newport. It had been in his family for a couple of generations. His pa ran off when he was little. His ma worked in a factory until her back gave out, then went on disability. He showed himself to be a prodigy at a young age. His ma didn't have much interest in academics but, as he was her only child, she liked what he liked. He liked learning. While half the kids in his class eventually dropped out – many of them as addicts – he became valedictorian with a thirty-six on his ACT. Then to Vanderbilt on a free ride. There, he met some people as similar to him as he could find, and he did his awkward best to form friendships, with some limited success as best he could tell. Then to MIT for grad school, and finally back home to East Tennessee to study and work at the world-famous ORNL.

He finishes reading and heads off to class. It's October in New England and the trees on campus are ablaze with color, like giant tiki torches. Dustin is a nuclear physicist, and he's taking an elective in Machine Learning and Artificial Intelligence (AI). Programming has become an integral part of his career over the years. With the advance of technology, new discoveries have fostered new and more complex puzzles that he can no longer solve by writing equations on a chalk board. These quantum challenges have grown too extensive even for computers. It has thus become necessary for computers not just to calculate, but also to learn and think.

Now, as he sits in a class about putting minds into machines, he tries to solve a mystery about the workings of his own mind. It's the most reflective he's ever been, as he studies the reflections of eight colleagues. Two of them are white Caucasian. The rest look Chinese or Indian, including the speaker – a lean young fellow who keeps adjusting his glasses and ending every third sentence with "…and so on and so forth." Dustin continues to watch, assuring himself that he's a scientist, not a stalker. By the end of class, he still has nothing, not a revelation or insight.

He takes the long way back to the hotel – the scenic route along the Charles River, the Boston skyline looming on the far bank. A couple of joggers run by, and he has one of his rare, fleeting thoughts of himself exercising. Nah.

He returns to pondering the matter of his dreams and begins to have doubts. Perhaps it's not one of his classmates, maybe someone he saw on the plane. Oh, but he didn't dream of her that first Monday morning, before his first class. And it's not anyone at the hotel; he hasn't seen anyone. He just goes straight up to his room. He can't even remember who checked him in. Maybe it's something he ate. Or even simpler, maybe there's no reason at all. Just one of those things.

He decides to settle on that answer for now, a feeble attempt at self-placation. He'll try to focus on his studies, stop dwelling on dreams and just enjoy them. But when he gets back to the hotel, he can't help but loiter in the lobby for just a minute. Sitting in a lounge chair, he stares at his loafers, intermittently peeking around. Nobody there and no one passes through; just the desk clerk. She's a young, attractive woman with pink hair, hair that he would've remembered if he'd seen her before.

He goes to his room feeling wholly unsatisfied, orders Chinese and reads. He can't concentrate for some reason and studying goes poorly. He paces a bit and looks out the window. It's dark out. Maybe some TV? Ugh! He'd rather exercise. By 10 p.m., he'd normally fall asleep, but he's not tired. Most of his evening has been spent wandering between books, online surfing, online chess and the occasional text. He thinks about sleeping pills, but doesn't want to mess up a chance to see Her. He isn't bored as he lies in bed, staring at the ceiling. He's looking forward to the rendezvous.

But he did mess up. He must have, for she didn't come. He wakes up the next morning having not dreamt, as far he knows. He fumbles around for his glasses to see the clock. It's only nine; he's slept about five hours. Tired and frustrated, he hits the pillow again, but can't get back to sleep. He gives up after an hour and gets up, grouchy for the rest of the day, with nobody at whom to grouch.

She doesn't come on Sunday either, and he starts to get concerned, if not despondent. He feels foolish about these feelings, but resigns to being a fool for now. By Sunday night, he also resigns to drug use, worried that he might otherwise sleep through class. The next morning, she comes.


She comes wearing a suit and tie. At first, she looks like his mother, then like Judy Garland; but it's definitely Her.

"Where have you been?" he asks.

"I don't know, baby." She kisses his neck.

He then realizes where he is. He's sitting on a toilet in a public restroom without walls while people mill about, paying him no attention. He's horrified with humiliation.

"Can you wait outside, my love? Just give me a few minutes," he asks her.

"Sure, baby. I'll wait forever if you want."

She steps outside a door. He finishes his business, then washes his hands. He washes them twice more to be sure. It's cheap soap and he still feels soapy. She reappears and takes his right hand. She gives his palm a quick kiss, then turns it over and gives the back a longer one.

She suddenly grabs it and starts running, pulling him along. Through the train station they sprint, but not to catch a train. In fact, it's trying to catch them, run them down. He tires quickly.

"Can we lie down?" he pleads. "I can't breathe." They repose on a plush, sprawling bed. "I don't know why you put up with me," he says, still abased. "Sometimes, I'm ridiculous."

She nuzzles up to him, her hair smelling like cotton candy. "Never mind, baby," she coos, her tone soft and sure. "You're always perfect to me."

He marinates in her tender affection and bakes in her warmth, and in the sunlight that pours from above.


Monday begins as a soft, sweet overture in accelerando. Dustin awakens, nestled in his pillow, a pool of saliva soaking his cheek. He jumps up feeling refreshed and dives into his day. He washes up, eats and even does a few jumping jacks. (He may have pulled something, but that's okay).

He looks through his stack and finds a fresh notebook. At the top of page one, he writes the title – Dream Diary. He recognizes the importance of these dreams in, if nothing else, how they've been affecting his mood. He's not sure if there's a pattern, but if there is, he determines to find it using good ole scientific observation. He divides the pages into columns. The big one on the right is where he'll describe his dreams. The other columns he labels with every variable of which he can think – Time Awake, Time Asleep, Food, Symptoms, and one called Miscellaneous. That one is for unforeseen stimuli that grace his day. If he smells a skunk or stubs his toe or talks to a hobo, he'll write it there.

Next, he resolves to control, and thereby eliminate, what variables he can. He'll eat the same thing at the same time, walk the same route and retire at the same time every day. He'll cease all texting and web browsing. He'll replace it all with one, deliberate, test experience each day. For his first one, he'll try talking tonight to the one white woman in his class. She's kinda cute and she sits alone in the café each evening during break.

But she's not there today and he returns to the hotel mildly disappointed, with nothing to log. The lull continues into Tuesday morning when he awakens without a dream. But he's well-trained; his career has been an exercise in patience and discipline. Science is nothing if not the practice of waiting for data, addressing the setbacks, and valuing – and sometimes publishing – the failures.

That night, his classmate is there. She's tall and thin with short, blonde hair smartly cut. She sips a steaming cup and studies at a laptop. He gets an herbal tea (lemon zinger) and walks by her. She doesn't notice. He walks by twice more before getting enough courage to approach. He's a bit nervous around women, and around men for that matter, but especially women.

He was once actually married for a couple of years to a colleague of his. They admired each other physically and intellectually, and it seemed to make sense. But they were always busy and didn't see each other much. They lacked the time, and perhaps the skill, to learn to love each other. Eventually, marriage didn't seem to make that much sense after all.

"Would you mind if I sat here?" he asks.

She studies him for a second. "Yah, that's okay."

She has a sexy, European accent of some kind. He doesn't ask. He himself has a slight southern accent which slips out when he drinks (one reason he doesn't drink). She looks about forty.

"I'm Dustin. Friends call me Dusty."

She's also a physicist. Ilka.

"I like this name Dustin," she says. "Vat does it mean?"

"I think it comes from a Norse name, Torsten, which is supposed to mean Thor's Stone. Go figure. I didn't see you here yesterday."

"Yes, I vent home ferda weekend and the airline canceled my flight beck."

"Oh."

A brief, uncomfortable pause.

"Vell, Dustin, vat do you think of this place?" she asks, looking around.

"What, the cafe?"

"No, this crazy beelding."

Ironically, the campus building to which he treks every day, The Stata Center, looks to him like a nightmare. A heap of clashing shapes and colors, of brick and chrome and galvanized steel, it was designed in the spirit of Deconstructivism. But to Dustin, it looks more like Tim Burton and Pablo Picasso got together and threw up. But he just met her and doesn't want to let loose, so he tempers his reply.

"Oh, ha. I don't think much of it. I'm used to it."

Not one for eye contact, she turns her eyes to her cup and traces the rim with a long, slender finger.

"It looks to me," she says "like something that vas spit out from a computer who is struggling to solve a problem. You know? A problem beyond its capacity."

"Hmm. An interesting thought. To me, it just looks spooky."

"Vell, you know, this is what Einstein said about quantum entanglement, 'Spooky,' right?"

Quantum entanglement is a phenomenon where two separate subatomic particles mirror each other's behavior for no apparent reason. It's also something Dustin tends to do when talking to women, and he now traces his own cup. To him, women are a natural phenomenon far spookier than quantum physics.

"I guess we'll call anything spooky if we don't understand it," he says. "Eighty years later and we still haven't identified a force between entangled objects."

"Vell, this is vie Einstein hated quantum mechanics, you know. It's the same reason I hate this Stata Center. Einstein vas seeking the same thing vee have always sought as physicists – the elegant, unifying simplicity. It is our human instinct. But the deeper vee go into the nucleus, and the furder vee go into the cosmos, vee amass a bigger and more complex and more disjointed pile of theories, ugly and counterintuitive like this ugly beelding."

"And computers haven't helped."

"No, and our AI technology vill never be as sophisticated as the seamless processes of human instinct, vill they? Faster yes. More powerful, yes. But our instinct knows best, and our instinct tells us that there is something wrong vith this pile, something missing, something simple."

"And so we search."

"And so vee search and research."

Dustin enjoys this conversation and starts to relax and slouch. He wonders if she could be the one, but he can't yet see how.

"I guess if there is a simple solution, it will only be found through the collaboration of man and machine."

"I don't think that vill be powerful enough. The type of intelligence vee need vill require the collaboration of millions of people, as well as machine."

"A hive mind."

"It already began vith the internet, didn't it. Life is redundant. That is also our instinct. Like the cell. The cell has a circulatory system – cytoplasmic streaming. It has its own nervous system – the membrane; reproductive system – the nucleus; respiratory system, digestive system, defense department, maintenance department, sanitation…"

Now she looks at him, her eyes livened with interest.

"It sounds like you've given this talk before," says Dustin.

"Given? No. Exchanged, yes. Just talking vith friends."

"Please go on."

"Vell," she says, leaning in. "Over time, our cells, they developed specialties and organized into communities. Then they organized into beings like you and me, using the same blueprints and same parts for each system. For example, your immune cells are soldier cells. They are armed with chemical veapons and they organize for the rapid response."

He picks up on where she's going and takes the ball. "Then," he says, "on the next level, people organized the same way."

"Yes! Vee have a circulatory system of highways and trucks. Vee even call them arteries. Vee have armies and farms and dumps. People really don't get many new ideas. Vee just follow our instincts and life repeats itself. It is our fractal nature."

"And of course, we have wired up a nervous system, first with switch boards and telephone wire and now with cables, computers and satellites."

"Yes. Nerves, but still no brain. Ven humans evolve to that level, then I think vee start to unlock the secrets of the universe."

"What about crowdsourcing?" he asks.

"It's a good start."

They continue to chat on about such things, then return to class, then to their respective hotels, him following his prescribed route.

The next morning, he dreams of a car crash. He's the driver, injured and trapped, but not in pain. She's in the passenger's seat, kissing his scrapes and bruises. There's a tap on his window and it's her, now standing outside, dressed as a policeman. She tells him to get back as she pulls out a large, heavy flashlight. She smashes his window, which prompts him to wake up.

He sits up, a little shaken. It's 10 a.m., a bit earlier than usual. Oh well, might as well get going. He makes a couple of notations in his journal, calls down for breakfast, throws on some pants and opens the door. Nothing there. No coffee, no towels. But the housekeeper's cart is parked right there. He scans the hall, left then right. The door to his right is ajar, held open by the metal door guard. The sound of a vacuum cleaner seeps through.

"She's busy," he thinks. "She won't mind if I just take what I need off her cart… Actually, maybe she will." He retreats inside for a moment to don a shirt, then returns. He knocks on the other door. No answer. Again. No answer. He pushes it open just a crack.

A woman vacuums on the other side of the room, her back to him. He opens it more and yells. "Excuse me. Excuse me! Do you mind if…" She doesn't hear him. He takes a timorous step in, then another. He lowers his voice, trying to find a volume where he'll be heard but not arrested. "Excuse me." Still no response. He creeps up to her and thinks about tapping her back. He makes a practice run, swiping her air with his finger. He makes another, then decides to follow through. He makes contact and she just about has a heart attack.

She drops the vacuum and spins around, wide-eyed and stumbling. She clutches her chest and lets out a yelp, hardly audible over the droning of the whiny machine. The moment he sees her dark brown eyes, he is also taken aback. He knows it's Her.

# EIGHT

She hardly looks the part. She's older, at least fifty, the lines of time having crept around her eyes and streaked through her hair. At 5'4" with a slightly stocky build, she looks to be Latina, or perhaps Asian. But it is Her. He knows it.

He raises a hand in a calming gesture and apologizes. "I'm sorry, I didn't mean to… I just wanted to ask you for towels, but you couldn't hear me."

She sees kindness in his eyes and relaxes. She's further tranquilized by the sincerity in his voice, and, for reasons that elude her, she's uniquely drawn to this pale, plain, pudgy man.

With even more sincerity, he asks the most frequently insincere question that men ask women. "Do I know you?"

For one strange moment, she transfixes on him, especially those eyes. She thinks hard without looking away. "I'm not sure. You seem very familiar," she says with a mildly Hispanic accent.

He sits down on an ottoman, stuck in his own head, oblivious to the peculiarity of his behavior. He rests his chin on his fist, stares at the floor and thinks. "Have you ever worked at MIT?" he queries.

"No."

"Attended MIT?"

"No, sorry."

"And I've never been to this hotel before. How about Tennessee? You ever been?"

Despite her attraction, she gets a little uneasy. "No, I'm sorry. I have to get back to work. It was nice to meet you."

He starts to insist "But I…" then finally realizes that this enthralling moment is only so to him. "Of course," he concedes, rising back up. "I'm staying in the room next door. If I could get some soap and stuff, I'd appreciate that." He tips his head in a small bow and starts to leave, then stops and turns. "But we haven't actually met. I'm Doctor Dustin Nye."

She offers a graceful handshake which he warmly embraces with both hands.

"Anna."

"Anna. Okay!" He smiles, nods again and returns back to his room. He plops onto his bed and stares at the ceiling, wondering and worrying about how well that just went. He regrets having introduced himself so formally. He wanted to impress her, but now thinks he may have come off snootily. He's always had trouble figuring out how people see him. For the first time since coming to Boston, he's more interested in *how* he feels than why. He's literally met his dream girl and she's magnificent. This might be what they call love.

He lies there a while and ponders such things. A short time later, the sound of her comes. She's busy at her cart outside his door. Like a kid who hears Santa in his chimney, he wants to run and see. But he's not a kid. He knows better and fights the urge. Better to wait and be cool, and hopefully see her again tomorrow. He cogitates a while about how that will go, when suddenly he realizes "The sign!" Better take it off now before he forgets. He creeps up to the door and listens. No sound. He peeps through the hole. Nobody. He cracks the door. Nothing but soap and towels. Anna and her cart have gone. He slips the forbidding placard from the handle, never to guard his door again.

For the rest of the day, he reads little and eats little. He goes to class that night but hardly pays attention. The lecture sounds like the hum of a vacuum. He takes the long way home. That night, he scraps the journal and starts a list of every possible place he could have seen her – every Boston café, store or library that he ever patronized, every show he ever saw, and of course, every hotel at which he stayed. It's a big project, but he's hardly tired. He finally falls asleep around four.

But he doesn't dream, as far as he knows. At least he doesn't recall anything when he's awakened at ten by a somewhat timid knock on the door. "Housekeeping," she announces. He lies in a stupor, not quite sure where he is. A second knock prods him upright.

"Hold on, please!" He's already dressed, having fallen asleep fully clothed the night before. He soaks his head in the sink and quickly combs his hair, then to the door. And there she stands, soaked in grace. He tries not to stare and she does the same.

"Would you like your room made?"

"Oh. Yes, please," he replies, stiffly trying to hide his eagerness.

She enters cautiously, looking around for others, like a cat in a new house. She thought of him briefly last night, wondering what he's like and wondering why she was thinking about him. Now, she again feels affected, though still not sure why. As best she can figure, he seems to have a vulnerable quality that endears him to her.

She starts in the bathroom while he paces the suite, plotting his next move. She takes her time and does a meticulous job, partly to impress and partly to stall for time. When she can tarry no longer and shine no shinier, she takes a breath and ventures out to change the bed. He sits on an uncomfortable chair and watches her work. He is thoroughly relaxed, as one would be after spending two weeks sharing adventure and tenderness with someone, even if only in dream. He tactfully begins conversation by casually dripping out a couple of items from his list.

"I know we've met before. Have you ever lived in Cambridge?"

"Yes, I think you're right. But no, I always lived in Jamaica Plain."

"Did you ever work at the Mandarin Oriental?" She hasn't.

"Caffe Vittoria?"

"Sorry, no."

A brief pause ensues while he ponders something else. "I love your accent," he says. "Where are you from?"

She's been politely answering him while busily working, but now she stops and faces him.

"I didn't think I have an accent," she says. "I'm from Argentina, but I've lived in America for thirty years."

"It's subtle but it's definitely there. It's fantastic."

She blushes just a little and eases her rear onto the bed's edge. "I haven't gone back there in years," she says. "It's like America now, all built up and crowded."

"Why did you come?"

"To America? Why does anyone come? It's America."

"Of course. Dumb question. When you're born here, it's easy to forget how great this place is."

"Yes, it's ok." Her posture relaxes. She has slid backwards to a more secure position and crossed her legs. It's the first time in years he's had a woman on his bed.

Sensing this gained ground, he continues his advance. "Are you in a hurry, Anna? Can I make you some tea or something?"

In a corner of her mind, she knows that she does actually need to mind the clock and, regardless of that, she could get in trouble just for accepting his offer. But as much as he knows that he knows her, she knows that she trusts him. And she wants to stay. She consents and they talk for the duration of a cup, exchanging a few basic facts about themselves. She's a divorced mother of two, living in her own home with her younger son, Eduardo. She's worked at the Kensington for five years, and in hotels for about twenty. She draws her last sip, thanks him, and stands up to go.

He also stands and walks her out. At the door, his voice lowers and his tone intensifies.

"I very much want to see you again," he declares.

"Of course. I will see you tomorrow," she replies, lightly attempting to deescalate the moment. "Just leave your sign off the handle."

Feeling slightly deflated, he returns to choosing his words more logically and strategically rather than passionately. "Yes, of course."

And so she leaves. He sets about trying to read but can't, and he goes to class but can't focus, and he goes to bed but can't sleep. He does eventually sleep but doesn't dream. The next day, she comes wearing makeup and exuding beauty. She again cleans his suite slowly and professionally. Again, they spend a few minutes sharing tea and trivia. And again, he corners her at the door as she's leaving.

"I very much want to see you again," he declares.

She looks at the floor and traces something with her sensible shoe. It's a question mark.

"I don't see a point," she confesses. "You say you're checking out this weekend. Back to Tennessee."

"Why does there have to be a point?"

She looks up into his longing blue eyes. "Everything has to have a point. I'm not a toy. Besides, you are so young and I am old."

"You're not old. How old are you?"

"You're a doctor. You tell me."

"I'm not that kind of doctor."

"Really. What kind are you?"

"I'm a… Look, I'll tell you all that stuff when I see you again. Surely, you can tell I'm not playing games. You're right. Everything has to have a point, and the point is this…" He hesitates, then swallows his fear. "I have been visited by the almighty force of Fate. It has a commanding grip on my throat, and it has taken the lovely shape of you. Can't you feel it?"

She massages her neck with a work-weary hand and contemplates his words. "Yes," she admits, "I can. But I don't say Fate; I say Chemistry. It is definitely there. Between us."

"It's so thick I can taste it in my throat. How am I supposed to just ignore it and go home?"

She shakes her head. "It is a strange thing. I don't know you at all and it seems we are not alike."

"Well, let's find out. Let's explore this thing and see if there's anything to it. Meet me tomorrow for supper. Please."

In the midst of her disbelief, a gust of amusement blows in and she smiles, still shaking her head. "Okay. Let's have a date," she says, then wags her finger playfully. "But you better not be crazy."

They decide to decide the details tomorrow by phone, and she leaves. He leans in the doorway and watches her go, watches her push her little cart down the hall. She looks back twice, then is gone. He retreats back to his room, fists and jaw clenched with elation. "I was smooth," he thinks. "I mean really smooth." Dr. Nye has tallied many accomplishments in his life – degrees, awards, publications. He's even been married. But this tastes different. A woman, a real womanly woman, is really, actually into him. He feels like a man.

Today is the last class and he skips it. Instead, he hops the T across the river to Copley Place, the upscale mall on the Back Bay, to hunt for a new outfit. He starts with the shoes – he once heard that women pay attention to shoes – and builds from there, relying on the tastes of the most attractive saleswomen he can find. He pokes around downtown for a while, picks up a book about charm, then back to the hotel for some reading and rehearsing, some contemplation and a full night of gratifying sleep.

He calls her early the next day and they decide on Italian in the North End. He wants to be a gentleman and meet her at her home, but she's still skeptical enough to prefer not. Instead, they meet at the Downtown Crossing T station where her Orange Line meets his Red. He finds her sitting on a bench in a black, modest, borrowed dress. To the discerning eye, it's a little small for her; to him, it's perfect. She has worn her hair down and had it done – a layered, wavy shag. She extends her hand for a shake and he gives it an old-fashioned kiss. They take the Orange up two more stops, sharing a car with some happy college kids. From Haymarket, they walk a couple of blocks through the crisp evening air, nudged along by an autumn wind charging off the bay. Carmelina's is as he remembered – comfy setting, comfy food. He orders the Sunday Macaroni, which they share while gabbing about the pictures on the wall, the food and the weather. As far as wine, she also doesn't drink.

The conversation veers. "So, you are a physicist," she says. "I admit, when I was in school, I thought physics was too boring, but I also wasn't very strong in it."

"To me, it is the most fascinating subject."

She pauses to chew. "I did some internet searching last night. There are a lot of different kinds of physics. What kind do you do?"

"I know what you mean, although there really is only one kind. Nature is nature and we study how she acts at the most fundamental level. It's true that she expresses herself in a variety of ways, which means various fields of study. But there's also a lot of overlap because we're all still talking about the same woman."

"What woman? She who?"

"Oh, sorry. I mean Mother Nature."

She leans back in her chair and gently replies. "I don't think that God is a woman."

"Actually, I'm not sure I believe in God."

She again stops, more to chew on his words than her rigatoni. "On Thursday, you told me that Fate brought us together, no?"

"Yes."

"Yes, that was very romantic."

"Thank you."

"You're welcome. And when you say Fate, that means it was meant to be, no?"

"Yes again."

"Yes it does. That means it's intentional. Which means someone must intend it."

"Correct."

Dustin listens but takes more interest in the mystical lines of sagacity that animates her face as she challenges him, seamlessly blending masculine confidence with a woman's elegance. Her eyes glimmer as she winds up her closing argument.

"And who is that someone?" she sweetly demands.

He throws up his hands in surrender. "Touché."

"Not touché. God."

"You think God is a man?"

"That is a different subject. We have no reason to talk about the quality of God until we agree that there *is* God. The alternative is ridiculous."

"Well, I don't know about 'ridiculous.'"

She stabs a giant meatball, holds it up and examines it, planning her phagial attack. But before she bites, her eyes turn back to him and she waves her fork with meaty admonition. "If you would be with me, you have to believe in God."

For the first time, he feels a little uneasy. "Are you religious?" he asks.

"I guess I am. I go to church every Sunday anyways."

"I see. Do you believe in the Bible?"

"Much of it, not all of it. I am Unitarian."

"I'm not sure what that means," he says. "I hope I'm not getting too personal or deep… or odd. I'd hate to scare you off."

"No, my dear. I like this. Let's dive in, especially since you are going home tomorrow."

"Okay, then allow me this – Do you believe in life after death?"

"Yes."

"And a soul?"

"Of course."

"Okay, then what is a soul?"

"My soul is my spirit."

"Your spirit. Something magical?"

"I think so, yes."

"Which means it's not physical."

"No, the body is physical, the spirit is not."

"Then what do you suppose makes up this magical self? What makes us who we are?"

"I don't know, Dusty."

It's the first time he's heard her say his name. The sound of her pronouncing it with that cute little accent gives him a shiver of delight.

"Let's think about this for a minute. It's not our memories. Most people can't remember half their lives, and that's before dementia."

"It's our character," she answers. "Our goodness."

"Or evil."

"Yes."

"But I can make a good person into a bad one by giving him drugs or brain damage. Do you believe in Judgement Day?"

"Yes, I do."

"Well, I can insert an electrode into a particular point in the brain and make a man violent. At another point hypersexual. Now how is God supposed to judge behavior like that?"

"I don't know. I'm not God."

"Fair enough. My point is that most of what people consider their soul is in actuality their mind, and I can prove a hundred different ways that the mind is a very physical thing."

Anna contemplates a moment about her soul and her impending death, and the prospect of spending her remaining days with a strange, agnostic, white, southern physicist; an alien in every sense.

"So," she says, "there is one part of me that you can't control with your physics."

"What is that?"

"Who I love."

He starts to worry that he's becoming distasteful. He never had much in the way of good taste and always had trouble reading people. He wants to bring up the topic of pheromones as a rebuttal, but thinks better of it.

"Anna, believe it or not, I agree with you. I think there *is* a soul. In fact, I *know* it. But there's good news and bad news. Just like with me, or with any man you meet, some good news, some bad. The good news is that the soul exists, which means that, in some way, there is life after death. The bad news is that the soul is still just another physical entity."

Anna shakes her head in flabbergastation. "I don't know what the heck you're talking about."

"How did we start this conversation? We started by talking about my career, what I do. I happen to have the best job in the world. You asked me what kind of physicist I am. I'm a particle physicist, a 'nuclear scientist' if you will. I study things at sizes so small that they are no longer things at all, no longer tangible. For the longest time, my work involved designing materials for various industrial and research applications. But three years ago, Fate and the good Lord Himself grabbed me by the horns and took me on a wild ride, and it has not let up yet!"

Passion fills his voice, but she feels concerned — at least a little — about a potential language barrier. Until now, she always thought her English to be almost perfect. Sure, she speaks Spanish at home; but for decades she's done everything else in English, including a couple of jobs working with the public, and she's never had a moment's confusion that she can remember. Even chatting with a nuclear scientist was effortless… when chatting about the food and the weather and the pictures on the wall. But talking with him about his profession makes her conscious of her bilingual status. If she ever learned the word "tangible," she has long since forgotten it; and an application, as far as she knows, is something you fill out to get a job. Perhaps, she thinks, he'll be one of those husbands who doesn't talk very much about his work; just comes home and eats dinner and watches sports. No, that doesn't seem very likely. Or maybe she can just learn a whole bunch of new words related to his profession. There can't be that many of them. Yes, that seems a plausible solution, should the need arise. For now, she'll just reply with an Oh-What.

"Oh. What?"

"Ok. Remember how I said that there's a lot of overlap in categories of physics? There's the astrophysicists. They study things on the largest scale possible — galaxies and universes and such."

There's one fancy English word that Anna knows that she's quite fond of using when the opportunity arises — oxymoron. "Universes is an oxymoron," she says.

"Oh? How so?"

"Uni means one. It can't be plural."

"Okay! Touché again! Anyway, the astrophysicists have this thing called dark matter. Ever heard of it?"

"Yes, I think."

"Dark matter is this stuff that's all through space. We don't know what it is because we can't see it. Yet, it's so massive that its gravity holds the universe together."

"But how do you know it's there if you can't see it?"

"Because of the way that galaxies spin. See, we think of galaxies as clouds of stars because that's all that we can see. But if that's what they were, then the outer stars on the edge would orbit slower than the inner ones."

While talking, Dustin has removed a lily from a vase on the table and dipped the stem in tomato sauce. He uses this floral pen to makes dots on a small, empty plate, concentrating the most dots in the center. He then turns the plate slowly with both hands and continues his explanation. "But these outer stars don't lag behind as if they're floating freely. They keep up with the inner ones, as if they're stuck to a plate. But we can't see the plate and we don't know what it's made of."

"I see. Very interesting."

"Hence, scientists try to figure out what it could be using math and data and building on other theories. They come up with all kinds of hypotheses – wimps and axions and machos and shmachos – theories as big as black holes right down to particles so small, they could hardly exist at all. Then these scientists devise all kinds of experiments, trying to find some of these things. They use giant tubs of Xenon and microwave tuners and… Anna, it's a multibillion-dollar séance is what it is. Anyway, I had the idea that, instead of focusing on the nature of dark matter, and designing an experiment around a particular particle that *might* exist, why don't we shift our focus to aim on the experiment itself. Let's design something so sensitive it can detect just about anything. And that's what I did."

Anna nods and politely smiles. He can tell that she's lost, but he doesn't seem to care. He would tell this story to a teddy bear if no one else was around. He merrily carries on.

"I designed a crystal, Katascopos Espionium, a very complex structure. It's piezoelectric and fractal to several levels."

"Piezo.."

"Piezoelectric means that the slightest agitation will cause it to generate an electric current."

"And the other one?"

"Fractal? The best way I can explain that is if you first think of an image. Make it something complex."

"Okay. Mona Lisa."

"The Mona Lisa? Really? Plain girl with a simple smile?"

"Only a man would say that Mona Lisa is simple."

"Hmm. Okay, the Mona Lisa then. Now imagine that it—"

"She."

"Imagine that *she* is composed of thousands of tiny dots, like a photo in an old newspaper. Got it?"

"Got it."

"Now imagine that you can magnify one of those dots as big as a picture, and when you do, you see it's the same painting, the Mona Lisa. That is a fractal. And if that dot was also composed of thousands of Mona Lisa dots, then you're fractal to two levels."

"I understand."

"Okay, good."

"But I didn't understand what it has to do with the soul."

He continues to draw for her a connection that she doesn't yet see, by continuing his story in the way he likes to tell it, the way he's told it many times before. When he finally does arrive at the point, she understands. And at that moment of understanding, she becomes more serious about pursuing a relationship with him. Clearly, she could never have envisioned such a man in her life. Yet now, just as clearly, she sees a man whose company she enjoys, and a man on a significant path, one of which she wants a part.

They carry on talking for a while until they finally succumb to the polite pressure of a waiter who increasingly wants to help (help them out the door). It's dark out now and they catch a cab. They head to Faneuil Hall, the brick Georgian marketplace where Samuel Adams railed against the king of England, walked around, did some window shopping, ate ice cream, and railed some more. Dusty and Anna proceed to follow in the footsteps of the noble patriot... minus the speech. By the night's end, he's decided to stay in Boston another week and she's agreed. She considers asking him to go with her to church in the morning but decides against it. He does accompany her back to Jamaica Plain, and walks with her the three blocks from the T station to her little, white colonial in the Latin quarter. The stairs creek a little and the porch light is out. There, at her door, guided only by his feelings and the clinical fluorescence of a nearby streetlamp, he kisses her sweetly and bids her good night.

He never does tell her about his dreams, but tomorrow he'll change his flight and extend his hotel stay solely because of them. He can cite no supporting data or logic, only a knowledge that he cannot even articulate. It's like a secret that he keeps from himself, locked away and beyond his ken, but nonetheless steering the ship of his life. This latest step in Dustin's journey – from the concrete existence of a Southern male to the abstract world of quantum physics, and now to the mystical realm of intuition – began in a single moment four years ago, in an old mine, half a mile under the Smoky Mountains.

# Nine

Four years ago, Dustin's team had converted a part of a mine into a lab in order to eliminate interference from the heavens. The half mile of Earth above served to screen them from the cosmic rays that constantly shower its surface. They had rigged an Espionium crystal to a powerful amplifier and suspended it in a case to keep out light. The entire contraption was immersed in liquid helium at minus 450 degrees Fahrenheit to eliminate thermal activity, and wrapped in a field cancellation coil to filter out any remaining electromagnetic radiation from electronics, people, and all unknowns. For months, the crystal remained perched in absolute physical stillness and silence, while scientists sat and waited to hear the slightest whimper of a cosmic mouse. What came was not a whimper but a roar, and it came not from a mouse but a man gasping his last breath. Weeks of sitting, staring at instruments and eating take-out finally took its toll on his obese, diabetic heart, and Dr. Frank Archer suffered a tremendous infarction. In the face of the assault, his heart reacted by twitching nervously instead of pumping, an event known as ventricular fibrillation. He died within minutes. Dustin could only stand there, petrified, while one man called 911, another ran to hunt for the defibrillator, and a woman performed CPR. When it was all over, everyone left early to recover.

It wasn't until the next day, when reviewing their recordings, that they realized what had happened. The crystal had gone wild, pinning the needle as high as it could read. The whole episode lasted only a second, but it happened right around the time of their colleague's demise.

In reality, if something happens twice, it's just a coincidence; three times, you may be onto something. But a single occurrence is just an anecdote, hardly even worth mentioning. Dustin and his team set out to see if this phenomenon was reproducible. But how? Kill another scientist? Nah. Animals were the logical alternative, maybe rats.

The problem was that people do not sign up to be interns and assistants to a particle physicist with the expectation of doing animal experiments. One assistant, Autumn Sumner, was a vegan. She requested and received permission to be excused from work on those days. The remaining team of four searched the web and found a company to sell them some rodents. They ordered a half dozen rats, another half of guinea pigs, and some supplies.

When the animals arrived, Dustin took the lead and euthanized the first rat on a table, ten feet from the crystal, injecting 20% Pentobarbital into its abdomen. The rat struggled and fought for its life, but couldn't bite through his metal mesh glove. The crystal exhibited no electrical response to the execution, so he moved the table closer and tried again. Still nothing. Four rats left and four scientists, so Dustin proposed killing the rest simultaneously. However, one assistant declined, so three. Someone gave a countdown, the three rats were killed, and the crystal stayed mum. They freed the last rat – put it on the elevator and sent it up to the surface.

Dustin got less cooperation about the guinea pigs; they were too cute. Those who did participate insisted that the animals first be given the halothane gas to put them to sleep. They went through four guinea pigs. Still no luck. They kept the last two as pets and cursed them with nerdy names – Quark and Lepton.

The next day, the team gathered to discuss their lack of results and determine the next steps. They had to consider that they were chasing the wrong lead, and that the tragic death of their colleague was just a coincidence after all. But Dustin asserted that it was far too early to entertain that possibility, and that people are much bigger and more complicated than mice. He reasoned that the only logical plan was to euthanize larger, more intelligent creatures. He had been researching the options and concluded that the best choice was dogs, beagles in particular. He put forth this idea in his usual, clumsy manner, and was instantly met with howls of objection from everyone except Dr. Beeks, his most dedicated assistant. Dustin persisted obliviously, thinking that his protesting peers would understand if they just had more information.

He explained how tens of thousands of dogs in the U.S. are used every year in a variety of experiments, and how beagles are preferred due to their docile, trusting nature. But the more he tried, the angrier they got, and Ms. Sumner actually resigned.

"I'm going to report you to… somebody!" she declared as she stormed out.

The team prorogued without decision… except for Dustin who, unbeknownst to the rest, had already made up his mind. He tried to purchase a dog online, but the two breeders he contacted claimed to be highly regulated and would only sell to certified biomedical research companies. So over the weekend, he adopted a shelter dog – a shy, yellow Lab named Brady. He kept Brady locked in his garage to avoid spooking his cat, Schrödinger. He was spooked anyways; and so was the dog, who paced and circled and made a racket. Perhaps he could sense his sentence like a death row inmate.

Late that Sunday night, Dustin took Brady to the lab to put him down. He placed him on a table, strapped a mask to him and titrated the gas to flow just enough to keep him drowsy. Two feet away and standing eight feet tall, the alloy column that housed the crystal loomed like a chrome god demanding a sacrifice. Dustin gave the gas not for mercy's sake, but out of necessity, for he had to put an I.V. in the dog's forearm and had never done it before. He had watched a few videos online and felt ready, but expected it would take a few stabs before he got it. Indeed, it took four before he saw the flash of blood that let him know he had entered the vein. Slip in the catheter, secure with tape and screw on the syringe. When he felt ready, he cut the gas, guessing that Brady ought to be fully alive in the minutes before he was fully dead. Brady didn't regain consciousness with much enthusiasm. He just trembled and bowed his head, clasping his eyebrows and looking pitifully up at his captor. Holding his breath, thumb squarely on the poison plunger, Dustin pressed death into dog and waited.

And with his last breath, Brady breathed life into that crystal, eliciting a response, weak and brief but measurable. A thrill coursed through Dustin's own veins, and he could feel his pulse in his thumb, which was still pressing the piston. A million thoughts raced through his head before he finally let go. He was definitely onto something, possibly of gargantuan dimensions.

But he also knew that a continuation of his current methods was neither a feasible strategy nor likely to be productive. However, he had ideas.

It had been three weeks since the awesome demise of Dr. Archer, and Dustin had spent it thinking and planning for this moment. He needed more data, which meant more studies which meant more death, preferably human death, as that seemed to produce the most dramatic results. Obviously, he couldn't achieve such a thing in a lab or on a regular schedule.

To solve the first problem, he would have to modify his device – make it portable. Portability meant going above ground and going unfrozen. For that to be possible, he would have to reduce the crystal amplification. Its signal, the first time when Archer died, overwhelmed the instruments and made it impossible to detect subtle variations. Above ground, it would be worse.

The crystal could still be kept fairly cold with reasonably small technology. More importantly, it could be kept at a constant temperature, which would allow the thermal noise to be subtracted from the data with some advanced coding, on which he was already working. Likewise, some modification to the programming, the casing and the field cancellation coil should be able to cope with the added radiation assaults.

But what of the second problem? The mass slaughter of animals already occurred every day to satisfy the carnivorous lifestyle of Americans. It would be easy to find a slaughterhouse willing to make a deal. But Dustin doubted his ability to overcome all those thermodynamic intrusions if he had to work with weak reactions, which is what he'd gotten thus far by working with animals. Nope, the subjects had to be human.

But from where? China? He'd heard somewhere that they execute a lot of people over there – dissidents and such. But China was so far away and strange, and the idea seemed too complicated and maybe even dangerous.

Then he thought of babies. Abortion – now there's a big business, *and* it operates on a schedule. He wouldn't even have to go far; probably a clinic right in Knoxville. He checked; there were two. One of them was that big chain, Liberated Loins. They had that slogan – Kompassion Is Loin Liberation. Perfect! He would call them tomorrow.

Meanwhile, he disposed of Brady and conjured a story, warping the truth just enough that he wouldn't get reported to somebody. Brady became Sparky, an old, cancer-ridden mutt who Dustin learned about when calling around to local veterinarians. Ole Sparky was about to be put down anyways, and the vet agreed, for a fee, to do it in the lab. The team seemed to buy the tale without a fuss, perhaps because they believed it, but equally because they were awed by the results. They too felt something big afoot.

The abortion idea didn't go very well. He spent hours on the phone, being punted from one office to another, one bureaucrat to another, even one state to another. The only thing that remained constant was that neurotoxic "music" that drones on and on and on when you're on hold – music made not to soothe your suffering, but to enhance it. He eventually reached someone who seemed to be the right person, the Senior Director of Medical Services out of New York.

Dr. Pia Pacelli sounded skeptical on the phone, but agreed to meet with him, so he flew to the city and had lunch with her in Little Italy. He prepared on the way by struggling through a book she had written. The Tao of Tiny Tim looked to him the same way that equations of quantum chromodynamics look to the rest of us. Nonetheless, he did attempt to casually refer to it during their meeting and did so with all the subtle tact of a particle physicist. If she was flattered, he couldn't tell.

"We're often favorable to supporting the scientific community when we can," she told him. "Especially when it brings funds to our program. And though you're not offering what we can usually get from private industry, that's not the main issue. The main issue is logistics. It's one thing to participate in pharmaceutical trials or to sell you fetal tissue, but you don't need anything like that. You want to be present during a procedure and set up all kinds of equipment."

"Well, it actually wouldn't be a lot."

"But we're not talking about lab rats here. We're talking about women in a very touchy situation, a very private matter. Even if I could find a facility to agree to work with you, *they* would probably have trouble finding patients to volunteer."

At this point in the discussion, Dr. Pacelli noticed Dustin copying her movements. He had done it once and she thought nothing of it. But he did it again, this time taking off his glasses, regarding them and replacing them right after she did. She didn't know what to make of it, but felt disconcerted and annoyed. The meeting turned further south when he further explained his research – the examination of matter, or perhaps energy, emitted at the death of human subjects.

"There are no dying human subjects in our clinics," she curtly corrected.

"I mean the babies… fetuses."

"Fetal tissue."

"Yes, that. When they die."

"They don't die."

"Um."

"Fetuses are not alive; therefore, they cannot die. I'm afraid you've been misinformed, and I certainly wouldn't want you to waste your time and resources, or ours. Thank you very much for lunch. It was nice to meet you and I wish you success in your research."

With that, she stood, donned her giant purse and her spring jacket, and left Dustin to sit, deflated and somewhat confused.

His flight home briefly crossed the sea, and he daydreamed from his window seat as he watched the glittering waves. He thought about how each sparkle meant that waves of light had traveled ninety-three million miles from the sun, bounced off of a single ocean wave miles away, then shined onto a tiny spot in the back of his eye, allowing him to perceive said ocean wave. Some simple pleasures were beyond his reach, but where he lacked aesthetic appreciation, he thrived in amazement.

Back at the ranch, Dustin invited Beeks over to brainstorm. At twenty-seven, Beeks was the only team member younger than he. He looked even younger than that with his round face, his overgrown, tight auburn curls and a dash of freckles littering his otherwise shiny cheeks. His pointy small nose turned up just a little, making you want to hang your keys on it. More importantly, his youth meant that he was still stiff of courage and limber in imagination. They sat on the sunporch drinking iced tea, and watching the cardinals and deer.

Beeks liked the idea of calling around all the veterinarians in the area and he proposed that they do the same with the hospitals and maybe nursing homes as well. "We could foster some connections, have a network of people on the lookout. If someone's about to croak or they're getting ready to pull the plug, they give us a call."

Dustin didn't like it. "Too low-yield. It relies on too many things going right in a short period of time. The hospital has to approve, the family has to approve, and in the middle of the drama of death, our informer has to have the forethought, the time *and* the desire to pick up the phone."

"It works for organ transplants," Beeks responded.

"Ya, but the organ donor system has been around for decades, nationwide. It saves lives. Everybody knows about it. Besides, we're in East Tennessee. Folks here aren't exactly dying left and right. For your idea to have a chance, we'd have to go somewhere crowded."

"Atlanta. Nashville."

"Bigger."

"Okay, like New York, Chicago, DC. Lots of death there."

Suddenly, an idea overcame Dustin and his baby face lit up with life. "Not just death. Sudden death. Those places get homicides and car crashes like Memphis gets rain. And at those scenes, we don't need anyone's permission. We just have to stay outside the yellow tape."

The excitement spread to Beeks. "And we wouldn't need informers," he said. "We just need one of those police scanners."

That settled it. They had a plan. They spent the next weeks working out the logistical and technical details. For the latter, they completed their design of a portable apparatus to house, insulate, refrigerate, amplify and record the Espionium crystal. The entire thing spanned three feet long, weighed nineteen pounds, and would never get through airport security. They dubbed it the DIKE (Device for the Investigation of Katascopos Espionium) and made three of them with carrying cases. They also constructed a stand – a metal frame with legs and round slots into which the DIKEs fit. The stand unfolded like a bed frame and was designed to hold the DIKEs half a meter off the ground and precisely four meters apart. The frame's joints were made to ratchet, allowing the DIKEs to be arranged in a selection of angles.

Dustin and Beeks would be the field investigators. The rest of the team would stay in Oak Ridge and analyze. They chose Baltimore for a location – not too far and a reliably fatal place. They bought a used pickup – the best option to manage their equipment. They met with the Baltimore police commissioner, fire chief and the directors of several hospital emergency departments. Nobody seemed helpful. Some were skeptical. The team was ready by July.

Or so they thought. Getting around Baltimore proved harder than they had imagined, and someone honked behind them at every red light. Really. Every single one. They half-thought it might be the same person following them around just to niggle. They got honked when they didn't block the box, when they didn't jump at the light change, and even when they failed to mow down a jaywalker. And the pedestrians themselves seemed to *try* to get injured, especially the ones downtown. Dustin sometimes imagined, as he navigated those tattered, crowded streets of chaos, that this must have been what driving was like through Saigon in 1975, trying to catch that last helicopter out of Vietnam.

They spent the first couple of weeks making two rounds – day and night shifts – at each police station, talking with whomever would give them time, making themselves familiar, and of course, always bringing gifts of coffee and donuts. They explained to anyone who would listen that "We're doing a study on trauma" and "We spoke with the commissioner" and "Please feel free to give him a call." From the friendlier cops, they learned a a few tips. One of them, Officer Dibble, was especially chatty and full of pearls such as

> - Stay out of the way.
> - MVAs (motor vehicle accidents) are obviously not as reliably fatal as shootings, but they happen in more concentrated blocks of time, i.e., rush hour. Homicides can happen any time of day, though not so much in the morning. They peak around ten to midnight and when it's hot out.
> - Nobody cares about the commissioner. Commissioners come and go like pop stars. If you want to talk to someone with influence, make it the FOP chief (Fraternal Order of Police) over at Lodge 3.
> - You can talk to who you want, but nothing goes further than appreciation.
> - Don't dress for work. Dress like a bystander but wear protective clothing – no shorts or sandals.

- Get rid of the pickup and the Tennessee plates. Baltimore residents hate rednecks and bigotry. Also, don't talk to onlookers. And think about packing a piece. (You didn't hear that from me).
- Stay out of the way.

Beeks knew what Officer Dibble meant by "appreciation" – bribery. Dustin also knew – donuts and a thank-you. (Dibble himself never knew that his two guests were mind-readers.)

They couldn't get different plates and it was too late to hunt for a new vehicle. They would make do with the truck while their staff worked on getting them a van or something. They got to work on July 15th.

They would have started a day earlier, but it had rained all day and their equipment was not water-friendly. Around noon, they fired up a pot of coffee, fired up their new police scanner, and sat back in their new efficiency, located among the brick row houses of the yuppie Federal Hill neighborhood. Their first break came three hours later – a major crash at the Interstate 95/Outer Loop Interchange. What they failed to realize, but soon did while driving to the scene, was that highway crashes cause traffic jams. Without an emergency vehicle, they were just as stuck as everyone else. They spent an hour in traffic and, by the time they arrived, the wreck had been cleared.

No more crashes, at least not on the highway.

And no more lounging around the apartment. They would instead sit in the truck and park on a main road, like Patapsco or route 40. They ultimately decided to post themselves in the parking lot of police headquarters. There, they felt central as well as safe, and had terrific radio reception. All day they tarried, mostly sitting and reading and talking and sweating. Occasionally, they broke to stretch or walk, or to make a run for alimentary input or output.

Dustin eventually nodded off, succumbing to the late hour and the hypnotic burble of police chatter, a miserable lullaby, a ceaseless stream of every kind of human misery reported in robotic, unimpressed tones. At 11:30, Beeks nudged him awake with news of an incident – a stabbing over on Purdue Ave. Dustin hardly had time to brush off his crumbs, wipe his saliva or fasten his seatbelt before his young partner was tearing down the expressway, urged on by a mounting chorus of distant sirens. They arrived at a narrow street blocked by people and emergency vehicles. A small crowd had gathered outside an apartment building, and Dustin gathered from the discussion that this was a domestic. A woman had stabbed her boyfriend and, apparently, he had it coming.

A policeman stood at the building's entrance and wouldn't let Dustin enter, and certainly not into the apartment. Even if he would have, there wasn't enough room to set up; and now the ambulance was arriving, and would soon whisk the victim away. Dustin started to realize that this Baltimore trip would not be as fruitful as he first thought. It seemed that too many stars had to align for him to be able to run a test. Such an alignment would come the very next night.


It was 1 a.m. They had found a twenty-four-hour pizza joint in a relatively safe area, Roosevelt Park, and were sucking down some coffee, each of them having already dozed off twice that night. They had left the scanner in the truck and were making do with a phone app when across came a 10-91 – gunshots fired in West Baltimore. They put down their coffee, plunked down a twenty, "keep the change," and sped down the Jones Falls Expressway. When the nice GPS lady told them to exit at Druid Hill Park, they found themselves on a well-kept road that hugged the southern shore of the Druid Lake reservoir. They were halfway to West Baltimore, headed west.

Under an overcast, moonless sky, they almost failed to see the park entrance that branched off to their right as they approached the end of the lake. But they did see it, so when they heard the explosions, they ended up skidding into the park, rather than crashing into the tall, wrought-iron fence that guarded the water's edge. Explosions? Gunshots actually, two of them, loud and close. Boom boom! Beeks jammed on the brakes and cut the wheel. He wondered if he'd been shot but didn't feel injured. Or perhaps he'd blown a tire, but he didn't really want to get out and check.

They were only stopped a second when a shadowy figure dashed across their path. They waited a moment and held their breath. No mention of anything crossed the airwaves. Dustin reached for the door. Beeks shook his head and grabbed Dustin's forearm.

"It'll be okay," Dustin reassured. "He's gone."

He opened his door and ventured out, diving into the hot, sticky darkness, a tar pit night. Beeks kept close behind. His fingers probed the dark while his eyes worked to squeeze some sight from the scant available light. They worked their way back east, away from the fleeing shadow and towards where they had heard the noise, across a bike path and into the tall grass along the water's edge. Dustin suddenly tripped and fell out of view.

"I'm alright," he announced, then quickly stood up, and finally thought to light up his phone. The cold LED mercilessly revealed what he had tripped over… or actually whom. Lying there on the ground was someone's son, resting his head in a pool of blood. He still pulled breath and his eyes roamed around as if watching the angels circling. His limbs were stretched, back slightly arched, wrists turned out and toes pointed downwards. This is called a decerebrate posture and it indicated that his brain stem had lost the ability to keep that balance between flexion and extension. Dustin didn't know about decerebrate postures, but anyone could see that the young man was dying. He and Beeks froze a minute. Beeks then phoned the police while Dustin ran to fetch the equipment. He returned and got to work fast, unfolding the stand and working it into the uneven ground, then placing the DIKEs. He all but ignored the dying young man until the time came to measure distances, at which point he tiptoed up to him, tape measure in hand. He then realized that he had a somewhat philosophical question he hadn't considered – where to measure from. Would those mysterious, dark particles emanate from the brain, the heart or from every cell? He decided on the navel – a small, central, reliable target. He didn't hesitate, for he didn't know when he would again have such an opportunity for such precision. He gently lifted the victim's shirt and placed his tape, taking care not to get his fingerprints on the pistol that peeked from the waistband. He finished setting up and they stood there, watching, the DIKEs humming away. Beeks turned to Dustin.

"Should we do something?" he asked.

"There's nothing we can do."

"We could pray for him."

Dustin thought for a second. "Sure. You go ahead."

Beeks bowed his head and Dustin followed suit.

"Heavenly Father," said Beeks, "we beseech you to save this young man's life if you see fit. And if you don't see fit, then to take him under thy mighty wing and grant him entry into thy kingdom. And ease the suffering that is sure to come to his family and loved ones. Whether we live or die, we belong to You, and though I walk in the valley of the shadow of death, I will fear no evil, for You are with me."

Death arrived before the police, though Dustin didn't know it. He kept the DIKEs running until they made him clear out everything and leave. Three of the officers didn't know him, and the fourth pretended not to. One called him a demon. They softened a bit when he explained his work, and more so when he showed them his list – names of sixteen of the friendliest officers he had talked with when doing his promotional tour, a list of references. They each knew someone on the list.

The next chance came a week later when an irate passenger shot an MTA bus driver in the chest while pulled over on Woodbourne, following an argument. The ranking officer on the scene knew about their study and accommodated them. He was professional and appreciated that they had a job to do. Such appreciation had long ago faded for the press, who he kept at bay. The gaggle of squawking reporters, naturally curious about the scientists' odd activities, lobbed questions at them. Dustin was also professional and ignored them. It was far too early in his project, and talking to them prematurely could only give him a lot of trouble. He would publish when ready.

Dustin stayed in Baltimore for another three months during which time he trained a second assistant to take his place. He then returned to Oak Ridge to run the show. Beeks and his new assistant continued to collect data for another year and a half. During that time, they received delivery of a nice, long, plain van. They also got to know much of the police department, on whom to rely and of whom to beware. Unlike Dustin, Beeks came across as a likeable fellow and the work became easier after Dustin's departure. In fact, when the right cops were on duty, they were good for a phone call, and Beeks could shut off the scanner.

They were present for a total of fifty-one deaths, including four crashes, three heart attacks, a stroke, a fall and forty-two homicides. They took readings at a variety of angles and through a variety of media, following strict protocols designed by Dustin. For testing materials, they used customized shields and casings made of lead, silicon and several alloys; and also a specialized container for liquids. They learned that these mysterious particles passed through everything, almost completely undisturbed. They hardly seemed to interact with normal matter at all, and didn't seem to dissipate over distance. These discoveries allowed Beeks to stop worrying about getting inside buildings or getting close to the scene.

More importantly, they learned that this dark matter was not matter at all. It behaved as a wave. This was a dark form of energy, a wave wholly different than electromagnetism, beaming from people at the moments of their demise, in all directions and through all things.

Dustin wrestled with the naming of this new breakthrough. He thought of calling it the Nye wave but didn't like the sound of it; never did like the sound of his own name. He settled on something pretty close, though. He simply dubbed it the Y-wave.

He published his findings on the second anniversary of the awesome death of Dr. Archer, about two years before he met Anna. His report was met with sweet excitement. Within two months, Popular Science magazine picked up his work. The producer of Good Morning Today called him a month after that.

The show's bubbly anchor, Cookie McGuffin, hadn't read the article before she attempted to interview him. She therefore didn't realize that the new entity had been boringly named after the second-most common variable in science.

"The Why Wave," she began, legs smartly crossed beneath an expensive, mid-length skirt, teeth biting lightly on the temple tip of fake spectacles. "You gave this astonishing discovery a profound and appropriate name. Why indeed. Why do you suppose the Why Wave exists?"

Dustin already felt about as nervous as a hen brooding a clutch of crocodile eggs. Some things made it easier, like filming in his home, and like Cookie's reassurances that "We're not out to get you," and "We'll do as many takes as we need." Other things were exacerbating, like the producers rearranging his stuff in order to shoot him in front of bookshelves, or the stunning Cookie McGuffin in her mid-length skirt with legs smartly crossed.

"Science doesn't really involve itself with questions of Why," he replied. "We leave that to the philosophers."

"But can you avoid it?" she asked. "I mean, after all, regardless of your background, you're the man who has stumbled on the place where the two worlds – philosophy and science – meet." Cookie got her last name from her Irish husband, but her gesticulations came from her Italian parents. She held up one hand for Philosophy and the other for Science, then clasped them tightly together. "Two great methods for seeking truth and, at their merger, one man stands alone, and that man is you."

"Well, I wouldn't say alone. I've had help."

"Yes, we've interviewed your team. They admire you very much."

Dustin suspected this was not altogether true.

"And of course, Frank Archer," he added.

"You're referring of course to Dr. Francis Archer, the one team member we couldn't interview, and the one you never got to thank. How do you feel about that?"

She asked him a lot about his feelings, a fact which later irritated him when he reflected on it. "I mean…" he thought "what does that have to do with anything?" She asked him how he felt about all the death he witnessed, and about his new-found fame. She asked him how he felt about the Baltimore press which, having been denied the scoop, reacted by coining stupid nicknames for him and Beeks, names like "Dr. Nye the Science Ghoul," and "The Doctors Grim." Dustin didn't think much about his feelings at all, but he did spend several days after the interview thinking of things he wished he'd said.

She asked some good questions too. She asked if he had any congealing ideas as to the origin of these "Why" waves.

He didn't.

She continued. "Okay, but would you go as far as to say that they are what could be called our life force?"

"I wouldn't. If there is such a thing, it implies that this is a stored energy, energy that is released when we die, unchanged. We don't know that yet. This could simply be a type of energy that is generated by the process of dying, much like heat is created from decay. The conversion from one form of energy to another."

This answer might have dampened another journalist, but not the ever-perky McGuffin.

"Okay, but if this is the stuff of life, does that mean that there's nothing magical about us? That we're nothing but physical?"

"Well, Ms. McGuffin, I don't really believe in magic. But if what you say is true, there's a bright side to it since energy can't be destroyed. It sort of means that we live forever, I guess."

"I guess it does!"

Within a year, Y-waves were being studied at research facilities around the world. The variety of perspectives produced novel ways to consider and analyze the entity. Its new fame generated a tsunami of societal cooperation, delivering tons of information to the shores of mankind. We learned that Y-waves are not just emitted from the dying, but also from living humans at levels just barely detectable. We also found that the flood of Y-waves occurring at the moment of death, though emanating slightly in every direction, overwhelmingly preferred a single vector. That vector seemed to vary depending on geoposition and time of day. We later figured out that it did not actually vary at all. From a cosmic perspective, the waves always flowed one way – towards Vega, the ancient North Star. That discovery led to a squall of excitement and chatter in both the scientific community and among well-informed layfolk. In some circles, it was proclaimed that the waves pointed the way to heaven.

Oak Ridge remained the vanguard of the expedition, and Dustin continued to make modifications in his equipment. But he couldn't find a way to improve on the crystal. He learned much about Y-wave behavior and interaction, but not enough about its nature, its essence. He believed that his crystal, although revolutionary, was nonetheless too crude as a transducer. A better crystal, he believed, would yield more detail. For weeks, he mulled it over constantly and read voraciously, looking for ideas.

He was in such a state one day, mulling and detached, while in the checkout line of his local grocer, buying some organic fruit and lentil chips. That seemed to be what they were all eating at the office these days.

"Mmm, I love kiwi," said the cashier, commenting on his purchase.

Dustin looked up from his Harley wallet to see a young girl with a bright smile. But it wasn't her face that caught his attention. It was the deep blue stone hanging from her neck.

"Do you ride?" she asked.

"No, not really. Say what is that stone on your necklace?"

"Oh this? My Lapis Lazuli. You like it?"

"It's interesting."

"Helps me with my migraines and it's also really stimulating. Harmonizes my spiritual energy. Isn't she beautiful?"

He whipped out his phone and searched the web. "Lapis?"

"Lazuli. L-A-Z—"

"Got it. A tectosilicate, moderate complexity."

"If you want one, we sell'em at my mom's shop. It's not expensive."

Puzzled, he asked "Why would I want one?"

"Because you like it, I think. I can tell," she stated, sweet and confident.

He thought a moment. "I guess I do. Yes, I'd like that – coming to see your mother's store."

She took a moment and wrote the address in beautiful penmanship on his receipt.

He left feeling somewhat surreal, being unaccustomed to friendly banter from pretty, young women. That same weird feeling returned that weekend as he pulled up to what he thought was the right address, but it didn't look like a shop. A house, big and white and Victorian settled comfortably back from the road, nicely tended with feminine flair. It looked more like a home than a store, or perhaps a small inn. He double-checked the address. Yup, that was it. He sat for a moment and hesitated. A thought flashed by – that this could be a teenager's prank and he might be trespassing. But he felt reassured when two women walked by and ignored him, an indication that they were guests, and that there were no big dogs around to eat him. They had left the house from a side door and Dustin followed their route back towards it, along a cobblestone path lined with crocus and daffodils. The path led him around the corner to the side of a small annex that had been obscured by trees. A shingle and a large bay window made for an inconspicuous store front. The sign read "Moon Children." Through the window, he could see people inside, and they could see him so there was no turning back. Unsure whether to knock first or just go in, he did both.

He entered a sizeable room filled with a sweet, unfamiliar fragrance. A menagerie of stone surrounded him – rows of bins and shelves displaying a panoply of minerals. Some were tumbled smooth and cut into geometric shapes or left to their own morphological devices. Others were too elegant to disturb and were allowed to remain in primordial majesty. Some beamed with stunning colors or sparkles or opalescence. Others brooded in subdued mystery. The girl from the grocery store flitted about an adjacent room. In the center of it all sat a woman on a stool, confident and clutching an iPad, talking with three more on a sofa. Her blonde hair hung dry and very long, with grey sprinkled throughout. Her skinny physique mismatched her robust voice.

"Welcome," she called.

Believing himself intrusive, Dustin felt the need to explain himself. "Hi. I just heard about this place and I was curious, that's all."

"We love curiosity here. Have a look around."

Hearing his voice, the girl entered. "Hi," she said to Dustin, then turned to her mother. "Ma, I was working, and this man liked my Lapis, so I told him about the store," she reported proudly.

"Yup, the Lapis is a powerful beacon," said Ma. "It's been captivating people for thousands of years. Do you use crystals?"

"I wouldn't say I use them," said Dustin. "I study them."

"I do too. But how do you study them and not make use of them?"

"Well, I don't know how. I study them over at the lab."

"Oh no," she said, raising a hand in protest. "You work there? You're not trying to make a crystal bomb or something, are you?"

"Oh no," he answered through nervous laughter. "Nothing like that."

He was briefly distracted by a young woman on the couch who held a ten-pound rock on her lap. It was a jet black piece of polished obsidian with an iridescent overtone, and she petted and admired it like a baby.

"No, I don't sense any destructive energy in you," said Ma. "Have a look around. If you have any questions, don't hesitate, okay hun?"

"Okay."

"You can ask me or my daughter Maggie."

"And what's your name?"

"I'm Krystal."

"Your name is Krystal and you deal in crystals?"

"Of course."

"Were you inspired by your interest to change your name?"

"No, my mother was inspired by the universe to name me Krystal."

"Um… oh."

Not sure what else to say, he proceeded to look around, and Krystal returned to her conversation. While he didn't know much geology, he recognized many of her pieces as being variations of quartz.

"Quite a collection," he chimed in.

"I brought'em from all over the world. I pick each of my stones with love."

"Um… oh."

He wasn't learning much, and he wondered if there was much to learn from this bunch at all. But he did feel he should buy something. He found some more Lapis Lazuli – a safe choice – and picked out an octahedral piece.

"You like the Lapis," said Krystal as he presented it for purchase. "She's a powerful stone. Good choice."

"Powerful how?"

"It amplifies your mind, gives you self-awareness. It also helps a bunch of ailments. Cleanse it and keep it in your pocket."

"Cleanse it?"

"Geez, I thought you studied these things. Yes, cleanse it. These crystals have been around forever. They've been touched by a lot of people and seen a lot of stuff, and not all of it good. They absorb all that negative energy."

Dustin played along. He didn't know what he sought, but he hoped that if he humored her, he might eventually find some insight amongst all this gobbledygook. "How do I cleanse it?"

"You got several options. You could burn some sage or bathe it in moonlight. Or you could buy this selenite charging plate."

The white dish was the size of his palm. He did a quick search on selenite – simple gypsum. He bought it.

"You ride?" she asked, eyeing his wallet.

"No, not yet" he replied. "Planning to." He wasn't. Motorcycles actually terrified him, but he always wanted to belong to something cool.

She declared him a very unusual man. "What's your sign?"

"Cancer."

"Oh my, a Moon Child!" Her face brightened. "Are you sensitive?"

"I don't think so. And I'm pretty sure I'm a Cancer."

"Well, you can be Cancer if you want. I'd rather be a child of the moon." She waited for him to understand. He didn't. "Same difference," she said.

"Oh. I don't really believe in Astrology anyways."

"You are aware, of course, that the universe is chock full of these massive things called stars."

Krystal delivered her snark with disarming sweetness, and the contrast left him a bit discombobulated. All he could do was nod.

"I thought so. And don't these stars exert gravity on everything, including you and me? Yes, they do. And don't they also move in predictable patterns? Which means they create predictable tides in every little creature. And they did so even when you were a baby in your mama's womb, and your little mind was still gelling."

"Maybe," he said and thought for a moment. "But the kind of detail and certainty that astrologers claim as knowledge… I don't know. It's also a stretch when they talk about predicting the future."

"Well, they've done pretty good with mine so far. Except you. I definitely didn't see *you* coming."

And with that, she handed him his purchase, which she had packaged into a lovely little bag stuffed with tissue and tied with a bow.

He thought about her a lot for the next couple of weeks, more interested in her than her trade. Eventually, she faded. He never even considered trying her voodoo, and the Lapis got lost in a drawer.

A month later, he decided to clean out his employee email. He only checked the account when HR called to bug him, repining that "You still haven't registered for your Triple-S."

"Triple-S?"

"Yes, your annual training – safety, security and sensitivity. Everyone has to do it, even the doctors. *Didn't you get my email?*"

When he finally did check it, he discovered this:

*Hi Doc. This is Krystal, the one who sold you the Lapis. After we met, I felt something in you and I got curious so I read up on you and holy cow!! There was a lot to read! I sense an intensity hidden inside you and I feel that your journey is leading you somewhere important. I want to help you if I can and also learn from you, I guess. Maybe we can learn from each other. Let's have tea.*

Holy cow, did she call him intense?? That word had never come within light years of his name, and would not again, even the next year when he would meet Anna. His first thought was to wonder if Krystal had romantic interest. But then, she had asked him to tea – a bad sign. He considered countering her offer with dinner – a little probe to test her waters. But then he thought better of it rather than push his luck.

He met her at a local tea house and was pleasantly surprised that she had dressed up. She wore make-up, heels and a knee-length sheath, and she looked beautiful. He felt at once proud to be seen with her, and also a little embarrassed of his own sneakers, jeans and polo. She ordered something Thai, and he followed suit. They mostly discussed his work, which he did with ease, having done many interviews by then. They discussed her knowledge of crystals and life force, and how it all fit together. She asked if he had followed her advice with his Lapis. He lied in reply, then presented it from his pocket as evidence that he had kept it with him.

They were both excited – she about the subject and he about her, particularly when she touched his arm in emphasis. At times, however, she could sense in him some skepticism of what she spoke. Eventually, she concluded and declared that his "sahasrara is all gobbed up."

"My what?"

"Sahasrara. It's your crown chakra."

"My what?"

"Your crown… oh Lord. It's the part of you that lets you think with an open mind. Your master chakra. We have got to get you cleaned out."

"We do?"

"Yes, we do. I mean all your chakras need work, but that crown is really crying for help." She waved her hands before him as if mapping out his flaws.

"Dang. Can you help me?"

"I don't know," she joked. "You're a project for sure. I may have to clear my schedule." She smirked. "Of course I can. Enlightenment is easy if you want it."

"I do."

"Tell you what. I have a place in Asheville; me and Maggie are headed there next weekend. We go once a month just to get away from all this nuclear geekery, no offense, and just ground ourselves, ya know? I have a guest room. You should come—"

He accepted emphatically. He was excited all week and even bought a couple of tie dyes for the trip. When they met again on departure day, she hung a gift round his neck – a plain black cord from which hung a piece of rose quartz. "It eases love," she told him. "And self-love."

She drove and he rode in the back. During the two-hour drive, mother and daughter mostly listened to gospel music, sometimes sang and sometimes talked. Maggie looked happy as ever, but no longer friendly and she mostly ignored Dustin. The change confused him and concerned him a little. Over her years, she had gotten used to the occasional strange-man sleepover, but she never liked it. As they wound their way through the steep cliffs of the Blue Ridge Mountains, she tolerated him.

Soon enough, the heights gave way to hills, and the quaint city of Asheville slowly emerged. Traffic was slow through downtown, almost as if by design, allowing the mimes and musicians and artists to vie for attention, attention which Dustin paid generously with alacrity and a rubber neck. Krystal kept driving and by noon reached her house – a light blue craftsman in a wooded neighborhood. The shingled bygone seemed to smile as it reposed in the shade of white oak and red maple. This house, like her other, had belonged to her father, Dr. Francis Metheuen, who had done quite well for himself as an esteemed author and scholar.

Maggie grabbed her bag and ran upstairs, and Krystal led Dustin to the kitchen to keep her company while she made sandwiches of hummus and tomato. Yes tomato. Dustin ate without a face, never revealing his enmity for the gooey fruit. But he couldn't fool her.

"I bet your diet is atrocious," she said.

"Actually, it's not that—"

"I'm thinking a complete overhaul, starting with a detox. Can you handle a juice fast?"

"If I drink anything too fast, I throw up."

"No, a juice fast. You don't eat anything. You just drink juice for a day or two."

"Um, ok."

"Great, we'll all do one. We'll pick up some groceries later."

After lunch, Maggie showed him to his room with renewed cheer. She had just learned that, this time, *she* would be the one to share Mom's bed and the man would be sleeping down the hall. He thought nothing of her sudden mood shift or the reason behind it. Later that afternoon, once the daylight had stretched too thin to burn, Krystal brought him outside to a bright part of the yard.

"You need some sun," she said. "Why don't you take off your shirt?"

She had him lie on his back, on the grass and close his eyes. Peeking through one eye, he saw her place pieces of clear quartz around him, six of them in a hexagonal pattern. She pulled up a chair, sat at his side, and spent a half hour whispering to him things both relaxing and instructive. His embarrassment eventually faded, and he even nodded off for a moment.

For dinner, she made what he thought was a salad. Until she put it in a blender. "Yummy yummy phytonutrients," she teased as he choked it down and washed it through with alkaline water. They spent the evening playing Scrabble, breathing incense and drinking peppermint tea. Besides the phytonutrients, he had a lovely time.

Until the next morning when he had to drink more juice. This concoction was less green and more fruity than the previous, and thus more tolerable, made more so by his hunger. They left soon after and headed for the River Arts District, a collection of old brick remnants of industry. Two dozen mills, warehouses and factories once hummed, churning their products into the market and dumping their excrement into the French Broad River. They eventually slipped into disuse and dilapidation as all things do, until some creative people adopted the area and coated it in bright, tacky colors. Now it hummed again, this time with music and mantras and the chatter of crowded tourists.

Krystal made a final turn down a drab side street, away from the hubbub of the river front, and pulled up to an odd building. The brick two-story, long and narrow, stood apart from its neighbors. Its street front spanned only twenty feet, making for a brief illusion of smallness until its depth – almost ten times as long – was noticed. It wore a staggered quoin pattern round its crown, like lines of age on a burdened brow. A rusty, iron balcony adorned each of its second-floor windows.

The ground floor had been boarded up, and they entered by a fire escape that ascended its side, leading to a steel door on the second floor.

Inside was much newer and comfier than one would expect. The entrance opened to a small lounge, around which were scattered assorted cushions, bean bags and low-lying furniture. Turkish lamps ornamented the room, as did beaded curtains and tapestries of Moroccan mosaic. Three young men sat in a corner and smoked hookah. They mostly ignored the newcomers until Dustin put on quite an impressive sneezing fit, his eyes watering from the smoke.

They hastened to the next room where a scent of burnt sage was fainter and easier on him. Its décor harkened towards India with Hindu and Buddhist symbolism. A long bar along the far wall was used to serve all kinds of healthy, revolting drinks. A hundred years prior, the same bar had furtively served alcohol during Prohibition.

In the center of the room, eighteen people sat in a circle on a padded floor. They ranged in age from Maggie up to 70-ish. Everyone had dressed either comfortably or shabbily, except for one older woman who wore the raiment of her Cherokee tribe. One man wore dreadlocks and a couple of others sported man-buns, and they all made weak attempts to squeeze out some bit of facial hair.

One man was clearly the leader or instructor of whatever this was, and Krystal introduced him to Dustin. His name was Joseph, but he went by Joe. He shook Dustin's extended hand, but never looked at him. Rather, he just smiled at Krystal and said nothing, until she mentioned that Dustin was a doctor of "Physics or something." Then he turned briefly towards him and whispered. "Very good, Doctor. I'm a doctor too, you know. PhD in Yoga and Meditation."

"Joseph has over thirty degrees and certificates," added Krystal. "And he's an ordained minister of Good Vibrations."

Dustin started a laugh, then choked it back on realizing she was serious.

"I have added a couple since I last saw you," Joe confessed. "I am now an authorized instructor in Keeping It Real, and I just finished a course in Rain Dance. Two more arrows in my armory."

"Oh, wow," she marveled. "Can you make it rain?"

"Sometimes. It's really hit-or-miss."

They separated and took places, and class began. It lasted around two hours. At some points, it seemed to Dustin like nothing more than light exercise – stretching and strengthening. Being too stiff or clumsy for much of it, he faked it or followed along as best he could. For him, it was largely an exercise in abasement.

At other times, they were asked to close their eyes and focus on their thoughts, or their breathing, or the universe, or the soothing words of Joe. This was much easier for Dustin, though he often found himself peeking around.

And there was other stuff. They sang and hummed mantras, some in English and some not. Two of the participants seemed particularly loud and enthusiastic, and he wondered if they were in competition. And there were rituals of hand gestures for opening chakras, and other larger movements, culminating in a ballet of the elements known as Qi Gong.

Some people remained after class to socialize and juice. Many knew Krystal and said hello, but she focused on speaking more with Joe. She explained to him as best she could about Dustin's research, his reach into "alternative science" to find answers, and the internal obstacles he faced.

Joe expressed some interest, though he mostly talked about Dustin without talking to him. "Yes, I can sense the burden in him, but there's also potential. It seems he's even gotten a lot out of this one session."

"I agree," she agreed. "But what do you think about his research into crystals and spirit waves?"

"Oh, I think there are some possibilities there. But really, isn't that mostly stuff that we already knew? I swear, Western science is so far behind the East. Every time they think they 'discover' something, we're like 'Ya? Duh?' I mean, they still think Columbus discovered North America, for Christ's sake."

"Well, I'm excited."

"Oh Krys. You are such an altruist. You always have a mission."

She took a second to look into Dustin's eyes before turning back. "I'd say he's more of a hobby."

At any other time, Dustin would have found this conversation as absurd as it was obnoxious. But now he simply wanted to fit in, so he simply smiled and nodded.

"I think you are on the right track," said Joe. "We should get him back for a cosmobiology profile. Also, I know crystals are your thing, but don't forget magnets, especially with all those nasty fields in his environment. There is a 25% synergistic effect when you use both together. That is a fact. Have you worked on his diet and eating habits?"

"Just started. We're doing a fast this weekend."

"Good good. You know, 85% of all psychosociospiritual issues have some underlying contribution from inflammation."

"I did know that."

"If not direct causation."

"I learned it from you."

"Excellent," he replied, putting an arm around her.

"It turns out that 78% of all statistics are just made up," Dustin quipped, feeling hungry and a little cranky.

A look of befuddlement crossed Joe's face and he paused for a minute. "No, I don't think that's right," he replied.

Krystal had a better sense of the mood and decided it was time to leave.

They spent the afternoon diving into the city, navigating street currents of Subarus and a landscape of bums and performers. They searched for nothing in particular. What they found were a couple of art galleries, an antique store and a tea house. They stopped at Pritchard Park to bathe in the rhythms of a huge drum circle, prostrating their mood to the whimsical shifts in cadence. On the outskirts of town, a hiking trail led them through wooded hills to the edge of exhaustion. Krystal tired first. Once she was satisfied that guest and daughter had been sufficiently amused, she headed back, heeding the call of bath salts and candles.

Throughout the day, Maggie had rewarmed to Dustin and peppered him with questions about his research. Now, as they made a final turn down the winding road to the cottage, she once again turned around and kneeled backwards in her seat to face him, her hands resting on the headrest, her chin resting on her hands, her seatbelt nowhere to be found.

"It's too bad you couldn't have met my Papaw. I bet he could've helped you. Don't you think, Ma?"

Ma agreed. "My father was an anthropologist," she said. "He spent a lifetime doing what you've just begun – looking for answers in other places." She thought for a moment, then continued. "You know, Dr. Joe was right. So much of what modern science thinks is discovery is really just re-discovery. You really need to take a deep dive into other cultures."

"I really wouldn't know where to begin."

"How bout the Tibetan Book of the Dead? Read that?"

"No."

"Okay, read that. How bout Raymond Moody?" she asked.

"Who's that?"

"He's right up your alley. Are you getting this down?"

"Got it. What about your dad?"

"What about him?"

"Did he publish much?"

"Yes, he did, and I am embarrassed to say I have not read any of his work. But he has boxes of stuff upstairs. There's bound to some of his books in there."

When they arrived back at the house, she showed him to an unfinished, dark attic that smelled of must and dust. Her parents' effects were scattered throughout, some in boxes, some not.

"Go nuts," she said. "I'm going to soak in the tub."

He gave her a nervous look, to which she replied "Don't worry; it's just stuff. I'm not sentimental."

He cautiously looked around, watching out for breakables and spiders. He didn't find anything scholastic until he looked in the eaves, which were stuffed with a dozen galvanized milk boxes, stored through a small opening, single file. One at a time he pulled them out, crawling deeper and deeper to get the next. Even with a flashlight, he reached the limit of his courage after eight boxes, and the rest remained stowed. The eight were labeled with hand-painted words, three of them faded beyond legibility. The rest were marked with categories – Communication, Kinship, Rites of Passage, Food; and the last box. Its hasp was broken, its lid stuck, and a layer of dust obscured its cryptic title – hanatos.

Hanatos? Dustin pried it open. Days later, he would remember to do a web search, only to be corrected by the search engine – "Did you mean *thanatos*?" The cross had faded away from the Greek word Thanatos, meaning Death, named for the mythical god of the same.

Inside the box were stacks of photographs ranging from polaroid to professional, and handwritten notes bound by rusted paperclips or contained in small journals.

There were pictures of the Dogon men of Mali doing their Dama funeral dance. The charnel dancers, strutting shirtless in hot-pink tassel skirts, could have been Burlesque showgirls were it not for their elaborate, ceremonial masks.

Other pictures were labeled with another Greek word – Nekromanteion – and chronicled the archaeological excavation, circa 1975, of a fantastic complex of subterranean halls and rooms. It turns out that The Nekromanteion, the "Oracle of the Dead," had been an ancient temple to Hades, believed to be a gateway to his realm, and a place where one could communicate with the dead. But Dustin didn't know that, and he breezed through them without interest, and through others about Indian funeral pyres, American seances, Tibetan sky burials, Japanese self-mummification, and the myriad other coping traditions documented in that galvanized box. Then one caught his eye.

An 8x10 Kodak, sharp and clear, and not nearly as worn as the face of the man it portrayed. He was black but his face looked white, painted so with lime pigment. He sat cross-legged in a dark room, eyes closed, naked as a newborn. Two ornaments were his only dress. One of them, enormous and white, hung from his nasal septum, hiding most of his lower face. It had been cut from the shell of a seasnail into a bi-curved shape, meant to resemble the tusks of the wild boar. The thing might have intrigued Dustin, were it not for the other. The other thing arrested him.

A headdress, perhaps a crown, adorned the man's aged, balding skull. Its jagged texture and gleaming reflections appeared to be crystalline. Its bluish tint seemed to fluoresce in the nearby candlelight.

There were notes attached which made clear from whom Maggie had inherited her exquisite handwriting. They began as follows:


*Of the most dangerous and savage primitives that I have studied, there can be little doubt that none possess these qualities more than the Asmat tribes of Papua. Indeed, had it not been for their previous adoption of my guide, Father Van Lith, I would have likely been welcomed during my first trip as a meal or perhaps a snack, rather than a guest, my head taken as revenge for some past wrong committed by another white man. And were it not for my own adoption this time, (completed in a strange ceremony which I have previously described), I would surely not have been privy to this most extraordinary ritual pictured here. It is only practiced in the remote village of Janepsto as far as I know.*

*For the Asmats, death is a way of life as much as life itself. The harsh conditions in which they survive are made that much worse by the unavenged ancestors who haunt their lives. These troublesome spirits need not have necessarily been killed directly. To the Asmats, all untimely deaths, including illness and accident, are no accident at all. There must be a culprit, be it man or monster, wielding spear or spell. And regardless of whether the offender is ever identified, the remedy remains the same: murder. Specifically, the head of an enemy must be claimed in order to exorcise and relieve the restless spirit, for the Asmats believe (rather wisely) that one's power and soul resides in the head. Indeed, it was their god Deso-ipitch, when beheaded by his own brother, whose blood spilled out to create the stars. The people of Janepsto believe that one of those stars fell to Earth in the form of this stone tiara. On a day that its sister stars are properly aligned (i.e., a conjunction of Mars and Venus), the tiara is placed on the most venerable head in the village and thence allows its wearer to hear the nearby spirits.*

*Thus, the Asmat culture is centered around the bidding of an insatiable, unavenged god, and the blood of that god gives voice to those who share his fate. Their lore and traditions form a closed, complete system, flawless except for the curious case of this fetish.*

*Though off topic, it is worth noting that there are no such crystals endemic to that region, and crystal workmanship is not an Asmat skill. Moreover, I was permitted to inspect it and, despite its unnatural shape, I could find no smoothed or cut surface to indicate that it had been altered at all. It is indeed as if fallen from the heavens, though clearly a rational explanation escapes me.*

*The Asmats are extremely animistic. They spend their days constantly coping with hundreds of spirits of all manner, in the village and jungle and at sea, using magic and ritual. This severe animism is partly because they are so primeval. They have been isolated for tens of thousands of years and their ways have remained as a time capsule. But it is also because their lives are so arduous, beset constantly by flooding and scarcity, war and malaria, not to mention crocodiles and boars. It is a familiar trade-off we see with all religions, particularly the primitive ones. We develop beliefs and rituals that make difficult lives more so, and in turn we gain the perception of control of things over which we have none.*

Dustin read on for a while, contemplated for another while, took some notes and moved on. But as he rifled through the rest of the box, he found no entry as curious as the case of the Maeto. And as he returned to his home and his life, and his research stalled for weeks and months, and as his understanding of Y-waves reached a plateau; so his curiosity about Asmats and Maetos grew like a crystal. Curiosity became interest, then fascination, determination, and finally planning. He would go to Papua and see this thing for himself.

His relationship with Krystal also grew for a while, until she saw him naked. They still keep in touch occasionally. When he became interested in interviewing local mediums, she helped him find the reputable ones. His meetings with the first few were simply open-ended conversations. As he became more familiar with their craft, he devised a questionnaire and expanded his inquiry regionally. Most respondents offered some form of guidance, healing and divination. A few claimed necromantic powers. None of them professed outright to be mind-readers, perhaps because it's easily tested, or maybe because they simply could not read minds. Only a mind-reader would know for sure.

In Dustin's mind, most of this smelled of nonsense, but he struggled to find a common thread within the data he collected, besides the props that were commonly used (tarot cards and such). Most of the psychics were women, but beyond that they varied in age, background, physical stats and every other factor of which he could think. He tried to develop a scoring system based on responses to certain questions, in order to identify the most intuitive mediums, but it didn't work. Intuition, he discovered, was too qualitative to be quantifiable. Those psychics who impressed him most were able to precisely describe imprecise things – his character, his emotional scars, his defenses, his feelings about his mother, stuff like that. The one variable he found to be consistent among the best psychics was a need for proximity. They couldn't read him over the phone or even across the street, but a few could read him in the next room. One woman read him only by pressing her forehead against his. He suspected this phenomenon was related to Y-waves. He couldn't prove it; it was just instinct.

Dustin had strayed beyond his expertise. He now enjoyed moderate fame and great importance, and had been given wide latitude and a big budget. However, this was fetched too far even for him, and so he had personally funded this side-jaunt, as well as most of the upcoming trip to Papua. As his funds dwindled, his psychic research ended; but in the dwindling months of that year, a love affair began.

# Ten

Now it's Sunday morning and he's on his way to meet Anna again, just hours after they parted. He's puzzled that she didn't visit him last night in dream, but he'll join her now as she heads to the 11:00 service at King's Chapel. He's not a churchy guy. In fact, he hasn't been in one since childhood, but he didn't hesitate at the invitation to accompany her and the chance to impress her. They'll go to her place afterwards and she'll make him lunch.

He again meets her at Downtown Crossing, from where they walk a block towards the central park known as Boston Commons, then right for two blocks down the Freedom Trail. The antique chapel stands right on the corner with only a narrow sidewalk to keep traffic at bay. Greco-Roman columns give a majestic face to the plain brick structure, making it look more like a bank than a house of worship – a bank with a graveyard to the side, where perhaps are buried loan defaulters and other such sinners.

The interior is far more impressive, at least to him. Its simple Georgian elegance seems opulent compared to the small, plain conference rooms of his Southern Baptist youth. He has surely never been in a church as grand. Choir song pours down from a panoramic balcony. The pulpit is enclosed and raised high on a wineglass stand, like a gazebo in the sky, its sounding board hovering like a halo. The hymns and sermons sound more subdued than what he remembers. But what they lack in enthusiasm, they recoup with a kind of divine tranquility that he imagines one would find in heaven, if there was such a place. In her opening statement, the minister welcomes everyone, "believers and doubters, seekers and skeptics," putting Dustin, a devout skeptic, at ease.

After church, they jump back on the orange line towards Anna's home. The further they ride, the more work-worn and weathered the newly boarding passengers appear, and the more perfect she looks by contrast. Along the way, he raises the topic of God and religion, and espouses his beliefs, or lack thereof. She listens sincerely, but as he continues, he reveals himself more doubter than agnostic, and she bristles. He senses it and takes a defensive step backwards, humbly suggesting that "there's nothing wrong with a healthy dose of skepticism." Then he stumbles, adding that "it's a sign of intelligence."

"You can also overdose and that's not so healthy," she cautions. "And you can be intelligent and also ignorant at the same time, yes? Then you can get arrogance, and that's a dangerous thing, right?"

"I guess…"

"Right," she continues. She takes his hand with one of hers, strokes his face with her other, and softens her voice, but not her words. "Arrogance and ignorance, they are like husband and wife, you know. They married a long time ago in Hell, and that is no place for you. Skeptic is okay, but it's not an award for you."

Award? Since they met three days ago, he's made occasional hints and references about his station and accomplishments, attempting to impress her. It has not worked, and that fact has impressed him. And now she's using his tactic to make a point. "Brilliant," he thinks, and loves her more.

Then he resorts to the standard argument. "What about Hitler and hurricanes and all of that? If there is a God, how can He permit such suffering?"

"I am ignorant too," she confesses, "and so I also gotta watch out for arrogance. When I think questions like that, I just remember that I don't know what God knows and I cannot think like God thinks. He judges me. I don't judge Him."

In the daylight, her street has less charm and more bars on the windows. Her front door opens to a living room/dining area. A kitchenette is off to one side, and in it a young man has buried his head in the fridge. He hears the door but remains immersed in his forage, only taking a second to call out "Hola, Mama," and only surfacing when she announces her guest.

"Eduardo, this is Dr. Nye, the man I told you about."

Eduardo mostly stays with his girlfriend, but comes home at least twice a week to do laundry, eat well and sleep in his own bed. He is handsome, sharply angled in face and form. His probing eyes, like his handshake, have a firm grip. He lowers his voice and greets Dustin with polite maturity. Inside, he harbors concerns. He trusts his mother's judgement and is happy to see her finally dating. He's also googled Dustin and learned quite a bit. But the sheer number of gaping differences between the two seems suspicious – of what, he's not sure. He makes a comment in Spanish which is met with maternal correction.

"Eduardo, honey, Dr. Nye doesn't speak Spanish, so we're gonna have good manners. We only speak English around him, okay?"

Eduardo usually misses church, but never Sunday brunch, and now she proceeds to cook up a feast. It's an unusually nice day, so she fires up the grill and makes steak strips (which Dustin relishes), blood sausage (not so much), chicken and grilled provolone.

The two lovers have a grand time, eating and talking and eating again, and Dustin stays late into the evening. Eduardo warms to him a little, despite finding him to be weird. He does find him interesting, especially when recounting his Baltimore adventures. Dustin, however, is entirely relaxed with Anna, and confident that he's impressed Eduardo.

The next day, he checks out of the Kensington and into another hotel so as not to affect her work. But he also asks her to call in sick, which she declines since she's not. She does manage to get a couple of shifts covered though, and for the rest of the week, they spend all her free time playing cards, dining out, shopping for a dress (the only gift she allows him), poking around bookstores and antique stores, holding hands and talking.

It turns out they do have a few things in common, both having grown up in relative poverty, raised exclusively by their mothers and excluded by their peers. They're both soft-spoken and a bit shy, though he's used to leading teams of people and she's just plain tough. They have magnetic eye contact, and they see in each other a presence of such familiar quality that they end up discussing reincarnation more than once. She has issues with the idea because of her faith, and eventually concludes that "I guess we'll never know."

To which he replies "But we *do* know. Look in my eyes and tell me that you don't know."

To which she has no reply.

The more she learns, the more she is fascinated by his work, as best she can understand it. By the end of the week, she can see herself venturing to Papua and he can see himself marrying her. After he returns home, they continue to talk daily, though they often don't have much to say. He helps with her frequent anxiety over her son, who she describes as "living like a mouse on a wheel." She helps his insomnia with her soft voice and sweet words. She soon shares his matrimonial sentiment and, in time, the inkling matures. When she visits him in Oak Ridge the following spring, he proposes marriage to her on the bank of the Clinch River, and she accepts. The daffodils bear witness.

She starts to scruple the next night after they dine out with some of his friends and colleagues. She has a terrible time, feeling misplaced at best, offended at worst. After his warm, brief introduction and a smattering of corresponding welcomes, she sits there mostly ignored, hands folded in lap, frequently shifting in her chair. Eventually, a professor's wife turns to her and asks the usual questions – "How do you like East Tennessee?" and "To what church do you belong?" Her replies generate amusement more than interest and lead to more questions. Another spouse joins in and the two of them converse with Anna for a while, sporting sickly sweet smiles to offset their genuine pearls, and answering her answers with bits of hyperbolic enthusiasm – "How *very* interesting!" and "Bless your heart!" Their condescension is of a quality and severity that transcends culture and smashes through language barriers. Ironically, the worst offense of the night is committed quite by accident and due to a language barrier. It turns out that when you say "I don't care to show you around town," it means in Oak Ridge the exact opposite of what it does in Boston.

As soon as she's back in the car, Anna unloads her exasperation. "If they want to treat me like a maid, that's okay! I'm a maid! But they are talking to me like a baby and that's not okay!"

Dustin agrees and apologizes, and apologizes some more, and she soon cools down.

"I don't know how this can work," she frets. "I'm like a square peg in your social circles."

On hearing this, he pulls over to the roadside to embrace her and whisper in her ear. "Oh Anna, I don't really have social circles. I only have you."

The next morning, he is still concerned enough about her state of mind that he whisks her off to the courthouse and marries her before a second thought can enter her head. She's still wearing the same dress from the night before, the one he bought her in Boston. They stop at a diner afterwards to eat some breakfast, chat, and watch others do the same. On finishing her last bit of sausage, she slaps down her silverware and decrees "okay, *now* you take me shopping." He smiles a big one and obeys.

They set about the monstrous, joyous task of preparing their new life, returning to Boston to get her packed and moved, and make dozens of other arrangements. She keeps her house for Eduardo and finishes out a two-week notice at work. They spend the rest of spring getting settled and adjusted –unpacking, redecorating, modifying habits and hygiene, and learning each other's ways.

They also learn some things about themselves. For example, Dustin discovers that he's rather chivalrous, if not overprotective of his new bride. He worries a lot when she's out, and buys her a gun and some training. He also learns that he's lousy at learning languages, after having resolved to learn Spanish from her. She discovers that she doesn't miss television that much after all, after having resolved to learn from him to live without it. She also realizes that she's still young and ambitious, and determines to return to school in the fall.

They're a quiet couple who have little in common besides a shared aversion to small talk and a sense of coziness when in each other's presence. They're generous in their own ways, taking pleasure in each other's pleasure. She likes to feed him, and he likes to be fed. She has a fondness for knickknacks, and he often finds himself, on his way home from work, searching estate sales and antique shops for something she might like. She regularly bathes him in compliments. His praise is not that verbal, relying instead on a look, a whiff or a touch. But his praise, like hers, is effortless and sincere.

They both have cold feet and wear socks to bed. He always falls asleep first. She rests her head on his chest and watches him and wonders, until she drifts off herself. They play chess and do crossword puzzles and form a very exclusive book club for two, complete with assignments and meetings and hors d'oeuvres.

He spends the rest of his free time preparing for their honeymoon coming up in July, when the rainy season of Papua gives way to a slightly-less rainy one, and also when the next Mars-Venus conjunction is due. He's already done a lot of research since his decision to venture there, research that has allayed most of his fears. For one thing, he's learned that the Asmats are no longer headhunting cannibals, their murderous heritage having been cleansed by decades of Catholic mission work. The world has encroached on them substantially since Dr. Metheun's visit, and made strides in civilizing them, exchanging their taste for blood and brains with one for tobacco and trade, and even clothes.

He makes arrangements for transportation, vaccination and translation. He tries to arrange accommodation but cannot secure detailed confirmation from such a remote village as Janepsto.

"They'll be expecting you," the travel agent reassures him over long-distant phone. "Bring gifts."

He shops for rugged boots and other gear. He wants to learn some of the Asmat language but discovers that there are dozens of dialects, and he can't find a lesson in any of them.

The flight is grueling, thirty-one total hours in the air over three connections. They stop for a day in Jakarta to recuperate in the hot tub of an airport hotel. They step outside for the first time on an airfield in Timika, West Papua for the final leg of their flight. As soon as they do, the humid island air punches them in the face. Dustin immediately starts sweating profusely; Anna not so much. The sweating continues as he crosses the runway towards the 11-seat Twin Otter, and for the entire one-hour flight. In fact, he'll continue to sweat with little abatement for his entire island stay.

Fear grips his chest and his hands grip the seat during the rapid, rough descent towards a small landing strip. They're met on the runway by the man who will be their guide – a swarthy, stocky fellow named Ahmed. Ahmed has a mixture of Indian and Oriental features, similar to the other Indonesians they've met this far. He greets them warmly and loads their luggage onto a jeep for a two-minute drive to the water.

On the way, Ahmed poses a question. "Oh Dr. Nye, are you still wanting to stay in Janepsto?"

"Yes, is there a problem?"

"No, there's no problem. It's all set. I was just surprised when you say that in your email. You know Janepsto is way out there. You can be more comfortable in Agats, stay in a nice hotel. You will still meet some tribal peoples. They come to Agats and dance for the tourists, make some wood carvings. You will have a nice time. Your wife too."

"I have business in Janepsto."

"Oh. Business?" He pauses to wonder what kind of business an American white guy could possibly have in the remote village, but he thinks better than to ask. "Did you bring some gifts?"

"Yes, three wrist watches for the chief or chiefs."

"Pshh," scoffs Ahmed. "Asmat got no use for watches."

"Well, I asked for suggestions, but you never wrote back. These are Movados. They're expensive." Dustin wipes his brow. "Besides, my options were pretty limited. You can only take so much on a plane or through customs. I have cash too."

"American dollars?"

"Yes."

"That's better, but we should stop in Agats and get some gifts."

Anna chimes in. "Yes, we'll do that. No problem." She turns to her husband and counsels him. "We can just return the watches."

A minute later, they reach their stop, a tributary of the Asewet River. A motorboat awaits them in the olive-green water. They board and speed away southward towards the river junction, located at the mouth. All conversation is drowned by the engine's noise, and by the view of mangrove trees frozen in eternal poses of interpretive dance. The wind gives Dustin a brief respite from the heat, as does the salty mist which smacks his face for violating the water's tranquility. His sweating returns as they slow at the estuary to make a hairpin turn west up the river. Off in the distance, they can see the line to the south where the brackish drink meets the deep blue of the Arafura Sea.

Three miles later, they start to smell the smell of man's pollution as they approach Agats on their right. The town, which began as an outpost of the Dutch government, was erected on stilts over a swamp, the swamp serving as both toilet and dump. They climb up to a dock and rent two of the many electric motorcycles buzzing around town. Dustin and Anna follow Ahmed through the network of wooden bridges that make up the roads, to a neighborhood where some shanties second as shops. They follow his advice to buy a satchel and fill it with cartons of cigarettes. The tourists today are Indonesian, Australian and Chinese; the locals mostly black, with broad features indicative of African origin.

Back to the boat and up, up the river for miles they go, following its branches, then its branch's branches, until the jungle becomes as thick as a wall and the river too shallow to go much further. It is then that they first hear the faint sound of chanting. The sound grows louder and closer and clearer, a muscular drone from muscular men, like legionaries marching into battle.

"Do be do be do. Do be do be do. Do be do be do."

Soon enough, they appear from around a bend in the river. Fifteen men stand in a canoe with an exquisite, effortless balance that takes years to achieve. They paddle in synchronicity with oars twice their height. Right behind comes another canoe with another dozen men. "Do be do be do. Do be do be do." They each wear a pair of rugby shorts and not much else. They have painted their faces and bodies with a white pigment in a variety of patterns. Some of the men are adorned with the same ornament seen in Dr. Metheuen's picture, called a bipane – large pieces of shell, curved like tusks or coiled like a cuscus tail, swinging from pierced nasal septums. Some of the men wear elaborate headdresses of cockatoo feathers, or necklaces of teeth that one hopes are not human. Some wear it all.

Dustin squeezes Anna's hand as the canoes pull alongside. She pats his back with her other. They can now see some young and old passengers squatting between the oarsmen. They've come along for the ride, come to get a first look at the strange visitors. These are not Asmats who dance for tourists. However, they do know Ahmed and give him a smile as they transfer him and his guests to their canoes, then permit the motorboat to leave.

Dustin feels as nervous about the canoe as he does about his hosts, but soon finds the craft unexpectedly stable. As for the Asmats, he is quickly calmed by the calm demeanor of Ahmed, who chats away with them in the strangest of tongues.

They continue upstream for another three hours, breaking only once to briefly rest and hydrate and urinate. Dustin and Anna say little the whole time. At one point, he thinks to check his phone.

"Oh, that not gonna work out here, you know," says Ahmed.

"I didn't think so, but I wonder how they knew when to meet us."

"They were expecting us today, you see, so therefore they place scouts along the river. They go to Agats once a week to get news and supplies. When the agency got your request, they sent me to talk with them because I know them pretty good."

"Do they have a radio or anything?" asks Anna.

"Oh no. You won't be able to reach outside while you're here. But you're not the first tourists they had, so relax yourself. Just don't get sick."

They finally land at a large clearing and make their way down a path, through muck and mud, among trees that stretch up to the heavens. As they walk, one of the elder tribesmen repeatedly shouts a threat to ward off any animals or demons that may be about.

As they enter the village, a row of women awaits them off in the distance, a stone's throw away. Ahmed immediately commands his guests to turn around and duck. He does the same, as do the boatmen, and for good reason. The women start yelling and throwing things at them — sticks and bones and clumps of dirt. The assault seems eternal but only actually lasts eighteen seconds, during which Dustin sustains a small laceration. For the first time, Anna too senses the cold sting of fright. But the fear recedes quickly as they turn back around to find greeting smiles. The women begin to dance and sing and chant; their long, exhausted breasts swinging side to side. The men join in. They surround the newcomers, swiveling their knees together and apart in rapid repetition, happily singing something that roughly translates as follows:

*Welcome white people. Welcome to our home.*
*We hope you stay a long time, but not too long.*
*Welcome white people. Welcome to our home.*
*We hope you stay a long time, but not too long.*

Ahmed raises his voice above the din. "The women, they throw things, you know, when people come back from a trip. They want to chase away the evil spirits that we might have picked up on the way."

Off to the side stands a heavily decorated man, too dignified to join in the merriment — the village chief, Honcho-ipitch. Despite his advanced age, he sports a powerful face and form, offset by a rather silly headdress of straw fibers made to look like long blond hair. After the celebration dissipates, Ahmed introduces him to Dustin and Anna. The chief greets them each with a nod and a firm handshake, a tradition Ahmed taught him years ago. Dustin is led away to sit and meet with him, accompanied by Ahmed and a few dignitaries, and trailed by curious, naked children. Anna is forbidden to come, despite Dustin's repeated requests. She is instead shepherded in another direction by some friendly, babbling women and more kids.

Janepsto has a smell that reminds Dustin of summer camp. As in Agats, the homes here have been erected on stilts, safely above the flooding that frequently washes the village. But this village has no roads; just a few, suspended, wooden walkways. The homes here are entered by ladder, some rather steep.

Dustin arrives at the "yew," a long wooden hall where the single men live, and where socializing and events take place. It is a steep climb up to it, one which the chief makes with remarkable speed. Inside, there are already a few men sitting or lying around – the ones who had been too lazy or boring to join in the welcome. One of them rests his head on a human skull, the site of which makes Dustin a little dizzy.

"That doesn't look comfortable," he nervously quips.

"Oh, that's he mother. He miss her," Ahmed replies.

They give Dustin a moment to micturate, something he has avoided for half the day, even refusing to make use of a perfectly good river. But now he happily streams off the side of the yew in a designated direction. Afterwards, he sits down with the chief and other leaders and eats cakes of sago. The patties are white and bland like him, made from the starchy trunk of the sago palm. He won't eat much else while in Janepsto. He certainly won't be eating what is brought out next – a bowl of sago grubs. He declines the fat little larvae as politely as he can, assisted by Ahmed's translational tweaks. In response, Honcho-ipitch simply shrugs and digs in with the others, relishing the delicacy. Still chewing, he leans and says something to Ahmed, who chuckles and replies. This annoys Dustin, who isn't paying Ahmed to leave him out of conversation.

"What?" Dustin barks.

"Oh, he just ask if all foreigners sweat so much."

After eating, Dustin presents his presents, including two watches which the chief examines, then slides one on each forearm. The chief then distributes the cigarettes. The cash he keeps for himself.

Dustin Nye is a brilliant man, and with his stomach now full and bladder now empty, his brain hums along at peak performance. But Dustin Nye never learned tact. If he was ever taught it, he didn't quite catch on. So, no sooner than the last village elder has swallowed his last bit of grub, does Dustin whip out Dr. Metheuen's photo of the Maeto and display it.

"Can I see this?" he blurts, tapping it with his pointer finger.

He hands it to the chief who instantly smiles, showing his four remaining teeth. Honcho holds it up to show his mates looking over his shoulder. Upon seeing it, they also smile and laugh as they recognize an old friend who has long since passed. The children laugh too, though they're not sure why. During this moment, one of the men in the room has become the center of attention as the others point to the photo, then to him, and make remarks. He is a noticeable figure, though Dustin hasn't noticed him until now. About 60 years old, he looks his age, unlike the others. He looks more Mulatto than Asmat with olive skin and features of Caucasian persuasion. Grey flecks his black, wavy hair as it rests comfortably upon his shoulders. But most striking are his eyes, blue and bright like precious gems.

"Who is he?" asks Dustin.

"The guy in the photo, that's he grandfather," says Ahmed.

"Can you ask them if I can see that headpiece?"

Ahmed complies, but the Asmats just ignore him. "I don't think they gonna answer you," he says. "Is better to wait. They don't know you."

They hand the picture back to Dustin who, after a moment's consideration, graciously offers it to the blue-eyed man, who happily accepts.

The day has stretched thin and the world starts to fade. Dustin asks to see his wife. Ahmed, who views himself as much a cultural buffer as a translator, thinks that his client's request will be perceived as weird and girly. So instead, he explains how far Dustin has traveled and that he wants to rest.

"He definitely didn't row here," one of them cracks. The others laugh, then bid goodnight.

Out on the yew's grand veranda, two woodcarvers have resumed their work, a flurry of shavings in their wake. Dustin steps over the new pile of mulch, one of many that litter the village. Ahmed walks through it.

The word "Asmat-o" means Tree People, and the wood carver, or "wo-ipitch," was once a revered position among them, when they used to sculpt their wooden brethren into totem poles and tools of war. But the Catholics did away with all that, and now they just make boats and ladders and such. Today, they're making dishware, lots of it, in preparation for tomorrow's feast. It's a feast to welcome their new guests, to welcome Ahmed's return, and the return of the astral conjunction.

Ahmed leads Dustin to the one-room home where they'll stay. It's not as big as the yew, but it's big enough to house the chief, his three wives, his two brothers, their wives, and offspring – twenty-seven mouths altogether. Off in a corner, Anna lies on the floor, resting her head on her luggage. She is crawling with youngsters who Ahmed promptly shoos away.

She greets her husband with a hug and scans his face for news or needs. She decides that he's dry and brings him water. They exchange details of their brief time apart. She was fed a lot, and she made herself useful afterwards by helping to mind and feed the little ones.

"Did you eat the roasted grubs?" were the first words out of his mouth.

"Of course."

"Of course?" he asks with a shiver.

"Of course. I'm not gonna disrespect these people on the first day."

"Did you like them?"

"So… it was interesting. I was grateful."

"I would have puked, respectfully of course."

"Of course."

They learn that night that Asmat hospitality does not include a bed. There are only two beds in the house, made from bamboo and rattan, and occupied by the chief's brothers. Honcho-ipitch himself likes the floor, and sleeps on his own skull-pillow. And what's good enough for the chief is good enough for his guests (minus the skull, of course).


Dustin awakens the next morning in virtual rigor mortis with a merciless spine demanding his full and constant attention. Anna aches a little but remains limber. She's been doing yoga for years, something she learned as she got older and heavier in order to alleviate the mounting strains of her job. She leads him through a difficult session after a thorough massage. Afterwards, he's still mostly useless but can move enough to poke around and explore a bit. She'll do it again nightly as a bedtime routine for the remainder of their stay.

Around midday, the drums begin in the village square. They are soon joined by singing and dancing and recitation of lore. Even the feasting itself seems to follow the drums' pulsing, primordial lead. They roast pigs, crocodiles, lizards and lots of fish, and Dustin eats it all. Just no bugs, please. The drumming continues late into the night, reverberating and penetrating through the hubbub, past the smoke, and deep into the jungle.

In the crowd, Dustin spots the blue-eyed man. He's accompanied by a blue-eyed woman with an even lighter complexion. In fact, she's almost as pale as Dustin. Sitting near them are two men nearly half their age, who also appear to be mixed race, though not as pronounced – presumably their offspring. Dustin points them out to Anna, grabs her hand and walks over. He greets the blue-eyed man with a nod and asks the blue-eyed woman if she speaks English. She doesn't respond, but instead turns to her companion with a look of confusion. He, in turn, speaks Asmat to Dustin who, in turn, apologizes and leaves to hunt for Ahmed. Dustin is intrigued by them, not just because of their incongruity, but also a strange familiarity that he can't pinpoint.

He finds Ahmed stuffing his face with bugs and flirting with a young woman. Dustin asks about the blue-eyed man.

"Oh, he the village Namer-o," says Ahmed. "He name is Yopokay."

"*His* name."

"Ya, *his* name. I forget sometimes, you know."

"Namer-o?"

"Ya, he like what you call a holy man. And the woman, that's he sister… *his* sister, Ohmati."

"I never knew there were white Asmat-o."

"Oh, it's unusual but it happens, you know. The Dutch sometimes made their way with the local women. She pretty white, though."

"Is he the one who talks to ghosts during the alignment?" asked Dustin.

"Maybe. I don't know about that thing."

Dustin heads back to Yopokay, dragging Ahmed along for translation. He introduces himself and says how happy he is to meet him, his sister and all the Asmats. Straight to the point, he then asks if he talks to ghosts.

"We all talk to them," Yopokay replies. "The ghosts of our ancestors, the ghosts of the forests, and the Holy Ghost."

"Then how are you, the Namer-o, different from the others?"

"Because I also listen to them."

"Do you wear the crown to listen? The crown in the photo?"

Yopokay turns to Ahmed and asks "Who is this guy anyways?"

Ahmed in turn shrugs and turns to Dustin. "I don't think this is a good thing to ask about too much," he tells him. "Like I say before, you know it's better to wait."

Dustin Nye, who is not a brilliant tactician, nevertheless finally understands the sensitivity of the subject and the need to build trust. He gets his first opportunity early the next morning when the Asmats put him to work.

He's awakened by three men speaking Asmat. Ahmed explains that they're supposed to fish today. He starts to dress, and Dustin stops him. "Stay with my wife today," he says. She needs you too. I'll be fine."

The men bring Dustin to the river and spend the morning fishing with hoop nets and taking turns watching for crocodiles. He makes some unsolicited improvements to their weir. He modifies its shape to further confuse the fish. He lays down clumps of brush and vegetation to make it feel cozy and safe, and builds a small dam upstream to slightly alter the current. All of it together makes a substantial improvement in its yield which, over the next couple of days, the Asmats notice and mention.

The feasting resumes around midafternoon, more subdued than before, and again continues into the night. It will do so again for the next three days, following the same schedule, uninterrupted except for a fight and a death. The fight is between two sisters who often fight about all kinds of things.

The death occurs when two men are hunting a cassowary, a bird similar to the emu but larger, with a bright blue head and big, ugly dinosaur legs. Sensing danger, the bird leaps at one of them and kicks him, plunging its five-inch foreclaw into his chest. He dies quickly. When his partner walks into the village carrying his corpse, his newly widowed wife wails and rolls in the mud to cool her grief. It is quite a scene, and everyone loses their appetites for a while. They have a funeral and bury him like the missionaries taught them.

Every day of the feast, Dustin finds an opportunity to corner the shaman and make small talk with him and his sister. Each time, he has that odd sense of familiarity like he felt when he met Anna, albeit not nearly as strong. He wonders if the same force of fate is at work, a force he suspects is related to Y-waves.

He is again put on fishing duty for two more days, followed by two days of helping to fell trees. He starts bringing along Ahmed and thence gets acquainted with his co-workers. He learns the general meaning of their frequent mutterings – they talk to spirits. In one instant, a man jabbers away at a palm tree about to be cut.

"He threatening the tree," Ahmed explains. "He warning it not to take revenge."

One of the men wants to get more acquainted with Dustin – a young man with a scar on his head, his torso painted white and red. He tells Ahmed something, to which Ahmed shakes his head in the negative. But the man persists, egging him on. Finally, Ahmed droops his head like a boy sent to his room.

"He asking to do papitch," he tells Dustin.

"Papitch?"

"Ya, he want to trade with you, your wife for his wife. Just for two days, more if you like."

Dustin stops and tries to think of the most diplomatic refusal he can conjure.

"Ahmed, please tell him that I'm very flattered but very sorry. The customs of my people are different, and that kind of thing simply is not permitted."

Ahmed turns to the young man. "He say no," he tells him.

It's obvious to Dustin from the brevity of the statement that his words were not translated properly. "Look, Ahmed," he snaps. "I chose my words carefully and I pay you to translate, not to just do your own thing."

"Do you want me to say your words, or do you want him to understand you? Because Asmat-o don't talk like that."

"Um… ok."

By his sixth day in Papua, the feasting has ended and the village is quiet. Dustin's back feels better and he's lost some weight, eliciting compliments from Anna. She has adapted quickly. She brought a sewing kit with her and mends their torn clothes, occasionally adding a small, embroidered butterfly by which to remember her. She also does a lovely reading of the Bible in Spanish, and has a small following that comes to see and hear her music without understanding a word. Everyone loves her.

After three more days of working and waiting, he grows impatient. It's been several days since he's seen Yopokay.

"I've been here over a week," he frets to Ahmed "and the one thing that I came for, nobody has even acknowledged that it still exists."

"Ya, but nobody knew that's why you came except you, until now."

"You know what? You're right. Let's go find the chief."

They find Honcho-ipitch where they expected – sitting in the yew with his entourage, smoking and relaxing. Today, he wears a crown of black cassowary feathers which creates a façade of spiky black hair. Dustin and Ahmed approach, greet and join in. Dustin attempts to sit like the rest but still lacks the flexibility to cross his legs, so he kneels instead.

"Dustin-man wants to explain something," Ahmed announces.

Dustin takes a moment to gather his thoughts, then says the following, with Ahmed translating as closely as possible. "Thank you very much for welcoming me to Janepsto. I like your people very much. You are good people and strong people. I want you to know that I did not come here as a tourist; I came as a student. I am trying to be a shaman, a kind of shaman for my people. I humbly ask that you teach me this powerful knowledge."

Honcho-ipitch ponders for a minute, regards his friends, then responds. "You must learn our language because Ahmed can't stay so long. He must go back to his family. And you must move to a different house because you can't live with me so long."

"I don't understand. I don't want to live here. I have to go back in a few days."

The chief scoffs. "It take years to learn shaman skills."

"Then may I just learn about the ritual of listening for ghosts, when the two stars become one?"

The chief sits and smokes while the others quietly mutter. Finally, he decides.

"You have been very good to us, you and your wife," he declares "but The Ghost-Listening is a powerful thing, you see. Is not for foreigners. But you are welcome…" Ahmed hesitates in his translation. "…welcome to be one of us."

"What does that mean?"

Ahmed interjects his own commentary. "It means they gonna adopt you. I did it. You not gonna like it. It's not bad, only strange. Worse than eating beetles, that's for sure."

Dustin, however, doesn't hesitate. "Not worse than coming all this way and spending all this money for nothing. Let's do it."

No sooner than he consents does the chief clap his hands and the others scramble away in excitement. They have gone to round up the village, all three hundred residents. Apparently, this adoption thing is going to happen right now. Honcho-ipitch remains seated, puffing away on what's left of his cigar, staring out the doorway. Dustin asks him about the whereabouts of Yopokay. Apparently, he's been holed up in his home, fasting and meditating in preparation for his big day.

"I have to ask you," says Dustin, "where does he come from? He doesn't look Asmat."

Honcho douses his stub. "His father came from the sea when I was a boy."

"The sea?"

Yes, the sea. That day, a band of villagers had made their regular excursion to the ocean to fish and hunt and collect shells, when they saw a man swim to shore. The people of Janepsto had never laid eyes on a white man before, not even a Dutchman. To boot, this one had starlight in his eyes, shiny and blue like the Maeto. He was brought back to the village and discussed.

He was thought to have swum across the sea from the land behind the horizon, the same land from which came their god Fumer-ipitch, he who carved the first Asmat people out of wood and breathed life into them. The white man spoke no Asmat and could not correct them. He could not fully tell them until months later that he was just a man exploring the region when his boat capsized.

Upon hearing this, a sudden realization smacks Dustin, flushing his skin and gunning his heart. The sensation that he kept having around Yopokay and Ohmati had not been familiarity but recognition.

"I have to see him!" he all-but-demanded.

"After the ceremony."

"Please, it's very important."

"After. The. Ceremony."

"Ok." Dustin calms a bit, then inquires further.

"Why did he stay so long? Why did he settle here and become Asmat-o?"

"He didn't have a choice."

They had considered killing the man and eating his brain, thereby absorbing his divine power. But wiser men prevailed with a longer view. They saw his arrival as destiny, a blessed solution to an impending problem. The problem was that their Namer-o (shaman) was aging and had no sons. He had two wives, one of whom was barren. The other had birthed two daughters. Clearly, this white angel with the starlight in his eyes was meant to conceive a successor. He was thus adopted and put to stud with both daughters, one of whom was also infertile. The other produced two children, a boy and a girl.

"Why did he go along with it?" asks Dustin. "Did he ever—"

Three men enter the yew, one as big as a tree.

"Time to be reborn!" they gleefully announce.

They grab him by the arms and all but carry him away. Down the step-pole and across the village to the clearing where, days before, the feast had taken place. Along the way, Ahmed does his best to fill in Dustin on what's going to happen. His description is surreal. A crowd is gathering, including a curious, clueless Anna. The villagers surround Dustin as each navigates for a good view. The circle widens when the chief arrives and tells them to spread out. Honcho-ipitch looks through the crowd and selects ten tall, older women to come into the center.

He announces to the crowd, his voice laden with strength and authority, "I like Dustin-man. We all like Dustin-man and he wife. They are two white people who can stay here all they want. I wish that they stay forever, but they won't. So today we gonna make that when they leave, they leave as Asmat-o. Wherever they go and wherever they die, they gonna go and die as Asmat-o! Today we reborn Dustin-man!"

And with that decree, the drums start pounding and the people start singing a joyous and friendly refrain. On cue, another man steps forward

– the ceremonial master. He is skinny and old, even older than the chief. He approaches Dustin and speaks.

"He say take off your clothes," says Ahmed.

"All of them?"

"Yes."

As Dustin undresses, the ten women line up single file, following the old man's instructions. They doff their grass skirts and trade-store shorts, and anything else adorning their groins, then spread their legs apart in a wide stance. They make it look easy, but for Dustin it's not. He's been fueled this far by scientific curiosity and his own momentum. But now, before he sheds his last vestige of dignity, he hesitates for a full three minutes while an entire village watches and waits and sings. He wonders what his wife must think, and what his colleagues would think. For that matter, what about Cookie McGuffin and her 1.9 million viewers? He is suddenly flooded with dread as he scans the crowd for any camera. None, thank God.

And just as suddenly, the dread disappears. Down go the skivvies and down goes Dustin as the old man directs him to the ground. He lies prone in the cool mud, wondering if he'll get a parasite. He lies behind a file of bare women, one who is bleeding. Forward he crawls between umber limbs, under a primal archway. As he advances, the women start to wail and moan, mimicking the pains of child labor with which they are so familiar. He ascends from the front of this symbolic birth canal, as traumatized and filthy as his first time through. He turns over on his back exhausted, and the women immediately disperse to make room for the three best-endowed among them. The three of them hover over him waving their pendulous breasts in his face. He recoils in horror from the suckling suggestion, a sight which makes the old man quip.

"I've never seen a man act like such a baby about acting like a baby."

Dustin rises to his feet, upon which the old man gives him a whack on his bottom, signaling the end of the ritual. The smack is shockingly hard and puts a tear in Dustin's eyes. The music stops and the villagers gather round to congratulate him and pat him on the back and invite him for a meal. Anna has left to fetch a wet towel.

On return, she pushes through the crowd and wipes him down as best she can, lovingly, annoyed. She's a cautious judge – good at understanding when she doesn't understand. But, at minimum, she feels disturbed by this vulgar pagan affair. They will talk later. Ultimately, she will conclude that his decision may have been right, but his haste was not.

"You didn't get successful by being impulsive," she'll tell him. "You are too intelligent to act like this."

"But our whole marriage began on impulse," says Dustin. "If it wasn't for impulse, we might never have been."

"Come on, that was not impulse. That's different."

Dustin thinks for a moment. He knows she's right but isn't sure why. "How so?" he asks.

"Because in impulse there's no thinking. It's just Do What You Want. You and me, we didn't start that way."

Dustin accepts her point and apologizes sincerely. She gives him a big kiss.

The day has been exhausting and he ends up napping part of the afternoon. He awakens around dusk with one thing on his mind – crystal crowns. He finds Ahmed and asks him to bring him to Yopokay, but Ahmed doesn't know the way. They ask a boy who leads them to a small hut on the village edge, set away from the rest, nestled in the woods. Ahmed announces their presence, and they climb up.

The room is darkly lit by a mud hearth in the corner. On the other side lies Yopokay, exhausted from his fast. Ohmati kneels by his side, giving him water. He speaks.

"He heard about your adoption," reports Ahmed. "He say congratulations."

The two siblings had not attended.

Dustin stares at them. "Thank you," he answers without a blink. Now he is certain. He can see it, especially in her – the wise and gentle jawline, the roman nose and high hairline. He had learned the sad fate of their father back in Tennessee, during his research of the Asmats.

Young Winston Vanderbilt, playboy, explorer and grandson of the great steel tycoon J.P. Vanderbilt, was the sole heir to the massive Vanderbilt fortune. Winston had used his family's connections with the Dutch royal family to get permission and assistance to visit the still mostly unexplored Netherlands New Guinea. He was tooling along the shore one day, about sixty years ago, through furious chop when his catamaran capsized, casting him into the deep. The guide who was with him chose to remain clinging to the hull as it drifted further out to sea. He was eventually rescued. But Winston swam for shore, clinging to two empty gas cans for flotation. He was never seen again. When inquiries were made, rumors swarmed the region – Winston was alive, Winston had drowned, Winston had been killed and eaten in revenge for Dutch atrocities. The matter became an international incident and a colossal investigation ensued, including a manhunt by land, sea and air. But no one ever came to Janepsto. It was too remote, even for that region, hidden just past peripheral vision. The search continued for two weeks, then died out, and the mighty Vanderbilts were left to swallow the bitter concoction of grief mixed with fading hope.

"I have to ask you something," says Dustin. "Is your father still alive?"

"No, he died."

"Well, I have to tell you something about him."

"You know our father?" asks Ohmati.

"No, I don't know him; I know *about* him. He was internationally famous."

"Oh, I don't know how to translate that," Ahmed reports.

"Ok, then tell them that I didn't know him, but I heard stories about him, and many stories about his family." Dustin turns back to the siblings. "Did he ever tell you about his family?"

Ohmati answers. "He talked a little about them, especially about he mother. He even taught us some of your language, but that was a long time ago."

"Did he ever tell you about their fortune? Let me rephrase that. Did you know that your grandfather was rich?"

Yopokay sits up and points a finger past Dustin. "That's our grandfather there."

Dustin turns around to see. There, in the corner behind him, rests a skull, well preserved, heavily decorated, and respected far more than your average Asmat pillow. The mandible has been secured with rattan. The orbits and nasal cavities have been filled with beeswax to keep out evil spirits. Red and gray seeds have been pressed into the orbital wax, patterned to look like eyeballs. The nasal wax is piled and caked and shaped like a nose. A bipane hangs from it. The skull rests atop a tripod made from three old bones, femurs from three enemies long since vanquished.

And resting atop the skull in full majesty, there it is – the Maeto. Its icy blue depths spark constantly in the fading light of the hearth. Its ethereal quality mocks those who attempt to capture it on film or in words. It beckons.

Suddenly, Dustin forgets about Vanderbilts and remembers why he came. "Can I try it on?" he asks.

"Yes."

Ohmati carefully lifts it off her grandfather and hands it to Dustin. It's heavier than he expected. He surveys it for a moment, then puts it on. But it's too small for his oversized cranium and just sits on top like a yamlike, sparking some laughter from the siblings.

"So Tiafay, you want to be Namer-o?" asks Yopokay.

*Tiafay* happens to be Dustin's new Asmat name, given to him by the chief at the end of his adoption ceremony. It means "Big Belly" and he's not very fond of it.

"I just want to learn what I can while I'm here, especially about tomorrow," says Big Belly.

He already knew the date of the confluence before he left America, relying on some online almanacs and his own calculations. The Asmats had not been as sure due to two days of overcast skies, but this night is clear. He takes off the crown and inspects it some more.

"Do you feel anything when it's working? Like a tingling, or…"

"What is this word, *tingling?*" Ahmed asks.

"Like a mild electric shock. Like putting your tongue on a 9-volt battery."

Ahmed thinks for a moment, then does his best.

"No, I only hear things," says Yopokay.

Dustin is in a bind. He doesn't think he'll learn much from this holy man. He needs to analyze the crystal. But despite his preparation, he didn't really think through this part. He bought a jeweler's kit before he left home, foolishly thinking that if the Asmats wouldn't sell him the Maeto outright, he might at least negotiate for a sample of it. He didn't anticipate just how sacred it would be to them, nor how far and isolated he would be from the protective cloak of civilization. And while he never really understood religious devotion, he knows it to be powerful and dangerous. So the jeweler's kit sits in his luggage as he sits in a hut in the woods, pondering his next move.

"Are there any stones around here that look like this?" he asks.

"There is no stone around here," Ahmed responds. "That's why they make everything from wood and bone."

Dustin returns the Maeto and returns to the previous subject. "I meant your other grandfather, your father's father. Did your father ever try to escape from here?"

The question elicits puzzled looks from the two siblings.

"They don't understand the question," says Ahmed.

"Ok, did your father ever try to *leave* here?"

"Why would he leave?" asks Ohmati. "He love us."

"Ok, never mind that. I have to tell you something. Your family is very rich. *You* are very, very rich."

Yopokay chuckles. "I know that."

"You do?"

"Of course. I got my own house. Even the chief don't got that. I got my family, I got the Maeto and I got respect from living peoples and also dead ones."

"But… oh, never mind."

In a way, ideas are like families – sometimes you get a lousy one, but it's the only one you got. Just now, just such an idea begins to form in Dustin's head as he notices a bowie knife among Yopokay's belongings. It's one of the few metal objects that he has seen in Janepsto, obtained in Agats during tourist season, traded for a wooden sculpture of a praying mantis. He ruminates while Yopokay attempts to educate him on some of the lore and history he'll need to be any kind of shaman. Dustin feigns attention for a while until Ahmed mentions the late hour.

"You go to bed," Dustin tells Ahmed. "I know enough words to get by. I'm going to stay the night and look after the Namer-o, if he permits. I'm sure Ohmati probably needs the break."

Yopokay consents; Ahmed departs. A little while later, Ohmati leaves too, and with her goes all remaining conversation. The house becomes quiet and the woods loud with critters. Yopokay looks weak but well-hydrated from occasional sips of cold broth. He'll need to urinate eventually, and Dustin needs a moment alone with the Maeto. There is no porch, and he figures Yopokay will have to climb down.

But Dustin figures wrong because shaman don't need no stinking porch. When the time comes, he just walks over, drops his drawers and pees out the doorway.

"Heads up, monkeys!" he announces, as he casts his urine into the night. It's his own little tradition, and the closest he gets to any kind of humor. He wobbles a bit and Dustin half-hopes that he'll fall – maybe more than half. The shaman returns to bed and falls quickly asleep. Dustin realizes that whatever he's going to do will have to be in his presence.

The embers are dying but the moon shines brightly, and he can still see his watch. He waits a half hour, then conducts a test. He slams two plates together. In response to the noise, Yopokay cracks an eyelid and stirs momentarily, then returns to sleep. Dustin waits ten minutes, then does it again. Same response. He repeats four more times over the next hour to be sure, and also to disturb Yopokay's slumber just enough that he'll sleep soundly afterwards.

Now he's ready. He cautiously takes the Maeto and the knife, and kneels by the entrance where the light is ample. From his pocket, he takes out a sweat-soaked bandana. He keeps it on him to occasionally try, in vain, to wipe even more sweat from his brow. He spreads it out on the floor and holds the headpiece over it. The crown shines intensely in his hand, seemingly resonating with the moonlight. In his other, he takes the knife and slowly, carefully starts to scrape the inner rim where hopefully no one will notice, using the broad edge so as to abrade and not gouge. Fortunately, the stone is fairly soft and yields a glittering dust that gently falls to the cloth. It clings to the dampness like lovers reunited. He continues slowly, diligently, quietly, until the bandana itself shimmers from edge to edge.

Fold it up neatly, put everything away, then pick a spot to lie down and try to sleep. But he can't sleep, and without wife or bed for comfort, he rises at dawn with a screaming back. While Yopokay still slumbers, he decides to leave, feeling sure he won't be missed. After all, today is showtime and the shaman will be busy.

He slowly lowers himself down the steps with little difficulty until he reaches the last, upon which his back suddenly zings him, sending him falling to the ground. He lies there a while, unable to move, staring up through endless trees. Eventually, he scrounges himself together and hobbles back to the chief's house. The bandana is sealed in a sandwich bag and returned to his pocket. It will stay there until he's back in Oak Ridge, checked upon frequently by the patting of a nervous hand. In four days, he and Anna will depart.

It would have been two days, but he finally succumbs to the Papuan germs that have been circling him like hyenas since he arrived. He develops two days of fevers and horrible diarrhea despite Anna fastidiously boiling every drop of liquid to touch their lips, and despite the emergency antibiotics that his doctor prescribed for the trip.

The séance itself ends up being rather anticlimactic, at least in appearance. Outwardly, it's just a guy sitting most of the day in the yew with his eyes closed and a thing on his head. But inside the Namer-o roars a tempest of thoughts and feelings and sweats and palpitations. It occasionally bubbles to the surface, causing him to utter secrets of the dead to two assistants who are assigned to sit at his side, listen and remember. The revelations include updates on the condition of dead relatives, complaints about living ones, accusations of theft and betrayal, and the unfortunate fate of a missing child. The accounts are sincere fabrications resulting from actual wave energy shining on the soil of Yopokay's understanding and experience, then fertilized into blooming detail by his own imagination.

On their day of departure, the entire village gives Dustin and Anna a warm sendoff, especially Anna, who will be missed and mentioned by the children for years. They return to Tennessee jet-lagged and exhausted, and Dustin takes a week to recover.


From his prized specimen, which he dubs Stardust, he is able to regrow a small crystal about the size of a marble. When his team finally gets it all rigged up, it responds well; in fact, too well. The moment they switch it on, it immediately issues a constant, maximum electrical output. And it stays that way – the needle pinned at 10 – despite the usual precautions to filter out signal contamination. But there is no contamination. It's just an ultra-sensitive crystal.

That crystal will eventually teach mankind that Y-waves are constantly showering the Earth. Most of them flow undisturbed through its magnetic fields, its core of molten iron, and through pitch-black depths of undersea canyons. Then they emerge to soar into the royal blue, then on towards the North Star – lost souls in search of a destiny.

Most, but not all. Some waves are blessed or cursed to be caught in gestating babies, and tasked to live out the lives they will live.

But Dustin need not be overwhelmed by the ubiquitous waves overwhelming his crystal. He does not have to be in a certain part of the world at a certain time of year like the Asmat-o. He doesn't have to rely on the gravitational forces of planetary syzygy to impose a calm in the waves long enough to hear the voices around him. No, he has technology. He tweaks the gain. He uses powerful computers, whipped by brilliant coders, to subtract the noise. All of this enables him to focus his crystal on a single, living subject. And what it reveals is a finely detailed, seemingly random, electronic fluctuation, like a fibrillating hand in alcohol withdrawal trying to sign a release form.

But the scribbles aren't random. Computer analysis discovers that the fluctuations that emanate from a single, living person repeats itself exactly every nineteen minutes - a pattern. And while parts of each pattern are common, the total pattern of each person is unique. It's like a fingerprint or a genome, or a radio show broadcast.

Yet, despite all his technology and his best techniques of neutron-scattering, the crystal defies all Dustin's attempts to determine its structure and composition. He learns that much of it is nothing more than simple calcite, but that's only part of it. Something elusive lies within, something that will not deflect a neutron, something stable with mass, but not of the baryonic world. Certainly not of this world.

The mystery haunts him and reminds him of the Asmat legend of the blood of Desoipitch. It will not be solved in his lifetime, which means the crystal won't be reproduced. This failure becomes increasingly problematic as the crystal opens new areas of study in a field already charged with excitement. As demand grows for its use, security measures are installed, including armed couriers and chain-of-custody protocols. The issue eventually turns political, bureaucrats get involved, and lawyers draw up long, wordy agreements to share the crystal and all its data.

But the worst headache comes from pressure on Dustin himself to reveal the crystal's origin. It comes from supervisors and colleagues, friends and strangers. Some even bug his wife, who has matriculated at the University of Tennessee to continue her psych major. She eventually turns to pre-law and beyond, ultimately becoming a civil rights attorney, one who is fond of saying "I'm not a maid, but I still have to clean up other people's mess." And she resists the pressure to betray the Asmats – they both do – he out of loyalty to the only people who ever made him feel accepted, she from a higher principle.

This resistance, combined with the mystical nature of Y-waves and of the crystal itself, creates an aura of mystery around Dustin, who gets increasingly famous. He even gains himself a small cult following and briefly becomes a figure of pop culture, even appearing in a few, awkward TV cameos. Unfortunately, he lacks the constitution to withstand all that admiration and attention, and his character starts to sour. He becomes arrogant and more vocally agnostic, if not outright atheistic.

All of this naturally chafes Anna who, without realizing, slowly drifts away. It starts with sweet habits being casually dropped. Her twice-a-day texts with nothing to say become daily at best and pragmatic. Their regular lunch dates die out and she's too tired to make tea after dinner.

She eventually finds herself missing him less and less, and not minding when he travels. And when he's featured or quoted in an article, she braces herself before reading it, closing one eye and squinting the other.

Had they spent more time together, their marriage would have likely ended. But she's busy – they both are – he working late and she studying at the library. They will eventually separate. When he retires from his day job, he'll finally accept a business proposal from Krystal, who's been bugging him for years to host a series of retreats. He'll make more money than he knew possible, feeding a delicious mixture of science and psychobabble to wealthy, aging hippies.

And years from now, when his fifteen minutes have faded but the pressure has not, he'll snitch about the Maeto, and foreigners will once again descend on the Asmats to take their stuff.

But meanwhile, a steady stream of discovery is already being extracted from the small sample on hand. A major finding comes out of Copenhagen, from one Dr. Jorgensen, a middle-aged neurophysicist with horn-rimmed glasses and a goatee, who found a way to combine his two fascinations – neuroendocrine pathways and college girls. He had long asserted that the pineal gland was not an inactive, evolutionary remnant, as commonly thought by his colleagues; but rather a busy and important structure that exerts significant influence over the hypothalamus, the nerve center of hormone regulation. Jorgensen is a pioneer in the field of Connectomics – the comprehensive mapping of the brain's connections. Despite his study being only tangentially related to quantum physics, his request to borrow the crystal was one of only seven to be approved among dozens of applicants. In his application, he discussed the pineal gland and its status as the only crystalline structure in the body. He also hypothesized that a person's Y-wave signature is not immutable, as had become the prevailing theory for no particular reason.

"The belief popularly held in society," he wrote, "that Y-waves are somehow the embodiment of that thing we call the soul, has found itself exerting undue *a priori* influence on scientific discourse. To accept such an assumption, we first must define our terms, and loosely define the 'soul' as that part of a person that is neither created nor destroyed, like energy or God. But to further posit that the soul, and thus Y-waves, are as constant as God, rather than alterable like energy, is a string of too many assumptions. Yet those assumptions seem to form the basis of the cross-sectional design of studies conducted thus far."

He thus proposed a longitudinal study, studying a few people over a long time instead of thousands of people just once. Specifically, he proffered studying women at a local college who were living in the dormitory. He was granted use of the crystal for two years. He enrolled a hundred women, but nearly half dropped out because they either hated dorm life or their roommates or both. What he found from the rest was that those roommates whose menstrual cycles synchronized (The McClintock Effect) had a corresponding change in their Y-wave signatures, specifically in a small segment which he dubbed the "menstrual gene." In that one segment, the frequency of electronic fluctuations between roommates became whole integers of each other. In other words, they harmonized.

These discoveries have opened the door to a new paradigm which researchers explore with fervor. In one study, they have found an entire set of wave "genes" that change over a much shorter period, possibly just minutes. This was demonstrated by a physicist from Bangalore, Dr. Shah, who examined the Y-waves of hundreds of Muslim pilgrims in Mecca, before and after the great Eid prayer. There was something about a half a million people crammed into a mosque, physically oriented around a central point and synchronized in thought and movement, that accelerated the harmonization of those wave segments.

Longer studies are also being done, studies on spouses, on families, lovers and even prisoners. Multiple other sections of the Y-wave are found to be mutable and harmonizing. The behavior of those segments, termed the "love genes," turns out to depend more on time and distance than on relationship or personal feelings. Over a long time, strangers are more likely to harmonize, and harmonize more thoroughly, than newlyweds over a shorter period. Indeed, this harmonic tendency appears to be independent of sex, age, income, education, political affiliation, or any other factor they can think to test. But the data is inconsistent; harmony cannot be predicted based on time and distance alone. For reasons unknown, some people just don't click…ever.

They don't click like Dustin and Anna did hundreds of years ago, in the city of Agra in Northern India, when they spent years together and loved each other deeply. She would feed him millet seeds and radishes, but he always preferred to sneak into The Man's room where, in a bowl on a stand, he would find the sweet, sweet mango.

III

At some point in the story, lots of people have sex with each other and some foul language is thrown around. Adolescents everywhere rejoice.

# IV

# List of Named Characters

Captain Christopher Younas: leader of missions for the Magellan space agency

> John Younas: war hero and Christopher's grandfather (deceased)

> Anthony Younas: co-director of Magellan and Christopher's father (deceased)

> Sarah Younas: Christopher's mother

> Sammy Younas: Christopher's brother

> Patrick "Patches" Kendrick: Christopher's friend

Officer Flanagan: a Dundo customs officer

Jacob Baja: returning Cobblestone

> Ann Baja: Jacob's mother (deceased)

Agent Stucky: Magellan official assigned to escort Jacob Baja

Mimi Sparrow: chairman of the Magellan Commission on Personnel Affairs

Mr. Hastings: a Magellan commissioner

Mr. Garcia: a Magellan commissioner

> Kerry Nelson: the former Mrs. Garcia

Dr. Shane Salter: scientist, discoverer of Santagati's disease

Dr. Richard Santagati: scientist, rival of Dr. Salter

Mr. Lipton: a Dundo detective

Baldric Silver: retired co-director of Magellan

Peter Panther: a prominent criminal in Dundo's underworld

Dr. Creeper: a criminal surgeon on Dundo

Henrik Jallolaby: retired vice president of pharmaceutical company, and murder victim

Otto Frye: a.k.a. Otto the Oppressor, Dundo's most notorious convict

Specialist Romano: a corrections officer on Dundo

Superdoctor Haruto Silver: a Dundo scientist, designer of the Galahad for Operation Ptolemy

Goink Bedoink: killer clown, sterilizer of women

Dr. Mary Money: a physician on the moon Argos, working for the Mao Corporation

Mr. Hand: an agent assigned by the Mao Corporation to assist Dr. Money

Luke: an employee of the Mao Corporation residing in Sector Z, on the moon Argos

Cyrus: the foreman of Sector Z

"Crazy" Joe Gallo: another Sector Z worker and creator of "the finger"

Sinumbre': a supervisor at a supply distribution center on Argos

Victor Lahab: a quality control officer on Argos, and a patient of Dr. Money

Victor Gall: a supervisor at Central Supply, on Argos

Silbin Lee: a purchasing officer at Central Supply and a patient of Dr. Money

# Eleven

On the planet Dundo, a customs officer watched a shuttle descend from orbit. On an obscure frequency, someone was speaking aviation. "Dundo radar 157, Phoenix 1252 at flight level 750,000. Requesting information and waypoint instruction." The officer scanned the vessel's stats. They were arcane but still in the archives. They indicated the shuttle to be at least 300 earth-years old, about two lifetimes. The message repeated, calmly and patiently, in a manner so robotic that he concluded the sender must either be machine or soldier. A slight change in inflection soon told him which. The repetition continued, giving him time to first be confused, then recall a faint memory of his training, then to consult his P&P manual. "Hang on," he blurted, and the repetition stopped.

According to the rules, the next task would be easy. He had to call an air traffic controller. There was one on call just for this purpose – when a pilot with outdated technology needed to land. Decades earlier, Dundo's engineers realized that their thick atmosphere was ideal for a network of air buoys and they created a system, using magnets and GPS, that rendered most of human air traffic control obsolete.

But officer Flanagan knew this was more than just a foreigner who had come a long way. This was a Cobblestone, and a very old one. The mysterious owner of that voice, and any passengers, would have to be delivered to the bigwigs at Magellan – the modern version of NASA – for debriefing. And a Cobblestone? Flanagan didn't know what a cobble was and he had never seen a stone. But everyone knew about Cobblestones. The unkind term had found its way into common usage.

Before explaining Cobblestones, a bit of human history is in order. Fifteen thousand years prior, Earth reached a major milestone of technology – a giant leap forward in speed. A new discovery enabled space travel at 31.3% the speed of light. On the floor of the World Congress, an apocalyptic fight ensued over what name to give the invention. Centuries before, Congress had stopped bothering with anything besides naming things and resolving to name things. On this issue, the Stupefaction Faction ultimately defeated the Cuck Caucus. The new thing would forever be called a Warp Drive, not Hyperspace. Ironically, the deciding vote took place on International Jedi Appreciation Day, rendering the victory even sweeter for the Faction.

Long before the Warp Drive, mankind had learned to survive very long times in space. But without speed, we wasted time puttering about the Solar System, exploring dead, dangerous places and collecting mostly useless information. After Warp arrived, we spent thousands of years exploring dozens of star systems and hundreds of worlds. And when Earth finally became too crowded, we colonized.

We never did find a planet as suitable as Earth. We never even found a completely safe one, and we soon learned just how fragile we are. Each of our colonies only became possible by overcoming multiple hazards, hazards in the form of insult (radiation, temperature, weather, poison) and deficit (water, oxygen, minerals). Eventually, we flourished, making use of our ingenuity and lots and lots of time. We eventually passed a point when most humans still had a basic knowledge of Earth but had never been there. However, even after those thousands of years, our standard of living advanced very little, and in some ways regressed, because we spent most of our resources and ingenuity on simply surviving in harsh places.

We also never found alien life. After a while, the hope and excitement that we once had about that prospect faded away, replaced by despair and a doubt among many people that there was, in fact, any other life in the Universe. Ironically, both hope and despair were born of the same flaw – arrogance. The Universe, of course, is teeming with life, but man was too pompous to know just how small he is, and too ignorant to understand that it would take him millions of years to find the nearest, living neighbor.

All of the early exploration was accomplished by trial and error, mostly error. Eighty-five percent of all missions never returned. Miscalculations and malfunctions caused missionaries to meet their fates very suddenly and at high temperatures, as they hurdled towards a star or through an atmosphere, or into a rock. Sometimes a large planet, or even a black hole, unexpectedly appeared too near to one's path, and turning in space is not easy. Some unfortunate souls never reached any destination. Their destiny was to hurdle through space at warp speed forever.

These early explorers were eventually dubbed Cobblestones because their ashes served as pavement for future, safe travel. At first, recruitment was easier than you might think. The benefits included a very generous life insurance policy. Poorer people with few prospects saw it as a way to secure a comfortable living for their families. Some were brave patriots, risking their lives to advance the human condition. But hatred, not love of mankind, motivated many more.

The hatred came from a lifetime spent packed into a crowded planet, so crowded that some recruits joined just for an opportunity to spend the rest of their days in peace. In fact, the recruitment brochure devoted pages to explain the long-forgotten concept of privacy. In language quite elegant for a government pamphlet, it described what it's like to hear your own thoughts, or to be alone in the bathroom. These foreign ideas seemed pointless to most, but stirred the imagination of enough people to fill their ranks.

A new corps was thus created, the Pioneers Corps. The Pioneers signed their lives away, spent four years in training and were launched. Those who returned received a hero's welcome. But that was a long time ago on another planet.


For now, on Dundo, protocol was followed. The old shuttle was modern enough to be controlled remotely, and the air traffic controller landed it without problem, from his home, in his underwear, while eating a sandwich. The hangar was sealed, its air flushed, and its temperature raised back above the freezing misery outside. A landing team boarded the shuttle and assisted its one passenger into a wheelchair. They scrubbed, vaccinated and fed him, then filled out forms and brought him to Flanagan's office.

The plain office had no windows. In fact, no windows existed anywhere on Dundo. They were too unsafe and expensive. Instead, a virtual window hung on the wall – a monitor which broadcast a live stream of some lovely scene on some far-off planet. Of course, live streaming between worlds meant that the images were at least weeks old, if not years. Flanagan quickly scanned the stranger with his eyes, trying to cloak his curiosity under a veil of professionalism. The man appeared his stated age of 82, still young by Dundo standards. He appeared more fit than expected, lacking the atrophy so common after a long space voyage. He had the big bones characteristic of Dundo natives (known as Dundoers).

Flanagan began. "Captain Jacob Baja?"

"It's pronounced Baha, sir," Baja replied.

Flanagan looked up at him. Baja sat in a wheelchair, dressed in the same, silly, white jump suit issued to all new arrivals after scrub-down. Yet he still exuded confidence, professionalism, and other nameless qualities that compel respect. Flanagan looked into his serious, sterile eyes.

"They said you were wearing a uniform. Are you a soldier?" he asked.

"It was my father's uniform, sir," said Baja.

Flanagan read some more. "It says here that you were born in space. So you couldn't have enlisted. Yet, you clearly *are* a military man. Did you take The Oath?"

"I was raised in a military family, sir. And, yes, I did take an oath."

"Very good," said Flanagan. "Welcome to Dundo. It seems you're someone special, and I will be escorting you to the colony myself."

"Thank you, sir."

Flanagan brought his guest across the building and up a ramp, which ascended into the center of a large chamber. At first, the room seemed round to Baja, until he realized that it was decahexagonal. Each of the sixteen walls featured a small door, one of which Flanagan opened, revealing a plain closet just big enough for the two seats contained within. In a corner hung a small box which dispensed pills. Flanagan took one, then held out another for Baja.

"Sedative?" he offered.

"No thank you, sir."

"I need 'em. I hate these things," said Flanagan.

He helped Baja into a seat, sat in the other, strapped them both in, closed the door and hit a button. Within a second, Baja was lying on his back and could feel the sensation of moving very fast in the direction of his head. He was in a pod – a pneumatic tube much like the canister at the bank, except that this one moved about forty kilometers per minute, the speed of a bullet. Were he able to see outside of the cross-country plumbing through which he sped, he would have seen a malevolent, unlivable world, cold and barren, the terrain impassable. He would have beheld skies permanently overcast with thick, poisonous air, under constant assault in all directions by lightning.

Around twenty minutes later, they arrived at a small building called a Lift Station. The one-room rectangular structure had four doors in each of its long walls. They entered through one door, crossed the room, and exited through another. The exit revealed a similar closet, except bigger and without safety straps. In the corner was another dispenser from which Flanagan took two pieces of gum. "You'll need this," he said, handing one to Baja. He shut the door, hit a button and the lift began to slowly descend. During this time, Flanagan's sedative wore off and he became chatty, telling Baja some history of Dundo, as best he knew it.

Dundo differed from most colonies, which were usually some type of constructed, surface biosphere. Dundoers were troglodytes. The caves in which they dwelt were, at this location, eight kilometers below the surface. But they weren't the random, rocky structure one would imagine. They had been formed millions of years ago when Dundo churned much hotter, violent with volcanic activity. In the antral layer of the crust, giant, fantastic crystals had formed. But like the brightest stars, their existence was fleeting. An era of acid rains dissolved them, leaving a cavernous network shaped like overlapping starbursts. The centers of those bursts were chambers large enough to build towns or factories or farms; their rays wide enough for highways and pipelines. The temperature was comfortable and weather was nonexistent. Then, humans came and coated everything with a thermoset polymer. Eventually, they discovered a large aquifer to provide water. Everything else, including air, was manufactured.

On arrival, the lift opened to an alley. The ground cover there was a thick, brown, plastic material with a surface coarse enough to grip, but smooth enough to keep clean. Upwards, Baja could see above the buildings to a ceiling which had been painted sky blue. A short way down, the alley led to a road busy with scooters and pedestrians. They crossed the street and entered a building, a rehab facility. An oxygen mask was put on Baja's face just as he started to wobble with wooziness. Here, he would gradually be acclimated to Dundo's air and altitude. Here, he would live for the next two to four weeks, until he had strength enough to walk under the heavy weight of Dundo's severe gravity. He would get regular injections to thicken his bones, lest he suffer one of Dundo's hard falls. He'd be taught some basic laws and customs and have access to a library.

And use the library he did, in all his free time. The therapists thought this peculiar and sometimes tried peeking over his shoulder. But he was secretive and guarded his business.

As soon as he had sufficiently adapted, an agent of the government, Agent Stucky, came to fetch him. It would be Baja's first trip out of town. Within town, people got around by scooter, golf carts and other small vehicles. But between towns, they took the Tube, a network of pneumatic tubes similar to the ones on the planet surface, but smaller and less rugged. The tubes circumvented each town in rotary fashion. They passed between towns via the narrow passages described earlier, called Ray Ways, or Rays for short. Much like air traffic, Tube traffic was directed by magnets and computers. Specifically, one massive computer controlled a network of a million magnetic switches. Magnets were also essential in making Tube traffic quick and efficient, eliminating friction by suspending the transport pods.

Agent Stucky had a car waiting. As they rode through town, Baja saw many things for the first time. Two of them struck him most.

One was the sight of children. He had known one before, the only other child on the ship on which he had grown. She was born just two months after he, and they were naturally very close. In fact, they had been intended for each other by their parents since before birth. But she died at the age nine of leukemia. Now, the sight of children left him with a weird combination of joy and sadness.

The other was the buildings. They were so tall! Having never seen a town before, he did not appreciate the unique nature of Dundo planning. Building in caverns meant conserving space, and the Dundoers decided early on to build upwards before sidewards. As a result, no building stood under ten stories tall, leaving lots of space for yards and sidewalks and plants, and decent parks. The main streets were concentric rotaries, the side streets straight and radial. The buildings were rock, many of them black volcanic glass like obsidian. Rock was the one raw material of which Dundo had plenty. Most construction material came from the hot, unsettled regions of the planet, where the caverns lay closer to its mantle. Drilling rigs extracted the magma, which was then processed and molded.

They rode the Tube for over an hour and traveled several hundred kilometers, stopping only once in another town to replenish air. The agent spent much of the time briefing Baja on what to expect, on proper manners and protocol when standing before the commission. Baja spent an equal amount of time ignoring him.

Hundun-5 was one of several towns built for the administration of government. On arriving there, Baja first noticed the ceiling, which was not sky blue. It was striped, each of the twelve stripes a different color. This had been done to please the various color constituencies. Of course, the people of Dundo were not twelve different colors, but they *liked* different colors, and this posed a dilemma for the planning commission. So the ceiling committee produced the kind of solution that committees usually do.

The town was overbuilt. Compared to the previous town, it looked crowded and poorly organized, and there were no children. Most remarkable of all were the blindfolds. Nearly everyone not driving was wearing one. Passengers, pedestrians, and almost anyone who had time could be seen groping and fumbling about, some being assisted by the non-blindfolded. Baja thought to ask, then thought better. Even Stucky, after arriving at Magellan and entering the building, stopped at the security desk and grabbed two blindfolds. He offered one to Baja, who declined.

"What are you? You hate blind people?" asked Stucky.

"I'm not sure. Am I supposed to?" Baja replied, having never known a blind person.

Apparently, it was Visual Impairment Awareness Day in Hundun-5. Stucky donned the blinder, took Baja by the arm and gave him directions. They eventually reached a closed door which had two knobs, aligned vertically. One knob was at standard waist level, the other a few inches below.

"Which knob do I turn?" asked Baja.

"It doesn't matter," replied Stucky. "They're just knobs. The bottom one is for the vertically challenged." The door opened to a conference room where five commissioners sat, blindfolded, and one clerk stood, fully sighted. On entering the room, a clerk barked at Baja.

"ARE YOU HEARING IMPAIRED?" he asked.

"No, sir."

The clerk then lowered his voice, took a deep breath, and recited the following.

"Are you visually impaired, mentally impaired, physically challenged, vertically challenged, calorically challenged, extremely nervous, sexually insecure, suffering from overactive bladder, or require any other accommodation that was heretofore unanticipated?"

"I, uh," Baja stammered.

"No, sir, he is not and does not," interjected Stucky.

"Very good," the clerk replied. "You are hereby notified that you have the following rights during this meeting. You may stand or sit. You may speak any language you choose, and an interpreter will be arranged. If you are shy, you may whisper. You may use the bathroom at any time, as long as you raise your hand. If you do not have hands, you may raise a foot. If you do not have feet, then you may interrupt. You may request lie detection at any time."

Baja had read about lie detection, a biochemical test. Apparently, a strain of bacteria had been genetically engineered to produce a particular chemical whenever lies were breathed upon it. You simply had the suspect repeat the statement over a petri dish, then you added a reagent and, if it turned red, the suspect had lied.

Baja's stoic expression cracked a hint of curiosity. "Pardon me, but if I was going to lie, why would I ask for lie detection?"

The clerk snickered. "Not you. The commissioners. The Firepants Act provides that any citizen of Dundo may submit to lie detection any employee of the government with whom said citizen has dealings, at the time of those dealings."

After everyone was seated, one older woman, Mrs. Sparrow, peaked over her blindfold at Baja. "Let me be the first to say that we are honored to be in your presence," she said.

"Here here," echoed the others, pounding desks with fists.

"A returning member of the Pioneer Corps," she continued. "I don't think we've had such an event since I was a child. It says here you went out to Alpha Lyrae, some twenty light years away! Goodness!"

"Twenty-five," said Baja.

"Beg your pardon?"

"It was twenty-five light years, madame."

"Indeed!" said she. "Well, you certainly are a hero and shall receive a hero's welcome if I have anything to say about it. Now, shall we begin?

"First of all," she continued, "Were you witness to any actions of the crew that would qualify as a violation of Dundo law? Harassment, rudeness or unkindness?"

Baja was puzzled. "Madame, I am the only remaining survivor. I don't see how any of that would be relevant."

"It's relevant for the record," she replied. "Merely a formality, my love."

"Then the answer is no."

"Very good. Next question – During your voyage, did you encounter any life other than your shipmates?"

Baja shook his head.

"Let the record indicate that Captain Baja answered in the negative," announced the clerk.

Mrs. Sparrow continued. "Now, did your crew mount a successful landing on this target planet, #5309, and if so—"

"Captain Baja," interrupted another, rather rotund fellow named Hastings. "We have been unable to board the Bucephalus. It doesn't seem to want to accept our access code."

"Yes, I changed the code," said Baja, matter-of-factly while regarding his nails.

"You changed…Captain, that ship and all data, recordings and samples on board are property of Dundo. You are required to—"

"I am not required to do anything, sir," Baja huffed. "You will get your ship when I'm finished with it. Until that time, it will remain in orbit, under lock."

A moment of silence ensued while the commission digested his words. Mr. Hastings removed his blindfold and leaned forward.

"Captain Baja," he said. "I understand you don't have counsel here today, and our laws and customs are likely foreign to you. What you may not understand is that vandalism and/or theft of state property could, in the very least, jeopardize the indemnities to which you are entitled, as well as inheritance. That would include the significant back pay owed your parents."

Baja remained calm. "So, instead of a hero's welcome, you would leave me a homeless, penniless Cobblestone. I'm sure that would make a terrific story for the press."

"We prefer not to use that term. We—"

"Captain," chimed in another fogey, still blindfolded. "The ship is a dinosaur. We have no use for it except the data it contains. You understand? The data. I'm not sure why you're giving us this trouble, but we need to know if you're worth the bother. So please tell us, did you indeed reach the target planet. Did a party land successfully? Were the proper scans made and samples collected?"

"To my knowledge," said Baja "the answer is yes to all your questions. Honorable commissioners, please understand. The Bucephalus is the only home I ever had. Everyone I have ever known died on that ship, including my parents. It takes time to move out. Now I will return her to you, and even prepare a full report, though I have signed no contract and have no obligation. However, I need time, at least several more weeks. And I need lodging, my money, and access to my shuttle."

Mrs. Sparrow spoke up. "Captain, you are surprisingly eloquent and a bit shrewd for someone so new to society. Of course we will give you time, and give you what's yours. Shall we agree to meet again in, say, six weeks? Terrific."

Thanks and goodbyes were exchanged, and Baja began to leave. As he reached for the door, Mrs. Sparrow also removed her blindfold.

"One more question, sir," she said. "To prepare for this meeting, we tried to research as much as we could. But much information regarding your parents' departure was classified, off limits even to us. I'm talking about banal details that would normally be of no interest. Do you know of any reason for such secrecy?"

Baja held the doorknob for a moment (the top one), perhaps to search his memory or to contemplate a response, then left without a word.


The commission spent a few minutes murmuring before the clerk announced the next order of business – Consideration of commission assignments for Captain Christopher Younas.

"What is this, Crazy Captain Day?" grumbled one member.

Captain Younas was neither crazy nor a bad captain. However, he was the kind of man who inspired nasty comments by those who knew him.

Into the room walked a man, 6'1" of slender build, fairly muscular but not excessively. A swarthy fellow with rugged features and wavy hair, he was handsome on the outside by any standard. He sat down, kicked back his chair on two legs, and put his feet on the conference table. He snickered at the blindfolds. "What is this, Pin the Tail on the Donkey? It's more fun in space, you know."

He was right. The popular ancient child's game took on new dimensions when played without gravity. In space, where voyages take months or years, travelers spent much time finding ways to pass time. A bored crew would often secure the liquids and breakables, turn off the gravity and play gravity games. Marco Polo was another popular one.

Mrs. Sparrow was not a woman to lightly suffer a smartass. She replied calmly, perfectly pitched and on-target. "Captain Younas, it would be very kind if you would return before this commission on Hearing Impairment Awareness Day, for you are much more tolerable to the deaf than the blind."

Younas was amused, not offended. He had some admiration for Mrs. Sparrow, and enjoyed exchanging verbal jabs. "Touche'," he said.

Chris Younas was the grandson of John Younas, a famous war hero immortalized in schoolbooks. And John was indeed a hero – a pilot, brave and honorable early on. But then he became famous, and then a politician. Celebrity and power eventually made him slimy, as it often does to formerly great men.

On Dundo, thanks to technology, life expectancy reached almost two hundred Earth years. Longer lives meant longer retirements, which meant saving more money. That meant having children later in life, which worked out fine because that same technology meant that women remained fertile into their sixties.

John Younas was sixty-two when his son Anthony was born. By then, John was well underway to becoming a bastard and Anthony learned very few of his father's earlier, good characteristics. He, like his father, became a pilot first, then a government man. In a blatant act of nepotism, John saw to Anthony's appointment as a top Magellan administrator. Anthony excelled in the position, performing more than competently. Unfortunately, he wasn't just smart. He had that special mixture of intelligence and viciousness – cunning. But Magellan had little use for viciousness, so Anthony was a powerful but poor leader.

Christopher was not as smart as his father, who had died a few years ago. He was a playboy and, like his father, a hunter. He hunted big game and had taken three excursions to Planet 80-T, where one went for such things.

The naming rights for most settled worlds had been sold to corporations, though many had been mangled over time. 80-T, for example, had once been called AT&T. By this time in history, very few people still knew that, or knew the origin of the name "Dundo". It would be centuries later when a box would be discovered in the lowest level of the Archive Repository. The box would contain papers – relics from a time when people still used paper. One document, after much effort by a team of linguists, would be sufficiently translated to reveal the planet's original name – Dunkin Donuts World. Instead of enlightening, the revelation would deepen the mystery, as nobody knew what a donut was.

Chris Younas had also been a hunter of women and was thrice divorced. But those hunting days were over due to illness. As the human race spread from Earth to other worlds, new living conditions created new diseases. Infectious diseases arose from mutation, or from new opportunities for old germs that had not previously been pathogenic. Younas, in his travels, had contracted one of them – Santagati's disease, also known as Ball Rot. A particularly nasty venereal disease, it's just as it sounds – a slow, painful, festering necrosis of the testicles for which the only cure is castration.

Notably, Ball Rot was also the first disease named out of vengeance instead of vanity. Indeed, Dr. Shane Salter, the biologist who isolated and identified the virus, was a vain man; too vain to name such a ghastly thing after himself. Instead, he would name it after the man who almost beat him to the discovery, Dr. Richard Santagati. A relationship that started decades earlier as cutthroat competition, then deteriorated into bitter personal venom, would end with Santagati being awarded the dubious honor he had sought without thinking.

Younas finally succumbed to surgery months ago, and though hormone replacement allowed him to keep his masculine features, he lost his libido. That was sadly the only trait of his personality which had softened. Paradoxically, after his surgery, he became more terrible because he was self-conscious. He had heard the name, "Younas the Eunuch," and was determined to prove his manhood.

One way he endeavored to do so was to torment his only child, a nine-year old boy from his third marriage. Weeks earlier, he had taken him to the park and tried to teach him to hit a ball. When the boy didn't show aptitude, Younas would grab him and bark. "Slide your wrist down! Elbows higher! No, not like that!" Then he would shake him a little and interrogate him.

"Are you a dunderhead?"

"No, sir."

"Are you a dunce?"

"No, sir."

"Then what are you?"

"I'm a DunDo-er, sir."

"Then DunDO it!"

Again, Younas tried and again the boy failed, at which point Younas recoiled like a cobra, then struck with verbal venom. "Stupid!" he yelled. Some heads turned at that moment, and the boy shriveled like a punctured, inflatable bunny. Younas felt a bit guilty right after. But guilt is easily swallowed when washed down with a crooked cocktail – one part finger-pointing, one part self-pity.

He soon forgot the incident and now focused on getting back to work. He was more adventurous and less ambitious than his father, and he was bored. He wanted a mission. He was an explorer, but not a Cobblestone. He was better trained, better equipped and less brave. His job had been to conduct Phase II studies of worlds that had already been mapped and crudely analyzed. He led big teams on big ships, loaded with big, fancy equipment – thermometers, barometers, particle detectors, sonar, spectrophotometers, seismometers, vehicles, lots of sample containers and lots of assembly kits. There were kits to assemble bases, drilling rigs, communication towers and even ice breakers.

In the conference room, Mrs. Sparrow pressed on. "I must confess to being a bit perplexed. We were told you're here because you seek to return to active status with Magellan. Yet you begin this interview with your feet firmly placed in the one place that they are not welcome." She lowered her blindfold to glare. "Perhaps you're giving us a demonstration of zero gravity."

At that moment, Younas's smirk vanished, his voice lowered and his posture straightened. "Interview? I'm qualified and credentialed," he said. "This hearing should just be a formality."

"Then you have otherwise completed your recredentialing process?" asked another.

"You bet," responded Younas. "Flight hours, continuing ed, physical cert, psych cert, anal probe. Every deadline has been met and every fee paid. It's all signed, notarized and delivered, baby."

It was at this time that a Mr. Garcia spoke up, no longer able to suppress his hostility. Younas knew the source of his animus. Two years earlier, Younas had laser-tattooed his name on Kerry Nelson while she lay drunk, naked and passed out on his bed. At that time, Kerry Nelson was Mrs. Kerry Garcia, and Younas had placed the tattoo where Mr. Garcia would be certain to see it long before she did, if he was any kind of man. Apparently he was, and now he sat on this commission.

"This is not a done deal, Younas," Garcia seethed. "You still have the interview, and the interview means you only fly if we decide you fly, so you'd better start becoming more impressive and less emetic before we adjourn."

Younas was floored. "What? Me? You can't," he stammered. "You have to approve me if I'm qualified. I have rights. Qualified *and* experienced. Otherwise, that's some sort of discrimination, I'm sure. Maybe cuz of my father."

"Captain," Mrs. Sparrow calmly bristled. "First of all, it is not a right to be entrusted with the lives of dozens of people, not to mention equipment worth vigintillions of pesos. Second, if there ever was any paternally-based discrimination, it was always in your favor, a fact you would acknowledge if you were being honest. And yes, you are a talented pilot and missionary, but a deeply flawed leader. Those who have worked with you or under you simply detest you. You have been demonstrably bad for morale, bad for recruitment and retention. Performance scores for those around you have been predictably and chronically below average. You've been the cause of dozens of complaints, several lawsuits and probably one suicide. In short, despite your talent and your famous last name, you are simply not worth the trouble."

At this point, Younas's talent and training went into action. He excelled under stress, and this ship was clearly plummeting to disaster. At that moment, he convinced himself that he was contrite. His demeanor followed his lead.

"Although I can't confess here to any of the charges you listed," he said, "I wish I could, at least to some of them." He paused for thought. "You all know that I was recently ill. And sure, a lot of people wouldn't see it as a serious illness, though I was septic for a spell. But for a guy like me, it's the kind of disease that can change your life, open your eyes. They say hormones affect our brains, and they're right. In that way, I wouldn't call what I had a sickness but a treatment, maybe even a cure. It made me realize that I was sick in other ways."

Younas was not a great actor, but he was good. He took another dramatic moment of silence. He then wound up and delivered his punchline. "It's one thing to find out you have a disease. But when you find out you *are* a disease, well, where do you go for that?"

"Then you're a changed, man?" challenged Garcia. "Is that what you're telling the honorable members of this commission?"

"I'm saying I've started down that road," Younas meekly replied. "I think if you review my psych eval, you'll see that."

Hastings chimed in. "Captain Younas, we are neither shrink nor pastor. We are only here today to determine if you are suitable for the job and, if not, what steps need to be taken, if any."

"What are your goals?" asked Sparrow. "What do you hope to accomplish?"

"Ma'am?"

Sparrow tried again. "To put it another way, why do you keep coming back to a career for which you seem ill-fitted?"

Younas's answer came easy. "First, I love to fly. Those of you who know me know that. And it's ironic, but being cooped up for months on a ship is less claustrophobic than being on Dundo, you know? Once you've seen a real sky, it gets hard living underground after a while."

Sparrow tried to wrap up. "Well, thank you very much for—"

"There's also the service part," added Younas. "A guy like me spends a lot of time focusing on himself. When I've been out of work for a while, I start to get sick of myself. This job, this career helps me refocus on working for others, for my shipmates, for Dundo and mankind."

Sparrow paused to make sure he had finished. "Thank you, Captain. We need to discuss. Why don't you go find some lunch and return in an hour."

Upon returning from break, Younas learned his fate. He would be reinstated after he had completed approved training courses in the following subjects:

- Compassion for the Calorically Challenged
- TransSpecies Sensitivity
- Menopausal Mindfulness
- Passion with Compassion: Sex Worker Sympathy
- Understanding Nerds and Weirdos

The decision annoyed Younas but also impressed him. It was a good move for the commission. It got him off their back for a year or two, since the courses were not scheduled consecutively, and the commission only met four times per year. They hoped, he figured, that during that time he would either lose interest or be unable to maintain his credentials.

Later that day, he sat on his balcony while the town's backlights gradually dimmed to simulate the fall of night. He watched the small lights projected on the cavern ceiling. They were supposed to look like stars but were generated randomly, without any basis in astronomical reality. Still, they looked pretty, even though they amused him. He continued to watch through the advertisements that were projected regularly onto the cavern "sky." He watched and sipped his cocktail.

Younas had a drinking problem. He didn't drink regularly and only occasionally drank excessively. His problem was that, when under the influence, he became a sadist. It was a problem that sometimes caught up with him, as it would a month later.

He was taking the class on Weirdos. During the first two classes, another student gave him a few looks of familiarity. He also recognized her, but didn't know from where, and didn't care because she was fat. But he would care after the third and final class. He was walking down a side street when he suddenly found himself on the ground, being kicked from all sides by the same woman, her husband and a third man.

"Sick bastard!" she yelled. There was little else to clue him as to why this was happening, until she added "Stay away from my kid!"

Aha. That statement, along with one more stomp on his head, jarred his memory before he passed out. He had been at a social gathering some time back, mixing boredom and alcohol into an ornery state. He fired up a conversation with a young boy, about his son's age. During the chat, he convinced the boy that he was good friends with the boy's parents. He gradually gained his trust, at least enough to deliver his punchline. He confided that the parents were keeping a secret. The boy's mother, lied Younas, was dying. The boy was old enough to keep the secret for several days, just long enough to become very ill and depressed.

The day after the assault, Younas awoke in the hospital and declined to press charges. He rarely pressed charges. He had a weird moral code of get-even-ism, and now everything balanced. Besides, he knew he had a much bigger beating coming from the family of Patrick Kendrick.

"Patches," as Patrick was known, was mildly retarded. He was just old enough and smart enough to make his own decisions, but young and stupid enough to make bad ones. His worst decision had been to befriend Younas, who he admired and visited frequently. Younas took advantage of the situation to amuse himself by convincing Patches to get one tattoo after another, one piercing after another.

Then one day, Younas had a few too many drinks and determined to convince Patches to pierce his own eyeball. It was a hard sell, but Younas had talent.

"No, it's not over the colored part," Younas told him. "Of course nobody does that. You do it in the corner, near where the eyelids meet."

"I never seen anybody do that," Patches contested.

"You're right. I've only seen it once myself. But I never forgot that guy. He was totally sick. You would be razor edge."

Younas drove the sale home by offering to help him do it.

Our involuntary nervous system is very protective of our eyes, but it can be overcome. That day, Younas could not overcome it enough to complete the piercing, but did manage to do serious damage, resulting in hemorrhage, infection and partial blindness. That's the kind of man Christopher Younas was when he drank. But even he did not suspect vengeance when he got the call.

# TWELVE

As we age, the fatty layer at the base of our skin melts away, resulting in wrinkling. The veins that were suspended in that layer no longer are. Any kind of traction tears them, and the skin bruises easily. For similar reasons, the brain also shrivels in the elderly, and the so-called *bridging veins* between the brain and the skull become more vulnerable to the same, shearing forces.

However, unlike the skin, the brain is enclosed in a vault. So when an intruder smashed Sarah Younas in the face with her best frying pan, her skin had the entire world in which to expand. Thus, her face became bruised and swollen with hematoma. But the blood that rapidly accumulated in her skull had nowhere to go. It could only push on her brain, squeezing it through the small hole at the base of her skull. Her brain stem was compressed, her breathing stopped, and she died quickly on the floor of her kitchen.

Mrs. Younas had been a widow with just a few, close friends. She was level-headed, pleasant and good. So, when her son Christopher got the call, he never suspected vengeance. He reacted first with disbelief. It didn't make sense because of SITS.

Centuries ago, the universal adoption of the Surgically Implanted Tracking System had nearly eliminated all premeditated crime from humanity. It was simple – at birth, every person had a device implanted that would emit a radio signal throughout one's life. The signal was weak, but strong enough to be detected and recorded by a local positioning system. With the spread of humanity to new worlds came less crowding, and with that, a renewed interest in privacy. Authorities needed a warrant to access and review tracking data.

The tracking devices were originally inserted subcutaneously, but that proved easy to remove by determined, nefarious types. Now they were inserted at birth, deep into the umbilical vein near the liver. Babies were delivered in rooms heated to body temperature, which allowed the vein to remain patent long enough to do the procedure.

A man like Younas, who never knew life before SITS, could not conceive of passionless crime. But his mother was too boring to stir passion. He concluded that the culprits must have been irrational – either intoxicated or crazy. In any case, SITS would give answers.

His second reaction was indifference. It had been years since he had seen or spoken with his mother. She lived hundreds of miles away and they had not been fond of each other. Instead of sadness, in typical narcissistic fashion, he was upset that he was not upset. He felt that he should be sad about his mother's passing, and he didn't like the idea of something else being wrong with him.

He next reacted with dread. The traveling, the red tape, the family members, ugh! It was worse than he expected, as the first person he saw at the funeral home was his third ex. She had heard about his latest mistreatment of their son, and greeted Younas with yelling. "What the hell is wrong with you?" and "Why don't you just do everyone a favor and kill yourself?" She sometimes lowered her tone and got serious, pleading with him as she had done so many times before. "If you really love our son, if you really want him to have a chance at being a normal, healthy, happy kid, just stay away from him, huh? Give him a chance. He deserves a chance." Etc. etc. blah blah.

Younas let her tire herself out, then brushed past her to see his brother, who he loved. Sammy Younas was the only man that Chris would hug, and a long, tearful embrace did Sam now give. Sammy, unlike Chris, could cry. He differed from the rest of the Younases in many ways, and thoroughly from Chris. He too had a government job – a low-level bureaucrat. He had neither smarts nor ambition, but he was honest, loving and happy-go-lucky. He was the only person in the world who never criticized Chris and never scolded him. Were it not for those big, brown Younas eyes, Chris would have been sure that Sam was adopted. He sometimes wished that Sam would be more like him. But deeper inside, he wished the reverse.

"Why would anyone do this, Chris? To Mama? It doesn't make any sense at all," Sam protested through tears, still hugging his brother.

Chris gently reassured him. "Soon. We'll find out soon."

Sam let go and turned to embrace his own, beautiful family – a wife and two daughters. Meanwhile, a well-dressed stranger pulled Christopher aside. He was some sort of constable.

"That may not be entirely correct," the officer said.

"Excuse me?"

The detective, named Lipton, explained. "I'm saying it may not be that easy to bring this case to justice. Not soon anyways."

"Aw, man," scoffed Younas. "Are you telling me this was done by someone connected?" He meant government connections.

Lipton lowered his voice and looked around to ensure nobody else heard. "I'm saying we don't yet know who did this."

The whole notion was alien to Younas, and he took a moment to process it. But Lipton had heard of such cases.

"How is that possible?"

"Before I say, I need to ask you," Lipton began. "Was your mother involved in your father's business in any way?"

Younas answered quickly and certainly. "Not a smidgen."

Lipton opened a satchel he had been carrying labeled "Crime Stuff." He said "I want to show you something." He pulled out a crude device with a monitor. He pushed a few buttons and held it up for Younas to watch. A map of Sarah Younas's flat displayed on the screen. A single point of light wandered through it.

Lipton pointed to the dot. "You see that? That's your mother's tracker. She's moving around, doing her thing, moving, moving. Then right there, she stops. That's when she's murdered."

Younas rubbed his rough chin, then completed Lipton's point, which was a lack of a point, or more accurately, lack of two points. "There's no second person in the flat," he said.

"Killed by a ghost," said Lipton, clicking off his machine. "And actually, these are called just that – Ghost Crimes. There's only two possible explanations for them. Either someone in the government was powerful enough to have the data removed, or someone went underground to have their tracker removed. That's very expensive and usually only happens in organized crime. I'm thinking, in your mom's case, the latter very unlikely. And if it's the former, then I figure *you* are the key to solving this."

Younas raised his hand haltingly. "Look," he said, "I haven't had contact with my mother in years. I have no knowledge of any involvement she had with Magellan or any other part of the government. She was just a housewife, and I really don't know why anyone would want her dead."

"That is quite a definitive statement," said Lipton. "Do you mind if I put it through lie detection?"

Younas consented and Lipton again reached in his bag, pulled out an envelope, and opened it to reveal a petri dish. He uncovered the dish, held it four centimeters from Younas's mouth, tilted it to a 45-degree angle, and had Younas repeat his statement. He then opened a small bottle and carefully squeezed out three drops of indicator. Younas passed. Lipton thanked him and asked him to call if anything came to mind.

"I'll call you if I think of anything, but I aint gonna rack my brain," said Younas flippantly. "I don't know anything and couldn't care less if this is solved."

Lipton quietly nodded, then went over to talk to Sammy. At that moment, Christopher realized that the case was indeed important to solve for Sammy's sake. But, unfortunately, several weeks passed without a clue. Younas even paid a visit to Baldric Silver who, along with Andrew Younas, used to run Magellan.

Younas, who was a neat freak, didn't like to visit old Baldric. His flat was immersed in piles of memorabilia, interspersed with half-hidden, half-eaten bits of food of sundry ages. There were geological samples from worlds light years away, samples enough to fill a museum. What's worse, sometimes Younas would find something he thought a space specimen but turned out to be an old morsel. The entire place seemed to be coated with a fine film. And to make matters ironic, Baldric always insisted that guests remove shoes.

"Christopher! Come in come in," he said with a pat on the back. "I am so very sorry to hear about your mother. She was a wonderful person." He lowered his voice as if being spied. "You know, I always said she was too good for your old man, God rest their souls. Are you doing ok? Ok good. Tell me, did they ever find out who committed that senseless, awful crime?"

Baldric's timely knowledge did not surprise Younas. Though he looked a hermit, Baldric still maintained plenty of contacts at Magellan. And though he sometimes acted a coot, Younas knew it was an act, and that Baldric Silver was still as slick and sharp as his own father used to be.

"No, and I wanted to ask you about that," replied Younas. "If anyone would have any information or insight into the motive of this thing, it would be you."

"Oh Christopher, you came all the way over here to ask me that? You could have called."

"I wanted to ask you in person."

"Captain Younas, this doesn't seem like you to care so much, even if it is your mother."

"It's for Sammy," said Younas.

"Oh, of course. Then I'll tell you what I told the police, and I passed lie detection. Sarah Younas was a good woman and a homemaker, nothing more. Every day, she made Andy two sandwiches to take to work, one for the commute and one for lunch. She had dinner hot and ready when he came home. He never involved her in the agency, never brought his work home, and I highly doubt he ever confided in her anything that was classified."

"He must have," countered Younas. "It's the only thing that makes sense."

Baldric put a hand on Younas's shoulder. "Christopher," he said, looking far off. "Do you know how human sacrifice was born as a tradition? Millions of years ago, some poor bastard was murdered, and the next day it rained. The point is, sometimes there is no connection, it just looks that way. SITS is an aging system. It needs renovation. Perhaps your mother's killer is simply the first one to expose that fact."

Ever a cynic, Younas assumed that Baldric was full of it. But he also knew that he could not match the old man's wits and, besides, he had done all he could. He had gone "above and beyond" like they say. He knew it, Sammy would know it too, and that was good enough. He would give Sam a full, empty report when he went to visit him in a few days.

Sam had invited him over for supper with the family, an event which Chris routinely told himself that he hated. Mrs. Younas would make meatloaf *again* (he craved it). The two brats would climb on him and bombard him with their incessant yammering (he loved it), and Sam would spend the evening flashing his silly grin.

It all came to pass except the grinning. Chris couldn't remember ever seeing his baby brother so down. Sam was still in the clear, however. Officially, he was not yet nuts. Years ago, the Dundo legislature passed, in conjunction with the Dundo Psychology Association, a resolution declaring twelve weeks to be the normal human duration for healthy grief. That time period had been determined by a committee of experts. Centuries earlier, the same kind of committee had determined that there was no such thing as magic, and that love was strictly a physiological process. Such bold statements came with advances in mankind's understanding of the Why Wave.

They passed the evening reminiscing up on Sam's balcony. They both agreed that their mother had been a saint for staying with the old man all those years. They also discussed the consequences of her death and the task of helping the kids to cope. But most of the time they spent just trying to understand why.

"I've been over this a hundred times from a hundred angles," said Sam. "I've poured over every aspect of my job and everyone I work with. But my brain just gives me bupkis."

"Ya, me too," said Chris, as he stood up to leave.

Sam also rose to give Chris one of his famous hugs. Sam's hugs were strong and sincere, like he hadn't seen you in years and would not for years more. This one was longer and more pathetic than what Chris was used to, but he didn't mind.

Through his tears, Sam whispered something equally unusual. "We have to find God, brother."

Standing on a balcony, three stories up, on a sad but peaceful evening, Chris Younas had exactly 2.9 seconds to ponder that statement. Then he felt it – a sharp, hot slap in his face accompanied by the taste of blood on his lips. And though briefly stunned, Chris was still holding Sam, but Sam had let go.

And as he realized what had happened, Chris, a man who could not be alarmed, shook with terror from the yawning exit wound at the corner of his brother's neck and shoulder. A moment later, he was again Captain Younas. He gently lowered his dying brother, then rushed past the still unaware family to do a self-check. In a mirror, he saw himself covered in blood and tissue, but without injury.

Sam's wife grimaced with horror at the sight of his gory appearance. Her girls launched a pitiful mix of screams and wails as he grabbed them and ordered them to follow. He rushed all three down the hall to the neighboring flat and told everyone three things: This is an emergency, call the police and stay here.

Suspecting that this murder was also untraceable, he sprinted down the hall, then raced down the stairs towards the exit. He had quickly assessed that Sam had been shot from across the street, probably the ground floor. Younas was no cop and no hero, but he was brave enough to keep running across the street, then along the front of the other building, looking in all the doors and windows. As he ran past one flat, he noticed the lone occupant lying on the floor. He stopped, doubled back, hopped the gate and entered.

The man lay dead, probably for several hours by the look of him. Younas cautiously and quietly inspected the apartment, careful not to touch anything. He ran through the building, searching the halls and knocking on doors. Nobody had seen anything.

Unsure of what to do, he went back to Sam's and awaited the police. His brain was a din of racing thoughts, the loudest of them being the realization that these crimes did not orbit his mother, and that he was the likely center of these events. But that thought, though increasingly obvious, still baffled him. He had many enemies and had been threatened many times. He even owed a couple of bookies. But he could think of no offense so heinous, nor any foe so depraved as to make conceivable the idea that someone would kill his family. But there it was, as plain as the Sammy stains on his shirt. This meant that others were in danger – his son, his relatives, maybe his friends.

Back at Sam's there were lots of questions, lots of crying, and lots of police. Sam's wife went to stay with her mother. After a phone call, Younas's ex did the same. The next day, his fears were realized when Lipton called to inform him that his brother had indeed been killed by a ghost. Even before he got the call, he had made up his mind to take a trip to his old stomping ground, Brooktown.

Brooktown, one of his favorite hangouts, was where one went to do things that were at least turpitudinous, if not illegal. Geology played a large part in its nefarious evolution. Its uneven cavern floor had plenty of craters and gullies. Before the cavern could be sealed and made livable, these irregularities had to be smoothed, so they were filled in with plain old sand. But the sand could be easily excavated, leaving a nice hiding space under the plastic ground. A small space could store contraband. A larger one could hide people engaged in illegal activity. So came to be Mount Brooktown, a mysterious pile of sand that appeared one day in the town park. Over the years, it continued to grow until it was big as a building. It naturally attracted children who would naturally climb and play on it, then sink to the center and die of asphyxiation. The town dealt with the problem the cheapest way possible, by covering the whole thing in cement. But kids still got hurt and sand still kept appearing. The town resealed the mound several times with softer material. Then, one day, the sand stopped coming. The crooks had dug all they were going to dig. There it stood for a hundred years, a giant eyesore covered in graffiti. Then one day, an imaginative young artist came along, carved it into an abstract shape and painted it. After that, it was still an eyesore, but a little fancier.

Another problem that arose from the illicit deconstruction was that the secret, underground chambers were not always properly sealed. As a result, the residents of Brooktown sometimes endured flooding or leaking gases that occasionally made their way through the Dundo crust.

Now, Younas headed there to hunt down the one guy he knew that might know how to get a SITS tracer removed. Peter Panther was a criminal multitasker, a busy fellow with hands in lots of pockets and a long list of associates. He was also a Feline. Younas didn't like Felines. He thought they were ugly and dumb.

The story of the Felines goes back centuries. Long ago, the unhappy people of the world found a new craze in which to immerse themselves and mutilate themselves. They took the concept of Crazy Cat Lady to a whole new level. First came the societies and the clothes and the customs that Kitty Kulture adopted. Then came cat worship and cat marriage. Then came the surgeries, the bizarre public behaviors, and other cries for attention and belonging. Inevitably came the court orders declaring that cat people were, in fact, cats.

Eventually, with advances in genetic engineering came the ability to design children with feline features. After a few generations of inbreeding and improvements in the lab, the modern Felines evolved. They had high cheek bones and small, pointy ears. But it was their eyes that came the closest, and their eyes that most bugged Younas. They were cat's eyes, vertical and fluorescent.

He also hated the way Felines rolled their R's. Through years of self-imposed isolation, the Felines had developed many strange habits. They even hissed when threatened.

Younas had tried calling Panther but couldn't reach him, so he checked the most likely spots. He went to the dog fights; Felines loved dog fights. He checked the Haters Club, where all kinds of illegal topics and views were openly discussed and exchanged.

Next, he checked the Sadist Society. The Society was like a brothel, except you didn't pay for sex. You paid to beat the snot out of someone, a person called a Punching Bag. Bags, like whores, often had costumes and could play roles, most commonly those of infamous celebrities. It was an obviously brief career, and exclusively attracted Dundo's most desperate wretches.

Younas made his way down a short side street which dead-ended at a small grocery store open unusually late. He entered and greeted the clerk. "Hey, Skippy, how's things?"

Skippy smiled. "Chris, how you doin'? I ain't seen you in an ice age."

Younas knew The State had suppressed the story of his mother and would probably also for his brother. The State quashed all news it deemed likely to be embarrassing. That was fine with him, for he didn't feel like talking about it, so he didn't tell Skip that a tempest of fear and anger and sadness raged within him.

Instead, he grinned and lied. "Ya, I've been trying to lay low, get back to work, etc." Some more small talk before he got to the point. "Skip, I'm looking for P.P. You seen him?"

"Ya sure, Chris. He's downstairs. Go on down."

Skip welcomed him behind the counter and opened a well-concealed door in the floor. Down went Younas. The stairs ended in a cement hall, dimly lit, resembling a bomb shelter. He passed several doors from which could be heard muffled noises from soundproofed rooms. Younas recognized the sounds – the yelling, the whipping, the whimpering. It also smelled familiar – a sickly combination of sweat, Moondust (a commonly smoked stimulant), and a hint of blood. Occasionally, when the beatings intensified, a whiff of urine or feces joined the mix.

The last two rooms were open, an office and a break room. In the break room, a couple of enormous bouncers relaxed. In the office stood a single, small desk at which sat a shirtless, overweight Feline. He glanced up at Younas, then raised an index finger, signaling him to wait.

Peter Panther then went back to concentrating on the task at hand. He opened a small case and pulled out two droppers, one painted black to protect the contents from light. From the case came other items – a razor, an alcohol swab, pair of tweezers and some packing strip. He cut off a section of packing strip. Onto it, he squeezed two drops from each bottle. With the last drop, the strip lit with a glow of ultramarine blue. He continued to ignore Younas as he proceeded with care and concentration. He scrubbed a small area of his forearm with the alcohol, then made a small, but deep incision. The next steps he did quickly, before he could bleed too much. Using the tweezers, he stuffed the entire strip into the incision. He then covered the wound with a chilled, moist wash cloth which he held firmly in place as he reclined and relaxed.

Within a minute, his entire body emitted the same blue glow, save his yellow cat's eyes. The irises contrasted eerily with his blue sclera and white teeth, teeth that radiated a silly grin. He looked quite content and detached, and Younas knew that he was high from Trizzian salt. A rare and expensive mineral, the salt was only found only on Stivus-7, a remote moon. It awakened your deepest and fondest childhood memories, replaying them in your mind's eye with vivid clarity.

Panther stared off distantly. The cadence and pitch of his voice changed, and he began to talk like a child, babbling to someone named Buttons. Younas knew that he would be occupied for the next couple of hours.

"Geez P.P.," he said, as he left for the break room. "You could've talked to me before you got started with all that."

Compared to the rest of the complex, the break room was rather opulent, and Younas took in some refreshments and conversation. In came a scrawny fellow, drenched with sweat, breath slightly labored, forearms scratched up.

"Man, I wish I had known about the place sooner," he said. "It's great exercise and keeps me from killing my boss."

Sitting across from him, one bouncer leaned forward and stared firmly in his eyes. "Oy, you want to know how the other end feels?" he asked.

The man looked perplexed. His smile shrank. "What?"

"You've got a razor peeking out of your hand tape," the bouncer said calmly. "You know the rules. No cutting." He then moved with a speed which did not surprise Younas. He had seen it before. The bouncer grabbed the man by wrist and nape, and wrenched his arm. "Out you go," he said, as he marched him down the hall.

Panther was grumpy when he finally came around, suffering the drug's depressive postdrome. "Chrrristopher, I ain't in the mood for visitors," he cautioned. "Where you been anyways? Did you go soft when you lost your balls?" He then remembered something and mollified his tone. "Hey, sorrry about your ma. It's a very sick thing what happened." Panther had a way of knowing things that weren't in the news.

Younas, who was also not in the mood, replied "I guess you didn't hear about my brother."

Panther sat up and sobered up. He had not heard. "No, are you kidding me?"

"Yup," said Younas. "Shot by a sniper. Died in my arms."

"Chrrris, what have you done?"

"I don't know," Younas answered. "That's why I'm here. Turns out they were both ghost murders. I figure if anyone would know how to get a tracker deleted, it'd be you."

"Deleted? What for?" Panther scoffed. "If I want to whack someone I bring 'em down here. You know these vaults are SITS-proof."

"Ya, but," Younas countered "if you can't get someone down here. Maybe you can only get them in their own home, a long way from Brooktown."

Panther looked at his monitor, trying to ignore his guest. "Nah, I don't know about things like that," he said dismissively.

Younas thought about grabbing Panther's razor, lunging at him and holding it to his neck, or perhaps to one of his creepy eyes. But he knew that Panther, like his Punching Bags, had an alarm on his person, one that would bring the bouncers running. So he kept cool and instead tried flattery.

"See, I don't believe that," he said. "There's a reason, no there are two reasons why I came to you first, why I trekked down to Brooktown and spent all day looking for you. One is that you're the guy. There ain't no network of wires or people that runs broader and deeper than that head of yours. You know. You always know."

Panther raised a halting hand, but Younas pressed on. Younas was not a great actor, but he was good, and his current emotional state enhanced his talent, which he now milked. His voice cracked, choking back tears. He trembled just a little.

"But there's another reason." He pointed at Panther. "You're a decent cat. You always were. I figured if there was anyone who had the heart to help me, knowing the situation I was in, it'd be you. See, I remember things, like the time that guy died here, the guy with the really nice shoes. You remember that? It was nobody's fault, but the boys wanted to strip him. And you said no. You took his money and rings and even those shoes, and you sent them right back to his widow. Or how about that time you were gonna cut off that guy's finger who owed you money? At first, you just went for the left hand, you know, instinctively. But then you stopped. You remembered some people are left-handed, so you asked him. See? That's considerate."

"Alright alright!" said Panther, his hand still raised. "You're gonna make me cough up a furball. I'll tell you what I know if you'll just shut up. But I don't know much. My businesses are not routinely violent. But there's a guy, a doctor actually, Creeper."

"Creeper?"

"Ya, that's his real name. I don't know where he fits in. He could be a middleman or the actual guy who does the thing. What you do is make an appointment with him. I'm sure there's a code word or a phrase or something. I don't know it. But even if I did, if he doesn't know you, if he's not expecting you, you're gonna die. He works with people who do not mess around."

Younas sighed. "Well, Petey, to tell you the truth, I'm not sure I've got much longer to live anyways."

It was late. Younas rented a room and a mini-car. The next day, he learned that Dr. Creeper would not be seeing patients in the office that day, only the hospital. Apparently, he was a big-shot surgeon. On the Dundo web, it was easy to get someone's picture, usually in 3-D, and often in VR video. So Younas had a clear picture of whom he sought as he parked across from the hospital parking garage. All day, he watched through a scope as people left. Hours he waited until his mark finally showed – a tall, lanky fellow with somewhat oriental features, riding a bicycle.

On the narrow streets of Dundo, the prospect of surreptitiously tailing a bicycle with a car seemed unlikely. So Younas, who was still pretty athletic, got out and ran after the oblivious doctor. Creeper lived nearby and went straight home to his large, ritzy apartment complex. He checked in his bike at a small storage facility between the main entrance and the parking garage. While he did, Younas, who was a few meters away, changed his tactics, from skulking to stalking in plain view. He adjusted his pace, arrived at the entrance one step ahead of his prey, and held the door for him. He was struck by Creeper's size, at least 6'5". His thin bent torso and gangling arms had the air of a praying mantis.

In the foyer, Creeper turned right, bypassing the lift and continuing down a hall. Younas stalled in the foyer and watched the odd creature walk away, making note of which flat he entered. Customarily, downscale tenants, not doctors, lived on the ground floor. This twist concerned Younas, whose experience had taught him that small surprises often concealed big consequences. But at least ground floors are easy to surveil from outside, and it seemed that this mission could be finished sooner than he had thought. But outside, he learned that the doctor's windows were mirrored one way, so he went back in.

He listened at Creeper's door and heard nothing. He braced himself and knocked. No answer. He listened. No sound. He knocked again. Still nothing. He tried the knob. The door was locked, but not tightly. There was a slight give. He braced again and kicked it in.

Nobody home. He searched every room and found nothing until he entered the walk-in closet. There, the rug had been moved, revealing another secret door in the floor. Cautiously and quietly, he opened it a crack and peered through.

At the bottom of a ladder, about five meters down, there appeared to be a small, dimly-lit operating room. Off to the side, three meters from the ladder, Creeper hunched over a desk in a small alcove, writing, unaware. On Dundo, five meters is a long way to jump…too long. The element of surprise was pointless if the result would be to end up on Creeper's subterranean procedure table. So instead, he again opted for the tactic of stealth in plain sight. He moved quickly to avoid giving Creeper time to think.

He flung the door open and yelled, "Hello?" Without a pause, he began descending the ladder, speaking as he climbed. "I'm sorry. I knocked, but nobody answered. I hope I'm not—"

Creeper looked up and froze, his face fixed in a look of rattled concern. But he quickly thawed before Younas could finish his sentence. He opened one desk drawer, then another. Younas leapt off the ladder and tackled him as he reached for something in that second drawer. Creeper's head struck a wall, knocking him out. Younas rolled him on his back and mounted his chest. He pulled out his favorite hunting knife, a gift from his father. He held it near Creeper's throat and awaited his arousal, which came momentarily.

"Easy, big fella," he cautioned as Creeper tried to stir. He leaned forward, pressing his left palm firmly against Creeper's brow. With his right hand, he pressed his blade on the throat. "Now I'm guessing that you know enough anatomy to know that you're in a pickle right now."

Creeper stared back, looking mostly annoyed. He stayed silent, so Younas continued.

"I'm looking for a guy who can extract my SITS tracer, and I'm thinking that guy is you."

Creeper spoke up. "Corrupt," he said.

"What?"

"It's called corruption. I don't extract them, I disable them. But my clientele is small, I'm not taking new patients and I don't do walk-ins."

"Oh, I'm not a customer," said Younas. "What I am is the face of death if you don't give me what I want."

A hint of anger showed on Creeper's face. "I have friends, scary people," he said. "If you kill me, you will get caught. Everyone does. In prison, they will torture you, then they will kill you."

Younas replied by punching him straight in the face, still clutching his knife. He leaned forward even more, putting his face within kissing distance. His voice softened.

"Dr. Creeper, you look in my eyes and you tell me. Do I look like I'm worried about dying?"

Creeper looked for a second. "Not right now," he said. "But you will. What do you want?"

"I'm hunting a killer who's hunting me," said Younas. "A ghost killer. You're the ghost maker. So tell me who he is."

"I do not know who is he. I do not know who are you," replied Creeper.

Younas sat up a little and calmed a little. "Then give me a list. Even crooks keep records."

"It is not a big list," warned Creeper. "Not a high-volume procedure. I have not done a corruption in months."

Younas scoffed. With a wave of his hand, he pointed around the room. "Are you trying to say the mob built you this creepy little cave so you could do a couple jobs a year?"

"I do other things," replied Younas.

"Like what?"

A wicked glint flashed across Creeper's eyes. "I torture," he said with a slight smirk. "Sometimes for interrogation, sometimes punishment. Also, the occasional abortion."

Abortion had been banned in Dundo for over fifty years because of things learned from Why Waves. For thousands of years after their discovery, their cryptic energy remained elusive. We never learned how to generate them but we did learn how to receive, amplify and transduce them. Such knowledge initially proved of limited value, only good for a few tricks.

It was good for matchmaking, using a nifty gadget called the Wifinder. People would attend giant events called Affairs where women took turns being in the Hot Seat. The seated woman would don a device resembling a metallic hair net. It connected by cable to another one which the men lined up to try on. Once both nets were on, it only took a second for the two potential suitors to know if they were simpatico. Next.

Besides that, few other uses were discovered for Why Wave technology, and it was ignored for centuries. Then, about a hundred years ago, the Empathizer was invented. The first model filled a room, and people had to make appointments to use it. It was eventually miniaturized to the more marketable size of a book, which became popular at parties. Like Wifinder, it made use of helmets and cables, each of which plugged into the Empathizer.

You couldn't read minds with it. Thoughts and memories are not conveyed by Why Waves. Rather, it allowed the users to connect with each other on a level not previously possible by two incompatible or unfamiliar people. Even harmonious couples required years spent together in order to achieve the same sensation that the Empathizer provided within twenty minutes.

It soon found other uses. It became widely used in diplomacy, and government summits would routinely begin with an "Empathy Session." But the most profound step came when a transponder, the size of a microchip, was developed to replace the helmet. The chip could be inserted in utero and affixed to a baby's head.

Before that, abortions had been common due to the many decades that Dundo women stayed fertile and thus prone to unexpected pregnancies. But after this new technology, any public support for abortion was quickly replaced by outrage.

Dr. Creeper still performed them. And he kept lists of everything.

"All my records are stored here," he said, pointing to his temple.

Younas pressed the blade harder, breaking skin and drawing blood. "That's too bad for you," he said, "because I'm afraid that will not do."

Creeper's eyes suddenly bugged with fear as he felt the sharp edge creep closer to his carotid artery. "I also have a hard copy," he blurted. "If you will remove my left shoe."

"You do it," said Younas, and he moved to assume back control. With his right hand, he maintained the knife's position, albeit clumsily. With his left, he grabbed Creeper's left wrist. He then dismounted him, allowing him to sit up. As Creeper rose, Younas moved behind him and sat against him. His legs wrapped Creeper's waist, his chest pressed against his back, and he pulled the wrist into handcuff position. The surgeon leaned forward and, with his free hand, slipped off his left shoe. His middle toe looked like the others, long and crooked; but when he pinched the end of it, it clicked. He slipped the prosthetic toe off his foot. A connecting pin protruded from it, one which fit into a hand-held device – a crude, customized computer. Creeper kept the device in the same drawer as the alarm he had tried to trigger minutes ago.

Because the gadget could not transfer data, Younas rolled his eyes… twice… counterclockwise. That triggered the video recorder in his contact lenses. He would later review the data using the same lenses. Known as Eye Phones, they were used by Dundoers to read, communicate and some other things. You could tell when a Dundo teen was texting, for their eyes would flit about like they were having seizures.

While scanning the monitor, Younas relaxed enough to become curious. "Exactly how do you disable the SITS tracer?" he asked.

"I fry it with a magnet. Powerful magnet inserted laparoscopically."

On finishing his recording, Younas thanked the good doctor for his hospitality and left him with a warning. "I have these records now. You'd be wise to forget this whole thing, because if I get so much as a heebie or a jeebie, I'll send this stuff straight to the cops, and then you'll be as dead as me."

Creeper's records showed that he'd only done eight corruptions over twenty years. Younas didn't recognize any of the names. Over the next weeks, he did all he could to find his connection to any of them, but he was no detective. He was also impeded by caution since these were eight dangerous people whose notice he must avoid. He thus limited his investigation to web searches and cross-searches. He showed the list to Panther and a couple of others. He did manage to learn that two of them had died years ago. Beyond that, all taps were dry.


Meanwhile, another man who *was* a detective also sought a link to Younas. Lipton sat at home, whipping brain and body over a new case. Most Dundo police worked from home. Crime was rare enough that most towns had neither patrols nor stations. Instead, the police worked and lived in the nearest police township, in this case Hundun-65. Like the others, Hundun-65 had a jail, a prison, an armory, a courthouse, some small office buildings and a residential area.

This wasn't Lipton's case. The crime had actually occurred thousands of kilometers away, but he had been consulted because it was another ghost murder. Three in three months meant there was a link. There had to be. Yet the third victim was as remote in circumstance as in distance.

Henrik Jallolaby had lived 220 years, well beyond a life expectancy on Dundo. It seemed pointless to murder such an old man, but that's what happened when someone threw him off his tenth-floor balcony. Police conducted a thorough genetics check; the victim was unrelated to the Younases. Background checks and multiple interviews had so far failed to reveal any business or social ties either. He was a retired vice president of a pharmaceutical company. No criminal record. "Boring," thought Lipton.

Perhaps the victim bored him, but the case did not. This one had a witness, the caretaker. Lipton reread the notes of her interview:

*A knock on the door. Caretaker answered. Perpetrator pushed past her without a word. Young-to-middle aged male, brown hair cut high and tight, brown wide-set eyes, about 5'10". No scars or tattoos. Void of expression or inflection. He walked over to Victim and asked his name. Victim replied by asking the perpetrator for his name. Perpetrator introduced himself as Eris Drol. (Note: Not in database. Determined to be false and is, in fact, anadromic, backwardly spelling "Lord's Ire"). Victim then answered, "I am Henrik Jallolaby. What can I do for you, friend?" Perpetrator then grasped victim's hand and held it. He whispered in victim's ear for about a half minute. Victim was seated at the time. During that time, victim's face turned grave. Perpetrator then lifted victim, threw him over his shoulder, walked to the balcony and threw him off. Perpetrator left as he came, calm and quiet.*

There were still more interviews to be done, and Lipton was tasked with that of Chris Younas. The two men sat on Younas's balcony, sipped wine and discussed. Lipton showed a picture, a computerized composite generated by the witness. Younas didn't recognize him. The day before, he had submitted a list, requested by Lipton, of everyone he had ever known. From his memory and records, he managed to produce about five thousand names, minus a few that he chose to withhold. Now, he and Lipton reviewed some of the highlights, and cross-referenced a list made from Jallolaby's life. There were actually quite a lot of shared names, as Jallolaby had once lived on this side of Dundo. They also scrutinized Younas's tax records, looking for crossed business paths.

Nothing came from any of it and, in the end, Younas learned more than Lipton. He learned that these murders may not be personal after all, a thought which intrigued him. It was late by the time Lipton left, and the city lights cast strange shadows on Younas's face as he studied the drawing. Perhaps, he thought, these were not mob executions but were indeed some dastardly doings of high state.

He lowered the picture and gazed towards the sky. His brain continued. "It's one or the other. Either the tracer or the data was destroyed." Then a new thought entered his mind. "Unless there never was a tracer at all."

At that second, he could delve no further, for a sudden choking sensation demanded his attention. He pulled with desperation and futility at the fabric that wrapped his neck. The assailant had waited in hiding, in his shower. When ready, he had twisted the shower curtain into a rope. Now, he stood behind Younas and pulled with all his strength, his foot planted in Younas's back for leverage. Younas struggled, and the sum of forces caused him to fall forward, knocking over furniture, landing face down in shards of wine glass. The intruder maintained his grip and his foot, now standing firmly on his victim. He now held a terrific advantage, and he used the moment to grab his other tool, the curtain rod. He wrap the curtain, entwined the rod and turned, using torque to twist, and twist to choke.

Younas's head filled with blood and adrenaline, and he was getting dizzy. In moments, it would be drained of oxygen as well, and he would pass out for the last time. But before that, he was still sharp enough to remember the sharp thing in his boot. He bent a knee and reached. He grabbed his favorite hunting knife and began to saw frantically at the material. The sharp blade proved a fair match for the fabric, and it took endless seconds to cut through. But cut through he did, lacerating his own neck in the process.

The killer, Baja, looked around for a weapon while Younas caught his breath. Baja picked up a small, stone flowerpot and lifted it overhead. Younas rolled over and escaped, rolling away as Baja threw it at his head. Younas jumped to his feet, staggering a bit, blinded by some dirt from the pot. Baja lunged, knocking him on his back and landing on top. Younas was still clutching his knife, but he was stunned, blind, and easily disarmed. A few blinks gave him enough vision in his right eye to see the tip of that knife being plunged towards it. With both hands, he grabbed and blocked the attacking forearm. A struggle ensued, as Baja enlisted his free hand. But Younas was bigger and stronger, and held him off. Baja pushed harder, leaning all his weight in the effort, which gave Younas an advantage. He abruptly pulled the knife down and to the right, thereby redirecting his opponent's effort and inertia. Baja fell forcefully on his own right shoulder. As he tried to get back up, Younas scrambled and secured him in side control. A quick kimura move disabled and disarmed Baja, and Younas grabbed the knife. Rage, rage and wine overwhelmed any forethought as he sank the blade into Baja's heart. Still in a position of side control, he held it in place for a moment, wiggling it to expand the wound. His head rested on Baja's chest, his face soaked with blood.

After resting a moment, he got up to check the mirror because he still couldn't see leftwards. The eyeball poured blood, having been lacerated by a flying shard of flowerpot. He closed it and applied direct pressure for ten minutes. Still bleeding. Still holding the eye, he fumbled around the bathroom until he found his first aid kit. He pulled out the styptic laser pen, the one marked KEEP AWAY FROM EYES. He leaned towards the mirror, bit down on a washcloth and cauterized the wound. The bleeding stopped… almost. A bit more pressure, a bit more time, and eventually the oozing stopped. Next, he got two bottles from his kit, one containing saline, with which he briefly flushed. From the other, marked "Dr. Goewey's Stem Cell Solution," he instilled a few drops. Some gauze and tape made for a makeshift eye patch. That would have to do for now. He would avoid the police and hospital, for he still did not know if his government just tried to kill him.

He repeated the ordeal for his neck wound, then went back to look at the man who had taken his eye, and presumably his brother and mother. Baja lay lifeless. Younas stood and stared a moment, released an ugly scream, and gave the corpse a few good kicks. Then he calmed and sat on the floor to study Baja's face. He didn't resemble the picture very much, but he did look familiar; perhaps someone he knew or someone from the television. Younas searched him, but Baja traveled lightly. He had been dressed to prowl. In his pockets, Younas found a key, a durable snack and some pills. No identification and nothing more. A dead end. He rubbed his fingers through his locks trying to milk his brain for thought. One soon came – Eye Phone. With two fingers, he spread Baja's dead left eyelids and looked. Yes, there was a lens. He removed it, washed it and donned it. Looking through its files, he was first impressed by how voraciously Baja had read. The subjects were mostly on Dundo, its history, its politics, customs, geography and such. Baja had conducted a lot of web research, most of the tracks of which had been deleted. Besides that, not much else. Some travel logs and receipts, all meaningless to Younas's untrained eye. One item did pique his interest – a scheduled appointment for a tattoo. He rolled up Baja's sleeves and saw nothing. He lifted his shirt. Still nothing. He cut all clothing off the corpse and turned on every light; inspected every inch of skin, including between the toes, behind the ears, through the scalp and into the gluteal cleft. Still nothing.

Perhaps Baja had chickened out. But Younas, who had no tattoos of his own, still knew of one other possibility. He went to the kitchen, found some cooking oil, and proceeded to coat the body, massaging every pore. He found his UV flashlight and turned out all the others. In the dark, the cadaver glistened eidolically in the dim, blue light. Younas repeated his survey and there it was, on the left wrist, oriented to be read like a watch – a series of numbers and letters fluorescing yellow. He recognized the first 5 digits, DR65H, as being nearly identical to the DR65M header for all of Dundo's ship access codes.

He knew his next move and embarked on it without hesitation. He packed a bag, washed up and left for the airport. He didn't know what dangers he faced, but he was a seasoned explorer. He had been the first human to set foot on new, often hostile worlds and had lost nothing compared to his losses at home. He feared less the notion of flying into orbit to scout a mysterious craft than that of calling the police and waiting at home.

His eye throbbed and, by the time he reached the surface, he had a severe headache. At the Tube station, he coped by taking too much sedative. In the pod, he fell asleep. The drug gave him crazy dreams. They started off familiarly enough. He dreamed, as he sometimes did, about his brother around age ten. But this time, Sam spoke with an adult voice and not his own, and he talked about God instead of ball. He sprouted angelic wings which filled the room as they unfurled. Then, a wound appeared on Sam's neck, just above the clavicle. It rapidly deepened and expanded to include the shoulder. Blood cascaded as the crater grew. Younas panicked. He applied pressure, first one-hand, then two-hands, then used his shirt. The cataract continued as Younas despaired. Sam just shrugged and hugged him.

"Chris, you don't understand," he said. "When bad things happen, God is either testing you or punishing you, or using you for a higher purpose. You can't know which and you can't stop it. All you can do is try not to deserve it."

The dream changed after that, morphing into a more familiar scene. Younas found himself alone, buried alive, struggling to get out, struggling to breathe. This was a common dream among Dundoers and a recurring one for him. He remained asleep when his pod arrived and for an hour after, until someone discovered and wakened him. Groggy and weak, he staggered to a restroom and regarded the mirror. The bandage on his neck was blood-soaked. He was a sad and frightful spectacle. He tended the wound and changed the dressing, cringing all the while. A comb through his hair, a splash on his face, and a moment for mirror meditation; then off to the hangar.

Younas had a plane, a two-seater, another legacy from his father. He loved her and would kiss her on the nose before boarding. As she powered up, a series of harmonious tones mounted into a familiar symphony, pulsating and resonating pleasingly in his brain. He flew manually for the first few kilometers after departure. When he reached enough altitude, he entered Baja's code into the navigation system which thankfully recognized it. He sat back and relaxed as the Dundo Air Traffic (DAT) System took control, guiding him through the thick, psychedelic display of Dundo's atmosphere – a visual extravaganza of formations and systems, and mixtures of hydrogen, ammonia, oxygen, water, and other lesser actors.

He was treated to an encore when he reached the outer Plasmasphere. At that moment, Dundo's magnetic field was being distorted by its largest moon in such a way that it drew the solar wind straight to his area. The atmosphere around him, rich in ionized helium, lit up in fantastic streaks and plumes of pink. Soon enough, the atmosphere faded to black and he saw millions of miles into space. With rapid calculation, the DAT system put him into a wide, decaying orbit, the trajectory of which would meet that of the Bucephalus after three full revolutions. It would take several hours and he was still very tired. He fought off sleep, fearing more nightmares, but eventually succumbed. He both lost and won the battle, for he slept without dream, and so got some painless rest.

An alarm woke him up, notifying him of his arrival. He looked around and saw the Bucephalus rapidly approaching him from the rear. At that point, the DAT system shut off, returning him to manual control. He descended, allowing the other ship to pass overhead, then he came up behind it. The strange craft had unfamiliar markings. Cuboid in shape, it spanned four stories. Three contiguous sides were concave. Those surfaces were iridescent, composed of material designed to harness either signals or power or both. The remaining, opposing sides were convex, each one of them different. The history of what must have been a long journey was written on them in scars – radiation burns and dings from debris. One convex side was opaque with hints of transparency peeking through. It had once provided a window for the living quarters before the decades scuffed it useless. Two small propulsion engines protruded from two adjacent corners, right angled to each other.

Younas watched for a while as the ship raced through its orbit just ahead of him. One or both of its rockets would occasionally fire to correct the occasional drift. He wondered why nobody had contacted him, for he knew his presence must be known. A ship's crew was notified whenever someone used its access code. He decided it pointless to be either cowardly or coy, and so sent a hailing signal. No reply. He waited patiently, then tried several other frequencies. Nothing. He tried an audio signal. Still nothing.

When he had had enough, he sent a different signal. Using the access code, he beamed a boarding command, to which the ship responded. It rotated until one of its convex sides directly faced him. The top half of the exterior wall then lifted and curled inside like a garage door, revealing a small, empty bay. He entered and disembarked, and waited a while for someone to receive him. Nobody did, which made burgeon his suspicion that the ship was lifeless. All was quiet, save the music of familiar sounds – the low hum of understated ship power, the soft whisper of vents and pipes, the occasional crackle of electrical fields, the occasional chirp of an alarm, and the regular, foreign chatter between computers.

He strained to see in the dim light. The hangar was rectangular with a high ceiling, about two stories. At one end, he could see a section of the large window he had seen from outside. Two doors were centered in the long, proximal wall, spaced about six meters apart. Cautiously, quietly, he tried the closer one on the right. It opened to reveal a hall which extended nine meters before turning left. A door stood halfway down on the right. He peeked in to see a workshop cluttered with tools, machines and parts. In the far-right corner of the hall were a lift and ladder. He passed them both and turned the corner. The second leg of the hall was nearly identical – nine meters long, a door halfway down on the right. That door opened to a storage room in which he looked around. It contained all the basics – medical supplies, cleaning supplies, cooking supplies, communication equipment. There was also some basic equipment for exploration – protective suits, survival gear, testing equipment and a couple of ATVs. He sniffed a couple of containers, pocketed a couple of items and left. He continued to follow the hall to a third, identical section, off of which he found a small clinic. Still no life. He tended to his wounds and continued. At the end of the hall, a closed door led back to the bay.

He backtracked to the lift. It wasn't exactly a lift, though it was called that. Elevators were too piggish of power and space to be of use in a small ship. Instead, a vertical conveyor belt extended through a hole in the ceiling and floor. A velcro loop material covered the belt's surface. Another belt was the one that Younas wore around his waist and through his crotch, like a jock strap. Called a Flight Utility Belt, it had been standard gear for a millennium. Woven into its fabric were circuits, four transmitters and four buttons on the right hip. Each button caused each transmitter to send a different signal. A wide variety of machines were standardized to respond to these four, universal signals. The lift responded to two of them – one for up, one for down. The belt also happened to have something else woven into its back – strips of Velcro hooks. He simply backed up to the lift, pressed a button, and up he went.

The top, fourth floor was of little interest. Nonetheless, he searched every room – the rec room, gym, kitchen, dining area and farm – all in search of a clue as to why he was there.

Down to the second floor, the lift put him in the corner of another hall nearly identical to that on the third floor where he first landed. The hall traced a square path around the warp engine, which could be heard through its inner wall. Its external wall contained doors which led to a bathroom, a storage room and three living quarters. The first suite was furnished but empty, and did not appear to have ever been used.

The second suite was nearly empty, with only a few personal items to indicate that anyone had ever lived there, including some photos of a couple at various stages of life. The least faded pictures had the most faded smiles, the few without the little girl. Her curly locks and beaming visage still filled and warmed the otherwise barren place. Younas figured she must be dead, for a girl like that does not stop getting photographed. The later pictures without her seemed nothing more than obligatory.

Unlike the second suite, the third one still bore the faint stench of prolonged human presence. The place was a mess, filled with stuff, mostly clothes and such, but also a curious clutter of sculptures. Dozens of figures and dioramas of varying size had been tightly twisted into existence out of wire and strips of metal, the culmination of talent and lots of time. People and scenes from history and literature, as well as strangers, ships and animals lay strewn about – a stark contrast between the care and diligence of their creation, and the neglect and contempt that followed. Some pieces had even been stepped on. One sculpture was apparently but not obviously a portrait of Baja, or perhaps his father, its features distorted, wicked and grotesque. Baja's image was also present in several photos, all very old, all in the company of his parents, his father being his spitting image.

Younas proceeded to search and examine everything. After an hour, he found a case in a drawer. Secure and shiny, it looked like a business card case. An Optical Recognition Chip (ORC) nestled inside. About the size of a thumbnail, an ORC was nothing more than a powerful flash drive designed to interact with an Eye Phone. He held up the plain, black piece of plastic in front of his good eye, which still wore Baja's lens. At the ORC's center, smaller than a gnat, was a red dot on which he fixed his vision. He continued to stare and concentrate until he saw a flash of light, at which point he knew the data had downloaded.

The ORC contained a large library of books and Baja's own copious files. There were voluminous written notes and a video diary containing thousands of hours, organized chronologically. As per his nature, Younas skipped all that and went straight for the photos. Most of them showed Baja's parents in their younger years. They were from Dundo, well-educated and had lots of friends. He grew bored and impatient, and quickened his perusing pace until he was flying through them – candid shots, parties, trips, ceremonies, weddings. And suddenly, there it was, and there he froze. A picture of their wedding party, the Baja couple radiant and beautiful, to their side the best man and his wife, Andrew and Sarah Younas.

He took a moment to be astonished, then slowed his browsing to a more careful pace. He reviewed more pictures and indeed found his parents in many of them. They were so young that he barely recognized them. In fact, most of the pictures of Baja's parents were made in the first three or four decades of their lives, at least in these albums. The rest were taken aboard the Bucephalus.

Wait a minute. How could that be? The pictures showed that Baja's parents lived well into their crumbling years. He had heard of people spending years, even lifetimes in space, but everyone lands. "You reach your port, you're all cooped up," he thought. "You get off the ship, you stretch your legs, and surely you take a picture or two." He looked again. Nope, definitely no terrestrial shots of the parents beyond a certain age, and none of Baja himself. "Were they reclusive? Were they nuts? Did they spend all those years just orbiting Dundo? No, not on a government vessel."

Then a light went on as he remembered where he had seen Baja before – a big news story, months back, about a returning member of the Pioneers. Younas wasn't much for news, but that had caught his attention. He couldn't remember many details, partly because few had been released. Things were getting weird. These weren't assassins. They were Cobblestones and friends.

Next, he turned to the harder stuff, the written files. Most of them bored him – manuals, procedures, personnel records, military junk. Some of the ship's data was stored here, and he learned some details of its unprecedented journey – Beta Geminorum, round trip of fifty light years, 160 years spent in space. It had only spent a few months actually orbiting the destination.

The health records were unremarkable, except that Mrs. Baja had taken one drug for decades, called GestArrest. In the same folder, he found some literature on it and a phase-3 study. Younas had never heard of GestArrest. Its brief time on the market had been before his birth. Its makers had capitalized on the rising opposition to, and ultimate ban of, abortion. GestArrest offered an alternative – halting a baby's gestation for as long as the mother took the drug. Its slogan – "Don't kill Junior. Put him in Time Out." Its time on the market was short, only a few years. The manufacturer recalled it after long-term use was found to be associated with several problems, chief among them being madness and leukemia. The health records were mostly Chinese to him and he glossed over them. But he did pause to do a search on GestArrest. From what he learned, he deduced why, in the pictures, there looked to be an age difference of at least seventy years between Baja and his mother. He realized, on closer inspection, that she had spent much of her life in an early, but visibly evident pregnancy.

He took a break, ate a snack, and used the bathroom before tackling the video library. He sorted the files by size and ignored most of the small ones. Scanning the titles, he homed in on one called The Oath. It was about an hour long.

The scene centered on an adolescent Jacob Baja, kneeling on a floor mat from the workshop. He wore an oversized, slightly worn, military uniform and somberly bowed his head. Off to the side, his father and the other guy sat in witness, or perhaps in judgment. Standing beside young Baja stood his mother Ann, gently massaging his scalp. She exuded authority and, when the event began, it became clear that she was the master of whatever this was. On her head sat a diadem of leaves and twisted branches. She extended an aged hand which young Baja took and kissed. She smiled a loving smile and spoke in a soft, noble voice.

"Neither aeons nor armies shall this bond break," she said.

Lifting her chin and her voice, she marched around the room. She circled her son, sometimes reading, sometimes reciting a collage from various religions, philosophies and her own crazy creations. Her voice fluctuated, her hands gesticulated, sometimes raising to the heavens. Occasionally, she knelt beside him and they recited together. As strange as it was, the event seemed highly choreographed.

She recited from the Book of Skip, the self-proclaimed prophet from Planet Visa. Younas had heard of Skip. Everyone had. Skip had only two rules for his small band of followers, the Skippers – tolerate everything and judge nothing. The religion proved untenable. Their glorious compound soon fell into disrepair and decay. Supplies dwindled to nothing. The Skippers starved or deserted. Finally, when Skip had nothing left to offer but his tolerance, the Skippers killed him and auctioned off his body on g-Bay. Ironically, that is when Skipping really took off. The twelve-year auction was a spectacle across the human race, and Skip became a legend. It didn't take long after for him to gain martyrdom, then sainthood and beyond. A new generation of Skippers made some practical rule revisions, and the religion blossomed (or metastasized). The Book of Skip was a verbal tradition, memorized by his followers. His words were never written, so as to avoid discriminating against the illiterate. Whenever someone pointed out that the Book still discriminated against deaf people, the subject was quickly changed to The Damned Jews.

Mrs. Baja also performed some interpretive dancing in the style of the Gayalics. The Gayalics considered themselves pagans. They worshipped Nature and an unseen force of good that runs through it, a force called Gob. Whenever someone pointed out that Gob sounds an awful lot like God, Gayalics would quickly reply that Gob is different. Gob wears a nice hat.

At certain points in the ritual, the two men chimed in, confirming Mrs. Baja's declarations with an "Amen," or answering her questions.

"What do we want?" she would demand.

"Justice," they would sing in hymnal tones.

"When do we want it?"

"Now."

At one point, Baja's father left. He returned with a tray upon which lay some kind of desiccated steak with a tail. A steam or vapor emanated from it. Younas, who had been getting bored until then, sat up with curiosity. For one thing, it was unheard of for meat to be present aboard a ship. In addition, the dish itself was unrecognizable, even to Younas, who had some experience in processing game.

Mrs. Baja received the tray and laid it on the floor before her son. The two faced each other, the strange entrée between them. As she wept and stroked his face, she again whispered "Neither aeon nor army nor Armageddon itself shall this bond break."

With that statement, young Baja grabbed the meat with both hands and began to eat. The placenta was tough, and gustation was slow. It must have also been unpleasant, for he wretched twice or thrice. He never vomited, though, and got through the whole thing.

She spoke while he ate. "This bond, that nourished our souls and nourished your body for most of a century, will nourish you once again. It will not be broken, but rather become a part of you, as I am a part of you."

The tray was taken away and the second course brought forth – a large basin of water. Young Baja proceeded to wash himself in ritualistic fashion. He anointed his face and head. He purified his mouth, arms and feet. The baptism complete, he put the basin aside and turned to face the two men. They, in turn, got up and together lifted something off the floor – a small piece of machinery, perhaps a motor, attached to both ends of a chain. Baja bent forward. He braced his knees with his palms as they hung the chain on the base of his neck. As they reseated, he struggled a bit with his new necklace. A knee buckled as he adjusted his feet, his face grimacing but stern.

Ann now spoke. "Feel the burden of the oath you now take. Stiffen your back and strengthen your resolve." She paused for a few minutes, giving him time to obey, then continued. "Do you swear, my son, before the Almighty God and His witnesses, to live a life of honor and virtue?"

Baja grunted a bit, but his voice rang clearly. "I swear so," he replied.

"Do you swear to devote your life to the pursuit of justice for all and retribution for your family?" she challenged.

"I swear so."

"Will you always subordinate other devotions, oaths and loyalties to those of your God, your family, and this oath you now swear?"

He swore so.

"Then rise, my love," she beamed as the chain was removed. "Rise as a man, as a paladin, as God's sword of justice."

Everyone smiled and took turns embracing him. Then they sat to listen as he nervously began to recite a speech.

"My beloved family, I stand before you as a new man, a man made for a single purpose, a purpose not of my choosing. That's nothing new, really. In that, I share the company of billions of people through history, both kings and slaves. But in this age, when so many do make their own paths, it is a weird existence. I am simultaneously cursed and blessed, as if Janus had donned the masks of Melpomene and Thalia. In my life, I pledge to focus on the comedy of it.

"In the beginning, we all are evicted from the womb's sanctuary without any idea of the significance of our own births, if any even exists. We then spend decades gathering a lifetime of knowledge and experience. Yet we never come one inch closer than that new baby, no closer to knowing if that fateful day ever mattered at all. The benefit of a life of purpose is that little of it is wasted agonizing over such questions to which there are no answers. My purpose is my first and greatest birthday present, given to me by my parents, guided by God.

"From my father, a good man who served his fellow man with honor in this very uniform. This uniform, worn and faded from the loyal execution of duty, is a more glorious garment than the shiniest new suit. It is in this uniform and by these hands that our enemies will know lex talionis, in this life or in their grave. I swear it.

"And from my mother, my guardian angel, God's greatest mercy. There are no words to describe my love for you except to say that my true life's purpose is to please you. The gate of heaven lies at our mothers' feet. Oedipus was not so great a sinner. His iniquity lay in degree, not direction.

"But don't worry, dad," he joked. "Sleep easily, but have an extra helping of lard. Mother, I swear to you now that never, neither in this life nor long after heaven has reclaimed you, will you taste the bitterness of discomfiture."

There was more to the video, but Younas was getting bored again and his eye was hurting, so he moved on to other things. He rummaged through a closet which contained mostly dull, personal items – a wedding gown, some baby toys, more pictures, all that crap. Underneath it all one item stood out – a soft, green case about the size of a book. Its broken seal bore the familiar mark of Magellan – a cursive M superimposed on a sextant. A title, "The Columbus Mission," was emblazoned on the front. Inside he found something he had never before seen – printed material. It was not paper, of course, but rather pages of thin plastic. Still, it was quite novel, and novella in size. He flipped through it to find detailed maps of an unknown world, detailed anatomy of an unknown creature, and a dictionary of translation. Slouched on the floor, he sat up, went back to the beginning and read the background. Seven hundred and thirty-two years prior, the unthinkable happened. A Space-time Capsule returned.

The subject of Space-time Capsules had been briefly covered early in his training, but it was on one of his daydreaming days. A very simple project, the Space-time Capsule was a cheap, durable hard drive that contained the entire human history and volumes of information about us. A thousand years ago, a million of them were launched in a million different directions with one purpose – to litter a cold universe with the news that the human race once existed.

They were never supposed to come back, but one did. It had been rewritten with new data about another life form more advanced than ours. The news was kept top secret while communication went back and forth. Each message took decades to reach its destination. More information was exchanged, as well as kind words. Ultimately, inevitably, plans were made.

"This is incredible!" he shouted as he read on. The mission of the Bucephalus had been to journey to the nearest settlement of our new friends, whose name could only be approximated by sounding out the letters Pthlanjk. Because the round trip would take more than one generation, the crew had another assignment during their trip – to breed. Upon arrival, some members were to stay as ambassadors, while others would return home with data and samples. A complimentary mission of Pthlanjk-ians was to likewise do the same.

Younas's eyes widened. He jumped up, dropped the dossier, and raced down to level one to find the sample containers. He cut through the cockpit and entered the warehouse, which was just big enough for six, large shipping containers. In a corner of the room, a large structure housed one of the ship's propulsion rockets. It briefly released a muffled roar, hinting at the power within.

The nearest container he knew to be for small samples, designed like a walk-in closet of closets. He entered it and opened every door. Behind every door, he opened every smaller door, every drawer and every bin of every size. Everything was empty. A bit befuddled, he only said "Humph" and moved on to the next container – a single room that was also empty. "What the…?" The next two containers were temperature-controlled, one oven and one freezer. The oven was off and empty. But the door handle to the freezer felt cool. His excitement returned as he hoisted the door open with both hands. Lying within, in the center of the floor, lay a perfectly preserved, perfectly dead Ann Baja.

# THIRTEEN

A knock at the door awoke Baldric Silver from his chair nap. It was an odd knock, feminine in pitch but delivered with confident authority, like that of a small policewoman. He opened the door and smiled widely. "Mimi!" he cheered. He leaned in to kiss Mrs. Sparrow's cheek. She dodged and gave him a light hug.

"Hello, Baldy," she said, brushing past him. Her eyes scanned the place as she entered. With subtle stealth, she rubbed the nearest chair with her index finger, then rubbed finger against thumb. Having assessed the level of filth, she pulled a handkerchief from her purse. She patted her brow with it while he was looking, then placed it on a chair when he was not. Then she sat.

"What a nice treat. Can I get you something? Tea perhaps?"

"Thank you, no. I shan't be long."

He sat. "Well, I figured you were here on business. You wouldn't come otherwise."

"Now why would I need to discuss business with a man who's been retired for nine years?" She raised a thin, sharp eyebrow.

"Mimi, are you being sarcastic or sardonic?"

She smiled a small smile and politely lied. "Facetious."

He waved her on. "Come on then. Let's have it."

"Another murder victim turned up three days ago. Care to take a stab?"

He said nothing for a moment; just sat and looked concerned. "Chris Younas," he eventually guessed.

She leaned over and cheerfully reported, "Wrong." She smacked his knee lightly for emphasis. "It was our own space hero, Captain Baja. He was actually found at the home of Younas. Poor Christopher. We have him in special custody, you know. Letting him sweat for a bit. Obviously, given the sensitivity of the situation, we had to mop it all up, seize jurisdiction, seal potential leaks, etc. All courtesy of our friends at PASS."

The People's Agency for Special Security was a secret police force tasked with all kinds of government nastiness. Many people had heard of PASS, but only a few knew that it really existed.

"Pass-holes," grunted Silver.

Sparrow sat back and relaxed in her chair, feeling satisfied. "You don't like surprises, do you, Baldy? Well, I've got another one for you. I've been working with PASS quite a bit lately. It started when this Baja fellow turned up and so much of his mission was redacted beyond my clearance. I appealed upstairs and *they* couldn't access the files. Then I knew we had a problem, and I knew the problem was you. So we called PASS and went before the Special Magistrate to request agency collaboration. I must say they have been very helpful. You know, it turns out that one need not torment many of your lackeys in order to breach your wall of secrecy. You just need to find the right one, well-connected keystone and break him. And of course, we all knew who your most trusted lieutenants are. Or should I say 'were'?

"And then… well, you certainly were a busy, naughty boy, weren't you? But still I did not discover the extent of your damage until Captain Baja turned up muerto. It turns out he's the killer of two Younases, and an old man named Jallolaby who you paid to falsify drug data. I assume you were next. You must be relieved. We've been through Baja's things and I have a team scouring his ship as we speak. I'll soon know nearly everything about all this sordid business."

Silver was somber, his face grim. He contemplated a moment. "Then why are you here?" he asked bluntly.

"Oh, a couple of reasons. Obviously, one can't learn everything by combing files, particularly the Why. And that is an important question, isn't it? What was the point of this phony mission of yours?"

"The point!" he said angrily. He paused to calm down. "The point was the same as it had always been – Keep Going. Isn't that the Magellan motto? But our core was the Pioneer Corps, and it was dead. We couldn't recruit anymore. Mankind had new homes and new lives. And when life isn't that bad, nobody wants to explore space. And definitely nobody wants to start a family, to *raise* a family in space! On a Cobblestone mission? Are you kidding me? But that's what it takes nowadays, when the distances keep increasing exponentially.

He stopped to rub his temples. "You can't imagine all the converging pressures. Dear old mother earth breathing down our neck, budgets being slashed, mining companies needing to survive. Hundreds of jobs, thousands of lives. And then Fisher Labs came out with their report – piles and piles of Sillinium in the Beta Geminorum system. Oh Mimi, it was just too much."

Mrs. Sparrow sighed. "And your answer was to invent this cockamamie Columbus Mission. How in hell did you ever convince anyone of that ridiculous dossier?"

"It's like anything else," he said. "You start with the people you know, the people closest to you. Andrew went to his closest friends. I sent my own nephew and his annoying wife. I think I did them a favor, frankly."

"But you didn't really think it through, did you? You didn't think about the consequences, should the missionaries return."

"Are you kidding?" He puffed his chest. "I am a visionary, honey. You should be thanking me. How many bureaucrats, or corporations for that matter, are thinking one or two hundred years into the future? The fate of these Cobblestones and whatever tantrum they can throw is a small price compared to the benefits that Man will reap from this one, highly successful mission. We can manage any fall-out from this."

"We?" She shook her head. "Even now, your arrogance is stunning. This stunt of yours has done enormous damage to the agency. It is a major embarrassment. Just to keep it lidded, *if* we can, will sap resources and morale. And who's to say we can? Captain Baja is a fresh, famous hero." She looked aside and spoke to herself. "Oh my, I bet he still has press interviews scheduled."

She looked back to Silver. "Baldric Silver, the Silver Serpent. Isn't that what they used to call you? The living proof that perception of power *is* indeed power. You and Andrew spent decades turning the Dundo branch of Magellan into your own little fiefdom. Then he died. So unexpected and mysterious was that. And years after you were forced out, you were still running the place. You have no title. You can't fire anyone, can't suspend anyone, can't even revoke a meal ticket. Yet a full one third of our staff still answered to you. But I've been taking care of that, you see, dismantling your power base. I came to realize that there were three kinds of Silver Servants. There were the genuine votaries. Then there was the second group who simply feared the first group. And the third group were people who simply did your bidding out of habit."

Silver huffed. "You keep talking about me in the past tense, as if I don't still have the talent and the strength to bounce back."

"Oh, Baldy," she said, rising from her seat. "You still don't realize how far you've fallen." She calmly walked around his chair and approached him from behind. "The man who can't be surprised has another one coming." She leaned over to whisper in his ear. "I told you I came for a couple of reasons. A couple means two." He turned in his chair to face her as she reached into her purse. She pulled out a small device which resembled a key fob.

"What's this?"

"It's a present from PASS. It's one of those radiofrequency toxins, completely untraceable. This one activates a clotting factor. I just aim it at you and press this button, and I can give you a stroke or a heart attack. Or if I simply back up a step, I can give you something terrible called DIC. Yes, let's do that."

She took one step backwards, pressed the button and held it for five seconds. In that time, he barely had a second to raise a finger in protest. In the remaining four, his skin turned gray, then mottled like a marble statue; his eyes turned vacant, and he dropped dead.

# FOURTEEN

On the Bucephalus, Captain Younas felt exhausted from three things that drain a body – injury, travel and overwhelming emotions which now included bewilderment. The weird videos of the weird crew, the amazing Columbus report, the empty containers and now this cadaver. It was all too confusing. He decided to fight off sleep and review more video logs, but there were just too many. He did find a period, when young Baja would have been about forty, when the entries were much shorter and far less frequent. Some of them were only a few seconds long. During that period, Ann Baja had passed away, leaving her son as the last survivor of the Bucephalus. He didn't take it well. He often went days without eating and weeks without bathing. He also took to rambling quite a bit. Buried in one of his tirades, Younas found the reason that Sammy had been murdered.

"I will make Andrew Younas and Baldric Silver pray for the first time in their wretched, demonic lives," declared Baja. "They will pray for death, but it will not come. And if they're already dead, then I will make them cry out from their graves. And if they've somehow conned their way into heaven, then I'll torment them in paradise."

Younas didn't blink. He was numb from fatigue. A Sleep Box rested in the corner – a plain empty box that was equipped with sensory deprivation, temperature control and zero gravity. He crawled in and went out.

He was awakened sometime later by a man or woman in a government-issued hazard suit. The person summoned two others while Younas collected his wits and adjusted to the light. The three suits conferred a moment, then one grabbed his arm and gestured him to come. A man's voice said, "Here, take this," and held out a capsule.

"What is it?"

"Compliance pill. We're detaining you."

"You mean arresting me. I think I'll pass."

"Look, you can take it, or I can paralyze you. But if I do that, then I gotta carry you, and I ain't got the strongest back, so I'm liable to drop you."

Younas glared, then grumbled and glared, then took the pill. For the next 18-24 hours, depending on his metabolism, he would follow every command he was given. He was still able to make editorial comments and snarky quips, and snark away he did. He had plenty of opportunity, as he had to endure the double-barreled bureaucracy of going through customs and detention processing.

A litany of dumb questions, such as "What is your pain level on a scale of 0-10?" were met with such answers as "I got a 10 out of 10 pain in my ass called You."

"Do you have any venereal diseases?"

"I'm not sure. How's your mom been lately?"

"Do you require a translator?"

"¿Que?"

You can imagine.

He was scanned and decontaminated. His wounds were treated, but his eyesight couldn't be restored. He was read aloud twenty minutes of notices and disclaimers, and made to watch a video on jail safety.

He was back underground and had hardly stepped off the lift when he was blindfolded. Distress quickly pushed its way to the fore of his already crowded mind. Yet, he still managed to get out a wisecrack. "Aw, c'mon guys. Blind People Day was weeks ago."

He was transported a long distance by tube, taking several hours and needing several stops to stretch and breathe. Along the way, the compliance pill started to wear off and he became tempted to remove his blindfold. But whenever he began, the escorting agent simply said "Don't do that" and he had to stop. He kept trying occasionally, but there was still too much drug in his blood. After a while, he began feeling warm, then hot. This was a strange feeling on Dundo, and he thought he must be somewhere unfamiliar, somewhere remote. When he finally reached the end, he was helped from the tube onto uneven ground. To help with balance, he was allowed to remove the blinder.

He found himself in an unusually small cavern, no bigger than a mall parking lot, unsettled and unfinished with jagged walls. There were rocks here, something that few Dundoers ever saw in their plastic-lined lives. A few, crude roads had been smoothed out of the rock floor to allow the movement of heavy machinery. He saw machines of excavation, of mining and mystery. Most of them were manned and busy, making a horrible din. There were also air conditioners and, on exiting the tube, his breathing got better though his hearing got worse. His eyes also strained, for there wasn't the usual, artificial daylight that pervaded the towns of Dundo. Instead, a variety of search lights were strewn about on stands and hung from the ceiling or placed wherever needed.

They crossed a section of the cavern, walking towards the left, using the roads when they could, and circumventing a small green pond. On the other side, they entered a ray that spanned only about five meters wide. The lighting was worse, but the floor was smooth and straight. They followed it for about a kilometer, after which it ended at a manmade wall containing a door. Behind it, in a plain room, a large, well-dressed man sat at a desk, eyes fixed on a HoPS (Holographically Projected Screen). A minute later, he looked up, got up and accepted custody of Younas.

He brought Younas through a side door and down a staircase, landing in a hall with three prison cells. A tinted, amber plastic formed the front wall of each cell, allowing easy viewing inward but not out. Grey, stone brick comprised the sides of each cell and the back was unaltered, black cavern rock.

The first cell was an extraordinary sight for a jail – well-furnished and decorated, with music barely audible through the wall. A well-dress, well-groomed, very old man reclined in a hover chair and read. He descried the two passing men, then looked up, sat up and got up. Straining to see, he rapped excitedly on the window and yelled.

"Hey, Rome. Who's this, Rome? Another inmate? Hello you. What's your name?"

The agent, apparently named Rome, replied curtly. "It's a noyb matter, Otto."

As they passed the prisoner, apparently named Otto, Younas spied the next cell. As they approached the empty, dim room awaiting him, his rising fear overcame his waning drug. He stopped in his tracks and braced his feet.

"I don't think I can do this, Agent Rome."

"Not an agent. I'm a specialist," said Rome, tugging on Younas's arm.

"Specialist Rome?" asked Younas, stalling for time. "That sounds kinda awkward. Is there a short for that?"

"It's Romano, and no there isn't."

Being a much bigger man, the specialist soon over-came his resistance. He worked Younas into an arm lock and marched him from behind. He pushed a button on his belt, and the wall of plexiglass became one of misty gas, held in place by an electrical field. He gave Younas a final shove through and re-pushed the button. The wall returned to solid state and Younas found himself looking through from the other side, straining to see out.

"Romano, wait!" he yelled, pressing against it. "I don't even know why—"

Romano's voice resonated artificially through the cell. "Lower your voice. I can hear you in my earpiece."

"I don't even know why I'm here or how long or anything. You told that other guy I was a noyb matter. What is noyb?"

"It's None Of Your Business," said Romano, and walked away.

"How can it be none of my business?" thought Younas. He posed the same question aloud.

No reply.

Younas looked around. Light and furniture were both sparse, and there was nothing to do but reflect. He had been arrested before, but never put in a real cell. He had only been punished virtually. He had been made to wear the Horror Helmet and spent the weekend dreaming that a bear was chasing him. Sure, it was rough, but you eventually figure out it's a dream and it's not so bad.

This was different. This was reality, as hard as Dundo rock, and it made him claustrophobic. You would think that a man who spent years in space would not get claustrophobic. You would be mistaken. Younas never thought of his ship as a container. To him, it felt more like a flight suit which allowed him to escape the bonds of gravity and the boundaries of stone, and stretch and soar in the great expanse.

His fear rose. The brave captain had absconded. In his place trembled a man at the lowest point of his life, in the deepest part of a deep world, with no company except his own. He was not facing death or danger, but something much worse.

He occasionally tried to lighten the torment by trying to converse with his jailor, but Rome rarely responded. However, Rome did regularly speak to Otto, a fact unknown to Younas, who was only privy to silence. Rome frequently worked alone. For many years, he had spent long shifts with no company except this one prisoner, and they were friends.

After a few days, Otto convinced Rome to let him to speak to Younas. After all, Otto didn't know anyone, wasn't going anywhere, and didn't get visitors. And so, one day, Younas heard a new voice in his cell.

"Hello, friend!" it said pleasantly.

"Hello!" said Younas, excited and thankful for the interruption. "Hello! Thank you for being kind. Who is this?"

"I'm your neighbor, and this is a kindness for me as well. My name is Otto, and yours? Christopher? Ah, a nice Exxonian name. Are you from there? No? How are you doing? Are you okay?"

"No, Pal. I am light years from okay."

"Christopher, I wish I could tell you how to adjust or when you'll adjust, but I've been here so long I can't remember. Tell me, why are you here?"

"I really don't know. I mean, I have some guesses, but… Hey, is this some kind of trick? If it is, don't bother, cuz I got nothing to hide."

Otto paused to carefully plan his next words. "Sir, I understand your suspicion and I am sorry for it. Please believe me when I say I don't want to start this conversation on the wrong note. I won't ask another word about you. We can talk about me if you like. It's just been decades since I had someone new with whom to converse. This is… you are nothing less than a milestone in my life. I certainly don't want to blow it."

Younas scoffed. "Well, *that* certainly didn't come off a state script." He relaxed a bit. "I don't know, Otto. That sounds like a lot of pressure, being your milestone and all. Does it come with a badge? An employee discount? Just what exactly are you in here for, anyways?"

"It comes, young man, with the chance to know a legend. I am the last man standing in the musical chairs of life. I am the greatest scapegoat in the history of goats. My name is Otto Frye."

"You're Otto the Oppressor," said Younas. "I hope you rot down here."

The trial of Otto the Oppressor was legend. Younas was just a child then, but he remembered it.

On Dundo, thanks to creative misfortune, everyone was officially a victim of something. Everyone except Otto. It didn't used to be that way. Dundo once teemed with people who didn't suffer, or at least didn't know that they did. But their numbers shrank with the discovery of more and more illnesses and exploitations. As they dwindled, so too did the size of the government checks that came regularly to Dundo's ever-growing list of unfortunates. Eventually, the money ran out completely and a massive audit ensued. The State conducted, then reconducted an emergency census. In the end, they could only find Otto. But Otto didn't have any money. You couldn't tax him and couldn't sue him. But you could blame him, so The State did what governments do best. They put on a show.

Everyone watched the trial. At first, Otto worked furiously with his lawyer to find something, anything wrong with him. The few, feeble ideas they had were quickly shot down in court. For example, it was not enough that he thought of himself as one quarter feline. He had to actually be so.

And it was not enough that his mother had miscarried her first pregnancy. Otto was ruled a first born, thus discarding his claim of Middle Child Syndrome.

The judge even disallowed his claim of paranoia because everyone actually did hate him.

It was fruitless; Otto simply didn't have any problems. His lawyer then turned to contesting the charge itself. He went through the details of Otto's life and argued that Otto had never bothered or harmed anyone. If anything, he usually acted kindly to his fellow man.

The prosecution, in turn, started with an old rule in Dundo law. "If there is an injury, then someone must be liable." From there, they invented a new legal concept, the Deduction Deduction. Simply put, one could deduce Otto's liability by deducting everyone else.

"I hope you rot down here," said Younas. "I got an Unspecified Personality Disorder and it's been a hard slog, thanks to you."

Otto felt neither offended nor bewildered by Younas' impertinence. He remained pleasant. "I guess I should expect your contempt. I guess I even asked for it many years ago."

"Yes, you did. Why did you switch your plea anyway?"

"I was feeling old. I had grown tired of working and was getting tired of people even before I was indicted. By the time the trial was half over, I learned to detest them. I wanted nothing more than to get away from them and to be cared for, in comfort, for the rest of my days. And when the trial's outcome started to become uncertain, we found the prosecution very receptive to our overtures of negotiation."

"That's why your jail cell looks like a penthouse."

"Any material wish I have is granted. I am only deprived of company which, I confess, I sometimes miss. In return, I am the gift that keeps giving. My story is taught in every school. My image is broadcast regularly on the news to show that Old Otto is still in jail. You see, I give the people a way to deal with their problems, if not solve them. It's not just a thankless job. It's three steps below that."

"Ya, you're a damn angel of mercy is what you are. Say Otto, what is this place, anyways?"

"It's a PASS facility, the People's Agency for Special Security. You must be in some special kind of trouble. You may be here to be interrogated or tormented, or perhaps just to rot alongside me."

The last thought gave Younas a shudder. He yelled aloud to Romano. "Hey, Romano, why am I here? Hey, Agent Asshole, answer me."

Otto interjected. "You shouldn't speak that way to Rome. He's our very gracious host."

Younas retorted. "What are you, a Stockholm case? He's a jerk. He sprained my arm, threw me to the floor and spat on me."

Then Otto got weird. "You lucky bastard," he bemoaned. "What I wouldn't give to be spat on by Romano."

Younas was left speechless.

He soon learned that Otto frequently said bizarre things. Yet, even if he was nuts, he was someone to talk to. Ironically, that kept Younas sane, like how something rough can smooth something else. Besides, Otto was smart and very educated. He had done little but read for the past half century. They had long conversations, though Otto did most of the talking. He taught Younas to meditate and pray. The meditation helped Younas calm and pass time. Prayers seemed pointless since they never got answered, but he did them anyways just to mix things up.

Younas also found other ways to pass time. He exercised – push-ups, sit-ups, squats and jumping jacks. He managed to make a game or primitive art out of nearly everything tangible, including his food, with which he played. He also made games of the intangible, creating mental challenges for himself; for his memory, math skills and concentration. These activities naturally evolved into a routine, and soon his day became as regimented as a ship's captain. So passed his time until three weeks later when visitors interrupted. He was immersed in meditation when Romano and another man, equally large and serious, entered the cell. Younas had become quite good at meditation and didn't even notice them 'til Rome nudged him.

Rome held out a capsule in his hand. The other fellow held a device in one hand, resembling a short cattle prod; in the other, a C-shaped object with metallic terminals and three buttons in the middle.

"You have a guest," said Rome. "Pill or paralyze?"

Younas' heart raced. "Who? What guest?"

"Pill or paralyze?"

He thought a minute, then took the pill. The two men left Younas for thirty minutes, enough time for the drug to work. They returned with Mimi Sparrow and a small chair. She sat.

"Hello, captain."

Younas tried to speak, but a crying spell suddenly overwhelmed him. He had not cried since childhood. Now he sat down on the floor, put his face in his hands, and bawled. Mrs. Sparrow sat and stared calmly for a minute. Then she squirmed a bit and exchanged glances with her escorts.

"Why am I here?!" he demanded, angry but still crying.

"My dear captain, don't pretend you don't know. You've been on a crime spree. You broke into a government vessel, trespassed on government property, accessed classified information. Above all, you murdered a planetary hero."

The crying died down. "No, I did not."

"Captain Baja."

"No."

"Savagely."

"No."

"Left him to rot in your home."

"No no no! It was self-defense and you know it!"

"Well, for all we know, you killed your family too."

He rose to attack, but she quickly yelled, "Sit down!" and he was chemically compelled to comply.

"I demand lie detection," he said.

"You can't have it."

"What do you mean? It's my right."

"You have no rights here," she said, matter-of-factly.

He tried to digest those last words, but they stuck in his chest. He didn't know what to say.

She continued. "Are we clear? Are we calm? No? Then we'll give you some time."

They left. Younas immediately began to look around for a makeshift weapon, but everything in his cell was either immovable or soft and light, unbreakable and rounded at the edges. He could only find things to throw in anger, things of which he promptly made use. A brief panic attack followed, complete with palpitations, smothering and a sense of doom. Once it receded, he could think again, but in frenzied racing thoughts. One after another, they bombarded him like a shower of meteors, each one scorching his brain. That continued for a half hour, until he decided to change the channel.

He knelt on the floor, bowed his head, clasped his hands tightly, and prayed the longest, most sincere prayer of his life. Here is an excerpt:

"Dear God, Almighty God. I know, and you know, we both know that, of all people, I've got the least right of anyone to ask for anything; probably even less than old Otto. But they say I can always ask anyway, so I'm gonna. Here goes.

"Please, please God, I'm begging you, get me out of this mess. Please send me home and let me build some kind of life for myself. And if that's asking too much, then please tell me what to do. Give me the wisdom to know if I should kill myself or carry on. And if I should end it, then please give me the guts to do it. And if I should keep going, then please give me the patience and endurance to do that. But I'd rather you just got me out of here and, if you do, then I swear I promise you won't regret it. I'll make you proud. I'm not exactly sure how, but I figure I'll be like old Scrooge after he woke up, running around in his new soul, being kind and generous and all.

"They also say that You know what's in my heart even better than I do. If that's true, then please just give it a scan. Feel around in there and see how sincere I am. After that, please *please* God, just give me a little taste of that abundant mercy that everyone says You have."

He remained semi-prostrate for a while and was still so when Mrs. Sparrow returned.

"Oh good," she said. "You've smartened. Now, let's talk, shall we? How's your eye? It's mending well, I think. Though I'm sure it's blind and useless. That makes *you* useless as a mission captain, my friend. Not that you were ever going to fly again anyways, after all this." She paused a moment and studied his face.

"Tell me," she continued, "how does your future look about now? Even without prison? Pretend you could go home right now."

"It was self-defense. I never murdered anyone."

"Maybe not," she said. Her tone softened and her cadence slowed. She leaned in and launched a stare. "But we both know that your recklessness has killed in the past, and that the only reason you were never even charged with anything was because of dear… old… daddy." She shifted posture and mien.

"But none of that really matters," she said. "There are really only three things that do matter. A. You know too much. B. Nobody likes you and nobody will miss you, and C. I don't like you. But I do have a use for you, and I promise you that if I walk out that door without being satisfied, I will never again trek back to the saturnine ends of Dundo to see you. You will remain here until either you or I are deceased."

Younas folded his arms. "You're wrong about one thing," he said. "I *will* be missed by two of my ex-wives and at least one bookie. There will be inquiries."

"Then, I'm glad that we deleted all your SITS data from the point that you went to the surface. The only thing anyone will ever know is that you left in your plane and never returned. And if—" He tried to interrupt but she forced her way through. "And *if* you were discovered, by subpoena or by chance, then I assure you that we have planted enough evidence to thoroughly frame you. For now, State Press is reporting Baja's death as unexplained but not suspicious. He was, after all, in a physiologically unique situation. But all that can change. And if you think life is difficult when you're unloved, imagine being universally despised. Ask your neighbor there. Don't you have a son?"

Younas was beaten and he knew it, and he felt helpless and submissive. His only hope lay in his next question.

"What do you want?"

"I want to meet you halfway," she replied. "Well, maybe not quite half. You want to shed the chains of gravity and society and rock. You want the Void. And I never want to see you again. Therefore, I have a mission for you, one from which you will almost certainly never return."

"A Cobblestone. A monkey in a tin can."

"A Pioneer, yes. But this expedition will be unlike anything that has ever even been conceived. You would, Gob-willing, journey exponentially further and geometrically faster than ever before. Brand new technology. A century of preparation. We've recruited two crewmen. You are the only missing piece."

"Yes," he answered without hesitation.

"Yes?"

"Yes."

"Wonderful." She turned to the two agents. "Let's get him upstairs and get a statement." Back to Younas. "We'll keep you here another two weeks to cool your engine; wring out any foolishness you might contemplate. After that, you'll be released, and I'll see you a week later for orientation."

The "statement" of which she spoke was shorter and stranger than the contracts to which he was accustomed. This one contained extensive sections devoted to secrecy and indemnity. The listed duties were vague and broad, and the penalty for breach was prison. He read it aloud off the HoPS while being recorded – the Dundo way of signing things. Afterwards, he relaxed, and remained relaxed right up until orientation day.

This calmness would have concerned him were he not so calm. It was the kind of tranquility that comes with having no choice and therefore no regret. He had lost the ability to imagine any possible scenario, even outside of prison, in which life would be ok on Dundo. His impotence was complete. Even a visit to Sam's family didn't inspire any hope in him, just sadness. His only hope lay in the mysterious, impending mission ahead.

Orientation began in a classroom at Magellan, where Younas learned his fate from a parade of nerds in uniforms. They briefed him on Operation Ptolemy, a collaborative effort of the seven colonies of the Alpha Centauri Tri-Star system. Such projects, like most human interaction, could only occur locally with little involvement from Earth. That's because it took years to exchange information and ideas with Earth and decades to exchange resources and personnel. The Sirius colonies were twice as far. Fortunately, the Tri-Star system was largely self-sufficient except for a few elements, vitamins and symbionts; certain things which could not be found, made or sustained in space. Not like Sears.

Sears had been one of the earliest colonies, a lone planet orbiting a lone star, the lone Wolf 359. One year, about five hundred years after settlement, a single shipment of supplies was lost en route from Earth. A single asteroid in the Kuiper Belt had destroyed it. Among those supplies was Gadolinium, without which one cannot manufacture a sericulus. The sericulus was one of the few parts of the Sears air generators that still wore out, despite technological advances. Without it, nitrogen gas could not be made. Soon, the people of Sears were forced to breathe pure oxygen, a gas which is completely absorbed from the lungs into the blood. Without non-absorbable nitrogen, there was nothing to hold open their lungs' tiny air sacs where absorption takes place. The sacs collapsed and air couldn't get in. One point two million colonists asphyxiated. The settlement extinguished.

It was a failure on multiple levels. Time had worn away people's memories of their own fragility. It only takes two generations 'til you forget you're in space. Budget cuts had led to the streamlining of previously redundant supply lines, and to the dwindling of previously excessive stores. The centuries had also allowed laziness and sloppiness to creep into routine but vital procedures. Because of inadequate tracking and monitoring, nobody knew the shipment was lost until it was too late. Because of incompetent inventory, too late came too early.

Operation Ptolemy began, Younas learned, because Why radiation had been discovered in space. It was found, in fact, to exist all over the universe. It doesn't emanate from stars or nebulae, doesn't laze in a haze like the Cosmic Microwave Background, doesn't even travel in a straight line. Rather, it exists in a loose, complex network of currents, meandering through the galaxy and beyond. What form of energy or matter shapes these currents was unknown, but Why traffic seemed to be most thick and busy through the planets known to host life. Besides that, many other hot spots of Why activity had been observed in far off, unknown places. One area burned larger and brighter than the rest. From the photos they showed, even Younas and his one untrained eye was able to discern the blazing flare from the lacy mess. It resembled the eye of a nebula. That spot, they told him, exists outside the Milky Way, billions of light-years away, spanning hundreds in diameter.

"What do you make of that?" asked Younas. "Is that where souls come from?"

"Or maybe where they end up," someone replied.

"Or both."

There were dark spots too, only visible at close range, within our neck of the galaxy. Those were areas where the paths of Why Waves seemed to converge, then disappear; or, conversely, appear and then diverge; depending on their direction of travel. Those were places where Magellan suspected either black holes or wormholes existed. The nearest one was about eight hundred light-years that-a-way. That's where they were sending Younas. Upon learning this, he grew concerned, though not fearful. The math didn't add up.

"At this point, I'm sure you're confused," said the young lady who was presenting. "Yes, I did say eight hundred light-years, to which you say, 'Is that possible?' to which I say 'Maybe.' We're hoping you can tell us. You'll be testing two brand new pieces of technology that we think are going to be absolutely revolutionary – Metabulin and the Galahad. Let me introduce Superdoctor Silver." She gestured as an older man approached. He looked more hoary than silver.

Haruto Silver was not related to Baldric, as far as he knew. "Superdoctor" meant that he had spent thirty years in education and training. Had he spent another decade, he would have attained the degree of Guru and, after that, Master Guru. Instead, he spent another thirty years working on the development team for the Galahad. The Galahad was a vessel, essentially a sailboat. The design of the sail had been the great undertaking and feat. It was based on the idea of solar sailing, an ancient attempt to ride the constant stream of light and radiation that emanates from the Sun. Solar sailing had limited success for a bit, eventually rendered obsolete by discoveries in other areas. Many millennia later, the folks in Operation Ptolemy revisited the idea, attempting to harness the elusive Why-rays for propulsion.

Younas was given a virtual tour of a long, sleek, conical vessel, black in color, anchored to a large space station. The red star Proxima Centauri beamed brightly in the distance. The ship looked plain, with no markings or insignia, and no apparent sail, at least initially. But soon after, the Galahad began to extrude a long, thin object from its tip. The scene looked to Younas like a defecating fish, except that the excretion shined a metallic silver. Once the thing was completely unfurled, it quickly relaxed into its natural shape – a ring. The ring faced the ship, attached to it by three cables, its diameter three times the ship's length. The ring soon began to glisten and hum as it filled with mysterious power, and the space within it filled with a green field of energy. The field remained a flat disc for several minutes, then slowly began to pouch, gradually increasing in concavity from dome-shaped to hemispherical and beyond. All of the Galahad's anchors – to sail and station – became taut.

Younas tried to discern if anything was moving. The black backdrop of the universe didn't provide the perspective needed to tell, so he asked.

"No," answered Silver. "The Why forces are too weak, and the station is too massive to overcome the nearby gravitational forces very easily. But the Galahad is made from very light material. If we were to release it, it would slowly drift away. It would…it *will* continue to accelerate indefinitely. It and we will approach light speed, but never reach it."

Younas raised an eyebrow. "That is pretty astonishing, Superdoc. Frankly hard to believe. But…ok, so I don't have to try and live for two millennia, just eight hundred years. I guess I better take my vitamins."

"Not exactly. At those speeds, time will slow dramatically for you, relative to us. Why, you may spend only three hundred years in flight. Maybe less!"

Younas huffed. "Maybe. Sounds like you've got all the kinks worked out Doc. Look, I don't know if you noticed, but I ain't exactly built to last three hundred years. Don't let these good looks fool you."

Silver remained poised amid the sneering. "Yes, well, as my colleague said, we have two things to show you. Superdoctor Patel will cover Metabulin tomorrow, I believe. Yes, tomorrow."

Silver continued his presentation and Younas learned that, on board, there would be very few of the instruments he was used to. No need. Pioneer ventures were not the complex, Phase Two explorations for which he was trained. His only job would be to survive and, if possible, report his status. He realized that he would not even qualify as a Cobblestone. He was less than that – an expensive, glorified Space-time Capsule.

Other features of the ship included some modifications to the sleep boxes which would enable a primitive form of suspended animation, or more accurately, retarded animation.

There was also something called a crash tank. It was the second largest and second heaviest item on the ship – a tank filled with liquid, large enough for three people, with extra room to permit a comfortable deceleration. It was designed to contend with the tremendous G-forces that were anticipated when decelerating from near-light speed. What you did, when the time was right, was to get in the tank, put in the mouthpiece, turn on the oxygen, and pull the lever. The lever simultaneously did three things:

- It released a solute that instantly turned the liquid into a semi-solid gel, suspending you in gooey packing material.
- It cut power to the sail.
- It deployed the hydrogen scoops.

When the hydrogen scoops fanned out into full position, they looked like a pair of wings put on backwards. But they weren't backwards, for they weren't designed for aerodynamics. They were designed to provide drag against the interstellar medium of dark matter and hydrogen ions that exists in space, and to scoop some of that hydrogen. The hydrogen would be fed to the boron-11 fusion reactor, the heaviest thing on board, which bulged along the ship's dorsum like a primitive spine. The reactor in turn would power the ramjet, allowing the ship some sub-light, local propulsion.

For the last item of the day, Younas met with Mrs. Sparrow. Silver attended a portion of the meeting, during which Sparrow introduced him to Younas in more detail. Silver, it turned out, would be one of his two shipmates.

Younas didn't like it. "He's old and has no experience," he protested most unkindly. "I'm not giving tours. I need a crew."

"You need someone who knows the ship," Sparrow countered. "And no one does better than the good Superdoctor. He also happens to be the only man on Dundo who would actually volunteer for this mission. It's his life's work. Also, let's be frank, Captain; it's not that easy to find people who would fly anywhere with you."

"So where's my other shipmate? What is he, a plumber?"

"She."

"She?"

"*She* is a doctor. Dr. Mary Money, and she's not here. You'll meet her at the docking station a few hours prior to your farewell."

"And may I ask where she is?" asked Younas.

"You may. She's in a jail on Argos."

"Oh wow. I get to spend a millennium with a convict doctor with a stripper's name. Is she hot, too?"

His shallow jest masked a dark situation. Argos was a moon governed harshly by the Mao Corporation, which owned the rights to the rare elements they mined there. Those who went to work there had either been paid handsomely or sentenced there by a court. And Mao didn't build prisons. Lawbreakers on Argos were either sentenced to slavery or executed, depending on their status. Whatever cell was holding this doctor must have been pretty medieval.

"She is like you," Sparrow replied. "A troublemaker who knows too much."

"And so, like me, she gets a death sentence."

"A death sentence? Whatever do you mean?"

"C'mon. You don't expect us to survive that wormhole or black hole or wherever you're sending me."

She lay a hand on his shoulder. "Dear boy, we're doing no such thing. If anything, you're being granted longevity." She paused and pondered, and stared at her sensible shoes. "We're all condemned to die, of course. By the time you reach the hole, I and everyone you know will have long since passed. And if you're headed where I think you are, I may in fact reach your destination before you."

"Ya, but a life in slumber ain't exactly living, even if it's a thousand years. It seems to me more like dying a really long death."

"We shall see, I suppose."

"We shall."

Younas spent most of the next three days learning new and revised protocols, signing a bunch of releases, and sitting with a state reporter for a highly scripted, heavily edited interview to be released at a later date. He underwent more in-depth virtual training on the controls and operations of the Galahad. He also got a bunch of injections and even some minor surgery. His tracker cracker was outdated and had to be replaced. The cracker, a semiconducting chip, was embedded subcutaneously in the abdomen and used to relay a person's location and condition to various onboard and handheld instruments.

He also got something new – a central venous access port implanted into his chest. Dr. Silver got one too. The port would be used for the IV administration of Metabulin, a modified version of GestArrest. Unlike its progenitor, the new drug spared stem cells and only halted the division of differentiated cells. Metabulin also had other ingredients, such as a full set of adult stem lines, and a fresh batch of transcription factors, methylating enzymes, and all the other proteins a stem cell needs for healthy, epigenetic regulation. This concoction had been found in early studies to halt the aging process. The team at Magellan then decided that, as long as a person was sterilized of all colonizing bacteria, and shielded from oxidative stressors in the new and improved sleep box, then the Metabulin would keep him from dying indefinitely. The drug had a long half-life – ten years – and that's how often it would be administered. It also had to be dosed slowly, over the course of a week. All of this would be handled by a very simple, very durable, IV infusion pump.

On his last night in Dundo, Younas passed his time alone, doing what he had done most often – sitting on his porch, a little bit of thinking and drinking, and gazing up at a rock sky.


The flight to the space station took a week. The station orbited a remote moon, tucked away from the nosy and the criminal. It was also located in the path of a large current of Why-waves, a feature that had been essential in building and testing the Galahad's sail. Now, with construction finished, almost everyone had left, and the place felt more graveyard than shipyard. That all changed when Younas arrived with Silver and a small, noisy entourage, including a Magellan media team to film a documentary, a couple of vice presidents to give speeches, a flight crew and some well-connected spectators – fans of space or history or hoopla.

The station looked even plainer than expected, having been stripped of all the comforts that made it livable for twenty-plus years. In a conference room, they met a few scientists and engineers – members of Silver's team. They would perform the final steps to launch the Galahad and tuck in its crew. And there was Dr. Money, head shaved, drugged with compliance pills and accompanied by a guard who was probably bigger than necessary. Middle-aged and lean, she had beauty that still shone through lines of age and frustration. She wasn't comely in the classic sense. Her appeal flowed from an air of intelligence, especially in her face; the kind of beauty that drew respect from Younas, instead of lusty contempt. He imagined that Mrs. Sparrow must have looked similar in her younger years, except for the eyes. Dr. Money's were deep and concerned; nothing like Sparrow's cold, daunting beams.

Introductions were made. Dr. Money kept quiet and sullen. Younas was immediately enchanted. She was not. This was not the instant, mystical connection they had felt the last time they met for the first time, in a hotel room in Cambridge, Massachusetts. That happened thousands of years ago, and the Why-wave harmony between them had long since faded. This time, his was a simple attraction born of complex psychology, something with which Dr. Money was not burdened.

Nor did they grow any closer after spending the next 350 years together. That was because...
after the introductions and ceremony and speeches,
and after the final check, in which Younas confirmed that everything was as he had been taught, and Silver confirmed that everything worked properly,
and after the crew was sterilized, hooked up, knocked out and packed away,
and after the launch sequence was initiated and the Galahad cast off,
Younas and Money then spent those 350 years in simulated death. Even though they achieved such speeds that they themselves were, at times, more wave than matter; still, their lifeless bodies cast no Why Waves to mesh.

When they finally revived, confused and blinded by darkness, it seemed that only an instant had passed. And when they opened their sleep boxes, they still couldn't see. As they slowly regained orientation, memory and room temperature, they began fumbling around in the dark, guided intermittently by the flashing of emergency lights. An alarm was blaring. This was not in the training. Something was wrong. That fact became more apparent when they opened up Silver and found a long-dead, thoroughly desiccated corpse, like a big piece of jerky. Apparently, his IV pump had not been so durable after all.

Captain Younas noticed that he felt odd, as if watching himself in a movie. This sensation, called Depersonalization, has been known to occur in certain, post-traumatic, mental illnesses called Dissociative Disorders, and sometimes as part of near-death experience. But he wasn't suffering from either of those. He was just going really fast. The near-light speed slowed his body as well. Moving felt like wading through batter, or like his limbs weighed a ton, which they actually did. The drag he felt was the gravity of distant stars, and he was fortunate that there were none closer. After a while of being awake and upright, his mind started becoming blurred and tenuous, walking a tightrope of consciousness. He knew his time was short.

He grabbed Dr. Money by the wrist, which made her instinctively resist. "In the tank, Doc," he said and led her into the bath. Open the oxygen, mask on, pull the lid closed until it latches, get down, eyes closed, remember to relax and *not* brace yourself, blow your nose, grab the lever and here we go.

The solidification process happened nearly instantly. It tickled his ears and made him feel warm all over. The deceleration was more gradual but more painful, causing the slow onset of a tremendous headache and a wrenching of his spine that kept building, like being in a trash compactor. The pain quickly reached a climax, then slowly faded over thirty earth minutes. When the all-clear light lit, they emerged, dripping and glistening with the thick slime. They still couldn't see much and thus couldn't do much but sit on the floor and shiver a while.

"The lights should come on soon," Captain Younas reassured, without being too sure himself.

"Poor guy," she said, looking over at the late Superdoctor. His remains had been plastered by the G-forces against the side of his sleep box.

"At least he's done worrying," he replied. "I don't mourn anyone's death but my own."

She was not impressed, and demonstrated so by shifting herself away from his side. "What a wonderful philosophy you have," she said.

"Oh, *now* you talk," he joked, trying to lighten the mood. "You ain't said a word to me in, what, a thousand years? And you break the ice with sarcasm."

She rubbed her thighs, trying to warm up. "Do you think we were out that long?" she asked.

"No idea. And no idea where we are."

They looked around, straining to see. They were in the "belly," the one-room living quarters, and the largest chamber on the ship.

"Do you always start a new life with a woman with dark comments about death?"

"Well, I *have* been married three times. Maybe four. Who can keep track?" Her crack made him feel foolish, so he foolishly dug himself deeper. "What I meant was that life is a curse. We are the only living things that see our own death coming."

"As far as you know."

"As far as I know."

She slapped the side of her head, trying in vain to jar some gel out of her ear. He started to undress.

"Do you mind?" she protested.

"Not at all," he replied and continued to strip. "I'm cold and it's dark anyways. Besides, aren't you a doctor?"

"Not dark enough," she said, shading her eyes. "And not doctor enough."

They sat for a while in quiet.

"How long do you suppose the power was out?" she posed.

"Not very long, or we'd be choked and frozen. Backup won't last long either." He turned and saw in her face that he was making things worse. "The reactor should spark any minute," he added. "Then we'll be fine."

Not actually sure if they'd be fine, Younas decided prematurely to satisfy his nagging curiosity. "So how does a doctor – a woman doctor at that – land herself in a dungeon on Argos?"

She thought for a while about how much to tell this man who was handsome enough, but crude and bordering repulsive; this man who, in most respects, could be considered her mate, wed to her without ceremony in an arranged marriage, arranged by the government and fate.

"You can never get warm there," she said, shivering. "Bastards keep it cold."

# Fifteen

Many millions of years ago, the class D moon of Argos escaped the orbit of its mother world. It coasted through space for a brief time, free and happy, before it was bound to a new path round the nearby star. It thus became a planet itself of sorts, a situation about which, in time, it felt divided. It felt so because, millions of years later, it became tidally locked with its star. Without relative rotation, its one side was doomed to eternally face the burning rage of its new master; the other condemned to lonely darkness.

On the hot side of Argos, the intense heat and radiation forged the rare elements and compounds that would eventually attract prospectors. But it also melted equipment and incinerated personnel, and the booty could only be reached by drilling through from the cold side. So the cold side is where the Mao Corporation set up shop – a sprawling network of company towns dotting the moonscape. And cold is how they kept it, to keep the workers frosty and the machines running smoothly. There was no life on Argos, only labor. The company kept the world childless by sterilizing the few women who ended up there. Everything was battleship gray.

They used to castrate the men too, thinking of the added benefit of pacifying criminals. But they eventually learned something else, after a lot of time and extensive cost-benefit analyses. They learned that the lost productivity from decreased muscle mass, decreased energy and increased osteoporosis, cost more money than aggressive men and heavy security.

The female sterilization process was an ancient technology that had not changed for centuries. Safe and effective, the noninvasive procedure involved assaulting the patient's senses with certain, pungent sensations – the smell of pus and the sound of Beer Belly Polka playing over and over and over again for hours.

At the center of the process was Goink BeDoink, a.k.a. Goink the Clown, the full-time clown who won brief notoriety as a part-time serial killer. A weird-looking chap who rather resembled an overgrown, ugly baby, BeDoink was universally acknowledged as the un-sexiest male of our species. Prior to his execution, his flabby body and nasal voice were captured for eternity in high-definition, holographic recordings. Long after his death, the life-sized sight and sound of the naked clown, whining through his rotten teeth about his hemorrhoids and the price of a decent liniment, would be used across the galaxy to wither ovaries.

Of course, no procedure is perfect. There are always a few genetic variants – those women who end up on the extreme ends of the bell curve and find themselves immune, or even strangely attracted, to repulsive killer clowns. It was for them that the polka and pus were added measures.

It was partly for the money but mostly from compassion that Mary Money signed a three-year contract to serve as a staff physician on the moon. She toiled like everyone else, mending and maintaining the beaten bodies and suffering spirits of overworked men and women. The work overwhelmed her, and she struggled to keep up. In her second year, the bone pains first appeared.

It started with a single machinist who presented to her little clinic with diffuse body aches, particularly in his legs. He couldn't stand more than a few hours, and the usual corporate pressure was on to find something wrong or return him to full duty. With her limited resources, she couldn't find much of anything. He had some scattered, pinpoint bruising, but it was so mild she hardly noticed. So she did her duty and sent him back to work. But you can't fix someone with a doctor's note, and he only got worse. Soon he couldn't even walk, and the bruising got worse. The pinpoints grew and multiplied and coalesced, and his skin became a blotchy mess.

Then came the others – employees with similar symptoms. A few at first, then the avalanche. Over the course of a month, dozens of people flooded Dr. Money with pains and bruises and nosebleeds and bloody, swollen gums. Baffled and overwhelmed, she cried out for help. The company responded with a list of references and resources, and procedures to request said resources. When the debility rate reached a threshold, they sent an agent to assist and monitor her.

Mr. Hand was a handsome, fit young man with nice clothes and a big square jaw. As soon as he arrived, Dr. Money sent him straight into the field with a questionnaire, to call on the sick and gather what epidemiological data he could. His first discovery was obvious. All of the afflicted lived in the same housing sector, Sector Z. As soon as he realized it, he ordered a quarantine, closing the sector Z tram station for everything but supplies and doctor visits, and restricting Dr. Money's practice to quarantined patients only. He reassigned her other patients.

She cared and comforted as best she could, and ran what tests she had. She didn't learn much, except that their bones were thinning – osteopenic at first, then full-blown osteoporosis. She spent sleepless days poring through literature and consulting what colleagues she could from such a remote world and under the thumb of a secretive corporation. This was a disease unlike any she had seen or could find. In medicine, it's no fun being interesting.

Skin sores began to appear. Sores became ulcers and ulcers got infected. When gangrene set in, she knew that these people, now upward of four hundred of them, would start dying. Her hope – that this scourge might be self-limiting – was squashed. She started getting frantic as she raced to find a diagnosis under a flood of need and suffering. Mr. Hand, who had been instrumental in fast-tracking supply requests, turned quite unhelpful when she asked him to assist in dressing wounds. The sight and smell of putrefaction was enough for him to politely advise her of the limits of his assignment, then excuse himself, then step into the hall and throw up.

As the plague worsened, so did his behavior. When people started dying of sepsis and strokes and heart attacks and internal bleeding, he started sitting in on patient visits, uninvited. As a representative of the company, he now represented a shift in priorities to a defensive posture. He took notes and occasionally interrupted her patient interviews, informing Dr. Money that "you're not authorized to ask that."

He also stopped meeting with her to review his own findings. And six weeks after he arrived, he left. "I think I've learned all I'm going to," he told her. "I'll head back to the home office, write my report, and see what we can figure out. We'll keep sending supplies."

And he did, keeping one less worry off her tortured mind. And she thought nothing more of him until a week later when she tried to review his data. Before that, it had been years since she had picked at her face. But then she discovered that he had quietly revoked her access, and she scratched away in astonished horror. But though she was now in the dark, she already knew one key bit of information. She just didn't yet realize its significance.

# Sixteen

She didn't tell all this to Younas, who she had really only just met. When he asked again how she ended up in an Argos jail, she only divulged one little thing. "I killed someone."

"You?" he asked incredulously, then thought back to his own traumatic event. "Ya, me too."

They sat a while longer before he turned his words to the ship.

"Come on, ya flunky!" he ordered, and stamped his foot. And with that, the Galahad blossomed to high-tech life. "Fantastic." He went to look for towels and clothes.

She stood up to look around a bit at the living quarters that would be her new home, her new world. She gently ran her long, elegant fingers along the surfaces, probing like a blind man, seemingly lost in thought. She took a deep, calming breath.

"Amazing," she marveled.

"What? This tin tomb?"

She let slip a wry smirk. "You know, I used to do some research into Why waves back in my grad years. It's…" She searched for the best word. "It's awesome in the literal sense. And now here we are, actually riding the lightning, so to speak."

"Look Doc, first of all, our sails are down now. The other thing is this – I don't think that last thing means what you think it means, though it's still pretty accurate."

"Anyways, I'm still amazed."

"Personally, I've always been kinda skeptical of all this wave hype," he said. "I mean, if we're nothing more than packets of energy tooling around the universe, then why get trapped inside these lousy bodies? And why live our lousy lives?"

"I think it's like nerve conduction. Do you understand neuro-transmission?"

"I couldn't really say."

"It's like this. Our nerves, as I'm sure you know, are there to transmit electrical signals. But those impulses can only travel so far before they start to fade. Therefore, we have neurotransmitters, little molecules that take a message and physically walk it from one nerve to the next."

"So, you're saying I'm a neuro—"

"Neurotransmitter, yes, in a sense."

"And what exactly is this signal I'm supposed to be conveying?"

She sat a moment, wondering if he was serious, or at least could be. "Isn't it obvious?"

"No."

"Love, of course."

"Oh Lord." He shook his head. "I thought you were gonna say something profound. I didn't know we were writing cheesy novels."

Her smirk faded but her patience did not. "Is there any other aspect of our existence that is so universal as love?" she challenged. "So durable? So ethereal?"

"Ah, I don't know."

"Think about it. Think about this – Why waves were discovered thousands of years ago and after all that time, its most popular use commercially is people seeking love."

"Well, if you're looking for love around here, don't bother," he said. "Like I said, I've been through three wives and three divorces. I'm done with it. And in case you didn't notice (you should've, being a doctor and all, but maybe you're just not that good), I've got a little vacancy in the scrotal area, which is a blessing actually, cuz it means that I just don't care."

Now her patience was gone and she shook her head in disgust.

"You know, we may just be the two most condemned people alive. And yet I pity you."

Her words scorched his already-raw pride.

"Ya? Well, I never knew you could grow such a high horse just by feeding it BS," he retorted. "And I don't need your pity. Don't need it and don't want it."

"Fine."

"Fine."

Many minutes of awkward silence passed as they looked around and tried to ignore each other in such a small space. The belly spanned about five by ten meters, designed like a submarine to conserve space. The bunks were recessed in the wall. Nearly every other item of furniture or appliance was made to collapse, fold and stow with ease, except the crash tank and sleep boxes. The tank would henceforth serve as a table, counter and work bench. The boxes would fit easily enough in the ejector tube, and that was where her mind now turned.

"Shouldn't we tend to our colleague?" she more-than-suggested.

"Ya, let's flush the poor bastard."

Dr. Money, who originally hailed from Planet Visa, replied with an expression in her own language for which there is no translation on Dundo or in English, but which at least is not very nice. After they sealed the tube, she again made a suggestion that was not a suggestion at all.

"Shouldn't we say words? Pray perhaps?"

"You can if you want. I'll just listen."

She bowed her head and he watched. Her words were like her, modest and plainly beautiful. Then off went the last vestiges of the once good Superdoctor.

As soon as that business finished, he rushed off like a kid after the last bell rings, and headed to his comfort zone – the forward end where the instruments were arranged in an alcove. He settled into the cockpit, scrolling through one HoPS after another with competence but not confidence.

"We're still going really fast," he shouted out. He turned his attention to a periscope-like device and stopped a while to concentrate, his face pressed against the eye cups. "It's weird," he said and kept looking. "I don't see any stars." He opened a cupboard and found a small bottle which he also opened, and an ear plug. Cocking his head, he dripped several drops of a radiotransductive fluid into his left ear canal, then plugged it. With eyes closed, he slowly turned a dial on a panel and listened intently. "I don't hear any either."

He could, in fact, see and hear low levels of light and radiation all around, but it looked scattered and distorted. Logically, he assumed that they were immersed in a nebula and that the surrounding dust and gas was bending and splitting light, as atmospheres like to do. However, it was not bent light, but space itself, for they weren't in a nebula. They were in a wormhole, and its yawning mouth had begun to collapse from the presence within it of a massive object – a ship at near-light speed. The Galahad would escape, and its crew would never know what almost happened. But there would be no turning back.

He returned as she was stepping out of the refresher booth. It had sprayed her clean with a solution, blown her dry with air, and dressed her with a fresh coat of Insta-Dry liquid fabric. She picked red this time.

"I can't navigate if I can't see anything," he told her. "After we slow down some more, I'll just redeploy the sail at low-power, and we can follow the current. Hopefully not into an asteroid."

The intensity of the field generated by the sail was adjustable. Full power meant full sail. But at lower power, the field became permeable, harnessing just enough Why waves to cruise along, like tubing down a lazy river of lost souls.

She nodded her understanding and got started on her workout. Her muscles had not atrophied, but she felt quite stiff. Afterwards, she settled into a hover chair, activated her Eye Phones and began a nice long book. There was nothing to do but wait and see if death was coming. For her, it was a familiar ordeal.

# Seventeen

She had experienced it before on Argos, after Mr. Hand and the Mao Corporation abandoned her, leaving her to contend with the victims of a serious illness; not knowing if she would succumb to it herself, and why she hadn't thus far. If it was infectious, then it certainly was contagious, but a contagion to which she seemed immune… thus far. But she wasn't the only one.

A handful of people who lived in Sector Z had remained healthy for whatever reason. They, like she, were also overwhelmed, given their new duties of feeding and cleaning and tending to the sick, transporting them to doctor visits and disposing of bodies. Most of these fortunate unfortunates were convicted criminals and didn't mind easing their own burdens by helping along the demise of the gravely ill.

She might have given more thought to the well ones were she not so inundated by the sick. Indeed, the mountain of data that she and Hand had compiled consisted of every physical, social, familial, environmental and historical aspect of the afflicted. The healthy had been overlooked, despite being a much smaller group.

Instead, she turned her attention to experimentation. Unlike before, when she had focused on running tests despite a paucity of resources, this strategy had the opposite problem – overabundance. That's because she owned one of those molecular 3-D printers. It was a cheap office model, so she could not mass-produce anything. But she had some pirated software – a large catalog of medical chemicals – and she could make just about anything in small quantities. But where to begin?

She started with the most common antibacterial, antifungal and antiviral drugs. Her miserable patients were, like her, willing to try anything. But nothing worked, so she turned to the immune modulators and chemotherapy agents with which she was most familiar and most comfortable. The only results she got were side effects, which racked her with guilt and frustration. This wasn't science; it was fishing. But what else could she do?

As more people died, her job sadly became easier as her patient load lightened. She was debriding a wound one day when word came from company headquarters – a letter on her Eye Phone composed of three lines:

*Diagnosis: Spacebug # 35.*

*Discontinue rescue.*

*Commence mitigation.*

Spacebugs were a category of germs that had yet to be identified. Over thousands of years, as humans spread from Earth to other worlds, new living conditions had created new diseases. Infectious diseases were born from mutation, or from new opportunities for old germs that had previously not been dangerous. When a new disease was discovered on a new world, if a cause could not be identified, then it was assumed to be a new infection, and given the name Spacebug. There were, to date, 57 documented Spacebugs, which meant that this one had been seen before.

"Spacebull!" she yelled, startling the young man who was helping her. He had lucked out today and gotten patient transport duty, the easiest job going and a chance to get away from that dying hellhole, Sector Z. At the moment, he was helping to hold still the old wretch he had brought for a visit; helping to keep him from squirming in pain while she scraped dead tissue down to bone.

She apologized for her outburst, then suddenly noticed her assistant. It was the first time in weeks she noticed anyone besides her patients and her own tortured thoughts. He seemed better kempt and mannered than most of the workers on Argos.

"Say, what's your name?" she asked with a smile. "Luke. I like that. Nice to meet you, Luke. I'm Mary. You seem very young. How old are you?"

"Not quite sure, ma'am…Mary. I lost count after 40."

"Well, you certainly seem young and healthy. You've never felt sick through all this?"

"No, ma'am. Thank Skip."

"Are the other healthy people as young as you?"

"Not really. I seen some old ones and young."

"I see. Are there many of you left in your sector? I mean people who still feel well?"

"Not really, I don't posit."

She continued to probe. "How many do you suppose there are?"

"It's hard to say, ma'am. We don't see each other much cuz we're always so busy with the sick ones. Plus, there's some of us that hide out."

"Hide? From what?"

"From working. Or from getting sick. I do it myself sometimes."

"And I don't blame you. But try to guess. How many?"

"Couple dozen, I posit."

"You don't say," she said. She looked past him as her brain hummed with thought. "Would you do me a favor, Luke? I need to come visit your town; spend a full earth day. Would you take me there? Be my guide? Keep me safe?"

He answered without hesitation. "I don't believe there's anything I could prefer more than that, Mary. But I'm not sure the foreman'll go for it."

"Leave the foreman to me."

The actual, company-appointed foreman had died three weeks prior. As is always the case when chaos boils in a cauldron of isolation, those who bubble to the top are the meanest and hardest and shrewdest of men. All of these qualities resided in Cyrus, the new self-appointed foreman of Sector Z.

She tried calling but couldn't reach him, couldn't reach anyone. So she packed a small bag with personal effects and medical supplies, and boarded the tram with Luke and his charge of six patients, three ambulatory and three who he pushed in a converted warehouse cart. The moment the car doors opened at the Sector Z station, the rancid smell of death floored her. Luke didn't flinch. His olfactory receptors had long ago surrendered under the endless siege of strident stimulation, and opted for early retirement.

They trudged through the tiled roads to return the patients to their homes and their beds. They passed several flatbed carts, each stacked two or three high with bodies, bodies waiting for someone to come by and bring them to be liquefied. Bleak high-rises loomed quietly under the great dome, their vigil sometimes broken by a muffled wail of pain or grief rising from within. Rats everywhere.

The task was slow and arduous, made more so when families and flat mates, and entire buildings of people learned that the doctor had come. They descended on her, seeking answers or news, or simply compassion. It didn't take long for news of her arrival to reach Cyrus, and he was waiting when she finally arrived at his office.

He was an ominous figure. Muscular and towering at 6'4", he overwhelmed the adopted desk in his adopted office. He had a slightly lazy eye which he rather enjoyed for the mind games it afforded him.

"Welcome, Doctor," he boomed through a half-chewed cigar. "Welcome indeed. We were wondering if someone was going to come down here and tell us something. Bad enough they deserted us."

"Thank you. I wish I had more information for you. I can tell you that The Company thinks this is an infection, and that is also my prime suspect, but I'm not convinced."

"Not convinced?" Disgust contorted his face. "After all this time, you still don't have a conviction?"

She grew a little nervous. "That's why I'm here," she said. "I need more information. The kind I can't get from my clinic."

"How do you know this ain't a spirit?"

"Beg your pardon?"

"Oh, you beg my pardon? I said how do you know that this ain't a spirit of vengeance? How's The Company think they're gonna come out into deep space and rape this weird little moon for decades on end, and not stir something up?"

"I hadn't thought of that," she replied.

"No, you hadn't thought of that. But we thought of it, didn't we, Luke?"

"Look," she said. "All this time, I've only been able to study the sick, and I haven't gotten anywhere. I hadn't yet the opportunity to examine the rest of you. Clearly, something is immunizing you and there aren't many of you, thus it should be easy to find a common thread."

"Oh, you want a common thread?" A grin grew on his face. "That's why you came? A common thread? Luke, what's our common thread?"

"We're all from Annabelle," Luke answered.

"And what else?"

"We all wear the finger."

Until now, Dr. Money had not noticed the shriveled appendage that hung from a string round Luke's neck, for he kept it tucked inside his shirt, as did Cyrus. And while she had noticed that Luke was missing a finger, she hadn't thought anything of it. In fact, looking back, she now recalled that several of her patients had been short a finger, but such injuries were not uncommon for the miners of Mao.

It started when people first started dying in large numbers, and Crazy Joe Gallo decided he had enough. In a supreme act of his particular brand of defiance, he determined to tell this plague exactly what's what. Using a large rock chisel, he amputated his left middle finger, and dried the bloody digit in an astringent. He then drilled a hole through it and strung it up around his neck, like raising a flag of victory, his favorite gesture waving tirelessly at the world.

As desperation grew around him, and it became increasingly apparent that Crazy Joe was not falling ill, others decided to give his idea a try, especially those who knew him – the ones from Annabelle. Some who did so lived and others died, but those who lived dared not tempt fate. They assumed that those who died must have doffed the protective charm at some point, a mistake they would not themselves make.

"You wait all this time and you come all the way down here to learn what you could just asked us at the start?" Cyrus asked with mocking contempt. "You sure you're a doctor? Doctor Dumbass, maybe."

Luke let out a chuckle.

"You go on ahead now," Cyrus continued, waving her away. "Stay or go, makes no difference if you got no use."

Her poise never flinched. She stayed a few more hours in Sector Z, just long enough to make some badly needed house calls, and visit the makeshift infirmary that now languished, unstaffed. She then went home to read about Annabelle.

Annabelle was the first world to be colonized by Earth, settled by people wealthy enough to afford such endeavors before they became affordable. She was named for the founder's widow, and subsequent generations of governors refused generous offers from corporate suitors to rebrand her. A gilded society, Annabelle still had her share of ne'er-dowells, some of whom even ended up on Argos. The women of Annabelle were simply called Annabelles, the men Annabeaus. They all had some common physical features, reflecting the small size of the population and the kind of wealth that can afford to dabble in genetic engineering. Their hair was fantastic and their dark, ageless skin was particularly resistant to radiative insult.

It was their renowned genetics program in which Dr. Money now took an interest. As she read through its history, she learned that, from time to time, new genes or genetic procedures were discovered or perfected, then became politically trendy, then mandated on all new citizens. The mandates meant banning natural child conception for a full generation, enforced by forced abortion if necessary, and replacing it with in-vitro (test tube) fertilization. The new gene was introduced into each new zygote, either by splicing it onto the chromosome, or introducing it as an independent, replicating gene called a plasmid. Some genes were added that produced antibiotics, supplements and other drugs. Others were modified to alter cell membrane receptors just enough to resist viruses, while still preserving their function.

This catalog of Annabelle's genetic interventions became the new focus of her therapeutic trials as she cranked out new chemicals — treatments for diseases to which Annabeaus were immune. She got her answer in rather dramatic fashion on the fourth try, with an acid she made that Annabeaus produced naturally.

It was called Ascorbate, once known as Vitamin C. Within a week of daily dosing, all but two of the thirty-eight surviving sick began to heal. Within two weeks, many of them were walking again. She wasted no time in reporting her findings, and The Mao Corporation (a.k.a The Company) soon permitted her to transfer patients out of quarantine and into the central hospital. Sector Z was shut down for an undetermined duration and its remaining inhabitants reassigned.

But as expeditiously as The Company cleaned up the mess, it sluggishly investigated the origin, or at least it seemed so to Dr. Money, whose frequent inquiries were frustrated. Whenever she reached out for an update, Mr. Hand, who still acted as her liaison in the matter, offered little more than a canned corporate response. He became increasingly hard to reach and eventually stopped returning her calls.

That, of course, would not do. She had spent days and weeks and months sharing the agony of four hundred of her own patients, many of whom she had come to know and love. No, it would not do at all. She would have to go on vacation.

The Company processed her leave request with serpentine speed, quite happy to relieve itself of her, if only for a while. But she did not flee to some picturesque location. Instead, she went back to Sector Z to have herself a shake.

Eating was not one of life's pleasures on Argos, not even for volunteer physicians. All employees were assigned a feeding time and issued a cup embedded with a unique chip. Twice a day, at your scheduled time, you got in line at the food fountain. The fountain scanned your cup and dispensed a shake in a quantity calculated for your age, occupation and ideal body weight. Dr. Dudrick's Shake was a recipe famous throughout the colonies, formulated to sustain armies, settlers, and other large groups facing harsh conditions. It was hypoallergenic, imperishable and completely nutritious with a slight hint of honey. Dr. Money needed a sample.

She went alone this time, using an excuse that she had left her medical bag behind the last time. Sector Z now lay abandoned except for a small take-down crew assigned to strip the place clean – to dismantle, pack and ship every reusable thing. Groping eyes and childish tongues let loose as she walked past, but wicked hands were stayed by the presence of heavy guard. Professional security was the one budget item on which The Company never skimped. She asked one guard to show her to the food fountain, but the burly woman informed her that it was shut down and drained. Dr. Money nonetheless insisted.

When they arrived, she looked it over, removed her coat, and explained to the guard, who recognized her from past physicals, that she was conducting a study for The Company. She again asked for help, this time to open the tank and help her climb in. Plenty of residue remained inside and, by the time she finished, she had collected more shake on her clothes and in her short, dark hair than in her specimen cup.

Soon after, a favor from a friend in a lab gave her the answer she sought – no trace of Ascorbate. But why? Had it been forgotten? Was there a leak somewhere? Had it been added, then destroyed by a chemical reaction or physical insult? She listed these possibilities and others in the start of what would become a journal, which she disguised as the chart for an imaginary patient – Drumm, Conan – and tucked away among her medical records. This puzzle clearly reached beyond her knowledge but not her capabilities, for she was determined and highly intelligent. So she determined to learn.

But on a corporate moon, it's not easy to snoop around about things that aren't your business. People are there to work, not live; and on Argos, The Company kept recreation restricted. Being on vacation gave her more freedom to wander about, but not more access to information. She started with a deep dive into the loneliest of libraries – the generally accessible company manuals. From these tomes on procedures, policies, maintenance, repair and safety, she learned that she could learn a lot. For example, she learned that, since the diets were so constant, the supply chain logistics for nutrition on Argos was mostly automated. The Company imported some nutrients and manufactured others locally. Carbohydrates were produced at photosynthesis plants constructed along Argos' meridian of eternal dawn, where light and darkness merged. Some of the shake ingredients were shipped, others piped around. On Argos, the oil in the oil pipelines fed people, not machines.

As she read on, she began to formulate a plan. Working backwards along the supply chain, the first step would have been visiting the Sector Z kitchen, where the shake was mixed. But the kitchen had been cleared out and cleaned, along with any clues it may have held. She could only hope and move on to the next step – the regional distribution center, where ingredients were gathered, divided and packaged for shipment to five sectors, sectors V through Z. She requested a tour which the center foreman readily granted, thinking nothing odd of a doctor interested in nutrition.

She found the place as foreign as the moon itself. A tangled network of pipes and conduits ran into and throughout the sprawling building. Large, spherical containers, as tall as a man, were rolled around, pushed along tracks like bowling balls. And all the machines! Mixers and spinners and dryers and wetters, and machines for pouring and packaging.

The foreman assigned a pleasant young chap named Sinumbré to show her around. Sinumbré was knowledgeable, and when she finally asked him about vitamins, he explained that they mix up two different batches for each sector: Vitamix-1 and 2.

"Something to do with how the shake is prepared," he explained. "Vitamix-1 has your fat-soluble vitamins, Vita-2 the minerals and water-solubles."

The maker of Vitamix-2 was a modest contraption, relatively small and lacking the impression cast by the other machines of a grotesque, tentacled creature. It stood there, idle, trying not to be noticed. Behind it, a series of shelves bore stacks of heavy canisters, identical except for their labels and the contents within – various Vitamix ingredients. Dr. Money asked lots of questions, relying on instinct in place of skill.

"Do you run this process?"

"Nah, it's that guy over there in the orange helmet."

"Is he new?"

"Nah, he's been here forever."

"Is this machine new?"

Sinumbré looked askance. "That's kind of a weird question."

"I'm weird. Is it?"

"No."

"Has it been worked on lately?

"What? Why are you asking me that?"

Now she relied on well-honed skill and lay a hand of reassurance on his shoulder.

"Because," she replied "I have...I *had* a lot of sick patients, and I don't know why, and I'm trying to find out. I think the answer might be here somewhere."

"How many? Sick people, I mean."

"All of Sector Z."

Sinumbré's face darkened with sobriety. He nodded in understanding. "Horrible," he said. "We only heard about it a few blocks ago."

"How about these containers?" she asked, pointing to the canisters. She hardly noticed his change in demeanor. "How are they made?"

"Them, they're all imports. They come straight from Central Supply, all weighed out and sealed."

"Do you have any of the final product on hand?"

"No, ma'am. It goes out on the tram same day it's made."

"Well, I'd like to see a batch get made. Can we do that?"

"I'm sorry, Doc. We only do vitamins every fourth block. The next mix is coming up soon, though. In three quarts, I think."

When we humans left Earth to inhabit distant worlds, our descendants lived their lives without ever having known the pace of Earth's rotation or the cadence of its seasons. Some never even saw a sky. We held on to those units, the hours and minutes, that seemed to sync well with our own physiological rhythm. But our other standards of time were eventually traded in for a more practical metric system. A "block" was a hundred hours, a little over four days. A "quart" was a quarter block – twenty-five hours. Dr. Money would have to wait about three earth days.

# Eighteen

Time is not so clearly defined when traveling at high speeds and contending with gravitational fluctuations. One could not tell how much time passed before the Galahad left the wormhole, but however much it was, Younas hardly noticed. What he did notice, as he checked his instruments for the hundredth time, was the gradual appearance of stars all around, like nightfall in the desert.

Unfortunately, those fancy instruments wouldn't give him a location. The ship had a basic astral positioning system. It measured the brightness of each surrounding star and their relative distances and angles, then plugged it all into a program that worked like facial recognition. But this place was a face unfamiliar.

Once they had slowed enough, he redeployed the sail at low power, and they set about passing whatever time remained of their lives. With the loss of their shipmate, they had rations enough to last hundreds of years. And without his help and expertise, they had plenty to do. He got to work reading manuals, learning what he could about the ship – its operation, maintenance and repair. She learned from him what she could about space living, exploration and even some aviation. In turn, she taught him some respect, making use of gobs of time and her potent personality. He eventually, inevitably became fond of her, but his affection went unrequited.

In fact, quite the opposite. Despite his trainability, he could not be taught to be tolerable to her senses or sensibilities. They never shared any intimacy of any kind, it being both physically and emotionally unworkable. It's even hard to say they had moments of affection, certainly not coming from her. Pity was as close as she came when she gave him a routine physical, upon seeing the damage that the Ball Rot had wreaked on his privates. It was his picture of Dorian Gray. She was prone to pity. It was her weakness and her strength. With time's passage, he only became more irritating to her until she came to believe that lonely isolation might be preferrable to her situation. It wasn't his fault, just him. For one thing, he was stupid – an intelligent, educated, stupid man. But that wasn't it. She sensed something darker, something eluding her.

There is no earthly comparison, except perhaps the grave, for the quiet on a ship in deep space with no active propulsion. It is an entity so haunting that the occasional interruption – by capacitors charging or the heat kicking in – is as welcome as an air pocket in an underwater cave. And when there are no more books to read or things to learn or conversations to be had or even arguments, then comes a beast not found in graves – oppressive, utter boredom. Then you may yearn for death, as Captain Younas and Dr. Money began to… before the tocsin went off.

The frenetic wail of the siren echoed through the chamber, indicating that the Galahad had detected an object wider than a meter and denser than gas, within a million-kilometer range. Younas leapt to the cockpit like a castaway catching sight of a ship. He pressed his face against the scope and, through his one good eye, saw something round, spherical actually, and deep green.

It glittered iridescently in the light of a nearby blue giant, like a blob of bubbles lit by morning sunshine. It was about a million clicks out and seemed to be slowly moving further away, its trajectory tangential to the Galahad's. Its appearance puzzled him. It spanned about a hundred meters across – too small for a moon, too symmetrical to be a stray rock and too big for an organism. It *was* the right size and speed for a spacecraft, but it didn't look like any kind of vessel that he recognized. It had no trail to indicate propulsion, no identifying marks or signals, nothing even to indicate its orientation.

There are rules on land and in water but, in space, no need ever arose. There was no traffic, even in areas where hundreds of ships passed. Space is just too big, and the odds of two crafts coming within a thousand kilometers of each other were too small to stir even the most bureaucratic of busybodies. One custom did evolve, however, and eventually became codified by treaty – the Orientation Rule. The Orientation Rule created an Up. On a planet, orientation is natural – ground is down, sky is up. On a spacecraft, there are floors and ceilings. But in the void, there is no ground, no floor. The Orientation Rule simply required that the top of every craft be aimed towards Vega. Thus, two crafts that crossed paths at any angle and direction would have the same orientation. The Rule ensured that antennae would be properly aligned, allowing for identification and communication. Younas was in violation because he was lost; and that ship, if it was a ship, was no help.

He determined to pursue it. He killed the sail, reeled it in, fired up the propulsive engines, and began the slow process of turning. It took an hour to reset course, during which he lost sight of the thing. More hours passed before it was back in range, and by then he could see where it was headed – a small moon.

The moon's surface lay bare, unobscured by any apparent atmosphere, grooved in some places, smooth in others. It was a patchwork of distinctive areas of different shades of fuchsia, bordered by ophidian lines. There were no large craters to indicate eons of cosmic bombardment, but small points were sprinkled throughout, likely indicating volcanic activity.

The UFO continued its path towards and descent to the moon, and it remained visible until suddenly it wasn't.

"It's gone," he announced, still focusing intently. "Vanished."

"How so?" she asked. She had been standing by, eagerly awaiting news.

"Don't know. It could've incinerated or smashed to bits or dove into a sea. Here, have a look. You've got more eyes than me anyway."

She stepped up to the scope, failing to mention that she too was monocular, nearly blind on the left.

"Beautiful," she whispered. She continued to gaze for a minute, then began to look around, pitching and yawing and swiveling the scope at every angle, scouring the universe for anything. A glimpse of the blue giant briefly blinded her and she stepped back, eyes closed.

"You okay?"

"Yes, just seeing spots." She blinked it off and went right back to searching. After a while, she stopped in one position. "Either I'm still seeing things, or I've found the mother."

"Whose mother?" He reclaimed the scope.

"The mother of that little moon – Petunia."

It took him a minute to see it, as the effulgence of the star behind it mostly obscured it, leaving just a thin sliver of crescent. It gleamed with beauty – silver, white and blue – a hidden, precious stone. It was a small world, considerably smaller than Earth, but still much bigger than its satellite.

"What's Petunia?"

"The name of that moon."

"Who named it?"

"I did. Just now."

He plotted an extrapolation of the UFO's course and realized that it came from that planet. They both bristled with excitement and relief.

"Why Petunia?" he asked.

"It's a flower."

"Oh? And what about the mother world? What's her name?"

"Let's see… her name… is Susan. We'll name her after my own mother."

"There you go. Heavy lifting done. Let's just hope that, if anyone lives on ole Susie, they don't have other ideas about what her name should be."

"Oh God, if I may ever again lay eyes on another soul, I don't think I'll worry too much about naming rights."

She continued watching him with hope as he studied his monitors. For the first time in a long time, he didn't look too bad.

"Will we follow the object then?" she asked.

"Not without knowing what happened to it. This dinghy doesn't have any proper probes. Too dangerous."

"What then?"

He retreated from his instruments and thought a moment. "We'll wait and watch. We'll orbit the mother, Susan; study her best we can. See if she coughs up any more mucus balls."

Oops, he was ugly again.

Watch and wait they did, and learned a few things. They saw that, on its daylight side, Susan also appeared quite beautiful. Its blotchy geography was marked by swaths of blue ocean interspersed in its colder regions with areas of sparkling, silvery white. In the warmer land regions, salmon color faded to brown. Susan had a fourteen-hour day and, like its moon, didn't seem to have much of an atmosphere. Its substantial magnetic field indicated a core of molten iron.

Petunia moved slowly and, after three weeks, only finished half its orbit round the planet. Plumes billowed from its surface, confirming the presence of either volcanoes or geysers. Younas and Mary found no other moons or any other UFOs. No radio or microwave signals, or any other signs of intelligence.

By the end of three weeks, he had scoped out a region on Susan that he was confident had sufficiently even ground and moderate climate enough to attempt a landing. A meandering network of lakes covered a large part of it. But he took more interest in a peculiar structure in a barren area, located many kilometers from any lake. It looked large and round and cratered like a crater, or perhaps a volcano. But its golden color contrasted starkly with its surroundings and, at certain times of day, it shone brightly with reflected light. In addition, a long, straight ridge, or maybe a gorge, extended from its edge. The whole thing looked…well, it looked rather like a giant spoon. Of course, from orbital distance, images can converge and play tricks on the mind, especially when you have only one eye. In any case, he determined to land as close to it as possible.

As they descended, Mary's stomach swelled, pregnant with anticipation and giddy from the rapid altitude loss. The thought of leaving that ship, even in a space suit, filled her with such excitement, she wasn't sure she could ever return to it. The descent took half an hour, during which Younas instructed her on some of the procedures, such as donning the suit, preparing her life dolly, and checking and rechecking, and rechecking again, all her connections and seals. She carefully inspected the two-wheel contraption that would be generating her air, heat, pressure and power.

"Can't we just take the hamster ball?" she inquired.

"The ball is for one-man use and it takes forever to inflate. Besides, you never explore with the ball. If you get caught on something or stuck in a ditch, you're dead. You scout with the suits, then the ball later if it's safe. Actually, it's probably best if I go first, alone."

"I'm coming."

The landing went pretty smoothly, unlike the chore of suiting up, which she performed with great difficulty. It was hard enough as a novice, but as a woman, she had the extra fun step of catheterizing her urethra. Naturally, he offered to help and, naturally, she declined.

"What's the temperature out there?"

"Minus seventy-five right now. We have about six hours of daylight left. Can you hear me okay?"

They opened the hatch to a barren land, flat but rocky, granite and clay, and a smattering of limestone formations. Down the ramp they went, then carefully trained their footing on the uneven ground. Off in the distance, a mountain range beckoned. They went the other way.

With little else to do, they had spent much of their life in space keeping fit, and they had escalated their training during their weeks in orbit in preparation for this day. Nonetheless, the hike was taxing and they frequently stopped to rest. Within an hour, a bright beam appeared on the horizon as their visual vector caught the first light of their target, which had caught the light of the morning. They followed it like wise men until the world turned enough that the glare disappeared. By then, they could see what it was – a large, golden, metallic-looking structure, about the size and shape of a small coliseum. When they reached within a stone's throw, Younas threw a stone at it. If Susan had had an atmosphere, the thing would have rung from the blow with a thin, hollow clang. But there was no air, so no sound. They walked all around it, looking for an entrance or some kind of marking, but found none. It looked smooth and shiny as if made by hands, but plain and imperfect as if it had grown there.

It was met on one side by a long ridge of the same height – about fifteen meters tall. The ridge had hints of the same golden color, but appeared more earthy in texture and sheen, like an ore. They followed along the ridge for about five hundred meters, at which point it abruptly narrowed and sloped down to the ground. But it did not end. It continued to run along the ground as a clay-colored mound no more than two feet high and two feet wide. Actually, on closer inspection, it wasn't a mound but a gutter, its top side being concave. This gutter or track, or whatever it was, extended as far as they could see. They followed it for the next two hours, during which nothing seemed to change, not the land or the track. So they put down a radio beacon and turned around, determined to return to ship before nightfall.

# Nineteen

Years earlier on Argos, she had been equally determined to get back to the distribution center and watch Vitamix get made. Her tour guide Sinumbré had told her she'd have to wait about three days.

"Then I'll come back," she said.

"Sure. We just need to see the foreman first. I'm just a low-level super."

The foreman's office was not really an office at all; just an elevated, furnished platform in the center of the building from where he watched everything. She told him her story and her agenda, openly and thoroughly; and though he expressed sympathy, he also used words like "irregular," "inappropriate," and "unauthorized." He had not heard of any questions surrounding the Sector Z epidemic, certainly none involving his center, definitely nothing about any investigation; and he wasn't about to let her "nose around the store." She protested a bit and appealed to his decency, but he would not be moved. He bid her good day and hoped she enjoyed her tour. Sinumbré stood by without a word from his lips, but a face of growing invective. As they climbed back down, he assured her, with angry defiance and through clenched teeth, that she could return and *would* return.

"I had two brothers in Sector Z," he lamented, voice cracking with sorrow. "We ain't even convicts. We just figured we'd put in our time and make a pile of money is all. Now look at us." He pushed past her profuse condolences and continued. "You come back in three quarts. Take the 6:00 tram. Don't get off at the first stop. The next one. I will meet you there."

The second stop at the center was the employee entrance and 6:00 was before the first shift arrived. When she returned, he put her in enough work gear – overcoat, goggles, helmet – that she looked unrecognizable but not ridiculous. Then he put her in the break room to hide out for a while. When the time came, he brought her to the Vitamix area and introduced her to the technician as a quality inspector.

"Nothing to worry about," Sinumbré assured the tech. "Just let her watch your routine and answer any questions she has." Then he turned to the doctor, said he'd be back in a while, and left.

The tech went about his work, trying to ignore her. He opened a door on the Vitamixer revealing four round slots, then pulled four canisters from the shelf behind and placed one in each slot.

"What are you doing?" she asked.

"Loading the cartridges," he replied, then pointed and named each one. "B-complex, Ascorbate, Calcium, and your trace elements." He paused a moment, then added "I'm not sure what you're supposed to inspect. It's mostly automated. Just watching and waiting and troubleshooting."

"That's fine. Can you tell me how it works?"

"You see these tubes?"

Four hollow tubes with narrowed ends protruded from the inner side of the door.

He continued. "I close the lid, they puncture the cartridges, and the mixer draws up a measured amount from each one."

"Draw? Liquid?"

"They come liquid, end up powder. First, they mix in that drum right there. It shakes it up like paint. Then over there, the juice gets evaporated into paste, then spun and tumble-dried. That's the longest part. Then it's dumped in a sack, sealed, stamped and spit onto a pallet. Then it starts all over."

"One sack at a time? That doesn't seem practical."

"It's wasteful in the short run, but they say they save money long-term by customizing each package. Each sector has its own needs. It's all precalculated and programmed into the mixer."

"Then you load more cartridges?"

"Nope. One set for the whole day, enough for all five sectors."

"Okay, let's see."

He was right. It *was* a long and boring process. She spent much of the time reading, and he tended to other duties around the center.

Sinumbré checked in from time to time. Every couple of hours, the mixer dropped another ten-kilo sack of Vitamix-2 onto the pallet, until all four finished.

"Wait a minute, four?" she asked, as the tech prepared to leave.

"That's right, Sectors V, W, X, Y makes four."

"But you have enough for five, right?"

"Sure, but Sector Z just shut down."

"And what will you do with the leftovers?"

"I posit that's a good question. Dump it, I guess. We're supposed to return the cartridges to Central for reuse."

She saw no further use for artifice and began to shed her hot costume as the tech took the cartridges one by one to the nearby eye-wash station and dumped their remains.

"That's odd," he said, and she stopped to look over. "This one's already empty."

Empty of Vitamin C.

She approached him and grabbed it. It now weighed only about 2 kilos, light enough for her to handle and inspect, looking for a leak perhaps. She found none. What she did find was a small metal plug, as wide as a straw, soldered into place on the bottom.

She showed the tech. "Do your other empties have this?" she asked.

They didn't.

"What about the full ones?"

There were over two dozen of them, almost fifteen kilos each. She went and found Sinumbré to help. Sure enough, four other containers had the same signs of tampering, all of them labeled "Ascorbate". From high on, the foreman noticed the commotion and descended from his office.

"What the hell are *you* doing here?" he bellowed on recognizing Dr. Money. "Besides trespassing and earning yourself some trouble?"

"What the HELL is this?" she barked back with matching fury, and showed him the empty cartridge. "What is going on in your little distribution center? Why would anyone siphon off a worthless vitamin? It seems to me you have a demented little killer in your midst. Maybe you!"

People in the area started to look over. Over the din of machines, they could only hear yelling, not words. Nonetheless, the foreman got nervous and raised his hands in defense.

"Now look, Doc," he protested. "I really do not know what you're talking about."

"Oh, don't you? You have cameras all over this place. If this isn't you, then buster you'd better help me out due to the fact that, of all the people in here, you're in the best position to pull off this… this *atrocity*, or at least find out who did."

Her words released an avalanche of fury in Sinumbré, and he launched himself at the foreman, pinning him down and squeezing his throat. The tech slithered away, having already worked too long a day for any of this nonsense. Others came running to assist the poor doctor as she desperately tried to pull the assailant away. They succeeded, the foreman was saved, and nobody filed a report. People on Argos didn't rat. The punishments were too severe, and everyone was guilty of something.

By the grace of serendipity, a spark of wisdom ignited in the foreman just as his light nearly vanished, and he became much more helpful afterwards. He spent hours with the doctor and Sinumbré reviewing surveillance, but found nothing suspicious.


After that, she wrestled with the idea of filing a report with The Company. If she did, they just might look into the matter upon learning that someone had intentionally cost them a fortune and might do so again. Justice might be done. But if they did and it was, she would never know. Besides, there also existed the small possibility that The Company was behind this. It didn't seem likely; there were certainly cheaper and more efficient ways to downsize. Besides, this crime, this mass murder, seemed far too imaginative for such a bloated, public-private partnership as the Mao Corporation. She ultimately decided to keep on sleuthing it alone. No, not alone. That was impossible. She didn't have access and didn't know people. Except her patients.

She didn't quite know where to go next. The tech had said that his cartridges came from Central Supply, which she knew from her research meant Central Receiving and Processing (CRP). Argos had three central supply locations: CRP-P (Personnel Support), CRP-I (Infrastructure) and the massive complex called CRP-M (Mechanics) where all the mining equipment and other machines and machine parts were assembled, repaired and stored. Her interest lay in CRP-P, where they handled everything from boots to pillows to vitamins. But CRP-P was much larger and less accessible than a regional center. If it hid the answers she sought, she didn't know how to find them.

But she *did* know her patients, some of them very well; and she knew they were a great potential resource, particularly those from Sector T. Sector T housed many of The Company's white collars and chair fillers; and despite their softer existence, they seemed to frequent the doctor's office more often than the callused ones.

She returned early from vacation and was assigned some new patients, and most of her old ones. During their visits, she made a point to gab with the right ones about their work, looking for a way in. She found one…maybe…almost three weeks later in Victor Lahab.

Middle aged and middle management, Victor was a recent addition to her practice and a frequent customer. Though relatively healthy, he was somewhat of a hypochondriac, or perhaps just lonely, often presenting with vague or confusing symptoms of which no cause could be found. Sometimes, he had no symptoms at all, just "concerns" about this or that. His job title, Quality Control Officer, sounded as nebulous as his complaints. When she inquired further, it turned out that, among his other duties, he oversaw several CRP-P departments. On hearing that, she proceeded to tell him a partial truth – that some of her patients showed signs of deficiency and that she had concerns about the quality of the nutrients they were getting. Mr. Lahab, in turn, offered to put her in touch with another Victor, Victor Gall, who ran that particular division.

Lahab must have been a big cheese because Gall met with her soon after and was quite accommodating. But Gall was skeptical. After all, he had not heard from anyone else in Health, just this one doctor who was bypassing normal channels. Nonetheless, he reviewed with her many things – purchasing logs showing that their suppliers had not changed, batch logs showing that all supplies remained well within the expiration dates, and storage logs showing that proper temperatures and humidity had been maintained without interruption or power outage. Each of those records contained the signed names of all responsible parties, names that she had hoped to record surreptitiously. But the building was equipped with Eye Phone disruptors, so she relied on her big brain instead. When she later cross-referenced the list with her patient roster, only one name turned up – Silbin Lee in Purchasing.

Lee had lived on Argos for years, but she didn't remember him. He was not one for visiting the doctor, even when required, and luckily had missed several appointments, leaving him overdue for some compulsory scans and updates. This time, she called him personally to reschedule and this time, he skipped again. So she called him again and politely explained the Mao policy on mandatory maintenance and missed visits. He apologized and explained how busy he was and, by the way, he had been afraid of doctors' offices since childhood. She, in turn, expressed her sympathy and offered to make a house call.

"I'll sometimes do that for my Sector T patients," she lied. "I don't like to see people get in trouble."

After a moment's hesitation, he consented. Dr. Money never lied, and to do so gave her indigestion. But what she was contemplating made her sick.

Long ago, when the compliance pill was first developed, it also came in an injectable form. We humans eventually banned it by treaty after we realized the unethical nature and abuse potential of a compliance drug that could be administered involuntarily. Now Mary Money was neither unethical nor abusive. Quite the contrary. But she had run out of ideas and this lead, this Lee fellow, was her last long pass. Should it lead nowhere, she would be lost. That, of course, would not do. She had to shrink the risk. She had borne the sound of too much wailing, and felt the sting of too many nails sunk in her forearm by the clutch of agony. She knew nothing of manipulation, seduction or interrogation. What she did know was how to give a shot, and Lee was overdue for his booster of Multivax-Max. And she had a molecular printer with pirated software that had recipes for all kinds of banned substances.

She struggled with the dilemma until it brought her to tears. Then, at once, she calmed. She wiped her eyes, took a breath and nodded her head with decision. "Yes," she declared to an empty bedroom. "I'll do it."

# TWENTY

"I'll do it" is also what she also told herself on Planet Susan as the day started to wane. She had decided that she would, in fact, follow the orders of a man she disliked and return to the cramped ship that she abhorred. The thought of freezing to death was more abhorrent, and indeed the temperature dropped another hundred degrees overnight. They slept in their suits from sheer exhaustion. The next morning, they moved the Galahad to a spot near the beacon they had placed, and set out early from where they left off. It would have to continue that way – short expeditions, never straying too far – because of Susan's short days and harsh conditions, and because their ship was built and equipped for speed, not exploration. The Galahad could shuttle in and out of orbit but could not fly laterally at low altitudes. It didn't even have a window.

They resumed their march alongside the mysterious track which itself continued endlessly in a mostly straight direction. By mid-morning, it hadn't changed, seeming less mysterious and quite possibly pointless. But then a second track began approaching from the left. It eventually merged with the first. They continued to follow. Later on, another track, another merger, then another. They started to feel that they were headed in the right direction, to the root of whatever this thing was, and hoped they would not come to a fork. When the time came, down went the beacon and off they went back to the ship.

On day three, they found water. Or at least it looked like water – just a little brook that came within a few meters of their path, then wandered away.

"Christopher, do we have anything with which to collect samples?"

He loved it when she called him by his given name.

"Nothing on me, but I'm sure we can find something on the ship."

Some kilometers later, the brook wandered back, or perhaps one of its friends. It was bigger now, more stream than brook. More importantly, it appeared to be hosting some primitive forms of life. They were still and green like plants, some with colorful splashes, and they appeared to be rooted in the ground on the water's edge. But they didn't look like plants. They didn't branch or obey any kind of fractal geometry. Instead, they preferred weird shapes, no two alike, like sculptures in an abstract art show. They reached up to a foot tall and looked kind of rubbery.

She fell to her knees under the fateful weight of the moment. She went over to touch one, ignoring his expressed concern. The thing felt softer to her gloved hand than it looked. Its shape gave way to her touch, like pressing into putty; but as soon as she let go, it bounced right back to its original form.

"Ya, definitely need some samples," he said.

As they went further, the stream continued to widen. It eventually crossed the path of the track. The track neither crossed over nor through the water. It simply ended on one side and resumed on the other. Eventually, track and stream diverged again, and the two exiles faced a decision of which to follow. But the time had come to go back, and the decision could wait.

The next day, they chose the track, but nonetheless continued to see more and more water as they continued – bigger streams and an occasional river. They also saw more life forms, and the further they traveled, those too became larger and more interesting, more colorful and more complex in shape. Some of them actually moved, slowly adjusting their positions or changing their shapes, but remaining firmly planted on the margin of a stream.

They had to stop early on day six, having reached a river's edge with no way to cross except fly. Once again, the track they followed had simply ended at the bank and picked up on the other side. The next day they rested, giving their feet, and Mary's poor urethra, a break. The day after that, day eight, is when they saw *It*.

They had reached another stretch of dry, rocky land with no sign of life. They had been trudging for hours and were ready to head back when, all of a sudden – zoom! Something whizzed right by them, rolling down the track at jogging speed.

"What the hell?"

It was round, as big as a beach ball and dark green. If it was alive, it paid them no notice and continued on its way into the distance. They raced after it, their dollies bouncing jovially behind; but they were too tired and encumbered, and lost sight of it. They didn't sleep that night.

They reached lake country on the days that followed. The climate ran warmer there, though still below freezing. The ground was more even, but softer and somewhat hilly, making it hard to find a decent landing spot for the ship. Large and small lakes abounded, some as small as a pond or pool. Many of the ponds bubbled froth or sported halos of emanating vapor, some tinged with color. Some were frozen.

The life forms they encountered in the area moved in bigger and quicker and more pronounced ways. Some even changed colors – increasingly fancy colors. But still they stayed planted in place. More tracks converged and several more beach balls rolled by, none of which Younas and Mary bothered to chase. There was no point, for they were clearly heading the right way, slowly and steadily, to something big. They reached something big on day eleven.


They started the morning trudging up a gentle hill, reaching the top after a half kilometer and a half hour. From their vantage, they could see a lake off in the near distance – or perhaps an ocean – calm and still, stretching out to the horizon. On reaching the hill's downslope, they could see to its bottom and what lay beyond. A plateau stretched a half kilometer from hill to lake. It appeared to be a hub of some kind, met by tracks coming from several directions. As Younas and Mary drew nearer, it became apparent that this place hosted some kind of primitive but intelligent activity. Pits had been dug, containing various materials of liquid or semisolid form. Metal vats and other containers, large and small, were scattered around. Trenches and ducts crisscrossed the area transporting this or that, some assisted by pumps. Crude tools lay strewn about, some recognizable, some not. There were no sheltering structures of any kind. The whole place resembled an abandoned encampment.

Except that it wasn't abandoned. Dozens of those same green spheres, lined up in rows like troops, sat and soaked in the shallow waters along the shore. Now seen close up and motionless, the beings, which

Younas had dubbed Melons (without objection), looked to be alive. They didn't respire or perspire or even budge, but their surface had an organic quality. Younas and Mary observed them as closely as they dared, fearing to disturb them. Occasionally, another Melon would stroll in off a track and join the others, utterly ignoring the nosy visitors.

"Do you think they're sleeping?" asked Younas.

"I am worlds away from a guess. They could be, I suppose, or recharging some other way. For all I know, they could be communing in some grand meeting."

"Or maybe they're just having a drink."

"What I would do for a sip of cold, unrecycled water right now." She sighed.

"Don't get any ideas, Mary. That's not water; or if it is, it's not *just* water. Water freezes at these temperatures."

"And no sky means no rain, I suppose."

"No, no weather here. I figure all this liquid springs up from underground, nice and warm. But it can't last."

"What do you mean?" she asked.

"I mean liquid water is totally unstable at low atmospheric pressure. It has to freeze or evaporate. My guess is these lakes are vaporizing into space as fast as they're filled. They'll all dry up some day, and then it'll be goodbye to life on planet Susan."

She felt sad at the thought, and then at once grateful, grateful for her whole life and all the misfortunes that brought her to this privileged position. She was the only person (besides What's-His-Face) who would ever witness this rare, fleeting, miraculous place. She was even thankful for him.

They turned back from the shore to browse around the encampment and all the artifacts within. For hours, they examined everything as best they could through their cumbersome suits. Yet, despite their combined intelligence and experience, they could not deduce the purpose or point of any of it. What was done there? By whom? And what role did the Melons play?

It was precisely at noon, when the light of the blue giant obliterated the surrounding heavens, that many answers came to life. The Melons suddenly came ashore and busily rolled around like the start of a game of pool. They started changing colors, particularly when interreacting with each other. They didn't just change from one color to another like any dull chameleon. They displayed wild, rapidly changing patterns of colors, no two alike, in hundreds of different shades, most too subtle for human eyes. They appeared iridescent if not psychedelic, and possibly epileptogenic.

They also changed shape, often looking amoebic, to suit whatever activity in which they engaged; and they were an active bunch. This was clearly their town. If a Melon needed to handle a tool, it grew an appendage. If it needed to carry something, it involuted its surface into a pouch, then sealed it shut.

They went about their business, seemingly blind to the two astonished humans in their midst. They dug and poured and stirred and hammered and cut and molded and many other things, until past dark for human eyes. At one point, a train of thirty Melons rolled in from somewhere and joined the show. Younas and Mary were so entranced that they stayed and watched well past a sensible time, almost into the risky hours. Regret never crossed their minds until they had almost returned to the ship and could sense their little dollies struggling to keep them alive, the deadly cold slipping past their capacity. They vowed to each other not to let it happen again.

"Even if those things break into song and dance," swore Younas.

They didn't explore the planet any further. There was enough to see at the Melon Patch, as they called it, to which they returned day after day.

# Twenty-One

This was not the first time she had taken big risks in visiting strangers. Years before, on the moon called Argos, she planned to pay a house call to a strange man – a man who might have been a criminal – under false pretenses, and with the intention of drugging him for information.

Like him, she also lived in Sector T, so she planned to visit him at the end of the day, on her way back to her own abode. Sector T was a little more upscale – no roommates or bunk beds or long feeding lines. Silbin Lee was a little incongruous there. He had a harsh and hard look about him with his small, close-set eyes, low-set brow and a nose that looked to have been punched a few times.

Nonetheless, he behaved politely, though perhaps grudgingly so. He welcomed her into his quarters and asked that she call him Silbi. He gave short, straight answers to her routine questions, and obeyed her instructions as she went through her exam – stand up, sit down, lie down, stand again, blow into this, pee into that. When it came time for his shot – time to administer a vaccine surreptitiously laced with a homemade psychoactive drug – she became understandably nervous. As she approached the abyss, she started to shake, which made her more nervous, which made her shakier. Lee didn't notice. He hated shots and had his eyes tightly shut. Eventually, it was done, and she calmed soon after.

She continued her routine while she waited the expected seven minutes for the drug to take effect, then seven more. Then came time to test it with a silly command. She told him to stand on one foot and stick his finger up his nose. Surely enough, he did. But what did it prove? After all, a routine physical is already full of absurd things, and to a patient who didn't know any better, this would just seem more of the same. She realized that and decided to go further – something unmistakable. She sat down, crossed a leg and removed her shoe.

"Get down on the floor and kiss my foot," she commanded, waving the tired extremity.

As he got on his hands and knees, he realized he'd been drugged.

"What is this?" he demanded between kisses.

He wanted to attack but found himself lacking the will. Any notion he had was obliterated when he unexpectedly stood back up, causing her to react with fright and unmistakable orders.

"Back off! Go over there! Sit down. Sit on your hands. Don't move until I say."

He again obeyed and again asked "What *is* this?"

"I'm sorry," she replied, "but I can't explain right now. I have to ask you some questions. It's a Company exercise." She squirmed a bit as he glared in silence. "Questions about your workplace," she continued. "Again, I am truly, very sorry for this. Nonetheless, I need you to tell me if you know anything about vitamins being siphoned off from storage containers at Central Supply. So tell me."

A brief moment passed as he tried to resist. "Sure I do," he finally confessed.

A rush of emotion pulsed down to her fingertips from the sound of his words – relief that her reckless gambit was not for naught, and dread over what she had unearthed, and what he might say next.

"Are you involved?" she continued.

"Yup."

"But why? What could possibly motivate someone to skim a bunch of cheap nutrient?"

Now it was he who squirmed, unable to move from his position of discomfort.

"We skim a lot of things," he answered. "And who said it's cheap?"

"It's not?"

"I'm the Purchasing Officer. I know the prices of things and I'm the one who knows what's worth stealing," he bragged.

"Then this was for money?" she asked with horror.

"Sure, lots of it. Last centiblock, your little vitamin had a juicy spike in price. Couldn't resist."

A single tear slipped down her cheek. "But all those people," she whispered.

"Who?"

"Sector Z!"

"Oh ya, the Spacebug outbreak. Heard about that. What of it?"

"Never mind," she huffed and began pacing as if trying to generate power to her brain. She had neither planned for success nor anticipated its form, and she did not know what next to do. Lee didn't quite know what to make of her behavior. She was odd, and he worried that she might be loosely assembled.

He also didn't know, nor did she, that 1% of people were born with a slight variation of a particular liver enzyme, that those people metabolized the compliance drug rapidly, and that he was one of those people. But he was. As he gradually regained self-control, he continued to play along for a while, partly due to a kind of momentum of obedience, and partly to bide his time; for he too wasn't sure what next to do. Keeping him patient were the thin walls between flats, and her nervous grip on a Thug Zapper – the popular, nonlethal weapon of electrocution without contact, like a cross between a taser and a flame thrower. She also had an alarm.

Meanwhile, she continued to question him, getting the names of the others involved. He only knew a couple including the ringleader, Victor Gall himself. She asked if anyone else from The Company had questioned them. None had.

"Have you any idea as to why the Ascorbate became so suddenly costly?" she asked.

"Who knows? Maybe been a factory fire. Sometimes a shipment gets lost in space, struck by a meteor or whatever. The cargo spills out into Peter Tork's Locker."

She thought a moment. "Ok, here's what we'll do," she concluded. "You're going to turn yourself in. You'll confess everything you just told me. You won't mention me or anything that happened here this evening. Yes, that's the plan."

Unfortunately, she had no experience with the use of compliance medication, and her words were indeed a plan and not a command. This error gave Lee a moment to know her intention without being compelled to follow. It was time enough for him to become worried, and to think quickly, which he did. He first thought to stall for more time, time enough for more thinking. He had already learned that was he forced to tell the truth whenever she demanded information. But could he *initiate* a lie? Yes, he discovered that he could, as he clutched his sternum and declared with a groan that he had a crushing chest pain. He knew the look from years earlier when he had watched an old man dying as he robbed him, and now he breathed with labored breath and swayed with feigned dizziness. The charade struck her with three sensations simultaneously:

- Concern for her patient – the kind of concern that often persuades people to enter medical school, and would be especially strong in a person who volunteers to serve on Argos.
- Concern for herself – this development complicated an already difficult situation.
- Suspicion – Dr. Money was no fool.

"It could just be a panic attack," she said, trying to calm him as well as herself.

Coronary artery disease had become a relatively unusual cause of death with the development of the CAFS (Catheter-implemented Angiogenic Factor Seeding) procedure. Performed routinely when one reached middle age, the CAFS made use of fetal hormones and stem cells to grow new coronary arteries. But not everyone could afford the CAFS, including most of the workers on Argos.

"Lie yourself down," she said as she approached him. "That's it. On your back and be still."

She examined him again, listening to his chest with a wireless stethoscope, then scanning his heart with a handheld ultrasound. He started to sense his freewill accelerate. It felt weird, like the first tingle when the dentist's Novocain starts wearing off. He became tempted to try something. However, he still lacked the control needed for subtle movement, so when he did try to move, he suddenly sat straight up. She leapt back.

"Lie down!" she yelled, and he quickly found himself obeying once more. She paused a moment, not quite sure what to make of what just occurred. "Are you still having chest pain?"

"Yes!"

"Ok." From her bag, she took out another sonic device. It looked like a big wand, the end about as wide as a golf ball.

"This uses sound waves to break up clots. If you're having a heart attack, it should help."

She cautiously returned to his side. The fine tip of the wand was a marker and she used it, guided by certain anatomical landmarks, to draw strange, curvy lines across his left pectoralis. When finished, she turned it around, turned it on and lightly pressed the wide end against him. Lee could feel its gentle, pulsating vibrations against his chest wall as she slowly rubbed it along the route she had drawn.

The whole process took about ten minutes…or, it would have, except that halfway through, the rest of the compliance drug quickly wore off. He felt a surge of freedom as his liver dispensed of the last of it. She was perched at his left and fairly busy, and didn't see him testing his renewed independence as he closed his right hand, then opened it, then closed it again, finally clenching it into a fist. She never saw the right cross to her head.

She awoke sometime later in a daze, with a searing, throbbing pain in her left cheek, smelling an awful smell and feeling a heaviness on her chest. Slowly, she regained some sense and some vision in her right eye, and vaguely recognized the foul face of a man lying on her. Lying on her back, her left eye still blurred, she struggled both to breathe and to dodge his putrid breath. When he saw that she had wakened, he pressed his big paw over her injured mouth, eliciting a muffled scream of agony.

As her fog continued to lift, she realized that her body suit had been ripped away at the top, exposing her neck and chest. With his free hand, he continued his plundering march southwards, undeterred, even pleased by her return to consciousness.

Mary Money was not delicate. Her younger years had been spent in lower status, and subject to the whims and moods of three older brothers. She could fight; and long before coming to Argos, she had many times thought detailed thoughts about what she would do in a situation like this. But she had not trained, and now, upon knowing her circumstance, all she could think to do was to writhe in futility.

It didn't slow him much, but it did a little; and in that little extra time, she remembered her alarm. All Mao management and female Argos staff had one – a button planted under the skin, placed where it could be easily reached but not easily tripped, on the superior side of the right olecranon process. If you straighten your elbow, the bony protrusion on the back makes a little shelf at the top. Right there. Unfortunately, Lee also knew about it, and when he saw her reach for it, he grabbed her left wrist and pinned it to the floor.

Now, with both his hands busy containing alarms (one silent, one noisy), his scarred and greedy brain did not know what to do. But she did. His position had changed with his last move, bringing his head into better view, and with it his neck, and with that an opportunity, long shot though it was. The long shot was a short jab – two of them actually – which she fired off quickly, obliquely to the cricoid cartilage, just below his Adam's apple.

Crunch. The pain felt so sharp that he thought she had stabbed him, and he quickly grabbed his throat with both hands and rolled off her, onto his side and out of view. She could still hear him though, as he briefly tried cursing through hoarseness and pain. She heard his breath, guttural and loud, as he worked more and more to move air past the growing swelling in his throat.

She tried to turn and see him but was too weak. She reached for her elbow and pressed the alarm. "Silbin," she called. No reply. His stridor continued. "Silbi," she tried again, then slid back into blackness.


She awoke days later in a strange room with a strange sensation of weightlessness. It was an easy enough achievement on a small moon, and an important one in a hospital, being necessary to prevent bed sores and leg clots and such. The hospital bed worked like a hover chair, except that it relied on fine jets of air instead of magnetism. Her fingers gently probed a sore area near her temple that had been shaved clean. She detected two bumps, each about as wide as a straw. Her stomach boiled with dread at the thought of having undergone any kind of surgery on Argos, much less on her skull.

The two bumps were plugs that filled two holes that had been drilled. The first hole was for instilling a solution of enzymes, enzymes to digest the growing, clotted collection of blood that had been pressing on her brain. The second hole served to suction it out. Then the first again to pour glue to prevent further bleeding; and the second provided access for tools, tools to tack the dura (the brain's lining) against the inner wall of the skull.

She lay a while as the jets slowly rolled her like a roast. She didn't think about much with her bruised brain and couldn't remember recent events. Not yet anyways.

The Company gave her a block to recover before sending someone to question her, but it wasn't enough time. With her memory still too sketchy, they gave her a couple more. Meanwhile, she rehabilitated nicely, and was up and about within quarts. But they wouldn't let her leave, and she knew enough to know she was in trouble. When she finally started to remember, she asked about Lee, but the hospital staff either didn't know or wouldn't tell.

When The Company came calling the second time, it sent the same man as before. This time, she recognized him more clearly.

"Victor, right? Aren't you one of my patients?"

"I sure am. I'm also the one who got you in to see Victor Gall at Central, remember?"

She did. The Company had planted the agent, who called himself Victor Lahab, as a patient in her practice, in order to keep watch on what she knew and what she was up to. A decision had been made early on to give her some slack and even some assistance, in order to see what she might learn. The thinking was that an unwitting participant in their investigation might be an effective one. Lahab was actually not a lonely hypochondriac. Rather he was schooled in the art of deception and manipulation, and could steer a conversation with stealth. Now he shed all that.

"That's quite a slug you took. You almost died," he said.

"A man attacked me," she replied, instinctively palming the left side of her face.

"Oh yes, Mr. Silbin Lee. I'd say you returned the favor but good."

"Is he alright?"

He wouldn't say. She pleaded, but he wouldn't.

"Never mind him," he said. "Let's talk about you. We're doing house calls now, is that it?"

She already felt confused as to why this patient, this Quality Control bureaucrat, came to visit her. Now his question startled her, and she hesitated.

"Kind of unconventional, wouldn't you say?" he continued. "Might even say inappropriate."

"I made a few visits in Sector Z out of necessity, during the quarantine. I got used to it."

He sat forward with stabbing eyes and possibly a slight grin, winding up his next question. "Did you drug *them* too?"

She was mute with horror, and not just because she was caught. She felt appalled by the noxious sound of her deed being so plainly stated by the lips of another. She was appalled at herself.

"Nothing to say?" he pressed on.

Indeed, she had absolutely no idea what to say, so she remained silent. "Lee must have said something," she thought to herself. "But how much can this man actually know?"

As if hearing her thoughts, he answered. "Maybe I should shoot you up with some Compliance," he said. "That'd work."

Her heart sank as he stood up, moseyed cross the room, and sat at her side. He leaned into her ear and lowered his voice.

"We found traces in his blood, and in a syringe at the scene. We've been all through your office and your files. It seems you broke more laws and codes than a pirate. Now you are looking at spending the rest of your pretty little life on this rock as a slave of the Mao Corporation, and the only chance at all that you have of saving yourself is if you talk to me, *right now.*"

His words melted away any remaining hesitation, and she poured out her tale through tears and a migraine. As she did, his attitude changed a little. He thanked her for her candor and assured her that this embezzlement ring would be broken up, its members properly punished, and the vulnerabilities plugged up. But she had still broken laws and she knew too much. The whole situation threatened major embarrassment, if not scandal. She couldn't stay on Argos, and they couldn't let her go.

He left for a while to brief and confer with his superiors. On returning, his face looked as stern and illegible as when he left.

"We're going to have to lock you up for a while until we figure this out," he informed her.

She nodded her understanding, though she didn't really understand. Argos didn't have prisons; only a few, crude holding cells deep in the mines, meant for brief detention in the unusual event that someone became unruly.

She spent the next several months in one such cell, in near-constant discomfort, hardly able to sleep on pallets, her only furniture. She would have back pain for the rest of her life. She was brought once a day past gawking workers to feed and toilet. If she needed more than that, well, she had a bucket. The heat at this depth suffocated her, as did the ubiquitous dust. The mining never stopped, nor did the oppressive, mechanical noise and chemical smell that went with it. Even sight was hard in the dim, available light.

Her case was passed around while she waited and wept and prayed and slept and prayed some more. It passed from desk to desk, where it sometimes sat for weeks, waiting for a decision, a reply or an idea. Many calls were placed to many contacts who worked in this or that planetary jurisdiction – contacts who made a comfortable living facilitating a steady stream of labor to the Mao corporation. Someone in the PASS agency on Dundo actually replied early on that they might know someone in Magellan with a place and use for her. But it took forever to act on it, and several more eternities for the Magellan folks to discuss, consult, negotiate and finally make arrangements. And not until she was finally set to leave Argos did Victor Lahab reach out one more time to end to her last bit of torment. Silbin Lee, he informed her, had survived her throat strike – a complete recovery. However, The Company put him to death for his crimes soon after.

# Twenty-Two

"Hold on," demanded Younas. "Slam on the brakes and back it up. I thought you told me, many years ago, that *you* actually killed someone. Now you're telling me it was Mao?"

"Didn't I though? He would have lived were it not for my actions."

"Oh my, what a big, smelly pile of fiction! He beat you, he tried to rape you, end of story."

"Ok, but it all started with me, you see, with my commission of a felony. That's called a Felony Murder. It doesn't matter if I actually pulled the switch."

"Hey," he replied, throwing up his hands. "You can whip yourself all you want. I know it gets boring out here and I myself enjoy a good flogging from time to time. But I am a big fan of reality, and it's painful to watch your logical contortions. You're gonna give yourself a hernia. The guy was vermin; he got what he deserved. The Company, not you, gave it to him and the world smells better. The end."

She pondered his words for a moment, then persisted. "He was just a thief until he met me."

"As far as you know."

"Yes, as far as I know."

"Where I'm from, a guy like that doesn't get left to the authorities. He gets taken off world and gets fed bits of himself until there's nothing left."

She didn't flinch. "And you think that's okay."

"Sure as sheep dip. Been that way for generations. It's expected."

"Look," she said "you can choose to be moral or be morally fashionable. The twain rarely cross paths. By now, most of the customs and all of the people from your hometown have been gone for generations. Now, where do you turn for guidance?"

"Myself, I guess."

She rolled her eyes. "Oh, Lord."

They returned to the melon patch daily for several days. He even inflated the hamster ball for her, but she found it too problematic. They didn't explore beyond that, except to occasionally follow some Melons as far as safely possible when the Melons ventured to other parts.

The Melons could do metallurgy without fire. They practiced masonry, often venturing out to add or repair track. And they seemed to be avid chemists, though it was usually a mystery as to what they made or why. They also seemed to be involved in engineering, as some of them made gears and other machine parts, without any evident use for them. Younas contended that they made such things for use by a higher life form as yet undiscovered, and he wanted to explore more of the planet. But the Melons fascinated Mary and so they stayed put.

"You don't think they're smart enough to use this stuff?" she asked.

"I don't think they're smart at all. I think they have complex instincts, like bees or ants. And I know they're not advanced enough for space travel. Don't forget, the reason we're here is because we saw a spacecraft coming from this world."

She went to the patch every day and observed and took notes. He sometimes stayed behind on the Galahad. With her background in science, she made some fairly good guesses. For one, she concluded that color was their language. That explained the sundry colors playing hypnotically on their phosphorescent coats. No air meant no sound; they had evolved in a world immersed in silence. Judging by their appearance, they were a chatty bunch, only occasionally resting in a state of solid green. Green was their silence, gray their death.

She also concluded that they were solar-powered, having never seen them consume anything. No air meant no combustion. We Earthlings, in order to evolve beyond plant life, needed to move past photosynthesis. Moving and thinking simply require more energy than our leafy solar panels could provide, so we learned to burn chemicals. But on planet Susan, burning was not only impossible, it was also unnecessary due to a more powerful star, a thinner atmosphere, and the fact that the Melons spent most of their lives at rest. An array of advanced photoreceptors covered their surface, bestowing sight and harnessing as much energy from as many wavelengths as possible. One side effect of this evolution was that it precluded carnivorous behavior and therefore any instinct for violence.

Despite her insight, she could not guess the product of the Melons' efforts. It seemed like a lot of make-work, like bureaucrats trying to justify a budget. She figured that Younas must be right – that they were making components and ingredients to export to a far-off land, for an advanced purpose by an advanced life form. She had plenty of time, she figured, to discover all of it.

But she was wrong about some things too. They both were. For one thing, the Melons didn't actually deliver everything they carried. They ingested some. Although they were entirely solar-powered, they still needed a wide variety of nutrients. Their physiological functions were far more complex than those of their closest ancestors, and had evolved beyond their ability to synthesize all the necessary components. A Melon's body simply did not make all the parts it needed to run, and that was the purpose of all their endeavors – the procurement and manufacture of vitamins and nutrients.

Younas was right about one thing – the Melons weren't that bright. They simply followed the instructions that God had taught them. That is why they paid no mind to their gawking guests. Without a sense of curiosity or fear, they simply went around them.

But he was wrong about the presence of higher beings. The Melons were, in fact, the most sophisticated life on the planet. That became apparent one day, after three earth weeks on Susan. He and Mary were at the patch when all the Melons suddenly stopped their work in the middle of the day, put everything down, and rolled over to the shore. But they didn't enter the water like they had every evening. They just sat there in quiet green. Mary and Younas followed curiously but didn't see anything different about the Melons or the lake. But ten minutes later, there *was* something – a shadow on the water's surface, round and small, but growing rapidly.

Younas thought that something might emerge from the depths. Perhaps an undersea volcano had erupted, spilling its contents into the abyss. But Mary looked up.

A meteor or something. A big, green blob of a meteor in the sky. It was impossible to know how big or far, but it was falling fast. Younas was frightened at first, but as it neared, he recognized it as the object he had seen from space. Knowing its size – about as big as a football field – he quickly determined that it wouldn't kill them, as it was far from overhead.

But what a splash! Down into the lake it went, making such a wave that they had to run, lest their dollies get soaked. After a succession of waves, the lake settled down, but not completely. The surface remained finely agitated, like the approach of a slow boil. Then, all at once, a thousand Melons burst out of the water and rolled across the shore like amphibious invaders. The patch became suddenly crowded and abuzz with chatter. Many of the arrivals unloaded what looked like some kind of salt. Most of them then departed by track for other places. Within an hour, the patch returned mostly back to "normal," just a little more crowded.

Mary was wrong about something else too. She and Younas did not actually have plenty of time for discovery, not in the way she meant. She learned this fact in a hot argument, about six weeks after they landed.


They had already wandered around a bit, and found some other smaller Melon communities, mostly around the same great lake. They hadn't yet found any higher life forms, and he was increasingly curious about the mystery of Melon space flight and all the little, mechanical doodads they made. The two of them had become accustomed to surviving there and she had grown content with the idea of living there – settling in and spending what remained of their lives and supplies on Planet Susan. They spent increasingly more time apart, which made it easier. She had to get out every day. He often stayed behind to work on the ship or play VR games or find different ways to get high. He missed alcohol.

The fight began during one of their expeditions. They were sitting on a hillside watching Melon traffic from a distance – she trying to detect a pattern to their movement – when he began unpacking a mylar blanket. She assumed it was a new tactic to help them stay off-ship longer. But there was a problem.

"I see you only brought one," she said.

"Oh, they're not for us, Mary."

"No?"

"Ya, I've been trying to think of different ways for us to bring one of these critters with us when we leave. Then it occurred to me – probably could just throw one of these things over it. Ha! Sometimes the best answer is the simple one hiding right in your face. So I brought one along to try it out."

It took her a minute to unpack his entire statement and everything wrong with it.

"You want to bring a Melon to the ship? They're light-dependent. It will die! You know that. It might even die before you get it on board if you put that thing on it."

"Well, ya. I don't collect pets. I collect trophies."

"Trophies? You want to tack it on a wall? To impress who? That is a lousy, awful excuse to defile this… this sanctuary. We find this place, this pure and beautiful place. We're the first and probably last people ever to be here. And your first instinct is to muck it up with your muddy, stinking footprint?"

"Look, Doc, first of all, I ain't a scientist. That's you. I'm a hunter, Baby. That's what I do. Second—"

"You call that hunting? Ha!"

"Second, I'm a captain on a mission for the Magellan Interplanetary Agency."

"Oh, come on."

"And my mission, as best I understand it, is to find Paradise. And this is not it."

She lowered and softened her voice. "Listen, Christopher, please. What this place is… it's a second chance. For you, for us. You don't *have* to be a captain or a hunter."

She grabbed his hand and tried to make eye contact, but the suits made it hard to connect. He pulled away.

"I'm also a man and men don't change. Women never get that. I know. I had three wives, and they were all too smart to learn anything. Besides, we couldn't stay if we wanted."

She tried to ignore the mounting heaviness in her chest. "Why is that?" she asked.

"Because our fusion reactor isn't going to last forever. If we don't move, we'll stay alive maybe six months. The only way to charge it is to get back in space and back on track."

She took a long, sad pause. "I see."

With that, she sank into a deep depression. They saw each other even less. She spent her days sitting and watching Melons; not studying them, just watching them and thinking about things. People at the lowest point of sadness often fail to commit suicide simply because they lack the motivation to carry it out. Such people are actually at increased risk of it as their depression improves. But that rule doesn't apply when procrastination is the chosen method. We don't know if Mary Money was truly suicidal. People in such a state are sometimes not even sure of their own thoughts. What we do know is that her will to live could be measured by what time she came in out of the cold. Each afternoon, she waited a little longer before mustering up the stomach to return to that ship and that man. He pleaded repeatedly that she not take such risks. But his pleas were futile.

We also know that, on her last night alive, she still had some will to survive; for when he found her the next day, frozen, asphyxiated and blue, she was halfway back to the ship. He cursed her but didn't cry. He never cried. Cursing, however, was an old friend.

He decided to leave her remains on Susan, following what he thought would have been her wishes. Being unfamiliar with the ancient custom of burial, he decided to sink her in the lake. It was a tricky task, and he had to innovate with what he had. He did have about fifty meters of rope. He left her in her space suit, filled it with air and tied off the hose with a quick-release knot. The spectacle of her corpse slumped across his dolly was pitiful as he carted her from ship to shore. He dropped her twice during the arduous trip. On reaching the lake, he left her a while to scout around for some stones he had spotted along the way. He tied her with just enough rock to sink her body, but not her inflated suit. He tied the rest of the rope to her knotted hose and pushed her off into deep water. When she was out far enough, he gave the rope a quick jerk, releasing the knot and the air that it trapped. But the water was more buoyant than he expected, and she didn't submerge. So he brought her back to the ship and repeated the whole process the next day, using more rock. That time, he used enough, and she slipped out of sight into sunken repose.

# TWENTY-THREE

He spent another week camped remotely, far away from Melons, marinating in disconsolation, lacking the drive to wash or eat. He was self-pitying, self-loathing and lonely.

He also felt defiant, though there was no one around to defy. It was in that spirit that, as he crawled back to life, he prepared to capture a Melon. "Need to get samples, remember?" he reminded the air. He cleared out a cabinet large enough to store his prize. While at it, he threw out a bunch of things he either did not need or did not know how to use – the effects of his late crewmates. The scattered trash marked his first salvo on the previously pristine planet. Next, he punched holes in the edges of the mylar blanket and weaved his rope through them, leaving the ends long – a purse string. He then flew the ship back towards the best spot for his nefarious intent – near the melon patch. The next morning, he began suiting up. He took his time, knowing that the Melons would be "asleep" in the water until noon, and thus out of his reach.

He was therefore confounded when he arrived in the morning to find the patch swarming with activity. It was more crowded than usual, and a large evacuation seemed to be underway, with Melons lining up and filing out of town on a single track. This business was far too curious for Younas, and he determined to follow them. But they moved too fast, especially on those tracks, and he didn't know how far they planned to go. So he dropped his blanket, grabbed his dolly, and jetted back to the ship as fast as he could. He returned to the patch with all the radio trackers he had left – three of them. Fortunately, not all of the Melons were leaving empty-handed. Some of them were bringing things. He managed to affix one tracker to some kind of caliper just before a Melon picked it up. Nine of the Melons gathered round a pit, ingesting its contents – some sort of goo.

Into the pit went a tracker. The last one he managed to jam straight into a Melon while it was ingesting some kind of quartz.

Having finished this side task, he returned to his original mission and found his mylar blanket. Looking around for easy prey, he spotted a Melon lollygagging alone on the perimeter. It never flinched as he walked right up and threw that blanket over it. It certainly did after that, and its strength jarred him as it struggled to free itself. But he managed to keep it pinned down and eventually wrapped, sealed and tied it. Despite its strength, it was unexpectedly light, and he tossed the bundle over his shoulder like a sack of Christmas toys. The hike back was nonetheless difficult with one hand towing his dolly, especially getting back up the hill. He stopped twice to rest. Back on the ship, he tossed the bundle unceremoniously into the closet like a sack of dirty laundry, then fell fast asleep and forgot all about it. It would be weeks before he'd think of it again.

He awoke the next morning with trackers on his mind and found all three still functional. One remained at the patch; the other two had traveled far, together. They were near the edge of lake country, in the direction from which he had come when he first arrived on Susan. He checked on them several more times that day, and they continued to move … slowly… as anything does when checked too often. The following day, he got wiser and only checked them once…maybe twice. Surely enough, the two trackers were still together and still moving in the same general direction. After two more days, they finally stopped right where he had suspected, then concluded they were going – the big golden bowl. He fired up his ship and went to investigate. He put down for the night in the same place where he first landed on Susan almost six weeks before.

He set out on foot at first light. Now alone, he crossed the rocky terrain a little quicker than before, but not much, and it still took half the morning to reach the site. At one point along the way, he noticed that the ridge abutting the bowl looked odd, different. Its top edge almost looked to be moving – a writhing or shifting motion. Eventually, he could tell what he saw – Melons, hundreds of them, rolling along its crest, filing into the bowl like green gumballs coming off a factory line. By the time he reached it, the ridge was empty and the bowl full. They must have piled in like slaves on a ship, for he could see the fortunate few who rounded out the top of the heap.

"Helluva way to have a convention," he said, scratching his head in bewilderment. Suddenly, in the distance, he saw a couple of them who must have been left behind or fallen out. They were rolling along the ground at the base of the structure, and about to turn the corner out of view. He ran after them and, thanks to the terrain, actually gained on them. He was not more than a few meters away when, out of the blue, they disappeared!

What?

Yes, gone.

His brain jammed with shock and his feet followed suit. After a brief refractory period, he slowly advanced to the place where they had vanished and he discovered an opening. A small ramp led downwards under the building into the darkness. He tried the spotlight built into his helmet, but it was out.

Having led research teams to unexplored worlds, as he did for years, required a sense of adventure and gobs of nerve, and Younas had both. But only now, when he could think of little left for which to live, could he willingly descend such a hole. And down that hole he absolutely went, cautiously, crouching to the height of a Melon, taking care to not catch his suit, and gathering his hose and cords in a protective embrace.

The ramp only descended about three meters before his probing foot detected a smooth level surface – a floor. Some daylight shone from the entrance, but not much, and it took time for him to see anything. The two Melons were there and could see perfectly well. Something else also moved in the dark, something big and slow…and rhythmic. When his eyes finally adjusted, they reassured him that he had been right all long – something more intelligent than any Melon lived on planet Susan, or at least had been there at some point.

A large Foucault pendulum, at least three meters tall, swung freely from somewhere up in the darkness. Every day for a full lunar month, it had made its trip around the room which housed it. The length of that month was almost a perfect multiple of a day on Susan, which meant that Petunia's phases occurred at almost the same exact time of day each month… almost. But not exact enough, which is why a little magnet had been placed in the pendulum. Every day, Susan's magnetic field nudged the pendulum slightly off its course, and Petunia affected the field. The end result was that when moon and planet reached a precise position relative to each other, the pendulum tripped a switch.

Younas, of course, didn't know any of that. He only knew what he saw – a pendulum in the middle, some gears with a crank off to one side, and on the other side two Melons idled, waiting for something to happen.

What did happen, he wasn't sure. All he knew was it was something tremendous, as his teeth and feet suddenly vibrated, and a cloud of dust floated in from outside. The whole event lasted only a few seconds, after which the two Melons busied themselves resetting and recalibrating things. He rushed back outside as fast he could to see what happened. He turned around and, astonished, stumbled backwards, tripping over his dolly and landing on his back. He lay there for a while, still trying to believe and comprehend what he saw.

The coliseum was gone and so too the ridge. Not gone, actually, but standing straight up as a single unit, almost a kilometer away. The catapult had launched its cargo – a huge pile of Melons – at the moon. It now stood tall, a giant banner of achievement silhouetted against the sky.

Younas spent the next few days quietly recovering from his amazement. His intrigue soon gave way to envy, for those astronautical Melons now basked in the company of his first love, the abyss, and he was starting to miss her again. The longing grew as it always had, and within a week, he too left Susan.

# Twenty-four

He kept the ship on fusion propulsion and backtracked his way to where he first saw the Melon UFO. A large Why current flowed there, a safe spot to raise his sail. Anywhere else, he might catch the wrong end of a tributary and get sucked right back into Susan. Once the sail was up, he adjusted it to low-medium power, making it about as fast as a standard Warp Drive. After that, he didn't have much to do except relax and wait to see where the waves would bring him. It didn't take him long to get lonely and bored. He didn't miss people, just Mary. There was much to do between maintaining the ship, watching shows, playing games and reading; but none of it satiated.

Then he remembered the Melon. Might as well have a look. He got out his hunting knife, cut through the blanket and spread it apart to see. The corpse lolled, gray and dried and sad. It was decomposing quickly in the presence of oxygen. Some dust of decay billowed into the air, and he sneezed. The sneeze, in turn, stirred up a much bigger cloud of dead-Melon-dust, which got in his eyes. The dust didn't burn; just itched a little. Nonetheless, he made sure to thoroughly flush his one good eye. But it was too late.

A severe, allergic reaction ensued within hours. It started off as just a bad irritation of the eyes, with some puffy redness and lots of tearing. But the redness got worse, the tears turned to discharge, and the itching became a deep, deep ache. His lids swelled shut, sealing off his remaining vision. He burst into panic, which only heightened his state of disability. He probed around, trying to remember where he had put the rest of Mary's things. Once found, he fumbled through them, hoping to find something that felt like it might be eye medicine. No luck. He screamed. Nobody answered.

The dust settled. After two earth weeks, the allergy burned itself out, leaving dead tissue in its wake that would eventually scar, extirpating any hope that he might one day see again. With hope went his drive to do anything – eat, bathe, move. He lost nearly half his weight over the next several months and would have probably died if he had been active at all. As for his hygiene, decorum prohibits elucidation.

He wouldn't have minded dying, and as his worst depression began to subside, and his drive began to trickle back into existence, he certainly did contemplate suicide many times. But he was too afraid, imagining death to be much like his existence now except worse.

In time, if there is such a thing, he got better at distinguishing his dreams from his waking nightmare. In time, he started to develop strategies for getting around the ship, and routines for getting through his waking hours. He employed some of the things he learned in the PASS jail – physical and mental exercise, and meditation, but not prayer.

He invented some new mind games, being no longer able to play the mindless ones. Some of his own games were just as dumb, like seeing just how much physical pain he could endure, and thinking of ways to inflict it. Others were a little more advanced. For example, he spent thirty minutes every day, whether he wanted or not, climbing further up the Fibonacci sequence, picking up where he left off the day before. When that became too tedious, he pursued the end of the endless Golden Ratio.

He also started journaling, though he didn't have much to say at first. As his recordings grew, he sometimes enjoyed going back and listening to earlier volumes, and marveling at how stupid or how brilliant he had been. No longer able to watch shows, he immersed himself in audiobooks. In non-fiction, he consumed a lot of self-help and healing guides. When he had enough of that, he moved on to philosophy, and then religion. He eventually grew quite educated in some matters and his journals reflected it with thoughtfulness and creativity. He started to ponder his mission and the millions of souls who tugged him along.

Education, pain and solitude can be terrific ingredients to grow character, and with time (if there is such a thing), Captain Younas, whose beard had grown long and gray, and his bones sore and bent, sprouted some rectitude. Gratitude replaced self-pity, and with gratitude came patience. His journal became an exercise in both. It also came with humility, *real* humility, and he started praying again. He had a lot to pray for and little else to do. He said prayers he had learned and others he invented. One of his most frequent prayers went something like this:

"Lord, there is no God but You. Indeed, you are perfect, perfectly just and perfectly wise, and I have been nothing but wrong."

He would recite this over and over until it grew into an obsession, and he finally had to rein it in with ritual – five hundred repetitions, which took about an hour.

He also developed a ringing in his ear, or maybe it was a new ship noise. He couldn't quite tell. A constant "eee" sound. He quickly desensitized to it and hardly ever noticed it until one day, his ship came a little too close to a pulsar. A pulsar is a rotating neutron star that emits radio waves and other radiation at regular intervals; in this case, every two seconds. The emissions from this pulsar affected his ringing, changing the pitch to an "aww" sound. Now all he heard from his waking moment until the last light of consciousness was "eee-aww-eee-aww-eee-aww," in two-second cycles. This was much more intrusive, and respites of his notice were precious and infrequent. It carried on like that for days, gaining in volume until he could hardly bear it. Then, one night, he got the call.


Or maybe it was morning. All he knew was that he had awakened because, once again, his sight was gone and the ringing had returned. He couldn't exactly remember of what he had dreamt, but now he had a strong urge – to get up, walk over to the periscope and have a look into it. Perhaps he was still dreaming after all, for when he put his face to that scope, he actually saw something.

The heavens were once again bejeweled with points of starlight and in the center of his visual field loomed a big one, really big or really close, its light yellow-white. Out from the light came the shape of a man – a man just standing there in the middle of outer space, his stark form undiminished by the blazing star behind. There was no way to tell how big or far he was. The ringing became louder than ever – "EEE-AWW-EEE-AWW" – but went unnoticed.

Suddenly, the man spread a pair of white wings, vast and sublime. Then another and another. Three sets of wings overwhelmed his frame like those of an exceptional dragonfly. They grew and unfurled until they eclipsed the star, but not its light – his flaming, framing corona. This winged man grew larger and closer until he blocked out all the other stars, and Younas could see his gentle countenance and naked state.

A switch suddenly flipped in Younas's brain from mesmerized to startled, and he jerked away from the scope. He was in the dark again…'til he sensed someone behind him and quickly spun around. The same man stood before him, now no taller than he, wings tucked away. Younas felt his head fill with blood and his stomach with sour dread. His heart banged away at his chest like a man waking up in a coffin. He could see nothing else but this strange, naked man who stood before him, patiently waiting for him to relax.

Younas did calm, especially when he took a moment to look him over. The man's face was ageless, commanding and kind; his hair straight and white, cascading to shoulder-length. His body was reasonably muscular but, like his mien, unimposing.

Younas swallowed his fear; not fear of the stranger, but of the question on his own mind.

"Am I dead?" he finally asked. "Are you even real? Or am I dreaming?"

The man took Younas by the hand and sat him down, then sat beside him. He rested an arm on Younas's shoulders. His voice was soft and rich like fudge.

"Oh, Christopher. Angels come in death and dream, and also when awake. So as for my existence, no difference does it make."

"You know my name. Do you have one?"

"Yes, Eog is my namesake, and your acquaintance I am pleased to make.

"Yog?"

"Your effort counts, but 'Eee-og' is how it's pronounced."

"That's what I said – Yog."

Eog sighed a little, then smiled an angelic smile. "Yes, I guess."

"Are you my guardian angel? Or like an angel of death?"

"I have neither rank nor position. You've simply entered my jurisdiction."

Younas chuckled. "Why do you always rhyme your words?"

"Do I? Oh my."

"Never mind. So! If I'm seeing angels, then I must be getting pretty close to where I'm going." He smiled and rubbed his hands together like a fly.

Now it was Eog who chuckled and shook his head. He tousled Chris's hair. "My child," he said "the journey to Him is one of deeds, my dear, not of leagues or lightyears."

"Then I'm screwed," said Chris. "My life has been one lousy deed after another."

"Indeed, treacherous is a life spent pursing what one pleases. It is fraught with disaster like a surgeon who sneezes."

Eog could see Chris's hope fading as he spoke. "*But,*" he quickly added "there is no exemption to a chance at redemption. We all get one, Son. In fact, I know a good place you can start after we part."

Chris perked up a bit. "I don't see how I get a chance at anything. My life is nearly over. My world is long gone."

"Fear not. Space and time are His invention. He exists outside your conventions. If He wants it done, it's done."

"Hey, you can't use the same word twice to rhyme."

"Done rhymes with done."

"Ah, the ole reflexive property. Say, do all angels go naked?"

"Yes. We are not tainted by sin, thus we do not shroud our skin."

"Humph." A moment passed as Chris realized what he had been told a minute ago. He would have a chance at redemption. For the second time in his adult life, he cried. And for the first time in his entire life, he hugged a naked man (who wasn't really a man, so it didn't count). "Will I ever see Mary again?" he asked through receding tears.

"That decision is neither mine nor thine. But I do not suggest you invest much hope. I suspect she has grown beyond your scope. She has joined the ranks of the few unimpeachables, and she may be to you unreachable. Yet, eternity is a very long time. Chance becomes certainty down the line."

Younas felt a wave of renewed grief, but it quickly passed. He had already come to expect and accept years ago that she was gone from him.

"I hope I do," he said. "And I hope to see you too! You are as wonderful as anyone would expect an angel to be, and I appreciate you."

"You are very kind, but if you don't mind, I leave you with this final pearl – All praise is for The God, Master of All Worlds."

With that, he pulled Christopher in for one more embrace and spread his wings just enough to surround the two of them. The wings immersed them not in darkness but in light, soft and white to the eyes and touch. Christopher closed his eyes and hugged, and decided he had not felt such contentment since his time in the womb.

But it was not to last. Eog slowly faded, though his light remained a while, a warm bath of brilliance for a tired old soul. Soon enough, that too dissipated and, as it did, Christopher began to feel something familiar below his feet. It was the feeling of trillions of tons of solid ground and the accompanying pull of gravity. As the last tufts of heavenly light evaporated, he could see that he could see, and he found himself in a place that he could not place, but he knew that he knew it.

He was at a park and young again, and so too was the boy beside him, his only son. He was trying to teach him to hit a ball, but the boy just wasn't getting it, or maybe he wasn't listening. Either way, Christopher Younas was getting impatient. He could feel his anger rising.